PRAISE FOR *HOSTAGE*

"Hypnotically good. Should be a hit, might be a classic."
—Lee Child, *New York Times* bestselling author

"A nail-biter of a thriller with an unexpected gut-punch at the end—a fantastic read!"
—Shari Lapena, *New York Times* bestselling author of *The End of Her*

"Feels like a blockbuster movie: edge of seat, nail-biting, propulsive, compulsive, thrilling, and just so beautifully done."
—Lisa Jewell, *New York Times* bestselling author of *Then She Was Gone*

"When Clare Mackintosh goes high concept, she doesn't mess around… A true page-turner that will have producers lining up with movie offers."
—Linwood Barclay, *New York Times* bestselling author

"A propulsive read—*Hostage* will have you questioning 'what would you do?' at every turn."
—Karin Slaughter, *New York Times* bestselling author of *The Silent Wife*

"Fiendishly clever. Mackintosh takes domestic suspense to new heights in this tale of a kidnapped child, hijacked plane, and two parents' desperate fight to save their family."
—Lisa Gardner, #1 *New York Times* bestselling author

ALSO BY CLARE MACKINTOSH

I Let You Go
I See You
Let Me Lie
After the End

Nonfiction
A Cotswold Family Life

HOSTAGE

HOSTAGE

A NOVEL

Clare Mackintosh

sourcebooks
landmark

Published by Sourcebooks Landmark, an imprint of Sourcebooks
P.O. Box 4410, Naperville, Illinois 60567-4410
(630) 961-3900
sourcebooks.com

Originally published as *Hostage* in 2021 in Great Britain by Sphere, an imprint of Little,
Brown Book Group. This edition issued based on the hardcover edition published
in 2021 in Great Britain by Sphere, an imprint of Little, Brown Book Group.

The Library of Congress has catalogued the hardcover edition as follows:

Names: Mackintosh, Clare, author.
Title: Hostage : a novel / Clare Mackintosh.
Description: Naperville, Illinois : Sourcebooks, 2021.
Identifiers: LCCN 2020056398 (print) | LCCN 2020056399 (ebook) | (hardcover) | (epub)
Classification: LCC PR6113.A2649 H67 2021 (print) | LCC PR6113.A2649
    (ebook) | DDC 823/.92--dc23
LC record available at https://lccn.loc.gov/2020056398
LC ebook record available at https://lccn.loc.gov/2020056399

Printed and bound in Canada.
MBP 10 9 8 7 6

For Sheila Crowley

OPERATOR: What's your emergency?

CALLER: I'm near the airport... I can see... Oh my God!

OPERATOR: Can you confirm your location please?

CALLER: The airport. There's a plane...it's turned over. It's coming down so fast. Oh my God, oh my God!

OPERATOR: Emergency services are on their way, caller.

CALLER: But it's going to be too late—it's *[inaudible]*. It's going to crash, it's going to crash...

OPERATOR: Can you confirm you are at a safe distance?

CALLER: *[inaudible]*

OPERATOR: Caller, are you okay?

CALLER: It's crashed, it's really crashed, oh my God, it's on fire...

OPERATOR: Fire crews will be on scene in less than a minute. Ambulance too. Is anyone with you?

CALLER: The whole plane is smoking—it's *[inaudible]*. Oh God, something's exploded—it's like a huge fireball...

OPERATOR: Fire crews are on scene now.

CALLER: I can hardly even see the plane anymore, just smoke and flames. It's too late. It's too late. No one's getting out of that alive.

PROLOGUE

Don't run, you'll fall.

Past the park, up the hill. Wait for the green man, not yet, not yet…
Now!

Cat in the window. Like a statue. Just the tiniest tip of his tail moving.
Twitch, twitch, twitch.

Another road to cross. No green man and no lollipop lady—she should
be here…

Look both ways. Not yet, not yet…
Now!

Don't run, you'll fall.

Mailbox, then lamppost, then bus stop, then bench.

Big school—not my school, not yet.

Bookshop, then empty shop, then the 'state agent where they sell houses.

Now the butcher's shop, birds hanging from their necks in the window.
My eyes squeezed shut so I don't have to see theirs staring back.

Dead. All dead.

PART ONE

ONE

8:30 A.M. | MINA

"Stop that, you'll fall."

A week's worth of snow has pressed itself into ice, each day's danger hidden beneath a nighttime dusting of powder. Every few yards, my boots travel farther than my feet intended, and my stomach pitches, braced for a fall. Our progress is slow, and I wish I'd thought to bring Sophia on the sled instead.

Reluctantly, she opens her eyes, swiveling her head, owllike, away from the shops, to hide her face in my sleeve. I squeeze her gloved hand. She hates the birds that hang in the butcher's window, their iridescent neck feathers cruelly at odds with the lifeless eyes they embellish.

I hate the birds too.

Adam says I've given the phobia to her, like a cold or a piece of unwanted jewelry.

"Where did she get it from, then?" he said when I protested. He held out his hands, turning to an invisible crowd, as though the absence of answer proved his point. "Not me."

Of course not. Adam doesn't have weaknesses.

"Sainsbury's," Sophia says now, looking back at the shops, now that we are safely past the birds. She still pronounces it *thainsbweez*, so cute, it makes my heart squeeze. It's moments like this I treasure, moments like this that make it all worthwhile.

Her breath makes tiny mists in the air. "Now the shoe shop. Now the-e-e-e..." She draws out the word, holding the next in her mouth until it's time. "...fruit and veg shop," she declares as we draw level with it. *Fwoot and veg.* God, I love this girl. I do.

The ritual began back in the summer, when Sophia was fizzing with excitement and nerves over starting school, questions tumbling out with every breath. What would her teacher be like? Where would they hang their coats? Would there be bandages if she scraped her knee? *And tell me one more time, how do we get there?* I'd take her through it again: up the hill, across one road, then another, then on to the high street. Past the bus stop by the secondary school, then along the parade, with the bookshop, and the estate agent, and the butcher. Around the corner to Sainsbury's. To the shoe shop, then the fruit and veg shop, past the police station, up the hill, past the church, *and we're there*, I'd tell her.

You have to be patient with Sophia; that's what Adam struggles with. You have to tell her things again and again. Reassure her that nothing's changed, that nothing *will* change.

Adam and I dropped her off together, that first day in September. We took a hand each, swinging her in the middle, as though we were still a proper family, and I was glad to have an excuse for the tears that pricked my eyes.

"She'll go off without a second glance, you'll see," Aunty Mo said, seeing my face as we left home. She isn't an actual aunty, but "Mrs. Watt" is too formal for a neighbor who makes hot chocolate and remembers birthdays.

I'd made myself smile back at Mo. "I know. Daft, isn't it?"

Daft to wish Adam still lived with us. Daft to think that day was anything other than role-playing, for Sophia's sake.

Mo had crouched down to smile at Sophia. "You have a good day, now, petal."

"My dress is scratchy." It came with a scowl Mo managed to miss.

"That's nice, dear."

Mo leaves her hearing aid off to save on the batteries. When I pop 'round, I have to stand in the flower bed by the lounge window and wave until she sees me. *You should have rung the bell!* she always says, as though I hadn't done just that for the past ten minutes.

"What next?" I'd said to Sophia that first day as we passed the greengrocer, anxiety bleeding from her fingers to mine.

"Police station!" she'd said triumphantly. "Daddy's police station."

It isn't where Adam works, but that doesn't matter to Sophia. Every police car we see is *Daddy's car*, every uniformed cop *Daddy's friend*.

"Up the hill next."

She'd remembered it all. The next day, she had added more detail—things I hadn't seen, hadn't noticed. A cat on a windowsill, a phone box, a rubbish bin. The commentary became a fixed part of her day, as essential to Sophia as putting on her school uniform in the correct order (top to bottom) or standing flamingo-like as she brushes her teeth, swapping legs as she switches sides. Depending on the day, these rituals either charm me or make me want to scream. That's parenting in a nutshell.

Starting school had marked the end of one chapter and the beginning of another, and we'd prepared for the transition by putting Sophia into preschool last year for three days a week. The rest of the time, she'd been with me or Adam, or with Katya, the quietly beautiful au pair who arrived with matching luggage and no English. She spent Wednesday afternoons at language college and topped up her wages stacking shelves on weekends. After six months, she declared us *the nicest family in the world* and asked to stay on for another year. I wondered aloud if there was a boyfriend, and Katya's blushes suggested I was right, although she was coy about whom.

I was delighted—and relieved. Adam's and my working hours made it impossible to rely on a nursery for childcare, and we could never have afforded the nannies that many of my colleagues employed. I had worried it would be intrusive, having a stranger living in, but Katya spent most of her time in her room, Skyping her friends back home. She preferred to eat alone too, despite continued invitations to join us, and she made herself useful around the house, mopping the floor or sorting the laundry, despite my telling her she didn't have to. "You're here to help with Sophia and to learn English."

"I don't mind," she'd reply. "I like to help."

I came home one day to find several pairs of Adam's socks on our bed, a neat darn hiding the holes that wear through on the heel of every sock Adam puts on.

"Where did you learn to do that?" I could just about sew on a button and take up a hem—albeit wonkily—but darning was proper housewife territory, and Katya wasn't yet twenty-five.

She shrugged as if it was nothing. "My mother learn me."

"I honestly don't know what we'd do without you."

I'd been able to commit to extra shifts at work, knowing Katya would be here to do the school runs, and Sophia adored her, which was by no means a given. Katya had the patience for endless games of hide-and-seek, Sophia finding more and more elaborate hiding places as time went by.

"Coming, if you are ready or if you are not!" Katya would shout, each newly acquired word carefully enunciated, before stalking around the house, looking for her charge. "Inside of the shoe cupboard? No... How about behind of the bathroom door?"

"That doesn't sound very safe," I said when Sophia came charging downstairs to tell me triumphantly that Katya had failed to find her curled up on a shelf in the airing cupboard. "I don't want you hiding somewhere you might get stuck." Sophia had scowled at me before running off for a rematch with Katya. I let it go. My father chided Adam and me for overcautious parenting as frequently as I begged him not to be so laissez-faire.

"She'll fall," I'd say, hardly able to watch as he coaxed Sophia up trees or across stepping-stones, wobbling their way across a stream.

"That's how you learn to fly."

I knew he was right, and I fought my instincts to treat Sophia like a baby. Besides, I could see that she thrived on adventure and loved the feeling of being treated like a "big girl." Katya had understood that instantly, and the bond between the two of them had grown swiftly. Sophia's ability to handle change—of people, in particular—continues to be a work in progress, hence my relief when Katya chose to stay on. I had dreaded the fallout from her departure.

It came abruptly in June, just weeks after Katya had asked to stay, weeks after I'd begun to relax. The au pair's face was blotchy and tearstained, and she'd packed in a hurry, stuffing her suitcase with clothes still damp from the dryer. Was it the boyfriend? She wouldn't look at me. Something I'd done?

"I go now," was all she'd say.

"Please, Katya, whatever it is, let's talk about it."

She hesitated, then, and I saw her look at Adam. Her eyes were angry and hurt, and I turned just in time to see him shake his head, silently giving instruction.

"What's going on?" I looked at each of them in turn.

Adam had once joked that, in the event of a disagreement between Katya and me, he'd be forced to take the younger woman's side. "A good au pair isn't easily replaced," he'd said.

"Funny."

"Tell me you wouldn't do the same."

I'd given a mock grimace. "You got me."

"Well?" I said. They had argued—that was clear—but about what? They had only Sophia in common, unless you counted the crime dramas Adam loved and I hated, the only thing that would lure Katya out of her bedroom on a Saturday evening. If I wasn't at work, I'd go for a run instead, returning after a 10K to catch the dark, moody credits and the tail end of their critique.

But no one argued about crime dramas.

"Ask him," Katya spat—the only time I'd ever seen her be anything but sunny. A horn beeped outside—her taxi for the airport—and she finally met my gaze. "You are nice woman. You not deserve crap like this."

Something splintered inside me, a tiny fissure at the edge of a frozen lake. I wanted to step back, to leave the ice intact, but it was too late. *Crack.*

When she'd gone, I turned to Adam. "Well?"

"Well what?" He made it a snap, as though my question—my very presence—was an irritation, a nag. As though it were my fault.

I focused on that look I'd seen pass between them, on Katya's red-rimmed eyes and implied warning. *You not deserve crap like this.*

"I'm not stupid, Adam. What's going on?"

"With what?" Again, the faint *tut* before he spoke, as though his mind were on other, more cerebral matters and I was dragging him back to irrelevance.

"*With Katya.*" I spoke the way some people speak to foreigners. I had the sense that I had stepped into someone else's life; this wasn't a conversation I had ever needed to have before, ever thought I'd find myself having.

As he turned away to busy himself with something that didn't need doing, I caught the flames of guilt licking his neck. Truth slid into my mind like the answer to a crossword clue long after the paper's been thrown away, and my mouth formed the words I didn't want to say.

"You slept with her."

"No! God. No! Jesus, Mina—that's what you think?"

Every bit of me wanted to believe him. He had never before given me cause to doubt him. He loved me. I loved him. I fought to keep my voice steady. "What do you expect me to think? There's obviously *something* going on between you."

"She left Play-Doh all over the kitchen. I had a go at her. She took it personally, that's all."

I stared at Adam, at the red-faced bluster of his lie. "You could at least have come up with a plausible excuse." Not meriting the effort of a cover story hurt almost as much as the lie itself. Did I mean that little to him?

Katya's departure tore a fissure through our family. Sophia was furious, the sudden loss of her friend a bereavement expressed through smashed toys and torn-up pictures. She blamed me, for no other reason than that I was the one who told her, and it took all my moral fiber not to tell her it was Adam's fault. He and I circled each other: me bristling and bitter, him taciturn and filled with faux resentment designed to make me doubt myself. I held fast. If Katya was the crossword puzzle, now that I had solved it, I saw that the clues had been anything but cryptic. For months, Adam had been cagey about his days off and protective enough of his phone to take it to the bathroom while he showered. I'd been a fool not to have realized sooner.

"Up the hill," Sophia says now. "Then the church, then the—"

My hand tightens too late, Sophia's fingers disappearing from my grasp as her feet slip from under her, and the back of her head meets the ground. Her eyes widen in shock, then narrow as she assesses how hurt she is, how scared, how embarrassed. I intercept her decision, dropping my bag and swooping her up from the pavement, bumping in my haste against a man walking in the opposite direction.

"Upsy-daisy!" I say in a nanny's no-nonsense tone.

Sophia looks at me, lower lip quivering indignantly, her dark eyes searching mine for a measure of how bad her fall was. I smile to show it was nothing and tip up my head to find the shapes in the sky.

"See the dog? Standing up—see his head, there? And his tail?"

She won't cry. She never cries. Instead, she gets angry, inarticulate screams making it my fault, always my fault. Or she'll run into the road, to prove something only she understands. That I love her? That I don't love her?

She follows my gaze. A plane slices through the sky, clipping the clouds that seem solid enough to stop its path.

"747," Sophia says.

I breathe out. The distraction has worked. "Nope, that's an A380. No bump at the front—see?" I set her gently down, and she shows me her gloves, soaked through from the snow.

"Poor Sophia. Look, there's the church. What comes next?"

"Th-then school."

"So we're nearly there," I say, my bright smile a carpet for the mess swept beneath it. My bag—Sophia's bag, really—has tipped over, its contents spilled on the pavement. I stuff her change of clothes back in and retrieve the water bottle rolling away from us, my daughter's name playing peekaboo with each rotation.

"Is this yours?"

The man I bumped into is holding something toward Sophia. It's Elephant, his trunk fist-squashed and shiny from five years of love.

"Give it back!" Sophia yells even as she takes a step back, hiding behind me.

"I'm so sorry."

"Don't worry." The man seems unfazed by my daughter's rudeness. I'm not supposed to apologize for her. It contradicts what she's feeling, when what she needs is support. But it's hard to stay silent before raised eyebrows and judgment raining down on you for not teaching your child manners. I take Elephant, and Sophia snatches him from me, burying her face in him.

Elephant came from the house where Sophia spent the first four months of her life. He's the only thing she has from that time, although nobody knows if he really belonged to Sophia or whether he was scooped up the day she was placed in emergency care. Either way, they're inseparable now.

She holds Elephant by his trunk until we get to school, where she shows Miss Jessop her wet gloves, and I hang up Sophia's coat and put her hat and scarf into her bag. It's December 17, and the school hums with anticipation. Cotton ball snowmen dance across sheets of sugar paper stapled to display boards, and several teachers wear festive earrings, their flashing lobes sending a signal that could be celebration or alarm. The tiled floor is wet, chunks of snow stamped loose at the door then trodden through to the coat pegs.

I take Sophia's lunch box and give it to Miss Jessop as I continue to hunt through the contents of the bag. Katya used to empty it at the end of each day, wiping away sticky fingerprints and discreetly recycling the less desirable pieces of artwork. I always mean to do the same, then I sling the bag in the hall each afternoon and don't think about it until we're walking to school the next morning.

"All ready for Christmas?" Sophia's teacher is very slight, with smooth skin that could mean midtwenties or a well-kept thirty. I think of all the duty-free Clarins I've bought over the years and all the skincare routines I've started with good intentions, only to go back to wet wipes. I bet Miss Jessop cleanses, tones, and moisturizes.

"Sort of."

There's a clump of ice clinging to Sophia's spare jumper, the fabric around it damp and cold. I shake it out, then resume my fruitless hunt through bits of egg carton and empty juice cartons. "I can't find her EpiPen. Do you still have the one I gave you?"

"Yes, don't worry. It's in the medicine cabinet, with Sophia's name on it."

"My hair bands are the wrong color," Sophia announces.

Miss Jessop bends to inspect Sophia's plaits, one secured by a red band and the other with a blue one. "They're very nice hair bands."

"I always have two blue ones for school."

"Well, I like these ones very much." Miss Jessop turns her attention back to me, and I marvel at a teacher's ability to have the last word, when my own discussions with Sophia over "hair-band-gate" had lasted an entire breakfast and most of our walk to school. "Don't forget, we've got our Christmas lunch tomorrow, so no packed lunch."

"Got it. It'll be our babysitter picking up today. Becca. You've met her before, I think."

"No Mr. Holbrook?"

I hold her gaze for a moment, wondering if that smile hides something else. Disappointment? Guilt? But her expression is guileless, and I look away, refolding Sophia's damp jumper. Damn Adam for turning me into the sort of paranoid wife I've always pitied.

"He wasn't sure he'll be finished work in time, so it was safer to get a babysitter."

"Where are you off to today?"

"Sydney."

"On a Boeing 777," Sophia says. "With three hundred fifty-three passengers. It takes twenty hours to get there, and then they have to come all the way back, and that's another twenty hours, but they stay in a hotel first."

"Gosh! How exciting. Will you be away for long?"

"Five days. Back in time for the holidays."

"They have to have four pilots because it's such a long way, but they don't all fly at once. They take turns."

Sophia's learned the details of all the planes I fly in. There's a tour of a 747 on YouTube she must have watched a hundred times. She knows it backward, her lips silently moving in time with the narrator's. It's an impressive party trick.

"Sometimes I find it a bit creepy," I told my dad, my smile an afterthought to soften the confession. Adam and I had recently discovered that Sophia had not, as we'd imagined, been reciting the words of her favorite picture books from memory but was instead reading. She was three years old.

Dad had laughed. He took off his glasses and rubbed them on the bottom of his shirt. "Don't be daft. She's a bright girl. She's destined for great things." His eyes glistened, and I had to blink hard myself. He missed Mum as much as I did, but I wondered, too, if he was remembering a time when they used to say that about me.

The psychologist concluded Sophia had hyperlexia, the first positive diagnosis in a sea of acronyms and negative labels. Attachment disorder. Attention deficit disorder. Pathological demand avoidance. They don't put *that* on the adoption posters.

Adam and I had spent a couple of years trying to conceive. We could have carried on, but the stress was already beginning to get to me, and I could feel myself becoming *that woman*. The woman who knows exactly when she's ovulating, who avoids her friends' baby showers, and commits her savings to cycles of IVF.

"How much does it cost?"

I was somewhere over the Atlantic, spilling my secrets—some of them, at least—to the colleague I was working with that day. Sian was gently maternal, and we were exchanging life stories by the time the wheels had left the tarmac.

"Thousands."

"Could your parents help out a bit?"

I didn't tell her about Mum. It was still too raw. As for borrowing money from Dad, after everything that had happened... I shook my head and switched tack. "It isn't just the money. I'd become obsessed, I know I would. I already am. I want kids, but I also want to stay sane."

"Fat chance of that." Sian snorted. "I've got four, and I've lost another set of marbles with each one."

We were approved to adopt. It took a while, not least because we'd been very clear that we wanted a child under a year old. Adam's police work had exposed him to some of the worst products of the care system, and neither of us felt we had what it took to handle that. A baby would be easier, we thought.

We were offered Sophia when she was four months old, taken into care from a neglectful mother whose five previous children had gone the same way. The wheels of adoption move slowly, though, and the months when she was with a foster family and we were without her were endless. We had to show Social Services we were prepared, but at the same time, we were plagued by superstition, Adam going out of his way to walk around ladders and make black cats cross his path. We compromised by filling Sophia's freshly painted bedroom with everything we needed still in its packaging, ready to go back if anything went wrong.

The court order was granted when Sophia was ten months old, and

Adam raced to the recycling center with a car full of cardboard and plastic packaging. We finally had our family. The movies would have you believe that's the happily ever after. Turns out you have to work a bit harder for that.

Sophia runs off now to join her friends, and I watch her through the glass. Even this far into the term, there are still tears from a handful of children as they say goodbye. I wonder if their parents look at Sophia and think, *Lucky mum*, just as I look at the kids clinging to their mothers and think the same.

Back home, I leave a note for Becca, the teenager who looks after Sophia from time to time. I leave lasagna defrosting in case Adam's not back by suppertime, and I dump a clean towel on the spare-room bed, even though he knows full well where the airing cupboard is. It's hard to break a decade of looking out for someone.

"Why can't I just sleep in our bed?" he said the first time.

I spoke quietly. Not just because of Sophia but because I didn't want it to hurt either of us any more than it had already. "Because it isn't *our* bed any more, Adam." It hadn't been *our* bed since the day Katya left.

"Why are you being like this?"

"Like what?"

"So cold. Like we hardly know each other." His face crumpled. "I love you, Mina."

I opened my mouth to reply that I no longer felt the same, but I couldn't bring myself to say it.

We tried counseling, of course. For Sophia's sake, if not ours. Her attachment issues were deep-seated, a muscle memory from the months when crying didn't summon comfort. What would it do to her if we separated permanently? Sophia was used to Adam working nights—to my being away for several days at a time—but we always, always came home.

Adam was monosyllabic at best, as evasive with the therapist as with me. In July, he agreed to move out.

"I need time," I'd told him.

"How much time?"

I couldn't say. I didn't know. I saw him hesitate over the suitcases, nestled one inside the other like rectangular Russian dolls. Optimism made him pick the smallest. Human Resources found him a room in a house with three police recruits, full of enthusiasm and cheap beer, outdoing each other with their newfound uniformed exploits. "I can't have Sophia there," he told me. "It wouldn't be right."

So I made up the spare bed, and when I go to work, Adam stays here, and I don't know which of us finds it the hardest.

I change into my uniform and double-check my carry-on bag. Today's flight is a big deal. The last nonstop flight from London to Sydney was in 1989—a PR stunt with twenty people on board. Commercial flights haven't been possible—it's taken years to develop an aircraft that can handle the distance with a full passenger load.

I leave a note on Sophia's bed—a felt-tip heart with *love from Mummy* underneath, something I've done every time I fly, ever since she learned to read.

"Did you get my note?" I said once when I was video-calling to say good night. I forget where I was, but the sun was still high, and the sight of Sophia fresh from a bath sent a wave of homesickness through me.

"What note?"

"On your bed. I left it on your pillow. Like always." Homesickness made me unfair, wanting Sophia to miss me simply because I was missing her.

"Bye, Mummy. Katya and me are making a den." The screen wobbled, and I was left looking at the kitchen ceiling. I ended the call before Katya could feel sorry for me.

I turn up Radio 2 as I head for the airport, but guilt knocks hard enough to make itself heard.

"People have to work," I say out loud. "It's a fact of life."

I told Adam there'd been a shift change, that I'd tried to get out of it, but I'd be away for five days, and what could you do, really? Work was work.

I lied.

TWO

9 A.M. | ADAM

"The boss wants to see you."

Acid gnaws at my insides as I fight to arrange myself into something resembling normal. Has anything good ever come of those six words?

"Oh. Right." I sit at my desk, my hands suddenly too big, too awkward, as if I'm in front of a huge audience instead of just Wei's curious gaze.

"She's in with the chief at the moment."

"Thanks." I frown at my screen. Flick through the papers on my desk as though I'm looking for something. I've got a charge file to put together for a robbery; statements to take for an assault that could end up as murder if the guy doesn't pull through—work I need to focus on, that demands my attention—only instead I'm sweating into my collar and wondering if this is it. If this is the end. I sense Wei looking at me and wonder if he already knows what Butler wants to see me about.

Soft flakes of snow settle on the other side of the windowsill. Inside, an ignored phone call transfers from one empty desk to another until someone takes pity on the caller and picks up. I find the GBH file and scan the list of witnesses. I can be out of the office all day, dealing with this lot, and if I miss a message from the boss, well, I was taking a statement or on the phone to Victim Support. I stuff the file into my rucksack and stand up.

"On your way to my office, I hope?"

The voice is light, almost pleasant, but I'm not reassured. I've seen enough police officers welcomed with a smile into Detective Inspector

Naomi Butler's office before leaving half an hour later with the counter-signed copy of a formal complaint screwed up in their bitter fist.

"Actually, I've got to—"

"This won't take long."

Butler doesn't give me a chance to argue, walking out of the office and along the corridor toward her own so I have no choice but to follow. She's wearing white Converse with pinstripe trousers, a gray silk blouse tucked into a leopard-print belt. A tiny, silver ring circles the top of one ear. I follow her, a kid on his way to the head teacher's office, mentally listing all the reasons she might need to see me and ending up with the only one that matters. The one that could lose me everything.

When Naomi Butler took over as DI, she dragged the heavy desk away from the window and moved it to face the glass door she now closes, meaning I have no choice but to sit with my back to the corridor. I know with complete certainty that in the next few minutes, Wei will find a reason to walk past, with the sole purpose of determining what level of dressing-down I am about to receive. I straighten. You can tell a lot from a person's back, and I could do without Wei running back to tell the rest of the team I was slumped in the boss's office.

"How are things?" Butler smiles, but her eyes are flinty. They fix mine so firmly, it hurts, and I have to blink to break the lock. One point to Butler. The biker jacket she wears whatever the weather hangs on the back of her chair, and as she leans back, the leather creaks a complaint. There's a police radio on her desk, tuned to the local channel. Rumor has it Butler never turns it off, even at home, rocking up at any job that piques her interest.

"Great."

"I understand you've had some domestic issues."

"Nothing I can't handle." Surely she's not about to give me marriage guidance? I glance at the pale band of skin around her fourth finger and wonder who walked out on whom. She sees me looking—of course she does—and her smile disappears.

"You've got a job phone?"

I'm thrown off guard. It's a question, of sorts, but one to which she knows the answer, meaning this is merely her way in.

"Yes."

She reads my phone number from her notebook, and I nod. The urge to run away is so strong, I have to grip the sides of my chair to stop myself from standing up.

"Finance flagged your phone bill."

Silence hangs heavy between us, both of us waiting for the other to fill it. I crack first. Even when you know the rules, it's hard to stop yourself from playing the game. Two-nil to Butler.

"Have they?"

"It's significantly higher than anyone else's in the department."

I can feel a bead of sweat trickling down the side of my face. If I wipe it away, she'll see. I turn my head slightly, only to feel a matching trickle on the other side.

"I had that mugging victim. The one who moved to France."

The DI nods slowly. "I see."

More silence. I've never seen Butler in a suspect interview, but she's reputed to be shit hot, and right now, that doesn't surprise me. Her gaze is rock steady, and I can't find a way to return it that doesn't feel defensive, doesn't look guilty. My pulse races; a muscle in the corner of my left eye flickers. Butler can't help but notice. She'll see it all. And she'll know I'm lying.

She closes her notebook, leans back in her chair, as if to say, *The hard bit's over—we're off the record now*, but I'm not fooled. Every one of my muscles is tight, as though I'm on the starting blocks, about to take off. I think of Mina, on her way to work, and for all that I didn't want her to go, I'm glad it's another five days till I have to face her again.

"They're sending me an itemized bill," Butler says. "But if there's anything you want to share in the meantime..."

I find a frown, as if I've got no idea what she's talking about.

"Because I'm assuming you're aware that job phones aren't to be used to make personal calls."

"Of course."

"Right, then."

I take my cue and stand up. Say, "Thank you," without thought as to why. For the heads-up, I suppose, the chance to prepare a defense, although the world's finest barristers couldn't spin together enough of a story to get me out of this one.

What happened with Katya is the least of my problems.

Once Butler sees that phone bill, it's over.

THREE

10 A.M. | MINA

As I near the airport, I see the police presence that tells me another demonstration is under way. Development for the new runway started three months ago, and periodically a cluster of protesters forms near Arrivals to make their feelings known. They're no trouble, in the main, and—although I'd never go on record with this—I sympathize with them. I just think they're going after the wrong target. We've created a world in which we need to fly; that can't change now. Better, surely, to tackle the factory emissions, the landfill?

I think guiltily of the daily wet wipes I use and resolve to dig out my Clarins again. A banner's been stretched across the road. PLAINS NOT PLANES. They must have only just put it there—security's pretty tight around the airport. The police can't stop them demonstrating, but they take down their signs as quickly as they go up. It seems a pretty pointless exercise, given that anyone traveling to the airport either works here or has a ticket to fly somewhere. A sign isn't going to change their minds.

I slow for the roundabout, glancing to the left where a woman holds a placard showing a photograph of a starving polar bear. Seeing me looking, she thrusts it toward me, shouting incomprehensibly. My heart races, and I reach for the central locking, my foot slipping on the accelerator in my haste to pull away. The absurdity of my reaction—to a woman on the other side of the railings, for heaven's sake!—makes me cross with the lot of them. Maybe I'll keep using the bloody wet wipes, just to spite them.

After arriving at the car park, I lock my car then wheel my case to the shuttle bus. I usually walk to the crew room, but the pavement's slippery with gray ice thrown up from the roads, and what was fresh snow at home is slush here. I can't wait to touch down in Sydney and see sunshine, dump my bag at the hotel, and head to the beach to sleep off the flight.

In the crew room, there's the buzz in the air that comes with hot gossip or new rosters. I queue for a coffee and cup my still-cold hands around the plastic. A woman in civvies looks at me appraisingly.

"You on the Sydney flight?"

"Yes." I feel myself flush, half expecting her to call me out on it. *You shouldn't be here…*

Instead, she grimaces. "Rather you than me."

I look for a name badge but don't find one. Who is this woman, so full of opinions? She could be anyone from a cleaning lady to a finance manager. Hundreds of people pass through the crew room even on a normal day, and this is not a normal day. Everyone wants a piece of Flight 79. Everyone wants to make history.

"Santiago's fourteen hours, and that's not too bad." I smile politely, getting out my phone to signal that we're done, but she doesn't take the hint. She comes closer, pulling me toward her and dropping her voice as though someone might be listening.

"I heard something went wrong on the last test flight."

I laugh. "What are you talking about?" I speak loudly, banishing the tiny seed of fear her words have planted within me.

"A problem with the plane. Only they hushed it all up. They made the crew sign confidentiality agreements and—"

"Stop it!" I'm 99 percent certain I've never worked with this woman. Why has she latched on to me, out of everyone here? I scan her face, try to work out where she's from. Human Resources, maybe? Not Customer Services, that's for sure; no one would ever set foot on a plane again. "This is nuts," I say firmly. "Do you really think they'd launch a route without being a hundred percent certain it was safe?"

"They had to. Otherwise Qantas would have gotten there first— they've been working on it for far longer. The test flights ran with a fraction of the number of passengers and with no baggage. Who knows what'll happen with a fully laden plane—"

"I've got to go." I drop my half-drunk coffee into the bin, the lid crashing down as I snatch my foot off the pedal to walk away. Stupid woman—ridiculous to let her wind me up. But a curl of fear wraps itself around my heart. Two days ago, the *Times* took a press release on the race between Qantas and World Airlines and twisted it. How Fast Is Too Fast? ran the headline, above an article that hinted at corner cutting and cost saving. I spent an hour on the phone with Dad, reassuring him that *yes, it's safe; no, they wouldn't take risks.*

"I couldn't bear it if—"

"Dad, it's perfectly safe. Everything's been checked and double-checked."

"It always is." His tone was loaded, and I was glad he couldn't see my face. I didn't rise to the bait. Didn't want to think about it.

They took forty staff members on the three trial flights last year, monitored their blood sugar, their oxygen levels, and their brain activity. The cabin pressure's been tweaked and the noise levels reduced, and even the meals have been specially designed to combat jet lag. It's as safe as any other flight.

"Good luck!" the woman calls after me, but I don't look back. Luck has nothing to do with it.

But my pulse is still high when I slide into the briefing room a few minutes later. It's packed—not just the crew but a bunch of suits I mostly don't recognize.

"Is that Dindar?" I turn to the flight attendant next to me, whom I've flown with once before. I check his name badge. Erik.

"Yes, that is Dindar. He is here for the launch."

Figures. Yusuf Dindar, the airline's CEO, only makes an appearance on days like today, when a big launch means television cameras and kudos for the men (because they're all men) behind World Airlines. The race for the first London to Sydney nonstop flight has been neck and neck, and behind Dindar's self-congratulatory expression this morning is a flicker of relief that they got there first. He stands, waiting until all eyes are on him.

"Today, we make headlines!"

Everyone applauds. There are whoops from the back of the room and a flash of photography. Amid the anticipatory celebrations, I feel a chill in my bones.

Something went wrong…a problem with the plane…

I shake the woman's words away. Applaud fiercely with the others. We're making headlines. London to Sydney in twenty hours. Nothing will go wrong. *Nothing will go wrong*, I repeat, a mantra against the growing sense of doom I feel.

I know why she's rattled me. It's because I shouldn't be here.

Personnel drew names for the crewing, although whether we were winning the lottery or drawing the short straw wasn't quite clear. There was a flurry of messages on the WhatsApp group.

Anything?

Not yet.

I heard the email's gone out.

So desperate to do it!!!

And then an image: a screenshot from Ryan's phone. *Congratulations! You have been assigned to the inaugural London–Sydney direct flight on December 17.* He had captioned the picture with a crying emoji and *Twenty bloody hours!*

I messaged him privately. Offered to take his place. I didn't tell him why, of course—tried not to show how much it mattered—but he still held out for a swap on Mexico City, plus a bunch of gift cards I'd gotten for my birthday. *Crazy chick!* he'd concluded, and I had to agree.

And now I'm here. An interloper on the most important flight in recent history.

"I'd like to introduce the pilots for this historic flight," Dindar is saying. He waves for them to join him at the front of the room, and there's a shuffle of feet as people move to make way. "Captain Louis Joubert and First Officer Ben Knox; Captain Mike Carrivick and First Officer Francesca Wright."

"Carrivick?" I say to Erik as everyone claps. "He's not on the crew sheet I've got."

Erik shrugs. "Last-minute switch. I don't know the guy."

Dindar is still going. "There will be a number of invited guests on board." By "invited guests" he means people who haven't paid. Journalists, a smattering of celebs and "influencers" who will spend sixteen hours of the flight Instagramming and the other four drinking. "But I urge you to treat them no differently from our paying customers."

Yeah, right. The journalists might be here for a jolly, sure—*free business-class trip to Australia? Take my passport!*—but they're after a story too. Think *Daily Mail* meets TripAdvisor. LONG-HAUL NO HYPOALLERGENIC PILLOWS SHOCKER.

Once Dindar and the suits have finished congratulating themselves, we hold the crew briefing. Mike and Cesca will handle takeoff and the first four hours of the flight, then they'll take their break in the bunks above the flight deck. Louis and Ben fly for the next six hours before the crews switch again. As for the cabin crews, there are sixteen of us, split into two shifts. When we're not working, we'll be up in the bunks at the back of the plane, pretending it's normal to be sleeping in a windowless room full of strangers.

Someone from Occupational Health comes in to talk about the dangers of fatigue. She reminds us to stay hydrated, then demonstrates a breathing exercise that's supposed to help us maximize sleep during our breaks. Several members of the cabin crew start laughing; one pretends to fall asleep.

"Sorry," he says, jerking upright with a grin. "I guess it works!"

As we walk through the airport, in pairs behind the pilots, there's an atmosphere of fevered anticipation, and I feel the buzz of pride I always do before a flight. Our uniforms are navy, with emerald trim on the cuffs and hems and around the lapels. An enameled pin on the left breast pocket says WORLD AIRLINES; on the right side, there's a badge with our first names. Our emerald scarves when spread out are a map of the world, each country made up of a tiny repeat of the airline's name. For today, we wear a new pin. FLIGHT 79. MAKING THE WORLD A SMALLER PLACE.

An in-house photographer snaps us from all angles, and a whisper of *London–Sydney* follows us to the gate.

"Like being on a red carpet!" one of the crew says.

Like walking to the gallows, I'd been thinking. I can't shake this feeling—a single bad apple in a barrel of good ones—that something terrible is about to happen.

Some people get this feeling every time they fly, I suppose: a pool of dread at the pits of their stomachs. I've always thought how sad it must be, to spend those miraculous hours of flight clutching the armrests, eyes screwed shut over imagined disasters that never happen.

Not me. For me, flying is everything. A triumph of engineering, working not against nature but with it. Adam laughs when I geek out over planes, but is there anything more beautiful than an A320 taking off? As a kid, I moaned when Dad took me to the airport, where he'd stand by the perimeter fence, taking photos of the planes. For Dad, it was the photography that mattered—he spent equally long days by the river, getting the perfect picture of a heron in flight—but slowly, I found myself drawn in.

"Got a great shot of that triple seven." Dad would show me the digital screen.

"That wasn't a triple seven," I'd say. "It was an SP."

I loved to draw, and I'd sketch nose shapes in my notebook, no longer complaining when Dad suggested we spend Saturday at the airport. When we flew to see family, I never cared what films they were showing or what nestled within the foil-wrapped food trays. I pressed my nose against the window and watched the flaps moving up and down, felt the gentle movement of the plane in response. I loved it all.

So it's unsettling, this flutter in my stomach, the creeping sense of dread as we board the plane. The door to the flight deck is open, all four pilots crammed inside as they prepare the flight, and I feel a shiver down my neck.

Erik notices. "Are you cold? It is the air-conditioning; they always have it too cold."

"No, I'm okay. Someone walking over my grave." I shiver again and wish I'd chosen a different expression. I check the cabin equipment, something I've done so many times before, but today, it feels different. Pressure. Seals. Oxygen tubes. Fire extinguisher. Smoke mask, survival kits... Each one essential. Each one the difference between life and death.

"Get a grip, Holbrook," I mutter. I carry a box of tonic water through the business-class cabin to the lounge and help to stock the bar. The plane has a bespoke layout, supposedly designed to improve passenger comfort on such a long flight. There's a galley at the front, between the flight deck and the cabin, with two bathrooms and the stairs to the relief bunks hidden behind a door. Business class comes first, followed by their private lounge and bar—curtained off from the rest of the plane—and another pair of bathrooms. The economy cabin is laid out in two halves, with a dedicated "stretching zone" between the two, and more economy loos at the back. Three hundred and fifty-three passengers in total: all breathing the same air from the second the doors close in London till they open again in Sydney.

Business-class passengers board first, eyes already looking toward the bar and scoping out the beds as we check tickets and take coats to hang in the cupboard by the galley. There are too many crew members on board, with all sixteen in the cabin to greet passengers as they board. Half will disappear to the bunks after takeoff, leaving Erik, Carmel, and me in business class, Hassan in the bar, and four in economy. For now, with everyone downstairs, there is a sense of mania that seeps along the cabin. Twenty hours. Where else would complete strangers spend so many hours locked up together? Prison, I suppose, and the thought makes me uneasy.

Those in business class are offered champagne. I see one man knock his back as though it's a shot before winking at Carmel for a second glass. *Twenty hours.*

You can tell the troublemakers from the outset. It's something in their look as much as their behavior, something that says, *I'm better than you. I'm going to make your life difficult.* It isn't always the drinkers, though (although free champagne doesn't help), and this guy isn't giving me bad vibes. We'll see.

"Ladies and gentlemen, welcome on board Flight 79 from London to Sydney." As the senior crew member, I have the dubious privilege of addressing our passengers. There's nothing in my script that marks out today as special, but a cheer goes up regardless. "Please ensure all mobile phones and portable electronic devices are stowed for departure."

I walk into the cabin, noticing a large bag at the foot of a woman with long salt-and-pepper hair, wearing a green jumper.

"Can I put that in the overhead locker for you?"

"I need it with me."

"If it can't fit in the storage compartments, it'll need to go in the locker, I'm afraid."

The woman picks it up and hugs it to her chest, as though I've threatened to snatch it forcibly from her. "I have all my things in it."

I try not to sigh. "I'm sorry. It can't stay here."

For a second, we lock eyes, each determined to win, then she lets out a *tsk* of frustration and starts pulling out the contents of her bag, slotting jumpers, books, cosmetic bags into the numerous storage cupboards surrounding her seat. I make a mental note to double-check her seat when we land in case she leaves any of it behind. Once settled again, she loses her grumpy expression, looking out the window as she sips her champagne.

At the captain's announcement—*Cabin crew, prepare doors for departure and cross-check*—the collective excitement in the cabin grows. Most of the business-class passengers have already delved into their welcome gift bag, and one woman has already managed to change into her souvenir Flight 79 pajamas, much to the amusement of her fellow passengers. There's a special video message from Dindar ahead of the safety briefing, which everyone duly ignores because no one they know has ever needed it. Carmel and I collect the empty glasses.

"Hold your horses, darling. There's a bit still in that." A woman with twinkly eyes grins at me as she scoops her glass back from my tray and downs the remaining half inch of champagne. I remember her name from the boarding list—one of a handful that have already stuck in my mind. By the end of the flight, I'll know the names of all fifty-six passengers in business class.

"Do you have everything you need, Lady Barrow?"

"Patricia, please. Well, Pat, really. Just plain old Pat." She has a naughty smile—the grandmother who slips the children extra chocolate when Mum's not looking. "The title is my children's idea of a joke."

"You're not really a lady?"

"Oh, I am. I preside over a whole square foot of Scottish soil," she says grandly, then bursts into infectious laughter.

"Do you have relatives meeting you in Sydney?"

Something passes across her eyes—a fleeting darkness she hides with a lift of her chin and that naughty smile again. "No, I've run away." She laughs at the surprise on my face, then she sighs. "They're very cross with me, actually. And I'm not entirely sure I'm doing the right thing—I'm missing my dogs terribly already. But it's the first year without my husband and—" She stops abruptly and lets out a sharp breath. "Well, I needed to shake things up." She puts a manicured hand on my arm. "Life's short, young lady. Don't waste it."

"I won't." I smile, but her words echo in my ear as I make my way down the aisle. *Life's short*. Too short. Sophia is five already, the days hurtling past.

I tell people I came back to work because we needed the money and because Sophia's case worker felt it would help with her attachment issues, and both those things are true.

"But this is all caused by neglect, right?" Adam said when we discussed it. "The fact that for the first few months of her life, she was essentially abandoned?" The case worker nodded, but Adam had already continued, working through his thoughts out loud. "Then how does it help her for Mina to go away?"

I remember the stab of fear I felt, that the glimpse of freedom I'd seen would be snatched away.

"Because Sophia will learn that Mina always comes back," the case worker said. "That's the important bit."

So I went back to work, and we were all happier for it. Adam because he didn't have to worry about money; Sophia as she began the slow process of understanding that I'd always come back to her; and me, because parenting Sophia was tough—really tough—and I needed to get away. I needed the break, but more than that, I needed to miss her; missing her reminds me how much I love her.

Checks complete, I wait for the PA from the flight deck—*Cabin crew, take your seats for departure*—and slip into the jump seat nearest the window. There's a roar from the engines, then the tarmac picks up pace beneath us. The flaps extend with a thud, the air pressure building until it's hard to say if you're hearing it or feeling it. The tiniest of jolts as the wheels leave the ground. I picture the space beneath us, the lift of the nose as we soar from the runway. Improbably heavy, impossibly bulky for such a graceful, beautiful maneuver. And yet somehow it works, and we climb, the pilots increasing the thrust as we push up and up. The sky has darkened, nimbostratus weighing low above the ground so that it feels more like dusk than midday, sleet lashing the windows until we're too high for it to strike.

The bell chimes at ten thousand feet, and like Pavlov's dogs, there's a flurry of activity. In 5J, a petite blond cranes her neck to look down toward the ground. She's tense, and I take her for a nervous flyer, but then she closes her eyes and leans back in her seat, and her face stretches into a slow, private smile.

We're underway. Seat belts off, passengers on their feet, bells already summoning drinks. It's too late now. Too late to do anything about the voice in my head warning me not to take this flight. It's my conscience, that's all. My own guilt for engineering a place here instead of staying home with Sophia, for being here at all, when life could have worked out so differently.

Too late or not, the voice persists.

Twenty hours, it says. *A lot can happen in twenty hours.*

FOUR

PASSENGER 5J

My name is Sandra Daniels, and when I stepped on Flight 79, I left my old life behind.

I don't think I'd have even considered getting on the plane if it hadn't been for my husband. They say victims of domestic abuse try to leave six times on average before they're finally successful. I only left once. Sometimes I think about what that does to the median, about the women who've tried eight times. Ten. Twenty.

I left once and once only, because I knew that if I didn't do it properly, he'd find me, and if he found me, he'd kill me.

They say that on average, victims are assaulted thirty-five times before they call the police. I wonder what it must be like, to have only been hit thirty-five times. Not that I counted (and I've always been stupid at math anyway), but even I know that two or three times a week over four years is a lot more than thirty-five. Although perhaps they only mean the big stuff—the broken bones, the blows to the head that blur the edges with fuzzy, black stars. Not the slaps. The pinches. They probably don't count. Typical me: overexaggerating again.

It wasn't Henry's fault, not completely. I mean, I know it's wrong to hit someone—of course it's wrong—but he lost his job, and that does things to a man, doesn't it? Having to rely on his wife's income, being the one expected to put a meal on the table, clean the loo, and wait for the dishwasher repairman.

It didn't seem fair. As Henry said, he was the one who loved his work, while I'd just fallen into mine. A job, not a career. Henry was going places,

*while I was treading water. He was respected—good at what he did. I was...
well, he told me what he'd overheard at the bar, that time he came to our
Christmas do.*

*I stopped going out for work drinks after that. How could I, once I knew
what they really thought of me? Thick. Ugly. Incompetent. Not news, I guess,
but no one likes to have it confirmed, do they? My colleagues kept up the
pretense, though, I'll give them that: all smiles and* How was your weekend?
and Are you sure you won't join us? *I said I was busy, over and over until
they stopped asking.*

*When Henry got a job again, I was grateful when he suggested I hand in
my notice. I doubted I'd be missed. It was a new start in many ways, and
although it wasn't something we'd discussed, I felt sure it would mark the end
of Henry's low moods. I would be able to support him so much better, now
that I wasn't working, and in between the housework and the cooking, maybe
I'd join the gym or take a painting class. I might even make some friends.*

*Henry happened to see an advert for online fitness classes. They cost much
less than the gym, and I wouldn't have to drive anywhere, of course, so it
made perfect sense. I did start my painting course, though. I was terrible! I
mean, really terrible. Our first assignment was a pencil sketch of a vase, and
as Henry said, it could have been anything. I didn't go back. Silly of me to
have tried, really. Old dogs and new tricks, as they say.*

*I did make friends, though. On Facebook, of all places. "Pretend friends,"
Henry called them, although in many ways, they were more real than the
people around me: the couple next door, for example, or the woman who
delivered the Avon catalogues and sometimes stopped for a cuppa. I talked to
them, you see, my pretend friends. About cleaning, first of all—we were all
part of a Facebook group about household hacks—but you know what it's
like: you get to know one another. Wish one another happy birthday, that sort
of thing. Before I knew it, we were messaging privately.*

—He shouldn't treat you like that, you know, *they said.*

*I did know, somewhere inside, but having someone else say it made
the thought take root. The next time Henry hit me, I went straight to my
computer.*

—He did it again.

—You should leave.

—I can't.

—You can.

They say one in four women will suffer some form of domestic abuse in their lifetime. A quarter of all women.

I look around the plane, counting the passengers. Statistically, at least five women in this business-class cabin alone have been—or will be—beaten by their partners. The thought is both comforting and horrific.

The older lady, perhaps. She has twinkly eyes, but they glistened with tears when she spoke to the air hostess. Is she running away too?

Or the wife of that footballer—we all recognize him—for all that she's draped across him, immaculate with her glossy hair and berry lips. You never know what happens behind closed doors after all. No one ever knew what happened behind mine.

The cabin crew?

Why not? Domestic abuse doesn't discriminate. I look for their name badges and try them out for size. Is Carmel a victim? Mina?

Mina has a smile that reaches every part of her face, but the second she ducks back behind the curtain, it drops like a stone. There's something there, behind her eyes, something troubling her. She doesn't look like a victim, but then I didn't think I looked like one either, didn't think I was one, till friends helped me see the world for how it really was.

It's hard to find the words for how I feel about those "pretend friends" Henry was so derisive about.

How do you thank someone for saving your life?

Because that's what they've done. They opened my eyes to what he was doing and gave me back the confidence I'd lost.

When Flight 79 took off, I relaxed for the first time in fifteen years. Henry won't follow me to Sydney. He'll never find me.

I'm finally free.

FIVE

3 P.M. | ADAM

My meeting with DI Butler shot my concentration for the rest of the day, making every statement take twice as long as it should have done.

"Are you alright?" My first witness looked at the scrawl my shaking hand had produced and cocked her head to the side in concern.

I made light of it—"I think that's my line"—but I could see her throwing nervous glances at the paper as I added to her statement, and when I read it back, there were so many errors that I started again. My silent phone logged twenty-seven missed calls, the voicemail icon flashing red. How long does it take to pull an itemized phone bill? How long for Butler to scan the pages, to see the same number again and again, the digits in the far column running higher and higher. How long to end a career that took twenty years to build?

I'm late leaving the office, circling town twice in the hope of a parking space, before giving up and taking the car home. The wasted time means I have to run to pick up Sophia, snow clumping around my boots and slowing me down. I cut through the churchyard in defiance of the signs, and I pass a bunch of women coming the other way, their kids clutching paintings. Crap. They send the kids to after-school club if you're late and charge you a fiver for the privilege, even if you pick up five minutes later. It might not sound a lot, but right now, it's more than I've got.

I skid through the gate at nine minutes past.

"Mr. Holbrook." Miss Jessop frowns, no doubt working out how to tell me I need to cough up. "Sophia's already been collected, I'm afraid."

"By who?" Not by Mina; her flight left before noon.

"Becca. Your babysitter," she adds, as though I might have forgotten. "Did Mrs. Holbrook not tell you?" I can see her storing the gossip away for the staff room. *Things must be really bad between Sophia's parents. I don't think they're even talking now...*

"Yes, she did. I just forgot. Thanks." I force myself to smile, even though I'm furious with Mina for making me look like an idiot.

I sprint down toward the high street, catching up with them on the corner where the police station is. I slow to a walk. Sophia's hair—so dark and curly that people see a resemblance to Mina that can't possibly exist—explodes from beneath her woolly hat and bounces on the shoulders of her bright-red duffle coat, the plaits Mina always does over breakfast no doubt torn out by lunchtime. She's looking down as she walks, finding the patches of untouched snow between the well-trodden slush so she can sink her boots into them. "Hey, Sophia."

She turns around. Her smile's unguarded at first, then a wariness creeps over her face. I hate myself for putting it there.

"Hi, Daddy."

"Hi, Adam."

"Alright, Becca? How come you're here? I told Mina I was leaving work early today."

She shrugs. "I just got a text. I don't normally babysit two nights in a row, but it's an expensive time of year, isn't it, what with Christmas presents and then New Year's Eve. The Bull's doing this thing where it's twenty quid to get in, then there's drinks, and if we want to go on after..."

I tune out as we start walking home. Sophia dances around, a fish on Becca's line. I reach toward her other glove, but she thrusts her hand into her pocket, and I bite the inside of my cheek till I taste iron.

Bloody Mina. I told her I'd pick up Sophia. I texted her, for God's sake—put it in black and white. I can't send Becca away now without giving her some cash—not if she was expecting to be paid until I got back from work.

"Veg shop," Sophia says. "Sainsbury's."

It's typical of Mina. She bangs on about how I need to do my fair share, then she pulls a stunt like this and makes a tit of me.

"Now the butcher. Ugh. Now the 'state agent where they—"

"Sell houses, yes, we know. For God's sake, Sophia!"

I feel Becca's eyes on me as Sophia falls silent.

Easy to be a perfect parent when you don't have kids, when their strange little quirks are endearing instead of infuriating. Maybe if Becca had to listen to Sophia narrate her journey to school a thousand times or heard Mina reciting *Goodnight Moon* every bloody night for five years, she'd get it.

Mina won't look at her phone till she lands, but all this frustration inside me needs somewhere to go, so I take out mine. She reckons I'm the one *not communicating*, when she can't even sort out the simple logistics of who's picking up our—

I stare at my screen, at the message thread I've opened in preparation for giving Mina both barrels.

> No need for a babysitter. I've sorted an early finish tomorrow, so
> I can

My message lies unfinished. I have a sudden memory of the call from Custody, of thrusting my phone back into my pocket yesterday afternoon, because my suspect's brief was finally ready for disclosure.

I thought I'd sent it.

I was sure I'd sent it.

Heat rushes through me, remorse a close cousin of anger, the way it always has been. This has only happened because Mina won't answer her phone to me now, insists on me texting. Or emailing. Emailing! Who emails their wife, for God's sake?

It's easier.

Easier on whom? Not me, that's for sure. She can't bear even to hear my voice, can she? She'd rather keep me at the end of an email, where she can pretend I'm just some administrative headache she has to deal with for Sophia's sake.

"Stay, then," I tell Becca, and even I can hear the bitterness in my voice. I swallow it. "Fix Sophia's tea, maybe? She'd like that."

She hesitates, then shrugs. "Cool."

Is that what Mina would have done? Or would she tell me I'm wasting money we don't have? There was a time when I couldn't put a foot wrong in Mina's eyes. Now I can't do anything right.

Liar.

Cheat.

Not fit to be a father.

The worst of it is that she's right. I am a liar. I am a cheat. She can't hate me any more than I hate myself, can't know that just catching a glimpse of myself in the mirror makes me sick with disgust. How did it come to this?

Butler probably has that phone bill already. She'll have been through it with a highlighter, reading between the lines. Coloring in the end of my career.

What will I do? Being a copper isn't like most other jobs; you don't do it then move on, as if you worked in a bar or tried your hand at retail. It's like teaching or being a doctor. It's part of you. And I'm going to lose it all.

Ex-husband, ex-father, ex-copper. Things couldn't get much worse.

As we come to the edge of town, Sophia pulls free from Becca's hand. It's snowing again, and her wellies leave tiny footprints on the path. She takes the corner twenty yards ahead of us, and I call her name, but she giggles and runs faster.

"Race!"

I break into a jog. Around the corner, the street's empty. Gray slush from the road has spattered the pavements, and I search for the right-sized prints. "Sophia!"

"Chill. She's playing hide-and-seek," Becca says, several yards behind me. "*Oh no!*" she calls, pantomime-loud. "*Where could Sophia be?*" She grins at me, but I'm not playing.

"Sophia!"

A car passes us, and I look inside, clock the number plate, the driver, the direction of travel. It takes seconds to snatch a child. Minutes to make them disappear.

"Sophia!" I break into a run. "Come out right now. This isn't funny."

"She won't come out if she thinks you're cross with her," Becca hisses after me, then calls out in that singsong voice: "*I can't see her anywhere!*"

I stop so abruptly, I almost lose my footing. "Please don't tell me how to parent my own child." I turn in a circle, scanning the street. Where is she?

During any police investigation involving a kid, there's a moment when you think: *What if this were my child? What would I do? How would it feel?* Only a moment, though; if you let it go on for any longer than that, you'd never get the job done.

The moment is already a minute.

"Sophia!" So loud the sound rasps in my throat and I have to cough to clear it.

"*It's no good.*" Becca heaves a melodramatic sigh. "*We'll have to go home without her.*"

"No!" Sophia pops out from behind a wheelie bin and barrels into Becca. "I'm here!"

"Oh my goodness, you were hiding! I thought you'd vanished into thin air!"

Blood roars in my ears as I bend down, grabbing Sophia's arm and pulling her to me. "Don't ever do that again, do you hear? Anything could have happened."

"She was just playing—"

I cut Becca dead with a glare and make Sophia look at me. Her bottom lip wobbles.

"Sorry, Daddy."

My face feels hot, a sharp pricking behind my eyes. Slowly, my heart rate returns to normal. I give Sophia a quick smile. Release her arm and tweak her hat straight. "You scared me, Soph."

She looks at me, dark eyes holding mine for so long, it's as if she knows all my secrets. "Daddies don't get scared."

"Everyone gets scared sometimes," I say lightly. She lets me hold her hand the rest of the way home, and I wonder if she knows how much it means to me. I catch Becca looking at me, her eyebrows alone somehow managing to convey that she thinks I overreacted. She doesn't say so, of course. Not like Mina would. *You're such a doom merchant,* she says. *Always convinced the worst is going to happen.*

Guilty as charged. But that's because it so often does.

"Mummy's on a plane," Sophia says as I help her out of her wellies. I bang them together and leave them on the doormat, along with the boots I wear for work. Our house—2 Farm Cottages—is the middle one of three terraced houses that once belonged to the farm a mile farther out.

"That's right."

All three cottages have gardens that back on to a park where there are huge oak trees and a path that forms a figure of eight. In one half of the eight is a children's playground and in the other a small lake, complete with a tiny island with a duck house. There's a wildflower meadow that's a riot of foxgloves and cornflowers in the summer, with a path Sophia loves to run through.

"She's going to be on a plane for twenty hours, then she's coming home again, and that'll take twenty hours too, but she'll stay in a hotel in between."

"That's right."

"Clever girl," Becca says, looking at her phone.

"It's a Boeing triple seven, and it's got three hundred and fifty-three people on it."

"Yes." *Mummy, Mummy,* always *Mummy...*

"Where is she?"

I count to five and summon my patience. "You just told me where she is. She's on a plane."

"Yes, but where 'zackly?"

Are there other men who feel the way I do? Other men whose children only ever want to be with their mums? Are there other dads who constantly feel like the consolation prize, no matter how hard they try? I guess I'll never know, because finding out would mean telling someone how shit it feels when your daughter only ever wants someone else.

I get out my phone and bring up the tracking app beloved by plane spotters and far-flung family. "Mummy is..." I wait for the app to load Mina's plane. "Here."

"Bell-are-us."

"Roos. Like in goose. Belarus."

Sophia repeats it, studying the word on the screen, and I know she'll remember for next time. She never forgets anything.

"*Nostrovia*," Becca says.

"You what?"

She wanders into the kitchen, leaving her wellies in a puddle on the tiles. "It's Russian for cheers."

I move her boots to the mat and look at the blinking dot on my phone that represents Mina at thirty-five thousand feet. Soon, the blinking dot will move across Russia's airspace, and then Kazakhstan's, and then China's. Finally, it'll cross the Philippines, then Indonesia, and then, before Sophia and I wake up, she'll have crossed Australia and landed in Sydney.

"Twenty hours," I'd said when Mina told me she was going. "That's a hell of a shift."

"I don't run the airline, Adam."

I left a beat of silence before I spoke again, refusing to rise to the argument she was trying to start. "Still, it'll be nice to have a few days in Sydney at this time of year."

"It's not a holiday!"

I'd given up. We were standing outside school—a handover of Elephant, who'd been inadvertently left behind that morning. Sophia had thrown her arms around Mina, then nodded at me as if we'd met once at a networking conference: *And what is it you do again?* I'd been granted a few hours with my daughter, with strict instruction to return her by six.

Mina had kept picking. "Stop trying to make me feel guilty, Adam. This is my job."

"I know, I—"

"It's not like I have a choice." She'd flushed with anger, making a show of buttoning Sophia's coat. I could see her taking deep, controlled breaths, and when she straightened, you'd never have known anything was wrong.

"I'll miss you," I said softly. I wondered if I'd overstepped the mark, but her eyes glistened. She turned away, perhaps hoping I hadn't seen.

"It's just like any other flight."

Twenty hours, though.

The fevered expectation around this flight has gone on for two years. Perhaps I've noticed it more simply because Mina works for them, but

World Airlines has been there at every turn. TV adverts, showing the smooth action of the flat beds in business class and the stretched-out legs of passengers in economy. Interviews with the pilots who worked the test flights, and nostalgic comparisons with the fifty-five-hour "Kangaroo route" they ran in the 1940s, which stopped in six countries en route.

"In 1903," Yusuf Dindar had said a couple of days ago, on the *BBC Breakfast* sofa, "the Wright brothers defied gravity with the first sustained flight of an engine-powered aircraft. More than a hundred years later, we have the capability to keep one hundred and fifty tons of metal in the air for twenty continuous hours." He leaned back, a confident arm across the back of the sofa, and smiled. "The Earth's forces are strong, but we've proved we are stronger. We've beaten nature."

A chill runs across the back of my neck now as I remember his look of supreme confidence. I don't doubt he has the best team, the best planes. But nature can swallow a town, fell skyscrapers, slide entire coastlines into the ocean…

I snap myself out of the worst-case-scenario loop playing in my head. Mina's right: I'm a doom merchant. They've tested this flight three times. They've got the whole world watching. Their reputation, not to mention the safety of hundreds of lives, is at stake.

Nothing will go wrong.

SIX

17 HOURS FROM SYDNEY | MINA

We're somewhere over Eastern Europe, below us nothing but a swirl of cloud. I touch my fingers to the glass and tune my eyes into the shapes I would be finding with Sophia if she were here. *An old lady, bent over in a shuffle on her way to the shops—look, there's her handbag. A palm tree—look, there! You have to squint a bit...*

I remember looking for cloud pictures with my own mother, lying on my back in the garden while Mum picked at weeds in the flower bed. She kept the garden beautifully, never knowing the names of any plant but instinctively knowing where each should go.

"Plants need five things to flourish," she'd said. She was digging up a pretty shrub that had sported delicate white flowers last year but that this year had failed to thrive. I'd sat up, delighted by this chance to show off what I'd learned in biology.

"Water," I said. "And food. Light, to photosynthesize." I thought for a moment. "Heat?"

"Clever girl. What's the fifth thing?"

I screwed up my face. I couldn't remember there even being a fifth thing.

"Space." Mum carefully lifted the shrub from the ground, filling the resulting hole with soil and patting in the surplus around the neighboring plants. "These three were fine together when they first went in, but now this one's too squashed. It won't die, but it won't thrive. I'll put it somewhere else, and you just see—it'll be so grateful."

I think about that conversation every time I step on a plane, swallowing the guilt I feel at leaving Sophia. We need space to thrive. All of us.

I blink hard and leave the clouds to make shapes alone. Inside, the plane is bright and filled with chatter. The meals we're serving are carefully planned: the first to keep passengers awake, the second to encourage them to rest.

"They should give everyone a sleeping tablet," Erik said when we were looking over the menu. "It would have been cheaper."

I take a walk through the cabin, checking everyone has what they need. There are seven rows in total. A double row of seats runs along the two sides of the cabin, with a bank of four seats in the center. Screens enable each seat to be isolated from its neighbor, providing each passenger with a private cocoon. When they want to sleep, the bottom half of the seat slides forward, tucking itself beneath the TV screen and transforming the already-comfortable chair into a perfectly flat bed. Not a bad way to spend twenty hours, and very different from the economy cabin, where thirty-three rows of nine are afforded a three-inch recline.

"Are we nearly there yet?" asks a man in one of the center seats, traveling alone. I laugh politely, although he's the fourth passenger to ask the question, each convinced of their own originality. Behind him, a sweet couple has retracted the privacy barrier between them and reclined their seats to an identical angle. On their screens, the same film plays, with a synchronicity only achievable by design. Newlyweds, perhaps, although if they are, the passenger list tells me she's kept her surname.

"May I have another blanket?" The woman's in her late twenties, with a riot of auburn ringlets held back by a wide band. "I'm freezing."

"Ginny's part lizard. Needs a heat lamp to be truly happy." Her partner's older than her, lines etched on his brow. He smiles as he speaks, but his eyes don't sparkle the way hers do.

"Well, you'll be glad to know it's twenty-five degrees in Sydney right now," I tell them. "How long are you there for?"

"Three weeks." Ginny bounces upright as though propelled by the force of her announcement. "We're eloping!"

"Gosh, that's exciting." I think of my wedding to Adam—church, family photos, hotel reception—and of the week we spent in Greece afterward. Conventional, perhaps, but reassuringly so. It felt solid. Safe.

"Ginny!"

"What? It doesn't matter now, Doug—we've done it. No one can stop us."

"Even so." He puts in his earphones, and Ginny flushes, her excitement squashed. I leave them to their film, but although they're sitting just as close as they were, something's shifted between them, and I'm uneasy for them. For her. I feel a sudden sadness for the couple Adam and I were, on that Greek island, and for the way we have ended up. Every relationship changes when you have children, no matter what route you take, but a child with special needs places pressure on a relationship that neither of us was prepared for. My response was to search for solutions, to read everything I could about adoption trauma and attachment disorder.

Adam's was to run away.

He was physically present—when he wasn't at work—but emotionally, I started to lose him years ago. I don't know if that was when the affairs started, and I don't know how many there have been; Katya is the only one I've been certain of.

I asked him once. I'd found a bank card for an account I hadn't known existed, then realized he'd changed the passcode for his phone to one I didn't know.

"Are you having an affair?"

"No!"

"Then why change your code?"

"I put the wrong one in three times. I had to change it." The lie was written all over his face.

I'm summoned to a seat across the aisle, where an older man with round glasses and thinning hair is frowning at his laptop. "There's still no Wi-Fi."

"No, I'm sorry. They're doing their best to find out what the problem is, but—"

"Will it be sorted soon?"

I resist the temptation to press my fingers to my temples and gaze into an invisible crystal ball. "I don't know. I'm so sorry for the inconvenience."

"Only I need it for work." The man looks at me expectantly, as though the power to mend the Wi-Fi network lies entirely within my hands. "It's a very long flight."

"It certainly is."

The flight crew is almost ready for the first handover. Cesca and Mike will go upstairs to the relief bunks for six hours; by the time they return, we'll be halfway to Sydney. There's a second rest area at the back of the plane for the cabin crew, accessed via a locked door in the rear galley. Eight small bunks, foam barriers and a curtain between each. I doubt I'll sleep much during my first break, but it'll be a different story by the second. The whole crew will be back on duty two hours before arrival, with strict instructions from Dindar to be box-fresh for the landing photos.

We'll have a couple of days in Sydney before the return flight. It'll be great to explore the city but even better to revel in sleep undisturbed by Sophia's screams. She's had nightmares every night for months, no matter what bedtime routine we adopt, no matter where she sleeps. I wake, heart pounding, running down the landing to find her bolt upright in bed, stiff and unyielding in my arms for a second or two before she lets herself be held. "Maybe she's missing Katya," I said once to Adam. The implication was clear: the fault lay with him. He flushed, as he always does when her name is mentioned, and I let it drop, but something had nagged me like a sore tooth, and it wasn't until the following day that I worked it out. The nightmares had started *before* Katya left.

"Excuse me." A young boy—maybe nine or ten—puts his hand up and waves his fingers as if he's in class and needs the loo. Next to him, his mother is stretched out on the flat bed, her mouth slightly open beneath an eye mask with *Charging—do not unplug* embroidered on the satin fabric.

"Hello, what's your name?"

"Finley Masters."

I smile. "Hello, Finley. Would you like something to drink?"

"My headphones are tangled." The boy looks at me earnestly, and I feel the sudden tug in my chest that so often ambushes me when I'm away from Sophia.

"Oh dear, that's very serious. Let's see if we can sort it out, shall we?" I use my nails to pick at the knots in the cable, returning it to him with a smile.

"Thank you."

"Any time."

Finley's the only child in business class, although right at the front of the middle section, there's a couple with a tiny baby. He's crying, a kitten's mewl—not loud, but insistent—and I catch the anxious look between his parents. I smile at them, trying to convey that it doesn't matter, but they're fussing over the baby's clothes as though the key to his discomfort lies in the way his Babygro is fastened instead of the pressure building in his tiny ears.

I check the passenger list—Paul and Leah Talbot—and go to see if they need anything. Their baby can't be more than a month old.

"Three weeks and two days," Leah says when I ask. She's Australian, her hair sun-bleached and her face tanned and freckled. Straight, white teeth give her a wholesome, outdoor look, and I imagine her and her husband barbecuing on the beach come Christmas Day. Maybe Adam, Sophia, and I will do that one year—escape the cold and run off to the sunshine.

Still Adam, then? my inner therapist prompts.

"What a cutie! What's his name?" I ignore my subconscious. It's habit, that's all. Five years of being a family. Adam's made it perfectly clear where his priorities lie, and they aren't with his wife and daughter.

"He's a beaut, alright." Leah beams at her son. She's older than me—well into her forties, I'd guess—but in far better shape. "Meet Lachlan Hudson Samuel Talbot."

"That's a lot of names."

Her husband grins. "We couldn't decide." His accent is English but with the upward inflection at the end of a sentence that expats down under so readily acquire.

"You look amazing," I tell Leah. "I can't believe you've just given birth!"

The compliment embarrasses her, and she drops her lips to the baby's head, breathing in his smell. Her husband puts an arm around her, and it feels as though they're shutting me out, that I've said something wrong.

"If you need me to take him later so you can get some sleep, just let me know."

"Thanks."

I leave them, an ache in my heart as though I've swallowed a stone. Adopting hasn't taken away the grief of infertility, hasn't stopped the occasional but visceral longing for a taut, full belly or the barely there weight of a minute-old baby. Sophia is my world—you don't have to give birth to be a mother—but that doesn't mean it doesn't hurt to think of what might have been.

At the very least, I wish Sophia had come to us as a newborn. It could have happened. It *should* have happened. Her mother was already on a watch list; Social Services was hovering, the older siblings already in care. But there was a process to follow, and it robbed us of the first year of Sophia's life and Sophia of the ability to trust. It robbed us of the family we could have been.

Neither Adam nor I had been able to sleep the night before Sophia came home for the first time, for fear we'd mess it up.

"What if I never feel like I'm her real dad?"

"You will! Of course you will." I knew Adam was nervous—he'd taken longer than me to come around to the idea of adoption—but I knew, too, that he'd soon fall for Sophia. Families are built from love, not genes.

Only he and Sophia never seemed to bond. She was demanding, even as a baby, and wouldn't be settled by either of us. Eventually, she allowed me to rock her to sleep, but if Adam tried to hold her, she'd stiffen, screaming till she went blue. As she got older, she became more possessive of my time, shutting Adam out. "Be patient," I'd tell him. "One day, she'll come to you, and you need to be ready."

"Cheer up, love. It might never happen." I'm jolted out of my thoughts by the man behind the Talbots, whose long legs are stretched out beneath his tray, on which rests a water bottle and a book.

When I was at university, I worked in a pub full of bankers and wankers and undergraduates. The second I stepped behind the bar, my educational peers would become intellectually superior, subjecting me to *come on, love*s, and *alright, darling*s, as if we were *EastEnders* extras. This job gets like that sometimes. I know all sorts of cabin crew, with all sorts of qualifications. I know former paramedics, and university lecturers, and a retired police officer with late-onset wanderlust. Most passengers don't see that, though. They see the uniform, and they see a waitress.

Never mind the emergency training, the water safety, the ability to put out a fire or cut a passenger free from their seat.

I paste a smile over gritted teeth. "Can I get you anything else, sir? Some wine?"

"Thank you, but I don't drink."

"Well, I'm here if you need anything."

I'm grateful for this oasis of sobriety as the rest of the cabin gets progressively merry. I have a sudden yearning to be at home, cuddled with Sophia on the sofa, watching *Peppa Pig*. When I'm traveling, I remember all the good bits. Isn't that always the way? I even remember the good bits about me and Adam—the laughter, the closeness, the feeling of his arms around me.

A hum of noise comes from the bar, and I go to see if they need help. It's heaving, conversation rising in volume as more business-class passengers join the throng. Several customers are in their pajamas, the novelty still amusing them, hours into the flight. A couple stands at the bar, their body language flirtatious.

"Have you seen the corkscrew?" The barman—Hassan—looks harassed.

"No idea. It was there earlier. I'll get you one from the galley."

"This is why I only ever drink champagne. All you need is a glass. Or a straw!" The petite woman from 5J is at the bar. She has a deep, throaty laugh at odds with her appearance. She has long, blond hair and careful makeup, bloodred staining her lips. The man she's with can't take his eyes off her. He's stocky, not much taller than the blond woman, but with biceps bigger than her waist. His dark hair looks as if it would curl if it weren't clipped so short, and a thick beard covers half his face. The woman's left thumb is hooked into the back pocket of the man's trousers in that casual, automatic way two people learn to slot together. I feel a lump in my throat, remembering the years with Adam when our relationship was still new enough to be flirtatious yet familiar enough to be comfortable.

As I turn to go, there's movement in the corner of my eye: a swish of the curtains between business class and economy. I look back to see a dark-haired woman approaching the bar. She looks around as she waits, taking in the wide-screen TV on the wall and the baskets of sweet treats laid out for passengers to help themselves.

"Champagne, please."

Hassan glances at me. "I'm afraid the bar is for business-class passengers." He sounds nervous, his hands hovering near the champagne as though he might still serve her.

"I only want one."

It's tempting to let her have a drink then pack her back to economy, but there's something *entitled* in her manner that gets my hackles up. I step forward.

"I'm sorry. You'll need to return to the economy cabin."

"For fuck's sake. All I want is a drink."

I smile. "And all I want is not to be sworn at for doing my job, but I guess neither of us is getting what we want today."

"How are your pajamas?" She wheels around, spitting the words at an identically clad couple taking selfies.

"Um, they're very—"

"Do you know what we got in our 'souvenir gift bag'?" She waggles her fingers in violent air quotes, then raises her voice into a shout. "Fucking shortbread!"

"Okay, that's enough." I take the woman by her elbow, and she shakes me off.

"Get your hands off me! That's assault, that is." She looks around. "Is anyone filming this? She just assaulted me."

"Please return to your seat." Everyone in the bar is staring now, the passengers in business class craning their necks to see what's going on behind them. "This is for business-class passengers only."

"So how come he gets to stay?" She jabs a finger toward the stocky man, who is doing his best to ignore her.

"Because he's in—" I start, then I see the awkward flush that appears on the man's neck and the way he pushes his glass away from him across the bar, half-drunk.

"Sorry," he says, although it's not clear if it's directed at me or at his blond companion.

"For heaven's sake!" I direct this at Hassan, who chews his lip.

"They're together. It was quiet when they asked, and I thought…"

"Will everyone without a business-class ticket please return to your own seats," I say loudly, "where cabin crew will be delighted to take your drinks orders."

"Sorry," mutters the stocky man again. He gives a last, lingering look at the blond girl before shuffling through the curtain and back to his seat. I fold my arms and stare down the drunk woman. We lock eyes for a full minute before she gives up.

"Snobs!" She delivers her parting shot at full volume, and I feel sorry for the economy crew, who will need to spend the next fifteen hours refusing her alcohol.

I let out a breath, coloring at the smattering of applause that breaks out from the passengers in the bar.

"You've got kids, haven't you?" the pajama-clad woman says with a grin. "That was such a mum voice."

I grin. I head back to the galley, and for the first time since I got to work, I feel myself relax, the uneasy feeling finally shifting. My instincts had been right: something *was* going to happen on this flight, but it was nothing I couldn't handle. I've been doing this job for twelve years—it would take a lot to throw me.

When I was a child, Mum would always stretch her arm toward the sky as a jumbo jet soared overhead.

"Quick! Send love to Manii and Baba sido!"

"That plane could be going anywhere," I'd laugh. But I'd wave anyway, too superstitious not to. The habit became ingrained—like saluting single magpies—long after my grandparents had passed away and there was no longer a reason to visit Algeria or to send our love across the ocean. Even after I'd stopped going to the airport with Dad—far too cool, by my midteens, to be caught watching planes—I'd raise a self-conscious arm whenever I saw a plane. *Hey, Manii and Baba. Love you guys.*

Years later, we were traveling back from France, where my parents still kept a house. It had belonged to my dad's parents, a ramshackle place full of memories. I was looking out the plane window, on to clouds that looked solid enough to stand on. We had spent every school holiday in France, continuing the tradition now I was at college. While my mother flitted about, catching up with her friends, I'd see my father relax, away from the rigors of London life.

"I'd love to be a pilot." It was the first time I'd said it out loud, and it had felt audacious. Ridiculous.

"So be a pilot," Dad said.

That was him all over. *You want something? Make it happen.*

Way down at the front of the plane, the door to the flight deck had opened, and I'd craned my neck to catch a glimpse of the instrument panel, of the vast curve of glass that looked out on that carpet of cloud. Excitement thrummed in my veins. "It's really expensive."

"How expensive?"

"Like…eighty grand? At least."

He didn't say anything for ages, then he shrugged and rustled his paper and said, "Get the details."

Six weeks later, they sold the house in France.

"Go be a pilot," Dad said.

"But you loved that house!" I scoured my parents' faces and found nothing but excitement. "It was supposed to be your pension."

"Who needs a pension when your daughter's a commercial pilot?" Dad winked. "You can keep us in our old age."

My mother squeezed my arm. "We'll be fine. We're excited for you."

She took a photograph the day I left for training college, as if it were my first day of school. I stood by the front door in my black trousers and packet-fresh shirt, a single gold bar on my epaulettes.

I look down at the skirt I'm in now, at my manicured nails and my flesh-colored tights. I love my job, but this wasn't how it was supposed to be.

"Fancy a brew to take up?" Carmel holds a tea bag over an empty mug.

"Go on, then." It feels weird to take a break now, just a few hours after starting, and even weirder to know that when we wake, we'll still have hours to go. Below us, people will get up, go to work, come home, and go to bed, and all that time, we'll be in the air. It feels impossible, almost otherworldly.

Unlike Erik, who hasn't cracked a smile since we boarded, Carmel is lovely. Only twenty-two and about to move in with her boyfriend, who she clearly worships.

"He works in the City," she'd told me proudly as we sat in the jump seats, ready for takeoff.

"What does he do?"

She blinked. "He works in the City."

I'd tutted at myself. "Ah, yes, you said. Sorry."

She makes the tea, and I reach into the hatbox next to the galley for the small paper bag Sophia made me promise to bring on board. "Don't open it till you're flying," she'd told me. She'd come into my room as I was packing, used, now, to the sight of my case open on the bed.

I unfold the paper. It's one of the flapjacks we baked together on the weekend, and the syrupy scent makes my mouth water. One of the corners has been nibbled, and I touch the ragged edge where my daughter's pearly teeth have been.

Beneath the flapjack, spotted with grease, is a piece of paper. *For my mummy, love from Sophia xoxox.* I show Carmel, and she clasps her hands to her chest.

"Bless! Your daughter?"

I nod.

"Oh my God, cute or what? I can't wait to be a mummy. Bet you do all sorts of stuff with her, don't you? Painting and crafts and all sorts."

"Mostly baking." I hold up the flapjack. "Lots and lots of baking. She made these practically on her own. She's only five."

"Amazing."

I pull off a piece of flapjack and put it in my mouth, putting the note in my pocket and wrapping up the rest to have upstairs. I start wiping down the galley, getting everything straight for the next team. Someone's left an auto-injector pen lying on the counter in the galley, and I pick it up so it doesn't get swept into the rubbish.

"Any idea who—" I stop, my attention caught by a slightly scuffed label on the pen. A small white rectangle with a hand-drawn smiley face and a printed name.

Sophia Holbrook.

"Milk and sugar?" Carmel asks.

What's Sophia's EpiPen doing here? The smiley face tells me it's the one from her rucksack—Adam's simple but effective solution for keeping track of which pen lives where—and the label is undoubtedly the same as those with which I painstakingly named her shoes, lunch box, and water bottle.

I think back to this morning, after I'd dropped Sophia at school.

I changed into my uniform at home. Even if the pen had been in my jeans, there's no logical way it could have transferred from one pocket to another. Did I put it in my work handbag when I got to the airport? Years of doing this job has made me a creature of habit; my passport and ID live in my work handbag, along with hand cream, lip balm, a purse full of currency. I don't keep an EpiPen in my work bag; why would I? Sophia is never with me.

"Earth to Mina. Are you alright?"

"Sorry. Just milk. Thanks."

I drop the blue plastic pen into my pocket. There's no other explanation. I must have brought it on board.

How else could it have gotten here?

SEVEN

6 P.M. | ADAM

"Becca build a snowman with me," Sophia says, the lack of question in her tone less about my daughter's command of language and more about her character. She isn't asking me; she's telling me.

"It's nearly teatime. It's dark outside," I start, but her face clouds over, and I think, *Sod practicalities, and sod sensible parenting. Why shouldn't I be the one to make her smile for once?* "I guess we can have the outside light on. It'll be an adventure! I build excellent snowmen. The trick is to—"

"No. Becca and me build a snowman."

"Fine," I snap, as if I'm Sophia's age. Salt doesn't sting any less the more you rub it in. Is parenting supposed to hurt like this? And when it does, are we just supposed to take it?

Becca's in the kitchen, poking at a lasagna she's taken out of the oven. "Is this veggie, do you reckon?"

I take the fork from her and peel back the oozing crust of melted cheese. "There's veg *in* it."

She rolls her eyes at me. "Is that supposed to be funny? Did you know the methane from cows is twenty-five times worse for the environment than CO_2?"

"Try being in a briefing room with twelve hairy coppers. Cows have got nothing on them."

"Daddy says we can build a snowman!"

Becca shrugs. "If you like." She picks up her phone again to check the ever-present notifications, and I feel my own fingers twitch in response.

Addiction carries muscle memory, and my thumb can swipe its own way to a fix before any conscious thought emerges to stop it.

Sophia has the fridge open, rifling through the vegetable tray. She emerges triumphantly with a carrot. "Now a hat." She runs into the hall to find what she needs, and I put the lasagna back in the oven to keep it warm. There's a veggie burger in the freezer—probably left over from the last time Becca babysat—and I put it under the grill.

Bundled back up in their boots and coats, Becca and Sophia go outside. They scoop up armfuls of virgin snow, Sophia whooping with the novelty of playing in the dark, and I close the door, watching for a second through the glass back door.

My fingers meet around my phone. I move away from the door, but they're still too close, and I head for the bedroom. I take the stairs two at a time, my pulse quickening in anticipation, the way your mouth waters when it knows it's almost time to eat. I glance out the window, checking the girls are still occupied, feeling the rush of conflicting emotions that always comes when I look at Sophia.

"She's such a happy little soul," Miss Jessop had said at parents' evening.

Mina had glanced at me. "That's good to hear. She's... We struggle with her. Sometimes." *Sometimes.* Try most of the time. Another glance toward me, looking for support.

"Her behavior can be challenging," I said. "She has meltdowns—*epic* meltdowns. They go on for an hour or more." Life with Sophia can be like crossing ice, never quite knowing when it might crack. At the mercy of a five-year-old's emotions.

"She can be very controlling," Mina added. She was speaking slowly, choosing her words carefully. "Possessive. Of me, mostly. It causes some..." She hesitated. "Tension."

There was a pause as Miss Jessop took this in. "Hmm, I have to say this isn't something we're experiencing at school. I mean, I'm aware of her psych assessment, but to be honest, you'd never know to look at her. I wonder..." She looked at each of us in turn, her head tilted to one side. "Could she be picking up on any problems at home?"

The only thing that stopped me from losing my shit completely was knowing I'd be adding weight to her argument. I waited till we were off school property, but Mina got there first.

"How dare she! What, so basically it's our fault Sophia has behavioral problems? Nothing to do with having a birth mother who didn't remember she had kids half the time or the fact that she had two different foster families before she reached us?" She burst into tears. "Is it us, Adam? Are we doing something wrong?"

In a rare moment of togetherness, she had let me put my arms around her. "It's not us," I told her. She'd smelled different—a new shampoo, maybe—and it had made my heart hurt that a bit of her felt like a stranger. "At least it's not you. You're an amazing mum."

Alone now in what used to be our bedroom, I look at my phone. I open my messages, and the familiar rush of shame and fear comes flooding out. I've fucked up so badly. I've got deeper and deeper into something so toxic, I can't get out of it, and I've dragged Mina and Sophia into it too.

My daughter's face flashes into my mind, tearstained and confused. Too scared even to speak. It was Katya who'd done the talking, after Sophia had stopped crying and was huddled in a blanket in front of the TV, as if she were ill.

"I not do this any more." Katya went upstairs.

I followed her up. "Please, Katya—"

She hauled out her cases from under the bed and started throwing in clothes. "No more lying. Is finished."

"Don't tell Mina, I'm begging you." Things between us were already bad. We were hardly talking, and Mina had begun to question me in a way she never had before. Where had I been? What time had I finished work? Who was I on the phone to? "She'll leave me."

"Is not my problem!" Katya had turned and jabbed a finger at my chest. "Is yours."

I close down my messages and open Facebook instead, bringing up Mina's profile. I thought she might block me after she threw me out, but nothing has changed. Her relationship status still says *married*, and it's pathetic how tightly I cling on to it as a sign of hope. She's updated her profile picture. It's a selfie, unfiltered, taken in the snow somewhere I don't recognize. She's wearing a hat with a fur pom-pom, and icy flakes cling to her eyelashes.

I've fucked up so badly. I've lost the only woman I've ever properly loved.

I met Mina after a rugby match, when she barged in front of me at the bar.

"You're welcome," I said, in that passive-aggressive, British way that enables you to take it back if you'd missed the *excuse me*.

She half turned, one hand holding up a tenner to keep her place at the bar. "Sorry, did I just jump the queue?"

There was nothing sorry about her expression, but by then, I didn't care. Her hair was crazy—wild curls that fell across her face and swirled around her shoulders when she spun around. On her left cheek was a painted England flag, on her right, a French one.

I pointed at them. "Hedging your bets, I see."

"Half French."

"Which half?" It wasn't very original, but she laughed anyway and bought me a drink. We took them outside, walking by tacit agreement away from the throng that had spilled onto the street and around the corner, where we perched on a wall.

"My mother's French." Mina took a sip of her pint. "French Algerian, technically—she moved to Toulouse before I was born. My dad's half French, half English, and we came to England when I was six." She grinned. "I'm a mongrel."

When I went to get another round, I was gripped by the fear that she might vanish, and I pushed my way through to the bar, telling myself all was fair in love and war.

"What took you so long?" she said when I got back. The glint in her eye belied her cross expression, and I grinned back.

"Sorry I'm late."

Mina was training to be a pilot—just a few weeks into a residential course. I'd never met a pilot before, never mind such a young and insanely attractive one, and the rush to my head had nothing to do with the beers I'd consumed.

"It's really not that glamorous," she said. "Not yet anyway. We're in classrooms, like school, and there's more math than you could possibly imagine."

"When do you start flying?"

"Next week. Cessna 150s."

"What are they?"

Mina grinned. "Let's just say they're a long way from the Concorde."

I went home with her. I would have gone anywhere with her. And when I had to leave, she was so insistent that she'd call, that she wanted to see me again, that we had something exciting, something *important*, that I never asked for her number in exchange for the one I gave her. I never doubted she'd call.

Only she didn't. And when I finally plucked up the courage to go 'round to her flat, she'd moved out. No note, no text. I'd been ghosted.

"You fucking idiot," I say out loud.

I had it all. The woman I loved. A family. And I fucked it up. I lost Mina once, and when I got her back, I drove her away, and if I'm not careful, I'm going to lose Sophia too. It's always been Mina she's clung to, and now that I'm not living here, it's a fight just to stay in her life. Attachment disorder takes years to overcome; it's not enough to be with Sophia on birthdays and special occasions or every other weekend. I need to be here when she scrapes her knee and when she feels scared at night. I need to show her I won't abandon her.

I swing my legs off the bed. Maybe I can help finish the snowman, and Sophia can put his hat on and wrap a scarf around his neck. Even if she doesn't want me to help, I can still watch. I can tell her what a good job she did.

I run down the stairs, newly determined to be—what's that word I see everywhere now? *Present.* I put my phone in my pocket, pleased with myself. I ignored the texts; I didn't respond. That proves I have resolve, whatever Mina says.

The hall floor is wet, a trail of melted snow leading into the downstairs loo. They've finished.

"Pair of softies," I say as I come into the kitchen. "Couldn't hack the cold?"

Becca's sitting on the counter, playing something on her phone. I look around the empty kitchen.

"Where's Sophia?"

"Outside. I came in to make some hot chocolate."

The kettle has recently boiled, steam rising from the spout, but there are no mugs on the counter. "You didn't get very far." I push my feet into the wellies I keep by the back door.

Our garden is a small rectangle with a padlocked shed in one corner and a sorry huddle of pots where the patio is. Beneath the snow, a concrete path leads to the shed. Neither Mina nor I are great gardeners; it's a space for Sophia to play, that's all.

Only she's not playing now.

The garden is empty.

Sophia's gone.

EIGHT

PASSENGER 2D

My name is Michael Prendergast, and when I got on Flight 79, I turned left.

Whenever I flew long haul as a child, my parents would be seated in business class, me behind, in economy. Mum and Dad would take it in turns to pop back and check on me, giving me the boxed chocolates from their coffee as a peace offering.

"You don't need the extra space," my mother said. "And besides, once you turn left on a plane, you'll be ruined forever: you'll never want to turn right again."

I couldn't see her point. We had enough money to turn left every time we flew, whether it was a weekend break to Lisbon or the fortnight we spent in Mustique every year, at the villa belonging to one of Dad's clients. Why slum it when you could travel in style?

Five hours into a trip to Antigua, I snuck in to see them. It was late, and most people were sleeping, and I held my breath as I tiptoed down the aisle to where Mum was stretched out. I was a twelve-year-old beanpole, too big to share seats, but I squeezed in anyway.

"You're not supposed to be here."

"Just for a bit."

She gave me her unopened crisps and a bottle of fizzy water and plugged the headset in so I could watch TV. I flicked through the channels—four times the number I had back in economy—but I hadn't even had a chance to choose when a shadow loomed large beside us.

"Sorry," Mum said. She gave an oops—you got me! *smile to the air stewardess and pulled the headset off me.*

"Come on, you." The stewardess smiled back at Mum, but her fingernails dug into my shoulders as she walked me back, and my cheeks burned with shame. I hadn't been hurting anyone. What harm would it have done to leave me there? As for my parents, how dared they treat me like a second-class citizen?

When we landed, I watched the passengers up front disembark first, scrutinizing their clothes and luggage, mentally compiling a list of labels around which I wanted to build my life. My parents had Louis Vuitton; I had a carry-on case that came free with a briefcase Dad bought.

"When you earn your own money," Dad said, *"you can have whatever suitcase you want."* He would bang on and on about understanding the value of money, when a grand is a grand, whichever way you look at it. Pocket money was a fiver here, a tenner there, when some of my mates got twenty quid a week.

"It's not about the money," Dad said when I was almost eighteen. I was trying to talk to him about it calmly. Man-to-man. *"It's the principle."*

It so *was* the money. Once, on a flight to Mustique, there were seats free in business class.

"I see you're seated separately," the woman at the desk said. *"I could offer you an upgrade today for just three hundred."*

Three hundred pounds! I'd seen Mum spend more than that on a pair of shoes without breaking a sweat. My heart skipped with excitement. It was finally going to happen! I imagined myself stretched out beneath a soft blanket, flicking between films and mainlining Coke.

"He'll be fine in economy, thank you."

My mouth fell open. *"But—"*

Dad glared at me, cutting off my protests before turning back to the check-in woman with a smile. *"Kids today, huh? Don't know they're born."*

She glanced at me as I sniffed back the tears I knew would only provoke another rant from Dad, then gave him a tight smile. *He's like this all the time,* I wanted to tell her. It isn't the money *or* the principle. It's just how he is.

I twisted in my seat the whole of that flight, resenting every galling glimpse through the curtain that closed me off from my own parents. As I picked at a cardboard sandwich and drank my carton of juice, I wondered what was being served in business class. I imagined soft, warm bread rolls, beads of condensation on glasses filled with freshly squeezed orange.

Fortunately, I had Grandma. I spent hours 'round at hers while my parents were working. We watched reality TV and laughed at Nigella making sex faces over chocolate mousse and discussed the merits of Burberry over Hugo Boss. She bought me presents, slipping designer shirts into Primark carrier bags for me to smuggle home. Grandma lived in a massive rectory with its own swimming pool and stables and enjoyed what she called the finer things in life.

"*I'm to blame for your mother's expensive tastes,*" *she told me over a cream tea one day.* "*We used to hit Oxford Street on a Saturday morning and shop till we literally dropped.*"

"*Last weekend, she gave me twenty quid to buy a pair of jeans,*" *I said miserably.* "*Twenty quid!*"

Grandma's lips pursed into a cat's bum. "*Well, that's your father's influence. Your mother was never mean till she married him.*" *She snorted.* "*It's not as if it's his own money to begin with. Gold-digging parasite, that's what he is. He met me and your granddad—God rest his soul—took one look at this place, and had a ring on your mother's finger quicker than you could say* inheritance." *Grandma didn't mince her words.* "*Well,*" *she said darkly.* "*He'll see.*"

"*See what?*"

But she wouldn't tell me, and it wasn't till she died that I realized what she'd meant. She'd cut them off. Both of them. Her will made it quite clear that not a penny of her vast estate—or indeed her actual estate, swimming pool and all—would go to my parents.

She left it all to me.

Dad went ballistic. "*It's far too much. She can't have meant it.*"

They were in the kitchen, their voices carrying up the stairs to where I sat on the landing, my back against the wall.

"*It's what she wanted,*" *Mum said.* "*She really loved him.*"

There was a pain in my chest like I'd swallowed too fast. I couldn't imagine life without Grandma, and the sudden transition to millionaire— insane though it was—wouldn't make up for losing her.

"*She must have lost her marbles. We'll have to contest the will.*"

"*She was sharp as someone half her age. You know that.*"

"*You're not just going to accept it, are you? That money should have come to us!*"

"*To me, technically,*" *I heard Mum say, but Dad didn't acknowledge her.*

"The boy's eighteen, for God's sake. He's completely irresponsible."

I waited for Mum's counterargument, but it didn't come. I swallowed. Fuck them. Fuck them both. I didn't care about the money—not like I cared about Grandma—but I wasn't giving it to my parents. I didn't have to put up with them anymore. I had my own house, enough money to do what I wanted.

Life was good, and not just for me: I wasn't tight like my parents. For every pound I spent on myself, I spent two on other people. I'd buy spontaneous rounds for strangers in bars, ending the night surrounded by new friends. I showered girlfriends with flowers, chocolate, jewelry, and the more I spent, the more they loved me. I made large, public donations to charity and brushed away the applause that made my insides fizz.

And—of course—I turned left. Always. As Dad said, it wasn't the money, it was the principle.

There are people on Flight 79 who have never traveled business class before; you can tell from the way they open every drawer and work their way through every button on the control panel, calling the flight attendant to ask how the bed works, whether the movie channels are all included, what time they'll be serving food... I sit back and let it fall into place around me like a Savile Row suit.

The flight attendants buzz between one passenger and the next, and idly I compare the two female crew members. They're both attractive, despite the years that separate them. The older one's clearly the boss, her eyes flitting over every seat, searching out any detail that might detract from our comfort. Her gaze falls on me, and I freeze, suddenly twelve again.

Come on, you...

Fingernails, gripping my shoulder...

She smiles. "Can I get you anything else, sir? Some wine?"

"Thank you, but I don't drink." I haven't for years. I prefer the buzz of caffeine to the thick head of alcohol.

"Well, I'm here if you need anything."

I breathe out. Funny to still feel like an impostor, so many years afterward. "Thank you."

Everything is under control. I have a business-class ticket. I have money in my pocket. Life is finally going the way I wanted it to go.

NINE

12 HOURS FROM SYDNEY | MINA

The rest area is more crawl space than room, the walls curving inward till they become roof, the shape of the plane as clear here as in the cockpit. The floor is made up of tessellated mattresses, reminiscent of school gym mats, separated by curtains that hang from the ceiling like in a hospital ward, each bunk the size of a coffin.

We were all too wired to sleep. Only Erik pulled the curtain around his bunk, leaving the rest of us to talk in whispers.

The remaining crew—seven of us—sprawled on the floor, exchanging the sort of passenger gossip that can't safely be had in the galley.

"There's a guy about halfway down—no word of a lie—must be thirty stone," said one of the crew from economy.

Carmel made a face. "Poor guy. He must be so uncomfortable."

"Poor guy next to him, you mean! He's got the aisle seat, and I keep getting the trolley stuck. I'm like: *Um, would you mind moving your... um...stomach?*"

They all roared with laughter, cutting off abruptly when Erik harrumphed from within his curtains. We all knew what it was like, trying to sleep when no one else wanted to, but there was a childish atmosphere in the air—a midnight-feast-at-a-sleepover vibe—that made us all giggle, pressing our hands over our faces. The passengers wouldn't be disturbed at least: no sound travels between the rest area and the cabin. When we're up there, we're completely sealed off.

I was only half there. Half joining in with the snog-marry-avoid game and Carmel's interior design decisions, half trying to work out when I'd last seen Sophia's EpiPen.

It had been in the rucksack yesterday morning, I was sure of that. I always check it when I take out her lunch box and flask, and there's no reason for me not to have done so yesterday. Could I have taken it out when I emptied her lunch box after school? I never had before, and even if I did, that still didn't explain how I'd brought it on to the plane.

Could someone be playing a practical joke on me?

I remember Adam, years ago, creasing with laughter as he told me how he'd been "initiated" as a new police recruit. "My sergeant said we were going to freak out the new mortuary assistant by making him think one of the bodies was alive," he'd told me, barely able to get out the words for laughing. "So I get on the trolley, and they cover me with a sheet and slide me into the fridge. And I'm lying there, chuckling to myself about how I'm going to do the whole *wooooo!* ghost thing when they pull me out, only...only..." Another burst of laughter bent him double, and I couldn't help but laugh too, even though the idea of being surrounded by dead bodies made me shiver. "Only next thing I know," Adam went on, "I hear this voice from the corpse on top of me, saying, 'Bloody freezing in here, isn't it?'" He creased up, apoplectic with mirth at the memory of discovering he'd been the intended recipient of the joke all along.

Adam's world is one of stark contrasts. On the one hand, critical decisions and violent altercations. On the other, cling-filmed loos and mobile phones Sellotaped to desks, fake loudspeaker announcements summoning nervous officers to a humorless superintendent.

"Comic relief," Adam always says. A lightness—however childish—to counterbalance the darkness of a road death, a rape, a missing child.

Adam was already a police officer when I met him, and I've often wondered what he was like before, whether he's always had the sort of mood swings that pull him down into a place I can't reach. When we got married, these moods would last a few hours—a day at most—but as time went by, the black dog snapped for longer at his heels. The last year has been unbearable.

"Who are you texting?" We were watching TV—it must have been around this time last year—but Adam had barely looked up from his phone. Katya was in her room, Sophia asleep.

"No one important."

"You don't look too happy about it, whoever it is."

Adam's jaw was tense, his thumbs jabbing at the screen. I left it, snatching glances at him for the rest of the evening and unable to focus on whatever comedy series we were supposed to be watching. After Adam moved out and Katya was back in Ukraine, anxiety kept me awake till the early hours. I'd drift into a restless sleep, only to jerk awake when my phone beeped with a text. Adam, hit by remorse—or guilt—midway through a shift.

I'm sorry.
I miss you.
I love you.

I took to keeping my phone on silent.

One morning, there were six texts and two missed calls from him, and as I stumbled downstairs, hungover from lack of sleep, my phone flashed insistently. Instead of letting it ring out, I canceled the call, a small act of defiance I knew would hurt. Downstairs, it took me a moment to pinpoint the strange smell that pervaded the downstairs rooms. I checked the kitchen, wondering if I'd left something in the oven, but the chemical smell was strongest in the hall.

The doormat had been drenched in petrol.

In my sleep-fuddled state, I wondered if I had spilled something myself before going to bed or trodden something in from the road. I opened the door to get rid of the fumes, blinking in confusion as I saw Adam get out of his car and walk up the path.

"I tried to ring. Are you alright?"

He looked manic, as if he'd slept even less than I had. His gaze shifted about, jittery, as though he'd taken something, although I knew he never would.

"Why were you trying to call?" The crisp morning air had woken me up, pieces slotting into place to form a picture I didn't want to see. "What are you doing here anyway?"

"I need to pick up some clothes."

"At seven in the morning?" I didn't wait for his explanation. "I was about to call the police. Someone's poured petrol through the door."

I was surprised at how calm I felt, given the circumstances. Throwing Adam out had made me feel stronger, more in control; lack of sleep added a layer of distance to proceedings, as though I were viewing myself from above.

"What?" He looked around wildly, as though the perpetrators might still be hanging around. "When? Are you okay? Is Sophia alright?"

There was something off about him, as though he were keeping something from me. As though, I realized suddenly, he wasn't shocked at all.

"She's fine. She slept with me last night. I'll call 101 and report it."

"I'll do it—I'm on my way to work anyway. Less chance of it getting binned that way."

Later, when Sophia was in nursery, I changed the bulb in the porch light and asked Mo if she'd seen anything.

"Sorry, love," Mo said. "The doctor's given me something to help me sleep—I'm out like a light nowadays. There was a bunch of kids in the park a couple of weeks ago, though, trying to set fire to the rubbish bins. Could be the same lot."

I called the police to give them this extra information.

"We don't have a record of criminal damage at that address, I'm afraid."

"My husband reported it this morning. DS Holbrook. He's in CID."

"Looks like he hasn't got around to it yet. I can take details for you?"

Afterward, I messaged Adam.

> Did you make the report?
> Yes, all sorted. Not sure there's anything they can do, but they'll check known arsonists.

I stared at my phone. Why hadn't he reported it? And why had he lied?

Another message came through.

> I'd feel better if I was home with you. Just for a few days. I'll sleep in the spare room.

In the murky recesses of my mind, a thought began to take shape. Could it have been *Adam* who put the petrol through the door, in some pathetic attempt to make me take him back? Did he think he was some kind of knight in shining armor?

We're fine, thanks, I told him. I wasn't scared: Adam might be an idiot, but he wasn't a psychopath.

"You all should have gotten some sleep," Erik says now as we leave the rest area and climb down the steep spiral stairs to the cabin. "We have a long time before our next break."

"Thanks, Dad," someone mutters from above me. There's a stifled giggle.

Erik's right, we should have slept, but the chatter of the other girls had been a welcome distraction from the question of how Sophia's EpiPen had made it on to Flight 79. I can't help but wonder if Adam is behind it. Is he trying to make me feel guilty for leaving her? Or hoping I'll worry enough to need his support? Is this, like the petrol, some warped way of him being my knight in shining armor?

It's no one I'm working with, that's for sure. It's not like Adam and his mates, who have worked together for years and know each other's limits; I work with new people every time I clock on. Who plays practical jokes on a stranger?

Back in the cabin, my gaze falls on the man in 3F. Jason Poke has the sort of fresh face and dimples that make teenage girls melt and mothers say *watch out for that one*. You'd have to have been living under a rock to have missed Poke's Jokes, a cult YouTube channel that swiftly went mainstream when it moved to Channel 4. I remember an episode I watched with Adam, long before everything went wrong for us. Poke's dressed as a vicar—all prosthetic nose and gray wig—stumbling over the marriage vows before an unsuspecting couple. "To have and to scold—I mean hold." Cue muffled laughter from the congregation. Poke hiccups, slurs the next line. The camera zooms in on an elderly lady, her lips pursed, as Poke turns his back on the happy couple and swigs from a hip flask marked *communion wine*. The bride's mouth falls open. Behind her, the best man roars with laughter as Poke peels off his prosthetics, and a cameraman walks out from the vestry. "Just another of Poke's Jokes!" goes the voiceover.

"Classic!" Adam said, snorting with laughter.

"I'd go absolutely ballistic."

"Only at first. You'd see the funny side eventually."

"That poor girl." On the television, we were being treated to the same "reaction shots" we'd seen a moment ago. The bride horrified, her mother in tears. "All those months of planning, and that wanker turns up and ruins it."

"The best man organized it. Poke didn't just rock up."

"Even so."

I walk past Poke's seat, glancing at the screen to see what he's watching. I'm surprised to see an Auschwitz documentary, and I flush when Poke looks up and sees me looking.

"Sobering stuff," he says, his headphones making his voice too loud.

I must have brought the EpiPen on board myself. I remember transferring a magazine from my everyday bag to my work bag; maybe it got caught up in the pages. Or could Sophia have accidentally put it in the paper bag with my flapjack? That must be it.

I ignore the whisper in my head that says the pen would have been in Sophia's schoolbag, not mine; that surely it's a coincidence too far for it to fall from bag to bag not once but twice; that the pen was nowhere near the flapjack. I ignore the voice that reminds me of the petrol through the door, the dropped calls I've been getting recently, Adam's strange behavior over the past few months. I ignore it all. It's just an EpiPen. What would anyone have to gain from bringing it on board?

I wish I could text Becca, just to check everything's okay, but ground control says there's nothing they can do about the Wi-Fi. Dindar pulled out all the stops for this route—wider seats in economy, premium films, carbon offsetting, and free Wi-Fi for everyone, regardless of ticket class. In the in-flight magazine, a full-page ad urges passengers to live-tweet their journey using the hashtag #LondonSydney. He's going to hit the roof.

I look around the cabin, trying to identify the journos. The first, a sharp-faced woman who writes a column for the *Mail*, is so much like her byline picture that I hardly need to check the passenger list for her name, although I do, to be sure. Alice Davanti is the name she writes under, Alice Smith on her travel documents. A married name, maybe, or perhaps Davanti is a pseudonym, chosen for its glamour.

It takes me longer to spot the second journalist. It's no one I know by face or name, and without Google, I'm lost. I take a walk up and then down the aisles, glancing at laptop screens and into books. I notice that the man with the round glasses has slipped his wine list into a notebook, and as I pass him for the second time, he is using a proper camera, not a phone, to take the ubiquitous "feet up, watching a film" shot. Old-school. I check the passenger list: Derek Trespass. Despite his Wi-Fi woes, he looks perfectly comfortable.

I touch the EpiPen again, feeling at once close to Sophia and thousands of miles away. I think about the note I left on her pillow and wonder if she's found it yet. I wish I could text her. There's a Sky Phone in the flight deck, as well as the VHF radio the pilots use to check in with air traffic control every half hour and whenever we enter or leave a country's airspace. It's not unheard of for personal messages to be passed via these channels (I've been on flights where birth announcements were made, and when the World Cup is on, every England goal is celebrated), but this isn't an emergency.

"I'm thinking of painting the walls gray, with an accent wall in rose-gold wallpaper. What do you think?" Carmel is talking me through the apartment she and her boyfriend have bought.

"Sounds lovely."

"I'd like a soft-pink velvet sofa, but I wonder if it might be a bit much with the rose gold. What do you think?"

"Maybe." I look at my watch again. Time has slowed down, and I long for the end of my shift so I can go up to the bunks and draw the curtain around me. Maybe the Wi-Fi will be up by then, and I'll be able to message home.

A small figure creeps into the galley. It's Finley, too shy, perhaps, to press his call bell.

"Hello, sweetheart," I say. "Do you want something to eat?"

He holds up his headphones. "Could you—"

"Again? What on earth are you doing to them?"

Carmel takes over, unpicking the knots with white-tipped nails.

"Mine do this all the time. I wrap them up really neatly, then, when I want to use them, they're like spaghetti."

There's a shout from the cabin, the commotion building from both sides. I hear someone shout, "Get help!" and my heart sinks. It'll be the woman from economy, causing problems in the bar again.

But just as I'm about to investigate, Erik comes running into the galley, his habitual blank expression flushed.

"What's happened?"

He doesn't answer, reaching for the intercom and speaking with a calm authority that belies his agitation. "If there is a doctor on board, please make your way to the front of the plane."

"Is a passenger ill?" Carmel says, and I wait for Erik to snap at her about stating the bloody obvious, but he stares at her, and I realize he's shaking.

"Not ill," he says. "Dead."

TEN

PASSENGER 6J

My name is Ali Fazil, and I wish I'd never set foot on this flight.

The crew members are running down the aisles. There's panic in the air—people shouting and calling for help, standing up in their seats to see what has happened.

It makes me feel better, to be honest, to know I'm not the only one panicking.

All that time I've had to sit here, heart pounding and palms sweaty, watching everyone around me ignore the danger we're in. There must be intelligent people among them, people who read articles, people who know the facts. Why aren't they as scared as I am?

I know what you're thinking: you're wondering why I'd get on a twenty-hour flight when I feel the way I do about flying. But some jobs require you to get on a plane. You're not given a choice.

I can just imagine emailing the boss to say, Actually, I'm a really nervous flyer, and the thought of being in the air for all that time is stopping me from sleeping…

Never mind flying: he'd have given me my marching orders.

My sister told me I should quit, said it wasn't healthy to be at someone's beck and call like that, but she doesn't know enough to understand. There's a hierarchy, of course, like any organization, but we all pull together. We're like family.

I've tried to get over it. I've had hypnotherapy. Reflexology. CBT. Ironic for a psychologist, right? It doesn't matter what I do: the facts always win.

Do you know how many people have died in plane crashes since 1970?

83,772. Wouldn't that make you panic? Think twice about stepping on board?

The reasons are many. Sometimes it's as simple as running out of fuel. It happens to car drivers all the time, doesn't it? No one intentionally runs out of petrol, but something happens—you have to make a diversion, or you get stuck in traffic—and suddenly you're crawling to a standstill, fuel light flashing. It's a pain—you might be stuck on the hard shoulder for hours or have to walk for miles to fill a jerry can with enough to get you to the petrol station—but you're not going to die from running out of fuel.

Unless you're in a plane.

Because planes do run out of fuel, you know. They get diverted, or bad weather stops them landing, or someone's miscalculated, and you know it's the pilots who work out how much fuel they need, not some machine? Did you know that? Think about how many times you've got a calculation wrong, because you're tired or you've had an argument with your partner or a million other reasons. All they have to do is get that wrong and...

There's no coasting onto the hard shoulder on a plane. No hazard lights and grinding to a halt. There's no walking to the petrol station. There's just three hundred tons of metal falling out of the sky.

And us. Lemmings, plummeting to our deaths.

Sometimes it's a shattered windscreen—the pilot sucked right out of his seat. It could be fire: some idiot smoking in the toilets then chucking the butt in with the hand towels. Smoke slowly engulfing us till we don't know if we'd rather choke to death or burn.

And sometimes, of course, sometimes it's deliberate.

Everyone just sits there, eating and drinking and pretending it's totally normal to be suspended in the air, that there's absolutely no chance of falling out of the sky. No one reads the safety card; no one watches the briefing video.

I did, of course.

I made sure I knew where the exits are. The second I got on, I counted the rows of seats so that if the lights go out, I can feel my way to a door. I checked that my life jacket was under my seat, and if it were possible, I'd pull down my oxygen mask to make sure it's working.

I want to be ready.

More than 95 percent of people survive plane crashes, although that includes accidents that take place on the runway, so it's not a statistic you can trust. I doubt 95 percent of people survive a Boeing 777 plummeting into the sea or crashing into a mountain. I doubt 95 percent of people survive a fire when they're locked in a plane.

Everyone's standing up now, so I stand up too, and my throat grips tight. There's a man on the floor. They've called for a doctor, and she's leaning over him, but he isn't moving, and his face...

I turn away. I count the rows to the exit again; I check again for my life jacket, take out the safety information card, and turn it over and over. I wish I'd listened to my sister.

I thought we'd go simultaneously—one terrifying but mercifully brief explosion sending pieces of plane and bits of body across thousands of meters—but maybe I was wrong. Maybe we'll go one by one.

Maybe this man is just the first.

ELEVEN

7 P.M. | ADAM

"Sophia!"

Snow softens the night air, silence answering my panicked shout. I run across the garden, past the half-finished snowman, and rattle the shed door, the padlock still coated with snow. I squeeze my head into the narrow gap between the shed and the fence, calling her name even though the banked-up snow is undisturbed. The fence is six feet tall, so there's no way she could have climbed it, but I stand on a wobbly garden chair and look over regardless. "Sophia!"

When Sophia was about eighteen months old, Mina and I were with her at a soft play center when we noticed a woman paying us more attention than felt comfortable. As she edged nearer, I recognized her from the photo album Social Services had put together. It was Sophia's birth grandmother, only in her forties herself, and there with the youngest of her own children, born the same year as Sophia. She didn't do anything, but it was unsettling—a reminder of safety measures most families don't even need to consider as they post photos on Instagram and check in on Facebook.

We were paranoid for a time. Wouldn't go anywhere without looking over our shoulders; wouldn't leave Sophia in the car even as we locked the front door, the house just yards away. As time went by and Sophia's birth family made no attempt to get in touch, we relaxed a little, giving our daughter the independence she craved.

But things are different now.

The risk is greater, the consequences worse, and there's no one I can call on for help. Not Social Services, not the police. I've brought this all on myself.

"Sophia!" I grip the top of the fence, the wood splintering my fingers as I call her name into the silent park. A dim sulfur glow comes from the municipal lighting that edges the path, but there's no movement, only shadow.

In the spring—when I was still clinging to the pretense that I wasn't doing anything wrong—Sophia ran away. She'd been in bed, Mina and I watching TV in the sitting room, and we'd heard her footsteps on the stairs. A second later, the front door had banged. I looked up, saw the same alarm in Mina's face I knew must be in mine. We jumped up, ran outside—me barefoot, Mina in slippers—and split up, running in opposite directions, shouting her name.

Twenty minutes later, I'd come back to the house, frantic with worry. Sophia was eating a biscuit at the kitchen table, calm as you like. I put my arms around her, relief rushing into my embrace, and felt her stiffen for a split second, the way she always does.

"Where were you?" I demanded, relief turning to anger.

"Here."

She'd never left the house. She'd opened the door, then slammed it, hiding behind the heavy curtain we pull across on winter nights. She'd watched us run like lunatics into the street, heard the panic in our voices as we called her name.

"I wanted to see if you'd look for me," she said, and her tone was dispassionate, almost clinical, as if she were conducting a scientific experiment.

"It's not normal," I said later when Mina had checked Sophia was definitely asleep and I'd screwed a bolt on the door, too high for her to reach.

"Oh, that's a lovely thing to say about your daughter."

"I didn't say *she* isn't normal, I said her *behavior* isn't normal. She needs professional help. Counseling, *something*. It's not enough to stick labels on her and send us away with some leaflets. I mean, God, Mina, I don't know how much more of this I can cope with."

"What's that supposed to mean?"

I didn't know myself.

"You're going to leave us?"

"No!"

"Or maybe you want to give her back!" She spat out the words, but that wasn't the worst bit of that night. The worst bit was that, in the silence that followed, she realized I'd already been forming the same thought.

"Of course not," I said, too late for it to count.

I burst into the kitchen, where Becca's still sitting on the counter. "Sophia's not there."

"She was literally there a second ago." Becca's mouth falls open, and she looks around the kitchen as though I might be mistaken, that Sophia is right here next to me. "I just came in a minute ago." She slides onto her feet, her mobile clattering onto the counter.

"Which is it, Becca, a second or a minute?" I'm not interested in her answer. I call Sophia's name again, trying for the balance between *come out right now* and *I'm not angry*. "Could she have come in without you noticing?"

Becca's gone to the open back door, calling for Sophia over and over, her voice thick with fear. "I don't know. Maybe."

I search the house, snapping into work mode and moving systematically from one room to another. Tramping snow through the house, I look in the bathroom and in the airing cupboard, and I open the door to the damp cellar beneath the kitchen, even though Sophia can't reach the key. She isn't inside, and when I go back out to the garden, I see something I've missed. There's a loose board at the bottom of the fence, held in place by an upturned plant pot. Only the plant pot isn't there anymore, and the space where it was is empty of snow. I crouch down and lift the board, exposing a gap plenty big enough for a child to crawl through. Caught on the wood is a piece of red wool.

Behind me, Becca starts crying. "What if something happens to her?"

She's just a kid herself, but that doesn't stop me being angry. We're paying her to watch Sophia, not piss about playing Candy Crush or messaging lads. Worst-case scenarios race through my head, each one made worse still by a real-life counterpart. Murder, sexual assault, child trafficking—these are the foundations of my working life.

"Park," I say. "Now."

While Becca runs the long way—back through the house and around the corner, to the entrance to the park—I stand on the rickety garden chair and haul myself up onto the fence, throwing myself over and landing with a jolt that rattles my teeth. On the other side of the loose board is a patch of scuffed snow, where Sophia must have crawled on her knees. There are patches of grass where the snow has been scooped up and piled to the side, then a faint trail of pint-size prints, already half covered with falling snow. A few feet from the fence, half buried in the snow, is Elephant. My chest tightens.

"Sophia!"

I would never give her back. I never meant it, not really. Never truly imagined ringing Social Services to tell them we couldn't cope, didn't want to be Sophia's parents anymore. It was a reaction, that's all, to the hiding and fighting and not wanting to be held. It was envy, I suppose, of all the parents with straightforward kids.

"Sophia!" Louder now, unable to hide the panic in my voice as I run toward the center of the park. If this were a race, I'd be pacing myself, mindful of how far I have to run, but I don't know, don't care. I'll run all night to find my daughter.

It's already dark, the park lit only by the occasional lamppost and a soft, yellow haze from the housing estate on the opposite side. I use my phone as a torch, following the footprints and wondering how long to give it before I call 999. They'll scramble the helicopter within minutes; they'll fly over the woods and check the lake—

I stumble, my foot catching in a tree root, feel my breath grow ragged even though I've barely run a hundred yards, fear sucking the strength from my limbs.

"Sophia!" Becca catches up with me, mascara all over her face. "There's no sign of anyone by the entrance." She looks at the ground, at the prints she's kicked snow over, and she claps her hands to her mouth, a high-pitched moan echoing through the silence. Her hysteria forces me out of mine.

"Go and check the play park. I'll look in the woods." I think of the lake, with its little island populated by ducks. Sophia's constant questions. *How many are there? What are they called? How do they know when it's time for bed?*

Then, through the crisp night air, I hear something.

"Shhh." I grab Becca's arm, and she gulps back her sobs.

There it is again.

Laughter.

"Sophia!" We run toward the sound, my heart thumping the same beat as my boots. I think of the day Katya left, of Sophia's tearstained face. The fear and disappointment put there by *my* actions.

Sophia is on the other side of a small group of trees, throwing a snowball at a group of teenagers. One of them stoops, balls up a handful of snow, and throws it gently at Sophia's arm.

I roar at them. "Leave her alone!"

She doesn't look hurt, but my hands ball into fists. Closer, I can see they're not even teenagers; they're maybe eleven or twelve at most. Three sheepish boys and a girl who looks at me defiantly. Doing someone else's dirty work? I draw closer, not stopping till I'm close enough for them to see who they're up against. "Who sent you? Who told you to take her?"

The tallest lad curls his lip. "The fuck you talking about?"

"What are you doing?"

"This is a public place. We've got as much right to be here as you."

"Not with my daughter, you haven't."

Sophia's looking down at the ground. I pull up her chin so I can see her face. She knows she's in trouble, and she jerks away from me.

"How do we know she's your daughter?" the girl says. There's laughter in her tone, but the others take up the theme.

"She doesn't seem to like you very much."

"Yeah, you could be abducting her."

"Pedo!"

"Sophia, we're going home." I take her hand, and she snatches it away from me. *Please, Sophia, not now.*

"She doesn't want to go!"

"Kidnapper!"

"Pedo!"

I hold out Elephant, and Sophia squashes her face in his wet coat, then I get out my warrant card and snap it open. "I'm Detective Sergeant Holbrook. This is my daughter. Now fuck off."

They fuck off, running toward the housing estate, with a half-hearted *wanker!* once they're safely out of reach.

I look at my daughter, my heart pounding, trying to reach a level of calmness that won't scare her. "Why?"

"The snow's better here."

"You scared me. I thought someone had taken you." Tears prick my eyes. I drop to my knees, snow soaking instantly through my trousers, and hold out my arms. "Come here, sweetheart."

When Sophia was a toddler, all our friends' children were coping with separation anxiety while we were struggling with the reverse. Sophia's friends cried when they were dropped off at nursery or clung to their parents instead of exploring at soft play. "She's so confident," they'd say, admiring the way Sophia trotted off without a care in the world. "You'd expect her to be clingy, after what she's been through."

I know a lot about attachment disorder now. I know it's very common among adopted children, especially ones who were fostered before finding their forever families. I know the symptoms (in Sophia's case: a refusal of affection and inappropriate affection toward strangers) and I know the best way to deal with it. It isn't Sophia's fault—she's a victim of circumstance. I know that.

What I don't know—what I've never known—is how to stop it hurting.

It shouldn't matter how I feel, of course. It's Sophia who gets the help, and rightly so—any kid born to a neglectful mother deserves to be the focus of attention. I should be able to rise above it, to smile when she turns away from a cuddle and say, *I'll still be here if you change your mind.*

Try it.

Try it with the child you've brought up, the child you've loved as your own from the second you saw her. Try it, then tell me it doesn't break your heart.

Sophia looks at me, and without taking her eyes off mine, she holds out a hand to Becca, who hesitates for a second, then takes it. A lump forms in my throat, and I think I might suffocate.

"Um—" Becca starts, shuffling her boots in the snow.

"Just go back to the house!"

I drop back on my heels, and when they're gone, I sit in the dark in the snowy park, and I sob.

Half an hour later, Sophia and I are eating the lasagna Mina left, Sophia picking out the red peppers and leaving them on the side of her plate. Becca's had a salad and three slices of toast, the burger charred beyond redemption. I've locked the back door and closed the bolt at the top of the front door, just in case Sophia goes wandering again. I look at Becca.

"You should be getting home."

"It's okay. I'm not going out tonight."

"I can't—" I don't know how to finish without inviting scorn—or pity. Mina left Becca's money in an envelope. I can't pay her for the extra hours. "I haven't been to a cashpoint."

There's a tiny pause. "It's okay. I'll stay for a bit. Help you get her ready for bed."

I wonder how much Becca knows about what's going on between me and Mina. Did Mina say she doesn't trust me, doesn't think I'm fit to look after my own daughter? Did she ask her to stay till Sophia's in bed?

Maybe it isn't Mina. Maybe it was Katya who said I can't be trusted. They knew each other, but were they friends? How close were they? Did Katya confide in Becca, even though I swore her to secrecy? Paranoia crawls across me like an itch I can't reach.

"Can we have flapjacks?" Sophia asks. "They're in there." She points to a tin by the kettle, and I take off the lid and put it on the table. "I made them."

"Clever you." Becca takes one. "I like baking too. Did you know you can collect ingredients for free from outside? I made pine-needle biscuits, and you can use dandelions too. There are loads of foraging websites."

"That's weird." Sophia looks at me, bored by a conversation she doesn't understand. "I want to see Mummy again." I bring up the tracking app and slide it across to her. "Thanks, Daddy." She beams at me, a gorgeous smile that dimples her cheeks and makes me return it, unquestioningly. She is a mass of contradictions, with no comprehension that each time she pulls away from me, she drives a knife through my heart.

Of course she doesn't understand, Mina would say. *She's five! You're the grown-up. You have to be the understanding one.*

Sophia traces her finger along the line that shows the route Mina's plane is taking. "The passengers get lunch, then dinner, then breakfast," she tells Becca, "and in between, there are snacks and lots of drinks—whatever they want."

"Have you ever been on a plane?"

"Loads of times! I've been to France, and Spain, and to America…"

"Lucky girl. When I was your age, we used to go to a caravan park once a year. I didn't go abroad till last year, and that was on the ferry."

"Caravans are nice too," Sophia says kindly. She hops off her chair and onto Becca's lap.

People don't get the whole attachment disorder thing. They see Sophia dishing out cuddles and wanting to tickle the postman, and they see a girl who's affectionate, caring, loving. And she is all those things, but with a whole bag of issues that mean it's not always directed the right way.

"Well, I can't see a problem at all," my mum said, after she'd babysat for a few hours. "Sat on my lap, having stories—lovely little thing."

It would hurt Mum to be told that it's easier for Sophia to form relationships with people who don't matter to her. The postman, babysitters, grandparents she only sees every few months—she'll open her heart to them because she doesn't expect anything in return.

But us? We're the ones who matter. Loving us means getting hurt—or so her instincts tell her.

I start clearing our plates. "We only travel so much because of Mina's job. We wait at the airport on standby, in case there's space. Sometimes we just come home again, don't we, Sophia?"

"I don't like it when that happens."

"Me neither."

Sophia starts telling Becca about the fuel capacity of a Boeing 777, and the older girl laughs. "You really know your stuff, don't you?"

"I can fly a plane too."

"Oh yeah?" Becca's dismissive, and Sophia looks cross.

"I can. Tell her, Daddy."

"They had a families day at the airport," I explain. "Mina took her on a flight simulator—the sort of thing they use for training. She was pretty good; they both were."

"I'm going to be a pilot."

I wonder if the police station could hold an open day, if Sophia might enjoy sitting in a police car, trying on the uniform.

"Mummy wanted to be a pilot." I fill the sink with hot water, remembering that first time I met Mina. The photo she showed me of her in her uniform, the unadulterated joy on her face.

After Mina ghosted me, I made a half-hearted attempt to track her down. She wasn't on Facebook, so I went to the airport where the training school was. The security officer on reception wouldn't look up her name—said it was against data protection rules—but as I walked away, he called after me.

"Try the White Hart, around the corner. Most of the students drink there."

I nursed a warm beer until a group of students filtered in, midconversation about tomorrow's forecast.

Mina had dropped out of the course.

"She had a panic attack, the first time she took a plane up." Mina's former colleague struggled to keep the derision from his voice. "They almost crashed as a result. Total wipeout."

"Is that right?"

I turned to see an older man, sitting at the bar, one eyebrow raised in our direction. He nodded at me. "Vic Myerbridge. I'm one of the instructors. Ignore Xavier—he's prone to exaggeration."

"Mina didn't have a panic attack?"

Vic's answer was considered. "There was no danger of the plane crashing. And look, we get a lot of dropouts—it's a tough course. She's not the first to realize it wasn't for her, and she won't be the last. Sometimes things just aren't meant to be."

"I don't suppose you know where she is now?"

"Sorry, I wouldn't have a clue."

That was that, then. She really had ghosted me.

Three months later, I saw her going into a shop on the high street. I raced across the road, narrowly missing being run over, only to pull up short on the other side. What was I thinking? Did I really want to be rejected all over again, only this time in person?

But what if she'd just lost my number?

I was still dithering when Mina came out. She'd cut her hair. All those crazy ringlets were gone, replaced by a close crop too short to curl. It sharpened her features and made her eyes even bigger, and I experienced the same surge of desire I'd felt when we first met.

"Oh," she said.

"Hi."

"I didn't call. I'm sorry."

"It doesn't matter."

"Doesn't it?"

"Well…"

Mina took a breath. "If I were to call now…I mean, not *right* now, obviously, but if I were to call you some time and suggest we went out… would it be too late?"

There was nothing nonchalant about the goofy smile that split my face in two. "Great. Shall I give you my—"

"I have it."

"You still have my number?"

"I still have your number."

That Friday, after drinks and a curry, Mina came back to mine, and she didn't leave till Monday morning.

Not a conventional love story, perhaps, but ours.

"If Mina wanted to be a pilot," Becca says now, "how come she's an air hostess?"

"She changed her mind."

I'd tried to persuade Mina to go back to pilot training, maybe have some counseling to get over whatever had caused the panic attack, but she wouldn't be swayed. She took a couple of jobs, but she struggled to focus. After her mum died, she said she needed to take stock. "I've let her down," she had said. "Dad too. All that money they paid for my training, and now Dad doesn't even have the house they both loved. They just wanted me to make something of myself."

"No," I'd said gently. "They wanted you to be happy." And she wasn't happy—not joyous, the way she was the first time I met her. Tentatively, I suggested an alternative career, one that would still give Mina the travel she craved, the flying she loved. She wasn't sure at first, but she went to an open day, did some research, and eventually went for it.

I chuck a tea towel at Becca. "They're called cabin crew anyway, not air hostesses."

Becca's eyebrows lift. "PC much?" She laughs as she starts drying. "Hey, that's good: you can be PC PC."

"DS actually," I mutter, but Becca's talking to Sophia.

"Come on. Let's get you bathed and ready for bed so Daddy can read you a story."

"I want *you* to read to me," I hear as they go upstairs.

I hear the bath running, and I pour myself a glass of wine, draining half of it in one swallow, haunted by the memories I've dredged up. Mina and I got a second chance at being together, and I've ruined it all.

Upstairs, Sophia runs around, giggling, and I know Becca is pretending to be the bath monster and that soon—when the bath is ready—the bath monster will catch Sophia and turn her into a monster too, with a bubble-bath beard and foam horns. It's a favorite game, second only to "flying": Mina on her back with her legs in the air, Sophia balanced on Mina's flattened feet, arms and legs outstretched like a skydiver.

The doorbell rings, and I go to open the front door, my wineglass still in one hand. I pause, feeling the hairs on the back of my neck stand to attention. Sometimes Mo will come around when she sees my car outside, needing help with something, but not at this time of night, not in this weather. I put my glass on the ledge by the window and slowly draw back the upper bolt, checking before I do that Sophia is safely upstairs.

I was right to be wary. It's a man, six foot tall and half again as wide. His head is shaved to a polish, the only shadow a greenish tattoo encircling his neck. "Alright, Adam?"

"Do I know you?"

The man gives me a slow smile. He's wearing a black puffer jacket and jeans, boots with the leather worn through on the toes, exposing scuffed steel caps. "Nah. But I know you."

"I haven't got it," I say. I put one hand on the door, but he's too quick, stepping forward and propelling me back into the hall, up against the wall. My wineglass topples, the contents spilling across the floor. I bring up both hands, palms forward. "Listen, mate—"

"I aintcha mate. Don't fuck with me, Adam. I'm doing my job, like you do yours. You've got till midnight, otherwise…" He doesn't finish. He puts one meaty hand around my neck, pinning me to the wall. I deliver a swift punch to his stomach, but as I do so, he lifts his right arm and punches me square in the face. He releases me, and I punch him again, but blood's pouring down my face, and he takes my arm and twists it behind my back, banging my head against the wall once, twice, three times. He lets me drop to the floor, and I roll to one side, arms up around my face, one leg kicking him away. But the space is small, and I can't get clear, and a well-placed boot winds me so completely, I think I might pass out. He kicks me again and again, and I have no choice but to curl in a ball and protect my head and wait for him to finish.

It seems to go on for hours, although it can only be a couple of minutes. He stops, and I feel him standing over me, his breath labored.

"This is from the boss."

He hawks, and a second later, I feel a globule of thick saliva on my ear. He leaves me with the door wide open, spitting blood onto the hall carpet.

TWELVE

PASSENGER 17F

My name is George Fleet, and I'm a passenger on Flight 79.

When you're out shopping and you get hungry, you grab a sandwich, right? Or a burger? And maybe you eat in, or maybe you take it outside, sit on a bench—even eat as you walk. Right?

Now let me tell you how it works for me.

First, I have to psych myself up. Do I really have to do this? Am I hungry enough to put myself through it? Hell yes, of course I'm hungry—I'm always fucking hungry. Okay, so I have to eat. I'm sweating just thinking about it, but I'm gonna do it.

I'd like a burger, but am I going to bring that on myself? When the calories are right there, printed on the wall by each picture? Nope. Not gonna do it. A sandwich, then, so I join the queue, start looking through the glass at the trays of tuna and egg salad.

Did you know you can feel people looking at you? Never experienced that? You're lucky. It burns like acid on the back of your neck, even before you hear the whispers, the sniggers. Gets worse when I order, of course. Ham and salad, I think. That's okay. That's healthy.

"Do you want mayo?"

My stomach growls. Somebody laughs. I shake my head.

"Butter?"

Mostly I say no to that too. Swallow down dry bread rather than face the jeers. But sometimes—fuck it!—sometimes I want to eat what everyone else eats. What you eat, without even thinking about it.

"Yeah," I say. "Butter would be good. Thanks."

A snort from behind me. A muttered aside. I tap my card, take my sandwich, fighting to get out before the violent flush I can feel on my neck reaches my face, where they'll know they've got to me. I've heard it all. Fatty. Maybe try a salad. Ever heard of exercise? Oink oink...

I've always been big. Tall with it. Broad. And yeah, fat. At thirteen, I had bigger tits than the girls. On the first day of GCSEs, I walked into the hall to find they'd shipped in a load of chairs with desks fixed to each one, a gap on one side for you to get in. I thought I was going to be sick. I caught Mr. Thomas's eye, silently begging him to realize that there was no way I was going to get into one of those chairs, that they were made for fucking Hobbits, but he just looked at his clipboard and ticked me off his list.

I still have nightmares about it, you know. Wake up sweating in the dark, because for a second, I was back there, hearing the laughter of a hundred kids echoing around the gym, burning with humiliation as everyone else sat down and I stood waiting for them to haul in a table and a chair.

I never finished my exam.

So anyway. Buying a sandwich. Maybe I take it to the park and walk till I find a bench they haven't added those armrests to. They're to stop people from lying down on them, but you try wedging your ass cheeks between them when your jogging bottoms are made to order from BigBoys.com. Maybe you'd just flop on the grass, kick off your shoes, and enjoy your sandwich in the sun? Yeah. If I try that, I'm not getting up without some serious machinery.

By the time I've found somewhere I can sit down, away from the judgmental stares of people who think fatties shouldn't eat, my sandwich has lost its appeal. A man's still gotta eat, you know? Dropping five hundred calories a day is enough to lose weight steadily, they reckon. Well, that still puts me needing well over three thousand a day.

Funnily enough, I don't get out much. I've had enough embarrassment in pubs to know you can't tell a chair's strength just by looking at it, and I can't stand for long because of the pain in my hips. Ironic, really: I wanted to be a stand-up comedian.

I'm funny, you see. Maybe not now, not like this, but I can be. Only way to cope, isn't it—laughing at yourself? If you don't laugh, you'll cry, they say.

So on the plane, when I realized the seat belt wouldn't fit, I made a joke of it to the guy on my left. "I'm your airbag. I guess I inflated a bit early!"

He forced a smile, even though half my butt cheek was bursting under the armrest onto his seat. I wondered how cool he'd be after five or ten hours of leaning to the left. I'd seen his face as I lumbered toward the empty seat next to his. Fuck's sake. Why does he have to sit next to me?

I'd been given an aisle seat, thank God, which just meant twisting to the side each time the trolley passed, so I supposed I'd be staying awake for twenty hours. No rest for the wicked, isn't that what they say? I could have done with the extra room in business class, but there's a pecking order everywhere you go, and I've always been at the bottom of it.

I knew I wouldn't be able to get the tray table down, so I didn't even try, even though it meant saying no to every meal. I had energy bars in my pocket so I could eat them in the toilet—assuming I could get into it. So much to think about, so much in my head as the plane took off.

But I'm going to change everything in Australia. Lose weight, make friends, kick-start my comedy career. Flight 79 marks the end of a chapter I never want to read again and the beginning of a whole new one. I'm starting over.

I've never been happier.

THIRTEEN

11 HOURS FROM SYDNEY | MINA

The passenger's face is waxy and slick with sweat. The doctor—a woman from economy with a neat ponytail and stud earrings in the shape of horseshoes—sits back on her heels.

"I'm sorry."

Beside me, Carmel makes a sound somewhere between a gasp and a sob. I put an arm around her, as much to steady myself as to comfort her, because suddenly, my legs don't feel like my own. The news travels around the cabin in a shocked murmur, and those passengers who had shamelessly stood and watched sink slowly back into their seats. I see Alice Davanti craning her neck from the other side of the cabin. She sees me looking and sits down, slipping a phone into her pocket. Was she taking a *photograph*?

"What do you think happened?" I'm unable to tear my eyes away from the body in front of me, from his blank, staring eyes to the pale skin on his exposed chest.

The doctor peels off the defibrillator pads and gently buttons up his shirt. "Some kind of seizure. Heart attack, possibly."

"He did say he wasn't feeling too good."

Everyone turns. A tall man with glasses and a neatly groomed beard is standing in front of his seat. He's wearing a gray sweatshirt, and he plucks at the sleeve, as though he's uncomfortable at suddenly being the center of attention. "We were queuing for the loo earlier, and he had his hand pressed to his chest. A spot of indigestion, he said."

"He was knocking back the port like it was Ribena." At the other end of the cabin, by the entrance to the bar, soccer player Jamie Crawford has none of the other man's awkwardness. I couldn't name the team he plays for if my life depended on it, but thanks to the gossip mags in my hairdresser's and my ridiculous memory for pointless facts, I do know that he retired at thirty-four, owns a nine-bedroom house in Cheshire, and is miraculously still with his wife, Caroline, despite shagging his way through several girl bands. The pair of them are in tracksuits: his gray and hers salmon pink, with *love* picked out in diamanté across the chest.

"And he had two of them cream cakes," she says.

"Right. Thanks." I'm suddenly defensive of the poor man on the floor, whose life choices are being picked apart by complete strangers. "Perhaps everyone could give us some space now?" Jamie and Caroline drift back to the bar, and I turn to Carmel. "You okay?" She nods uncertainly. "I'll let them know in the flight deck."

I walk the few feet to the galley and pick up the passenger list, noting that the dead man's name is Roger Kirkwood. Crossing to the flight deck, I tap in the access code and wait the few seconds for the pilots to check the cameras that will show I'm alone. They buzz me in, and I feel the rush of conflicting emotions that always comes from being inside the cockpit. Instrument panels stretch in front of the two seats, with still more between them. Glass displays showing altitude, speed, fuel, and more. An array of switches on the ceiling shrinks the small space further; only the vast, bright whiteness outside stops it feeling claustrophobic.

I could have been sitting here. On the right, as first officer, or maybe one day in the captain's seat. It could have been me, leading the lines of cabin crew through the airport, briefing the team at the start of each flight. Me, welcoming passengers to their destination or walking through the cabin, midflight, like the head chef at a Michelin-starred restaurant. Feeling that extraordinary surge beneath my hands as a B777 takes off.

And yet.

The buzzing in my ears tells me I'm far from over it. I can keep it in check by breathing steadily, by looking away from the controls. By focusing on my job. But it's still there. The fear.

Ben is yawning widely enough to show off his tonsils. He stops when I tell them what's happened.

Louis is making notes on the flight plan. "Bugger." He looks up at Ben. "What do you want to do?"

"Right now? Kick back with a few beers and sleep in my own bed. But in the absence of that, I'd quite like this flight to go without a hitch."

"Bit late for that."

Ben looks at me. "He's in business?"

"Yes."

"Traveling on his own?"

I nod.

He drums his fingers on his thigh. "Leave him."

"You're sure?"

"Between the devil and the deep blue sea, aren't we? Dindar'll go ballistic if we abort his precious maiden voyage. Make sure the screen's up around his seat, then put him in it and cover him up. And turn the heating down a notch." He grins, and I swallow the bile that rises at the implication behind his words. We still have over ten hours left till we get to Sydney.

The protocol for dead passengers is one of those sections in a training manual you flick through, assuming the chances of needing the information are slim. But airplanes are cities, suspended in the air, and in cities, people live and people die. The gentleman from seat 1J won't be legally declared dead until we land, and our responsibility until then is the same as for all our passengers. To look after him.

Roger Kirkwood weighs more than it seems possible any person can weigh. Carmel and I take a leg each, and Erik and Hassan manhandle his shoulders. Together we drag him to his seat and heave him into it. Carmel is trying not to cry.

"I'll cover him up," I say. "You lot go and check on the passengers, make sure they're all okay. Some of them look as if they could do with a sugary tea or even a brandy. I know I could." There's a glass on the floor in the aisle, dropped as the man collapsed. A bloodred stain spatters the floor. I pick up the glass. There's a drop of liquid in the bottom but something else too—a grainy residue, like when you lose a biscuit in a cup of tea. I sniff it, but all I smell is port.

Soon after I started working for World Airlines, a woman nodded off on a short-haul flight to Barcelona and didn't wake up. The plane was full, and there was nowhere to move her to, so she stayed where she was, strapped in and holding her daughter's hand till we landed. Emergency diversions aren't uncommon, particularly if there's still a chance of saving a life, but I've heard of bodies being stretched out across three seats or even on the floor in the galley. One urban myth, shared with much glee when I was training, tells of the unfortunate crew who stowed a body in the loo, only to discover him trapped once rigor mortis set in.

I shudder as I straighten Mr. Kirkwood's legs. Someone—perhaps the doctor—closed his eyes while I was talking to Ben and Louis, but his mouth is open, his tongue swollen and lolling to the side between blue-tinged lips. He wears a wedding band, plump flesh on either side holding the gold in place. His next of kin won't be notified until we land and he's officially declared deceased, and I wonder if his spouse waved him off at the airport or whether they'll be at Sydney, waiting to welcome him home.

He hasn't used his blanket, so I take it out of its plastic wrapping and lay it across his legs, pulling down his rucked-up jacket, as though he might find the wrinkle uncomfortable. There's a wallet in the left-hand pocket, and I take it out to keep safely in the galley. It's rare we have thefts on board, and I can't imagine anyone being cold-hearted enough to rob a corpse, but nevertheless, I'll keep it safe. The wallet is black, an expensive but simple piece of folded leather. When I open it, a photograph falls out: a home-printed image on cheap paper.

I put out my hand to still myself, even though the plane is steady. It isn't possible. It's a coincidence, that's all; a similarity to be dismissed.

But it can't be. I know this face as well as I know my own. This is a photograph of Sophia.

FOURTEEN

PASSENGER 1B

My name is Melanie Potts, and I'm on Flight 79 to honor my brother's memory.

The flight attendants have covered the dead body with a blanket. I don't know what I expected them to do with it—where I imagined they'd put it—but it wasn't that. Everyone carrying on eating and drinking, watching movies, with a dead man just meters away from them. Surreal, really.

The only other dead body I've seen was my brother's. I didn't want to see him, but I wanted to say goodbye, and afterward, I was glad to have gone. It's true what they say, about the body being somehow empty. Just a vessel for the person who used to inhabit it. I guess, if you think of it like that, it's not so weird to leave a body in business class.

My brother was murdered by the police. Maybe that's not what the court records say, but I can assure you that's what happened. Six of them—each one bigger than my baby brother—hearing an accent, making a judgment, seeing what they wanted to see.

"It was necessary to use restraint techniques," one of the officers said in court, "as the subject was becoming increasingly violent."

Wouldn't you be violent if half a dozen cops were sitting on you? Wouldn't you hit and kick and bite to get free? That's all he did, my little bro, and they pushed him into the ground till he couldn't take a breath. Positional asphyxia, they call it.

I call it murder.

They give good lip service to rooting out the corrupt coppers, the violent ones, the ones with grudges. Every now and then, they'll hang one out to dry, *distancing themselves so they can say he did this to himself—it had nothing to do with us. But scratch the surface and you'll find hundreds of complaints of police brutality, thousands of incivility, of racism, bias, prejudice. They keep the law on their side because they are the law, because the Masonic lodges are full of judges and magistrates and power, and a handshake will sweep away the inconvenience of a council estate lad in the wrong place at the wrong time.*

So where did that leave me? Drifting, at first. Suicidal, for long enough for it to be my new normal. I'll be honest, there were days when I couldn't get out of bed, or if I hauled myself outside, I found my feet walking to the middle of the motorway bridge and looking down at the lorries and thinking, Just do it. Just end it all.

But I didn't. Because they'd have killed two people then, and what would it all have been for? What would my legacy be, my mark on the world? I'd be as unimportant—as invisible—in death as my brother was in life. In court. If I've learned anything from what happened, it's that you've got to make every day count.

I started to raise my voice. I wrote to MPs and uploaded videos on YouTube. I met other families whose loved ones had been murdered by the police or by prison guards or by negligent nurses in hospitals where fat-cat execs only cared about the bottom line. I spoke for us all.

The invitations came from all over the country. Pressure groups, women's institutes, schools, and charities wanting to learn and help. They came from the authorities too—from police forces and councils ticking diversity training boxes—and I swallowed my anger for long enough to deliver my message and take the check that would enable me to speak for free somewhere else.

People paid for me to speak overseas. Three years after my brother's death, I stepped off a first-class flight to Washington and had to fight back the tears. I was making my voice count; I was making his sacrifice count. And I was glad—so very glad—that I'd never stepped off that motorway bridge.

I had more to offer the world by staying alive.

FIFTEEN

8:30 P.M. | ADAM

Becca's shouting from upstairs, the ringing in my ears distorting her words. I try to shout back, but my mouth's full of blood, and I retch as it hits the back of my throat. It hurts to breathe, and there's a dull ache at the base of my spine and across my stomach.

"Adam? Are you okay? Who was that?"

I manage to get on to my hands and knees, crawling toward the front door. No one drives along this track unless they're coming to the farm cottages, but I can't risk anyone asking questions.

You've got till midnight.

I let out a groan. What am I going to do?

"Are you okay? I could hear fighting, but Sophia was in the bath and—oh my God, are you badly hurt?" Becca's halfway down the stairs, where they turn a corner. Her mouth drops open. "What the fuck?"

"*Where's. Sophia?*" Each word makes the pain intensify, nausea swelling inside me.

"Still in the bath."

"*Don't. Leave. Her.*"

"But—"

"*Go!*"

As Becca runs back upstairs, I retch again, prompting a sharp pain around my ribs. I drag myself to the front door and vomit onto the path, then I pull the door closed. I breathe as shallowly as I can—anything too deep or too fast is painful enough to make my head spin—and slowly

I move to my knees and then stand up, locking the door. A piece of broken glass slices through my sock, but the pain barely registers. I hear the bathwater draining away upstairs, and I go into the downstairs loo to clean myself up before Sophia sees me.

One eye has closed up completely, the bruised skin around it swollen and cut. The blood that covers most of my face and a lot of my shirt is thankfully just from my nose, which is twice its normal size. I fill the basin and wash my face, wincing as the water turns pink.

"Adam? You okay?"

I give a noncommittal *uh-huh* and take a look at my reflection. It's marginally less terrifying without the blood. I take off my shirt and leave it in the sink, emerging in an undershirt that's dark enough to hide most of the stains.

"Jesus."

"No, still Adam," I say drily. "Although crucifixion feels like the better option right now."

Becca doesn't laugh. She's at the bottom of the stairs, Sophia a few steps above her, looking at me in horror through the banisters.

"I'm okay, sweetheart."

"You don't look okay," Becca says.

"You should see the other guy." I try for a smile, and pain shoots through my jaw. I stop trying. "Not a mark on him."

"Who was he?"

I don't answer, and she follows me into the kitchen. Sophia hangs back, Elephant dangling from one hand. She's wearing Action Man pajamas and a fleece dressing gown covered in unicorns. Becca has plaited her hair, but it's still wet, dripping down her robe. I grab a tea towel and use it to squeeze the excess water away, glad of an action that means my daughter can't see my face.

"Does it hurt, Daddy?"

"It's a bit sore."

"Shall I call an am'blance?"

"No, I don't think—"

"I know how. Mummy showed me."

"I don't want—"

"Nine, nine, nine."

"Um, maybe someone should just check you over?" Becca says. "You don't look great."

I finish drying Sophia's hair and open the cupboard where we keep the first aid kit. I reach up, biting back a cry as a sharp pain makes black dots swim in front of my eyes. The room rushes up at me.

"Here, let me do that. Sit down before you fall down." Becca steers me to a chair. Sophia is watching me, eyes wide with trepidation and curiosity.

"No ambulance," I say firmly. "If I go to a hospital, someone will notify the police that a crime's taken place."

"So?"

"So maybe I don't want the police involved." I speak quietly, my voice casual, but my face making quite clear to Becca how I feel.

She holds my gaze, her eyes curious—suspicious, even. "How come? I mean, they're not *my* favorite people, but they're your mates, aren't they?"

She passes me a glass of water and a handful of pills, and I knock them back in one. I'm suddenly exhausted, not just from the beating but from the sheer magnitude of keeping everything together over the last few months, from the stress of lying to Mina, to Sophia, to everyone at work. This morning's meeting with DI Butler feels like months ago.

"I've messed up," I say suddenly.

Out of everyone I could confide in, a seventeen-year-old girl isn't top of my list, but sometimes it's easier to talk to someone with no skin in the game. I give a loaded glance toward

Sophia. Becca's swift to react. "Do you want to watch *Paw Patrol?*" She holds out a hand and leads Sophia into the sitting room. A moment later, I hear the familiar theme tune, and Becca comes back into the kitchen. She folds her arms. "That bloke who beat you up was Katya's boyfriend, wasn't he?"

I'm so taken aback, I can't answer.

Becca smirks. "Did you think I didn't know you were shagging the au pair? One of the mums told me when I picked Sophia up from school, wanted me to know in case you tried something on with me." There's a harsh tone in her voice now, as though any respect she was showing me before was just a pretense.

"Tried it on? I wouldn't—"

She laughs. "You wouldn't get a chance!"

"Christ." I rub my face, forgetting the state I'm in. The resultant pain is a welcome distraction from the knowledge that Sophia's friends' parents consider me a sexual predator.

"Bit of a cliché, isn't it?" Becca seems older than seventeen now, and I wonder how she acquired such a jaded attitude toward men. We're not all that bad, surely? "Old man sleeps with—"

"Old?"

"—Ukrainian au pair."

"For God's sake, Becca, I was not having an affair with Katya!"

There's a sudden silence, broken only by the strains of Ryder and his canine chums. It's clear from Becca's expression that she doesn't believe me.

"How come she took off, then? The way Mina talked about it, she obviously thought it was your fault." She gets up and pours herself a glass of wine as though it's her house, as though she's an adult, not a kid.

"You're not even old enough—"

"Want one?" She pours a second glass without waiting for my answer. There's something self-conscious about her swagger, her confidence, as though she's playing a part. I'm gripped by the thought that all her talk about my trying something on might have been an act too, that she's been leading up to something. Has Mina put her up to this? Is this some kind of—the idea feels preposterous even as I think it—honey trap?

My skin feels clammy. I take the wine from Becca and sip it, trying to get rid of the chalky aftertaste of painkillers, the blood at the back of my throat. My nose is too swollen to breathe through it.

"I never had an affair with Katya," I say firmly, or as firmly as I can with my head still swimming. "I never had an affair with anyone. But it was my fault she left." Becca leans on the counter, her head tilted to one side. "That man—or one like him—threatened Katya. Sophia was there too." I have a sudden flashback to that awful day, when Katya and Sophia burst into the house, both of them crying so much they could hardly speak.

Daddy! Daddy!

He say he hurt me. He say he hurt Sophia!

"Sophia didn't pick up on exactly what the man was saying to Katya,"

I tell Becca now. "But she saw Katya's reaction and was scared enough for it to give her nightmares."

I stare out the window. It's dark outside, and the shadowy outline of the garden is overlaid with my reflection. It's snowing harder now, soft dots of white floating past the window.

"I don't get it. Why wouldn't you tell the police? Why would you let Mina think you were having an affair when you hadn't done anything wrong?"

"But I had done something wrong." I stare past my reflection and into the garden. "I owe money. A lot of money."

The amount goes up every day. The overdraft, the credit cards—the one Mina knows about and the five she doesn't. The store cards, the car payments, the cash I borrow from people at work because *things are a bit tricky since Mina kicked me out.*

And the big one. The ten grand from a moneylender whose path I'd crossed at work—for all the wrong reasons. I borrowed it to pay off the worst of the debts, at an interest rate I didn't care about because it was only short-term, I had a plan, it was all going to be okay...

Only I couldn't stop.

"I've got a gambling problem."

Three years, and that's the first time I've said it, even in my head. I've told myself I need to cut down, that I'll only do the lottery once a week, only buy one scratch card at a time, not twenty quid's worth. I've stood outside the dog track on the third day running and had second thoughts about going in. In all that time, I've never called it what it is—an addiction—but that's what it is. And it has me at its mercy.

"The ten grand I borrowed is closer to twenty now," I tell Becca, although if she walked out of the room, I think I'd still keep talking. It's all spilling out, all the lies, all the shame. "They sent that bloke to frighten me by threatening Katya and Sophia. I begged Katya not to tell Mina. A few weeks later, someone came to the house when she was here alone and threatened her. She left the next day, and that's when Mina accused me of sleeping with her."

"You should have come clean."

"I know that now! Back then, I thought I could handle it. I just needed one big win to clear my debts, then I'd..." I trail off, hearing how pathetic I sound. *Whenever you're in trouble,* I hear from the sitting room, *just yelp for help!*

"And you can't tell the cops because you took money from a loan shark?"

"I can't tell them because I've been hiding a gambling problem for three years." I reach for the wine and top up our glasses. "I can't tell them because I'm drowning in undisclosed debt, which is a disciplinary offense." Becca puts her glass down, untouched, but I swallow half of mine in one go. Not the best thing to do after a cocktail of painkillers, but I'm past caring. "I can't tell them, because I could lose my job if they find out."

Becca folds her arms across her chest. She's trying—but failing—to conceal her glee, and I wonder if it's my downfall itself she's enjoying or simply the fact that she's the only one who knows about it. "You really are in the shit, aren't you?"

"Thanks."

"So what's your plan?"

I knock back the rest of my drink. I turn around, press my palms into the draining board, and lean forward as if I'm about to do a press up, feeling the blood throb in my bruised face.

"I have absolutely no fucking idea."

SIXTEEN

PASSENGER 40C

My name is Elle Sykes, and getting on Flight 79 was a final fuck-you to my parents.

I sat fourteen GCSEs. All the usual ones, plus further math, additional science, Latin, Mandarin, and general studies. My little genius, Mum used to call me, even though I'd shot up that year and could see the top of her head when I hugged her.

"She's predicted A-stars all round," Dad would tell people, and I'd roll my eyes and slink out of the room, away from the politely impressed murmurs. Tightness would travel from my stomach like an elevator, and I'd take big gulps of orange juice to push it back down. Sometimes I'd still be able to hear him—math, further math, and physics at A-level, I'd imagine—*and the lift would ignore my jabbing of the buttons and continue to rise.* It would be a shame to give up on Mandarin—she's the only one doing it in her year, you know—and of course, Latin's always useful. *The elevator would reach my throat, and I'd lean over the sink, mouth working like a fish on a hook.*

There were six of us in what the school called the Gifted and Talented group: four boys and two girls. The boys kept to themselves, of course, making it awkward for me to ignore Sally, who wore knee-length socks and had a casual relationship with antiperspirant. It wasn't that I didn't like her; it's just that we had nothing in common beyond our ability to come out on top in every exam. Sally preferred to spend lunchtimes doing calculus, while I wanted a fag 'round the back with mates who forgave me for being clever because I blew smoke rings and knew where to score weed.

And actually, I wasn't clever. Not Sally clever. Not high-IQ, natural genius, go-to-university-at-thirteen clever. I had a good memory and a quick brain, and I worked hard. The harder I worked, the better results I got, and the better results I got, the harder I was expected to work, and the better results I got. 'Round and 'round I went, until the fourteen A-stars that results day brought was accompanied, not by euphoria or even relief, but by a sick feeling in the pit of my stomach.

"Cambridge is in the bag." *Dad grinned as he drove me home. I leaned back, turned my head, and closed my eyes so the countryside passed in flickers of filtered light. Cambridge had turned Dad down, and the chip he had carried around ever since was the size of a sack of spuds. I had been planning to do medicine at Cambridge for as long as I could remember. I say* "I": *I think you can probably guess whose idea it was. Not that I minded—I had to do something, I supposed, and I had no real objections to being a doctor—but sometimes I wondered what would happen if I turned around and said,* You know what, I want to go to drama school, *or,* I've decided to focus on PE next year. *Actually, that rather appealed. Sports science, at Loughborough.*

I wasn't given the summer off, by the way, before results day. I had private tutoring every morning, with homework each afternoon. It'll really give you a head start come September. *My parents weren't loaded, and I knew the lessons meant huge sacrifices on their part, but a kernel of resentment was already starting to build. They never asked me,* Do you *want* tutoring? Do you *want* to learn Mandarin? How do you feel about taking six A-levels instead of three? *It was presented as a fait accompli, my parents bursting with pride and excitement at this new opportunity they'd negotiated for me.*

"Mr. Franklin says you can go into school on Saturday mornings," *Dad said, in the autumn year of my final term.* "Sally too. Interview prep." *Mr. Franklin was the head teacher of our school, a comprehensive that—despite excellent results—had never yet managed to get a student to Oxbridge.*

"Great." *I wondered if it was actually possible to die from mental exhaustion and whether the pressure that formed in my head like an electrical storm was real or psychosomatic. I thought about the next two years of study, of the summer before university, when I would no doubt find myself enrolled in extra study classes to prepare me for my degree. I imagined the top of my skull shattering into pieces, a single piece of knowledge clinging on to each fragment.*

千里之行，始於足下

$z^2 = x^2 + y^2$.

Fuck. This. Shit.

I couldn't do it anymore.

"I'm going to take a gap year."

My parents looked at each other before they looked at me. "I'm not so sure that's a good idea," Mum said. "Cambridge is incredibly competitive. Surely, they won't take you if it looks like you're not committed?"

"I guess if it's relevant experience..." Dad was thinking out loud. "Voluntary work in a field hospital, maybe? I'll speak to—"

"No!" It came out sharper than I'd intended. I took a breath. "I want to organize it. I want a normal gap year. Hostels. Traveling. Meeting people. Reading stuff that isn't on a course list. I want—" To my horror, my voice broke. "I want to be normal."

They said they'd give it some thought, but my mind was made up. I wanted some time out. I wanted to get drunk, get off with people, take drugs, go clubbing... I wanted to do everything my mates would be spending the next two years doing, while my mother sprinkled essential oils around my bedroom to help consolidate your learning while you sleep.

I'd get through my A-levels, then I wanted to get on a plane and get as far away from my parents as I could. I wanted to have the experience of a lifetime.

I wanted to live.

SEVENTEEN

10 HOURS FROM SYDNEY | MINA

When Mike and Cesca come down from the pilots' rest area, neither look as though they've spent six hours in narrow bunks, high up in the nose of the plane. Cesca's makeup is immaculate, the only giveaway a tiny pillow crease on one cheek. Carmel produces two coffees.

"Cheers." Mike Carrivick has gray hair and blue eyes that crinkle at the sides when he smiles his thanks at me. In a moment, he and Cesca will assume control of the plane, and for the next six hours, relief pilots Ben and Louis will sleep.

Mike takes a sip of his drink and lets out an appreciative sigh. "Everything going well?"

There's a second's pause.

"Not for the guy in 1J," Carmel says darkly. I leave her to brief Mike and Cesca, moving to the window, where the darkness reflects nothing but my ashen face. We're somewhere over China, around nine p.m. UK time, and still hours before dawn in the East. Here in the cabin, the lights have been dimmed: a gentle suggestion to passengers to get some rest. I glance across to 1J where the privacy screen shields from view the blanketed figure of Roger Kirkwood.

What was he doing with a photograph of my daughter?

Ice runs through my veins, my head full of grooming gangs, child traffickers, pedophiles. I think of Kirkwood's waxy face, his lolling tongue, and bile rises in my throat.

Was he the one who brought Sophia's EpiPen on board too? I'd assumed whoever left it there had intended for me to find it—some sick joke, or Adam trying to make me feel guilty—but what if they have it because Sophia might need it?

Because they're planning to take her too.

I press my forehead to the glass. Cesca and Mike are in the flight deck now, Ben and Louis briefing them on the journey so far. I need to talk to someone about this. I'll wait till handover has finished, then I have to do something. I have to get a message to Adam, to make sure Sophia's okay.

The glass Kirkwood was holding when he fell is still on the side in the galley. I pick it up and wipe a finger around the inside. Residue coats my skin. It isn't sediment, as I'd first thought, but a grainy powder or a crushed-up tablet.

Medication.

Did he take it himself, or did someone slip it into his drink?

If Roger Kirkwood was murdered, the whole plane is a crime scene: every passenger a suspect.

Every crew member too, says a voice in my head.

The call bell sounds, but I don't move. I feel eyes on me, and when I look up, Erik is staring at me. He looks pointedly at the call light.

"Can you get that?" I manage.

Kirkwood was carrying my daughter's photograph. That's not down to me, his death isn't down to me, but will it look that way to someone else?

Will it look that way to the police?

Erik huffs audibly but turns to check on the cabin, and I wrap Kirkwood's glass in a cloth and push it to the back of a locker.

When the flight-deck door opens and Ben and Louis appear, I feel a flush spread across my cheeks, and I turn away, certain I must look as if I have something to hide.

"Cesca and Mike are so nice, aren't they?" Carmel says to the two relief pilots. "Mike was on the last test flight, you know. He persuaded Dindar to let him be on the first official one. For his CV, I suppose." She makes drinks for Ben and Louis to take up while the two men take a walk through the cabin.

When the call bell rings again, I catch a glance between Carmel and Erik before Erik folds his arms across his chest and plants himself against the counter.

"I'll go," I say. He widens his eyes, as if my doing my job is a novelty, and I feel a swell of anger inside. He has no idea what it's like, what I'm going through. First the EpiPen, now the photograph. Someone's messing with my head. Is it any wonder my mind's not on fetching cocktails for Alice bloody Davanti?

When I get back, there's a queue for the bathrooms stretching into the galley. The sudden influx of people pulls my nerves taut. I need space. I need to be able to take off this mask of smiles and *how can I help you*s and work out what to do about Kirkwood. About Sophia's photo.

Is it even Sophia in the picture? There was so much going on, and all the shock of losing a passenger... I saw a girl with dark plaits, but did my brain make an association that simply doesn't exist?

She was wearing the same school uniform.

"There are more loos at the back of the plane," I say to the queue, trying but failing to keep the curtness from my tone.

The man with the glasses and the neat beard raises his hand a fraction, like a child unsure if he needs permission to speak. "One of them's blocked. They've sent us up here."

I grimace. I wonder how much of Dindar's research was devoted to how well the bathrooms would cope with a full load of passengers.

Ben and Louis return. They're in no apparent hurry to go upstairs, leaning casually against the counter in the galley, chatting to the passengers in the queue. Heat rises inside me, my skull so tight, it could burst. The other journalist—Derek Trespass—comes out of the loo and hangs around, asking Ben questions about altitude, maximum load, cloud cover. I just need five minutes with everyone gone, just a few minutes to look at the photo.

It could be a different child, couldn't it? Another five- or six-year-old with dark curls and a blue-and-white uniform?

Everywhere, there are voices—talking, laughing—and underneath it all, the incessant white noise thrum of the plane itself. I push through the throng—suddenly aware of how tired I am, how much my feet ache, my head hurts—and someone jostles against me, their drink spilling over my sleeve.

"This isn't the bar, you know!"

Everyone stops talking. Carmel widens her eyes at me.

"Sorry. I—" I swallow hard, tears pricking at the backs of my eyes.

"We're making the place look untidy, aren't we?" Ben cuts into the silence with professional joviality, dissolving the tension as quickly as I created it. "Let's clear off and let the crew do their job."

"I'm sorry," I say as the passengers drift from the galley. "I'm a bit—"

"You're doing the important job." He winks. "Give me a plane over people any day."

"It's just a bit busy, that's all."

If it isn't Sophia, then everything's okay, right? I brought the EpiPen on board myself without realizing. The man who died—I mean, it's awful, but it's got nothing to do with me, with Sophia. Not if the girl in the picture isn't her.

Ben picks up the drink Carmel's made for him. "We'll take these up and get out of your way. Thanks again."

And they disappear. I know I've been rude, but pressure is building in my head, and I *have* to see that photo again. I have to look properly this time, see the difference in features, realize how ridiculous I was to even see a resemblance to my daughter. Slowly, the queue for the bathroom thins out. A call bell rings, and Carmel goes, after the tiniest glance at me. I've not been pulling my weight, and it's starting to show. Finally alone, I take the printed picture from my pocket and smooth it out.

It is not a good photograph. Not the sort you'd frame or send to the grandparents. Not even the sort of accidental snap you keep for the memories it prompts. Sophia—and there is no doubt that it is Sophia—is sitting in her classroom at school. There is a display of painted butterflies behind her, and papier-mâché planets are suspended above her head. In the background, through the classroom door, I glimpse children in the cloakroom, shrugging off coats. This photo was taken at drop-off, then.

Has it been printed from the school website? I try to remember if I signed a permission slip—what the website even looks like—but there's a fuzziness in the foreground that would make it a poor choice for a promotional tool.

No, not fuzziness. A reflection. Someone took this through a window. I run my finger over my daughter's image—over her face, the curls around her forehead, the plaits that tame the rest into two neat lines over her shoulders—and terror fills my veins with ice.

One red bobble, one blue.

The photograph was taken this morning.

The plane banks suddenly to the left. A water bottle slides from one end of the counter to the other, stops for a split second, then slides back again as we roll to the right. In the cabin, people hold their drinks in front of them, trying to keep the liquid level as we pitch forward. Another violent lurch sends Alice Davanti, on her way back from the bathroom, sideways. She clutches at the seat nearest to her before gripping each one in turn to get safely back to her own. I call the flight deck.

"Everything okay? It's pretty bumpy back here." As I'm talking, the seat belt sign pings on, and Carmel and Erik take an aisle each, checking that all the passengers are safely buckled up.

"Sorry about that," Mike says. "Crosswind—had to turn to get back on course. It'll be a few minutes, I'm afraid." The water bottle that's been sliding back and forth in the galley makes its final descent, crashing onto the floor at my feet, and I hear Cesca's command in stereo, through the intercom and over the PA: *Cabin crew, please take your seats.*

We buckle up, and I stare out the window at the seemingly innocuous night sky. It'll be another six or seven hours before we'll catch a glimpse of Australia, yet I'm already five thousand miles from home. I miss Sophia so much, there's a physical ache in my chest, love and guilt so intermingled, they're impossible to separate. I shouldn't have left her. I shouldn't be here at all.

I squeeze my eyes closed, making silent, pointless promises. *Keep everyone safe and I won't leave her again. I won't fly...* I'm seized by the absurd thought that someone knows what happened at training school: that I survived when I should have died. That I cheated destiny.

"It is just turbulence," Erik says from the jump seat next to me. I peel my fingers from my kneecaps. He thinks I'm scared we're going to crash, but what I'm scared of is so much worse than crashing.

Why would Kirkwood have a picture of Sophia?

Could he be connected to her birth family? Years ago, we ran into her maternal grandmother at a soft play center, and I can still remember the visceral fear that gripped me when I saw her watching Sophia. Does the family want her back? In five years, they've never tried to contact us.

I can't shake the thought that this is punishment—karma—for all the times I've moaned about my daughter's behavior, for all the times I've clenched my fists and wailed to the ceiling, *I can't do this anymore!*

I wrote a note to myself once. We'd had a perfect day playing games in the park—Adam, me, and Sophia—and we rounded it off with hot chocolate, all three of us in dressing gowns at the kitchen table. Adam put Sophia to bed, and I got out my phone and wrote a note, in among the shopping lists and the myriad reminders to find a plumber and get my coil checked.

I love my daughter, it started.

I love the way she's memorized every fact on the information boards in the zoo. I love that she's confident enough to tell another family that, It's an ape, actually—monkeys have tails. *I love that she wanted to give that little boy another ice cream when he dropped his. I love how funny she is, and how clever she is, and how hungry she is to learn new things. Mostly, I love that she's ours, and we're hers.*

Three days later, as Sophia screamed that she hated me, that she wanted me to die, I locked myself in the downstairs loo and read the note over and over.

I love my daughter, I love my daughter, I love my daughter.

What kind of mother needs a reminder like that?

Me. I do. Because trying to remember that you love someone who is screaming that they hate you, who has hurled the tea you lovingly made them across the floor, is like trying to recall summer when it's minus two outside. It's trying to imagine ever being hungry again when you're groaning after Sunday lunch. They are transient, slippery sensations, too quickly forgotten, remembered in the abstract way but not *felt*.

I love my daughter.

I don't need that note right now. I don't need a reminder. I don't even need to picture my daughter's face or summon a memory. What I feel for Sophia floods through every vein, every nerve ending until it is all-consuming. Unqualified, unending love.

And fear.

I search my memory for details from the first half of the flight, but there's nothing that stands out, no sign that Roger Kirkwood was paying me particular attention. His wallet yielded nothing of use. A platinum World Airlines frequent flyer card, a photograph—a properly printed one this time—of what could be his wife and grown-up children, and a business card that tells me he was a sales director for a soft drinks firm.

Just as we're released from our seats, I realize something. The photograph of his wife was carefully inserted into the notes section of Kirkwood's wallet, the business card slotted in among the credit and loyalty cards. But the picture of Sophia wasn't technically *in* his wallet, merely slipped between the folded leather. It was, I think—mentally summoning the moment I retrieved it from his jacket pocket—not carefully filed there but crumpled, as though it had been pushed in hurriedly.

Could someone have put the photograph in Kirkwood's pocket without his knowledge? Did they kill him too? Is the person who brought Sophia's EpiPen and photograph on board a murderer?

I head for the bar, ignoring the muttered complaints from Erik that I'm shirking my duties.

Finley puts up his hand as I pass, and I bite back my frustration. "I'm a bit busy at the moment; maybe your mum could help. Shall we wake her up? She might be hungry anyway."

"She said not to. She hates flying, so she takes a pill that makes her sleep the whole way."

"Lucky old mum," I say between gritted teeth. I take the headphones, which are even more tangled than before. "Look, I'll do these in a sec, okay?" Finley's reluctant to let them out of his sight. "I'll give them back to you, I promise." He's too well mannered to protest, and I stuff them in my pocket, no doubt making the knots even worse.

The seats in the bar are upholstered in navy velvet with emerald trim, and the hundreds of tiny lights on the ceiling make it feel like a nightclub. All that's missing is the music. It's only when you look out the windows that you remember you're on a plane, nothing between you and the ground but thousands of feet of air.

"The man who died." I try to keep the urgency out of my voice as I speak to Hassan. "Did you talk to him?"

"I served him drinks. Small talk, you know." He glances at my hands, and I realize I'm screwing a pile of cocktail napkins into a tight ball.

"Did he say anything?"

"About what?"

I open my mouth, but nothing comes out. *About my daughter. About his drink tasting odd. About someone putting a photograph in his pocket.* Hassan nods toward Jamie Crawford and his wife, who are sitting in the corner. "He was talking to these two for a bit."

I cross the small bar. "I'm sorry to interrupt," I say. "I wondered if—"

"Yeah, sure." The ex-footballer smiles lazily and stands up, looping an arm around my shoulders. "Caz'll take it. Where's your phone?"

"No, I don't—" I take a breath. Try to calm down. "I wasn't after a photo. I just wanted to talk to you about something."

He shrugs, as if to say it's my loss, and sits down.

"You said the passenger who died was knocking back the port."

"Must have had about four in the space of half an hour."

"Did you see anyone—" I cut myself off. If I ask whether they saw someone spike his drink, it'll be all over the plane within minutes. We'll be forced to land, and the police will take over and... I think of Sophia's photo, of my prints all over the empty glass I wrapped in waste paper and hid at the back of a locker, and I start to sweat.

Caz leans forward. "What did he die of?"

He was poisoned.

I swallow. "Um. A heart attack, I believe. I wondered if you'd spoken to him at all?"

"They don't keep themselves healthy, that's the problem." The footballer sighs with the smug self-awareness that comes from having a personal chef and a fitness trainer on speed dial.

"We did speak to him, though, didn't we, Jamie?" His wife puts her hand on his knee, her fourth finger almost eclipsed by a massive diamond. "He was the one who was a bit pissed and kept wanting to buy you a drink."

"Oh yeah! I was like, *It's a free bar, but knock yourself out.*"

"Did you see him with anyone else?"

"There was a couple with a baby." Caz screws up her face. "A bloke who said he was a journalist, I think."

I don't know what I was hoping for. That they saw someone drug Kirkwood? Nevertheless, I'm frustrated. I thank the Crawfords and push through the curtain to the rear cabin, scanning the seats for the doctor who responded to Erik's call for help.

She looks up from her book as I approach, her expression a little wary. "Don't tell me someone else is ill."

"No, I—I just wanted to thank you again for your help."

The doctor flushes, clearly uncomfortable with the attention. "I'm only sorry it was too late."

The woman next to the doctor is eavesdropping unashamedly, but I press on. "Air traffic control is just taking details to pass on to the next of kin, and I wondered if you could give me some more information. What makes you think he had a heart attack, for example?"

"The history given by your colleague and the other passengers was consistent with a diagnosis of cardiac arrest."

"It couldn't have been anything else?"

"You asked for a doctor; you didn't specify pathologist." She's smiling, and her tone is misleadingly pleasant, almost humorous, but her eyes are flinty. "Would you like me to attempt a full autopsy? Perhaps I could lay him out on your fancy bar and poke around him with a cocktail stirrer?" The woman next to her suppresses a snort. The doctor glances at her, then looks back at me, and her expression softens. "It could have been a number of things."

"Such as?"

The doctor sighs. "Look"—she takes in my name badge—"*Mina*. I did what I could—which sadly wasn't a great deal—but..." She makes a small but deliberate movement with the book in her hands, and I take the hint.

On my way to the galley, I'm stopped by a passenger at the back of business class who snaps his fingers at me, his eyes still on his screen. He's playing a game, one of those mindless stacking puzzles that gets faster with each level.

"Coffee," he says.

I leave a pause before saying, "Of course," in the hope of extracting a *please*, but it goes unnoticed. In the galley, Erik and Carmel break off from their conversation, and as I make my passenger's drink, I have the distinct impression I've interrupted something.

I return to the cabin. "Your coffee, sir." I smile as I deliver it, then stand as if I'm waiting for a tip. He's tall and blond, with a face full of angles, as though each part has been carved separately then slotted together. "You're most welcome."

The man's jaw tightens.

"Really," I say as I walk away. "It's my pleasure."

In the galley, I catch another look between Carmel and Erik. "Is there a problem?"

"It's nothing," Carmel says. Erik snorts, and I stare him down.

He doesn't flinch. "Is it okay, that coffee? Did you manage to make it? Because it seems you don't have so much practice."

"What?" I'm too taken aback to form a proper sentence.

"Carmel and I, we have done everything. Meals, drinks, cleaning the bathrooms. You are doing nothing!"

"Erik, don't. The passengers will hear." Carmel looks nervously toward the cabin.

"I'm sorry." I pinch the bridge of my nose, feeling the telltale sting of tears. "I'm just tired."

"We are all—"

I thrust my hand in my pocket, tearing out the photograph of Sophia and holding it with shaky hands, but before I can say anything, Carmel has wrapped her arms around me and is squeezing me tight.

"Oh, bless you. You must miss her. Is she with her daddy? They'll be having a lovely time, I bet you. She's probably hardly noticed you've gone. You know what they're like." Over Carmel's shoulder, I see Erik roll his eyes before leaving the galley. Carmel releases me, taking the photograph and saying, "Aww," before folding it carefully and tucking it back in my pocket. "Lovely to keep her with you like that. Come on. Let's get you a glass of water." She keeps talking, as though I'm a child myself. "Is it the menopause? Mum says she's a slave to her hormones."

"I'm thirty-four!"

"Does that mean it is?"

"No, Carmel, it's not the menopause."

"Well, you just stay here. We can handle the cabin. Make yourself a nice cup of tea."

I see my reflection in the window, its edges ragged and indistinct, and picture someone standing by Sophia's school, a camera raised to the glass. My head is filled with white noise, but it isn't enough to block out my thoughts.

I shouldn't be here.

Carmel and Erik are clearing the cabin, trays piled high with glasses and dirty napkins. Carmel sweeps through, dumping her tray on the side, and I make my feet move toward it, dividing the rubbish, the dirty cutlery. Erik brings a tray, and then Carmel another, and I'm separating the linen when I see an envelope, half hidden beneath a napkin. It's light blue, like an old-fashioned airmail letter, with a single word, written in ink.

Mina.

"What's this?" I hold it up.

My efforts to help with the clearing have failed to placate Erik, who stares at me. "It is an envelope."

"Perhaps it's a tip," Carmel says.

Erik snorts. "For doing what?"

"From who?" I say urgently.

They both shrug, Carmel looking helplessly at the pile of rubbish they've cleared from the cabin. It could have come from anyone.

"Maybe it's a love letter!" Carmel says. "If it's from the guy in 5F, I'll be green with envy—he's lush."

"If it is a tip, you must share it."

The walls of the plane curve around me as if they're crushing me, my lungs too tight, my rib cage too small. I push past Carmel to the bathroom, locking the door and pressing my back against it as I tear open the envelope. Inside is a single sheet of paper, the same navy ink running in neat handwriting across the page.

I read the first line, and my world shatters.

The following instructions will save your daughter's life.

EIGHTEEN

PASSENGER 8C

My name is Peter Hopkins, and I'm a passenger on Flight 79.

Almost as soon as we'd taken off, people started moaning about the legroom. The woman next to me put her seat back, only to be kicked in the kidneys by the bloke behind. Apparently there's an etiquette to flying economy: you don't put your seat back till the lights go out. Who knew?

I think the seats are pretty comfortable, to be honest. I've certainly lain my head in worse places. Filthy mattresses in squats that smelled of piss; between cardboard sheets; in doorways of shops with grilles across their windows to keep out people like me. In friends' front rooms, and on the sofas of people I barely knew but who couldn't say no when I turned up in the pouring rain. Sure, the flat beds of business class would be nice, but you learn to take what you're given. I'm not planning on sleeping anyway. Keep your guard up: that's another lesson you learn when you've lived on the streets.

The powers that be could solve homelessness just like that. Remember when there was that royal wedding in Windsor, and for forty-eight hours, there wasn't a single person on the streets? 'Course, as soon as the happy couple jetted off on honeymoon, everyone got turfed out again, but the point is: there's enough beds. They proved it. The government could give everyone a basic income, make sure they've got a roof over their head and food in their bellies. But it suits them to keep us at the bottom of the heap. Not registered to vote, so we don't get a say; not paying taxes, so why should we get a say? It's all about keeping us in our place. Second-class citizens.

We need a revolution. A massive uprising, where we march on Parliament and overthrow the government. None of your poxy online petitions, signed by middle-class liberals who count a direct debit and a tut as doing their bit. An actual revolution. Direct action: that's the only thing that works. Playing cat and mouse with the cops through the back streets of London; wiping Vaseline over riot van windscreens and jamming potatoes up their exhausts. Small acts, big action. Like back in the day, when we'd been banging on about overcrowding in the night shelter for eighteen months or more, and they were doing fuck-all about it. A small fire: that was all it took. No one hurt, no real damage done, but that storeroom they'd been on about converting got sorted in less than a week. Twelve more beds, no more crowding, just like that. Direct action.

Mind you, if we're talking about overcrowding, you couldn't fit more seats in this plane if you tried. We boarded in a long line—shuffling forward like we were being herded into gas chambers—and squeezed into our seats, climbing over legs and holding bags above our heads so as not to clout someone with them. I thought then: I hope there's not a fire. *It's all well and good, knowing where the emergency exits are, but the chances of you reaching one are slim, I reckon. You'd be trampled underfoot. People clawing at you to get past. Every man for himself.*

Don't get me wrong—like I said, I've spent nights in far worse places— but when you think about it, it's pretty weird to voluntarily stay in three square feet for twenty hours, in what is essentially a mobile death trap. It's like those trucks you see in India, stuffed to the gunwales with cows and chickens and women with bags full of shopping.

And no one complains. They just sit there, grateful for their shitty little packets of nuts and the tiny bottles of wine given out with the judgment of a chemist dispensing methadone. Because they're off to Sydney! They're so excited! So grateful! So blessed! It makes me laugh.

I know what you're thinking. You're thinking I'd be the first to complain, right?

Yeah, I've got form for causing trouble, but I also know when to keep my head down. I'm onto a good thing. A ticket to Australia; my first ever passport; the promise of a bed when we finally touch down. A fresh start.

What do I have to complain about?

NINETEEN

The following instructions will save your daughter's life.

An hour from now, you will ask one of the pilots to leave the flight deck. You may use whatever reason you wish, but you will not raise the alarm in any way. The bathroom adjacent to the flight deck will already be occupied. When the flight deck contains one pilot only, you will request access and allow the occupant of the bathroom to enter the flight deck. Then, you will close the door.

That is all I will ask you to do, Mina, and if you do it, your daughter will live.

Don't, and she will die.

The letter drops from my fingers, my knees collapsing me onto the loo. Toiletries rattle on the shelf above the sink, and I'm no longer sure if the roaring in my ears is the plane or my own pulse, thrumming without pause between beats.

This is a hijack attempt. There is no other explanation. Someone wants to take control of this plane, and if I let them, everyone on this plane is likely to die. If I don't...

I can't even allow myself to think the words. It can't happen. She's five years old; she has her whole life ahead of her. She's done nothing to deserve this.

And the people on this plane have?

There are courses they send us on, to deal with threats on an aircraft.

There are code words. Self-defense techniques. Restraint systems. We're taught to be vigilant, to identify potential terrorists from their manner-isms, their appearance, their behavior.

It all seems so easy, in the classroom. Breaking for lunch, conversation spilling into the corridor: *Can you imagine having to actually deal with that?* Filling up a salad tray, buying a Diet Coke, asking who's around on the weekend: *It's Ladies' Night at the Prince Albert.* I remember the role-play scenarios we did, the negotiating we practiced. *Comply, but don't surrender* is what we're told to do. If only it were that simple.

I never thought it would be like this.

I imagined a loaded gun, a knife to a colleague's throat. I imagined shouts, threats, religious fanatics in pursuit of martyrdom. Us against them. Fast-moving, quick-thinking. I watched Hollywood films with men who pulled guns on glossy-lipped flight attendants, and I wondered how I'd cope, how I'd feel. I imagined the terror, the panic, the loss of control.

I never imagined it would feel so lonely.

Carmel raps on the door. "You okay, Mina?"

"I'm fine. Just coming." The words sound as false as they feel. I flush the loo and run the tap, staring at myself in the mirror, unable to reconcile the way I look with the way I feel. I am the same person I was at the start of this flight, and yet so far removed. I think of that awful day in September 2001, when the world watched the twin towers fall, watched thousands of people in New York City die before our very eyes.

If one person could have stopped all that, they would have done so in a heartbeat.

I would have done.

And yet.

If you do it, your daughter will live. Don't, and she will die.

I'm glad it's so late. If Sophia were still at school or playing with friends, there would be a million ways someone could get to her. But it's almost ten p.m. at home, and she'll be tucked up in bed, her dad downstairs watching Netflix. For all Adam's faults, he's a good father. He'd put his own life on the line before letting anything happen to Sophia. She'll be safe with him.

"Is it the letter?" Carmel says as I emerge. Her face is screwed up in concern.

"Letter?" The effort of feigning lightness almost breaks me. "Oh, no, that was someone complaining about the Wi-Fi—like writing a letter is going to fix it! No, I think I've got some sort of tummy bug, actually. I really had to dash for the loo just then."

Erik looks revolted. He backs away, leaving us alone, which is at least one problem solved. Carmel seems to have taken my excuse at face value.

"Poor you. My mum always says flat Coke's good for dicky tummies. Shall I get you some?"

"Thanks."

She beams, pleased to be able to help, and I watch as she rifles in the lockers for what she needs. She's barely into her twenties, newly loved-up with the boyfriend who works in the City. Not a bad bone in her body.

"I'm sorry, Carmel." My eyes blur, and I blink away the tears that are forming.

She turns to me, perplexed. "Don't be silly. You can't help being poorly." She stirs my drink vigorously, the bubbles rising to the surface and popping. "This'll help."

I take it, sipping and telling her *it's great, it's definitely working, thank goodness. I'm sure I'll be fine now*, and she rolls her eyes at another call bell and says, *No rest for the wicked*.

No rest for the wicked.

I look through the curtain into the business-class cabin. Paul Talbot looks at me hopefully. His wife has nodded off watching a film; baby Lachlan is quiet at last, wide awake in his father's arms. I walk the few steps toward them, pasting a smile on my face.

"I don't suppose you'd take him for a sec while I use the loo?" Paul says. "Every time I put him down, he starts crying."

I stare at them for a second, unable to compute that life is continuing as normal, that nobody knows I hold their lives in my hands. Lachlan opens his mouth—the gummy wind-not-grin of the newborn baby—and liquid guilt seeps through my body. Sophia has her whole life ahead of her. But so does this baby.

I swallow. "No problem." Lachlan curls into the nape of my neck, and my heart squeezes.

It was raining the day Adam and I met Sophia. We arrived at the foster family's house in a flurry of umbrellas and coats, nerves making me talk too much and Adam too little.

"Sophia's just through here."

She was lying on a play mat, an arch of farm animals above her. *My daughter*, I thought, wondering if I'd ever be able to say that without feeling like a fraud.

"She's so lovely. Isn't she lovely, Adam? Hello, Sophia, aren't you lovely?" I willed Adam to say something, worried our social worker might take his silence as a lack of commitment. But when I looked at her, she was smiling, looking in turn at Adam, who had tears in his eyes.

"She's perfect," he said.

Lachlan has the biscuity scent of newborn babies, warm and sleepy. The woman in the seat across the aisle from the Talbots scowls at him—or me. Her long, gray hair is in a ponytail now. If she has children of her own, they'll be grown up. She'll have forgotten what it's like to travel with a baby.

Anxiety grows big as a tennis ball in my throat, each swallow forced around it. Someone on this plane is watching me. Someone wrote that letter; someone knows exactly how I'm feeling right now—and why.

I walk past Alice Davanti, typing furiously on a miniature keyboard, and Lady Barrow, her eyes closed and her fingers tapping to the music playing through her headphones. I scan every passenger, paranoia making every nerve ending tingle: invisible spiders crawling down my spine, along my arms.

Who are you?

Jamie Crawford and his wife are still in the bar. They've been joined by a handful of others, including Jason Poke, who is drinking champagne and regaling a small audience with tales from filming.

"...complete sense-of-humor failure and lamped the cameraman!"

Everyone roars with laughter, and Lachlan startles, flinging back his head and crying out.

"The little man's obviously not a fan, Jason!"

Could this whole thing be a setup? A Poke's Joke? I look up, searching the ceiling for signs of hidden cameras. Lachlan follows my gaze, and his eyes widen at the scattering of twinkling stars. How many night skies has he seen in his short life? My throat closes, the fear inside me rising and swelling like the tide. No one—not even Jason Poke—makes jokes about terrorism. Not on a plane. Decades ago, maybe, but not now, not after all the terrible things that have happened.

There's another burst of laughter. The other journalist, Derek Trespass, has a notebook in one hand. Maybe he came into the bar to work or in search of a story. There's no sign of such dedication now as he tries to shoehorn his own stories into the gaps between Poke's.

"The deputy PM was the same—no sense of humor at all. I remember an interview back in 2014..."

On the other side, three other passengers have moved on to coffee. They're picking at the cakes laid out on the bar, Hassan putting out side plates and folded napkins. I hear snatches of their conversation as I carry Lachlan back through to the business-class cabin.

"We've been meaning to visit Sydney for years, but the journey always put me off. As soon as I knew we could go nonstop, I booked, didn't I, love?"

"It makes such a difference, doesn't it? Mind you, we're paying a premium for it."

"First nonstop flight—it's a privilege. We'll be all over the papers tomorrow!"

I have a sudden, sharp image of our plane on the news. Dropping from the sky, bursting into flames. Headlines scroll at the foot of the screen. No Survivors from World Airlines Flight 79.

I shouldn't even be here.

Adam and I have always taken time off work in the last full week before Christmas. Last-minute present shopping, a mooch around the German markets. Hot mince pies, a cheeky mulled wine or three. It's our tradition. Our time together.

"We could still do it." He had said it casually, but I could see in his eyes how much he wanted me to say yes. It was still summer, the conversation prompted by Adam's need to book leave. "It might be just what we need. Some time on our own."

"I'll think about it."

The crew lists for the London–Sydney flight came out the next day.

"Sorry," I told Adam once the swap with Ryan was complete. "I've been shafted with the Sydney flight. I'll be away all that week."

One tiny lie. And now here I am.

I shouldn't be here. Not on this flight. Not on any flight.

As I walk back through the cabin, several of the passengers look in my direction. Because I'm holding a baby? Because they want another drink?

Or because they wrote the note?

Not knowing makes me self-conscious, fearful of dropping the baby, my arms suddenly clumsy. I'm still looking at each passenger, but I don't know what I'm looking for. Someone confident—arrogant? Or someone just as terrified as I am?

The woman in 5G has red eyes. She passes a balled-up tissue from fist to fist.

"Are you okay?" I crouch, getting as close to her level as my knees will let me.

"Not really." Her voice is hard. Bitter. *People who hijack planes are out of their minds, aren't they? Unhinged. Radicalized. This woman could be either of those things.*

"Would you like to tell me about it?" It's all I can do to keep my own voice under control, but I know I have to stay calm.

The woman stares at the baby in my arms. "You think you have all the time in the world when you're young."

I hold my breath.

"Then you realize the clock's speeding up, and you haven't done half the things you meant to, half the things that matter."

I put a hand on the woman's forearm, and she turns to look at me.

"She's dying." She has pale eyes, the color of a winter sea, and she stares unblinking at me, tears unchecked. "My best friend. My sister, I used to call her, although we got on far better than any sisters I knew. She moved to Sydney twenty years ago to marry some idiot with a surfboard, and I promised faithfully I'd visit, only life got in the way." Her eyes fill with tears. "And now death's getting in the way."

"You're going to spend Christmas with her?"

"Assuming she hangs on that long," the woman says quietly.

"I'm sure she will," I reply, because I don't know what else to say and because this woman has nothing to do with the note I received. All this woman wants to do is reach Sydney in time to say goodbye.

On the other side of the aisle, one row back, is a man who looks

Middle Eastern, his dark skin highlighted by a fine sheen. My nerves start to prickle, instinct and prejudice working hand in hand.

"Is everything okay?" I force myself to smile. He's shaking, and I mentally tick off the warning signs. Nervous appearance; erratic behavior; traveling alone.

"Is the plane alright?"

"The plane is fine," I say carefully. "Everything is fine."

"I don't like flying. I took a Valium, but it's not helping."

"Everything's fine," I repeat. "Planes nowadays are very safe. Very secure. It's impossible for anything to go wrong."

"That's not true. There are crashes all the time. You see them on the news."

"This plane, though"—my voice trembles—"this plane is safe." I leave, forcing myself to walk slowly, the way I'd normally move through the cabin. I don't want to be holding Lachlan any more. I don't want such a physical reminder of the innocent lives on this plane. I hand him back to Paul Talbot.

Airlines run safety maneuvers all the time. Fire alarms, ditching drills, tests of standard operating procedures. They will have done dozens for this route alone, dotting every i, crossing every t. Could this be another of Dindar's tests? An elaborate PR stunt, designed to demonstrate how safe the flight is?

I know the SOP inside out.

The first step is to inform the flight deck of what's happened. My daughter's safety won't influence the pilots, I know that. It sounds callous, but I understand it. If someone's held hostage this side of the flight-deck door, they're not allowed to open it—not if it's a passenger, not if it's a crew member. Even if their own family was on board and they looked on the camera and saw a hijacker standing there, a blade to the throat of someone they love, they're forbidden to open that door. Sophia might be in danger, but it won't make a difference to Cesca and Mike. There are too many lives at stake.

The cockpit door clicks open, and I step inside. There's nothing but blackness through the vast windscreen, and I have a sudden feeling of falling, of tumbling down Alice's rabbit hole, spinning out of control...

"Hey"—Mike glances at my name badge, well used to traveling with strangers—"Mina, how's it going back there?"

For that second, everything is still okay. I want to make it last, to draw out the moment before all our lives change. They'll notify air traffic control as soon as they know. There's a silent code to tap in. 7500. *Hijack in progress.*

What happens then is out of our control. An emergency landing at the nearest airport or an escort from fighter jets away from highly populated towns. In a volatile airspace, there's even the risk of being shot down: a controlled explosion seen as a favorable option to letting a plane crash.

I swallow hard. That's not my call to make. My job is to keep the passengers safe, not the plane. My job is to tell Cesca and Mike that we have a hijacker on board.

"All good," I say. "Except…" My pulse thrums, and I finish my sentence in a rush. "There's a young boy in business who's desperate to meet one of you. A real aviation geek. Any chance you could pop through?"

In 2015, the copilot of Germanwings Flight 9525 locked his captain out of the flight deck and flew the Airbus A320 into the Alps. Everyone on board was killed. The response from airlines was mixed: half immediately instigated policies stating that pilots could never be alone; the other half made no such change, instead looking at how they could preempt the mental health issues that had surely led to such a tragedy.

World Airlines made no policy change.

"His mum's a bit of a cow," I add. "She's knocked herself out and left the kid to fend for himself the whole flight."

"I can't stand parents like that," Mike says. "It's not a bloody crèche."

"I'll go." Cesca stands, stretching. "I need a pee anyway."

I don't thank her. I can't speak. My mouth is desert dry, my lips sticking to my teeth, and as I walk out of the flight deck with Cesca close behind, bile burns my throat.

I'm a mother.

I have no choice.

TWENTY

My head is thick, the combination of wine and painkillers making me nauseous. I swill out my wineglass and fill it with water, blinking hard as the glass goes fuzzy around the edges. My ribs hurt, and the pain around my kidneys is a constant reminder of the kicking I had.

I've got to find a way out. I've got to pay what I owe to the loan shark and get his gorillas off my back, then I'll deal with the banks. Once the debt stops getting bigger, I know I can start making it smaller again.

All you need is one big win, says the devil on my shoulder.

I press my hands harder into the draining board.

I've always liked a flutter. Nothing regular, just a bet on the Grand National and the occasional trip to the dogs with the lads from work. A tenner here, twenty there. When Mina and I got married, we gave lottery tickets as wedding favors. *We won the jackpot when we met*, read the cheesy writing on each envelope. *Here's hoping you're as lucky as us!* Mina's aunt scooped a hundred quid; a couple of people won a tenner. It was fun, as it was supposed to be.

For ages, that was all it was. Mina and I would play the lottery whenever there was a big rollover. They'd email you if you won, but we still sat and watched the live show: it was the anticipation we loved as much as anything.

"Who would you tell first?" Mina would say.

"Nobody. I'd help people out secretly. Like a fairy godmother but hairier. And no one would know until I died, and then they'd make me a saint."

Mina threw a cushion at me. "Bollocks. You'd be at the Lamborghini showroom the very next day."

"Fair point. Red or yellow?"

"Yellow. We might as well be vulgar as well as flashy."

We never won. Never even matched three numbers. And in the beginning, it didn't bother me. The chances were so tiny—it was just a bit of fun. But as time went by and life got more stressful, I found myself buying a ticket on Monday instead of waiting till Saturday afternoon. All week, I'd carry that slip of paper around, and every time I opened my wallet, I'd think, *Maybe this week...*

I'd think how incredible it would be to leave work and for Mina to quit her job too. I'd think how Sophia wouldn't have to be afraid of being abandoned, because we'd never have to leave her. Not for work, not for anything.

When Saturday rolled around and we didn't win, instead of crumpling the ticket and chucking it in the bin, I'd stare at it, rechecking the numbers. I'd feel jealous of the winners, bitterly resentful that it wasn't us. I'd feel Sophia tense in my arms and think, *This would change if we won the lottery.*

I started playing every week.

"We'd do better to stick two quid in a jar each week," Mina said. "At least that way we'd have a hundred and four quid to show for it at the end of the year."

"Where's the fun in that?" I said, although it didn't feel like fun by then. I set up a direct debit—it seemed easier than finding cash each time—and then I thought I might as well increase our chances. When I got to five rows, Mina stopped me.

"It's only a tenner a week."

"It's five hundred quid a year, Adam. We could go on holiday for that." She canceled the direct debit, and on Saturday night, she'd turn the TV over after eight o'clock and watch something on the BBC instead...

"You should probably sit down," Becca says now.

"I'm alright." The words come out slurred, and she looks at me strangely. My tongue feels too big for my mouth, the insides of my cheeks dry and chalky. I grip the side of the counter. I protected my head as best I could while I was getting a kicking, and I'm fairly certain my kidneys came off worst, but now I'm starting to think I might have a concussion. I've had it once before—during a rugby match—and I try to remember how it felt, but the details slip away from me.

It was scratch cards that fucked me. I'm almost embarrassed to admit it, like an alcoholic abusing Babycham or a drug addict who can't lay off the cough syrup. I won two hundred and fifty quid on the first card I bought. Two hundred and fifty! I could have kissed the bloke in the corner shop. I took Mina out for dinner and bought Sophia the color-change unicorn she'd been wanting, and I kept twenty quid back as my scratch-card fund. That was the key, I decided. Never gamble what you can't afford. I'd use a portion of everything I won to buy more scratch cards, and that way, I'd never get in trouble.

Except I only won a pound that time, and then nothing at all the next time, or the time after that…

Everything's fuzzy. I'm vaguely aware of Sophia coming into the kitchen, asking Becca, "What's wrong with Daddy?" I hear Becca's response as though it's underwater, and I shake my head to clear it.

"I'm fine, sweetheart. Just a bit tired." The first aid box is still on the side, and I rifle through it, wondering how strong the painkillers were, because although my head's swimming, I still hurt all over. "Did you give me ibuprofen or paracetamol?" I ask Becca. If it was just one, I can take the other.

"Daddy?" Sophia's rubbing her eyes. This first term at school has exhausted her.

There's all sorts of rubbish in the first aid box—sticky bottles of cough mixture and an assortment of bandages—but no painkillers. I blink, shake my head again like a dog running from the sea.

"Where are they?" I turn and look at Becca, who stares back, her face unmoving. She doesn't look like a teenager anymore; she looks older, more streetwise, more *knowing*.

In among the pain and the fuzziness comes a sudden clarity. "Becca, what did you give me?"

My mouth is so dry, it's hard to get out the words, and through the fuzziness in my head, I hear them run into each other. *Whatdidyougiveme?* The pain in my ribs and my kidneys feel so distant now, they could belong to someone else.

"Something to help you sleep." Becca smiles, as if she's done something helpful, and I grapple to make sense of the situation. Did we even *have* sleeping tablets? Maybe Mina got a prescription—was she struggling with insomnia?—and left the pills in the first aid box, but why would she do that, and even if she did—

"Didn't it say on the packet what they were?" I think that's what I say, but the blank look on Becca's face suggests what comes out is something else entirely. Suddenly, her expression clears.

"Oh, I see! You think I gave you sleeping tablets by accident, when I meant to hand you painkillers?" She laughs loudly. "No, I'm not that stupid. It was intentional. I brought them with me."

I grip on to the counter to stop the swaying that could either be me or the room. Sophia's still in the doorway, looking first at me and then at Becca, and I smile at her, but she shrinks back.

"Is Daddy poorly?"

I don't blame Sophia for her wariness—the way I've behaved over the last few months has done nothing to help her trust me—but I need her to understand that right now, she's safest with me. I reach out an arm toward her, my hand trembling, trying for words I want to be reassuring, but which slide out in an anxious heap. *Sokaypumpkincometodaddy.*

Sophia pulls on her plait, twisting it hard around her fingers as her gaze flickers between Becca and me, me and Becca.

"Come over here, sweetheart." Becca holds out her arms.

"Sophia, no!"

It's too loud, too violent. She claps her hands over her ears and lets out a cry, running to Becca, who picks her up and rocks from side to side. Sophia wraps her legs around her like a monkey, her face buried in Becca's jumper.

Above Sophia's head, Becca smiles. It's triumphant. As though she's won a game I didn't even know I was playing.

I force a pause between my words. "*You. Need. To. Leave. Right. Now.*"

"I've only just started."

I start walking toward them, one hand gripping the counter because the room won't stop moving. "I don't know what you're playing at, but you've already committed a very serious offense." I speak slowly, my bone-dry lips fighting every syllable. "Administering noxious substances carries a prison sentence, and don't think they'll let you off just because you're still at school." The effort of making myself understood leaves me breathless, like I'm fighting through quicksand.

"I'm twenty-three actually. Surprise!" She keeps her voice light, almost musical, as if she's talking to Sophia, who's still hugging Becca tightly. Becca sways from side to side, reassuring her. "Stop right there, Adam."

I've been in countless situations like this. Drunk people, angry people, crazy people. I've driven through town centers with sirens blaring, adrenaline surging at the prospect of a punch-up, and I've held my own when outnumbered three to one.

I've been caught out too: the calm house call that suddenly turns nasty or the fight out of the blue when I've taken a prisoner back to a cell. It can come out of nowhere, but on some level, when you're at work, you're always ready for it.

I'm not ready now. Not physically, not mentally. Not when my body won't work, and not in my own house, with my daughter. Not when someone I believed to be a seventeen-year-old girl has turned out to be an adult psychopath.

"Let her go."

"I said stay where you are."

"And I said let her go."

Becca moves her free arm and smiles. I stay where I am.

Because there, in her hand, just millimeters from Sophia's neck, is a loaded syringe.

TWENTY-ONE

PASSENGER 7G

My name is Ritchie Nichols, and I spent the first half of Flight 79 playing games.

I don't understand people who say they don't like computer games. Which ones? I always ask. Because it's like saying you don't like animals. Or food. There are so many different games, it's impossible to hate them all. If you're not into combat, there are sport ones, or role-play, or strategy ones where you run around collecting shit. They're not my bag, but to each their own. On the plane, they only have puzzle games, but it passes the time at least.

Me, I'm into FPS (that's first-person shooter). Those are the games you can really get into—you're not looking down on a world, you're in it. You can play for hours, lights off, headset on. You can hear your character breathing, and once you're into the game, you can't hear your own anymore. You're one person—a mix of human and avatar, nothing between you and the bad guys except the barrel of a gun. When it goes off and the controller thumps in your hands, you can almost feel the recoil on your shoulder because everything else is there—the sweat, the noise, the blood…

I've played since I was a kid. My mother kept threatening to take the PlayStation away, but she never did. It was back when I was still going to my dad's every weekend, and she knew gaming was our thing, so I'd only end up at his place after school if I couldn't play at home. She gave up trying to make me come down for tea. She brought it up on a tray, and when she realized it went cold before I ate it, she made sandwiches instead. I didn't eat many of those either. I got a kettle and ate Pot Noodles while the next game was loading and stacked the empties outside the door.

It was all I wanted to do. It was all I did do. And it wasn't just me. There were a bunch of us from school—we'd go multiplayer all evening and smash up zombies till gone midnight. More than once, I pulled an all-nighter, then bunked off double science to sleep in the disabled loos. I spent most of my lessons working out the strategy for that night's session, and I reckon no one was more surprised than me when I got enough Cs to stay on for A-levels.

I was seventeen when I started playing simulator games. You could take laptops into lessons, and there were loads of study periods where you could do what you liked as long as you were on-site, but if they caught you playing violent games, you'd be in the shit. I raced bikes first of all. Thought I might even get one. Then I flew for the first time, and I was hooked. Commercial planes, fight jets, World War II biplanes—I flew them all.

Everything went wrong when I got to uni. The stuff I'd found simple at school wasn't simple anymore, and it was easier to stay in my room than go to tutorials and be made to feel stupid. Mum shacked up with some bloke she'd met ballroom dancing, and they turned my room into a walk-in wardrobe for all their sequins. Gaming was the only thing worth getting up for, and I was getting better and better.

"Shame you can't make a living out of it," Dad said, bang in the middle of another argument about how much money he was sending me and how he hoped I'd have something to show for it at the end.

Uni kicked me out halfway through the second year. I got a factory job I lost the first week, and that's kind of what's happened ever since. Just me, the job center, and a shitty room in a shitty house in the shitty part of town.

Just as I'd hit rock bottom, things started looking up. I made some friends—real friends—and slowly I started to feel good about myself again. I started working out, got some confidence back. I still gamed all the time, but I ate properly too. Even went outside from time to time.

One of my mates put some work my way. They knew I was a shit-hot gamer (their words, not mine), and they needed my skills. They needed me. And—suck on this, Dad—they would pay me for it.

Gaming became my job. Testing out new releases for developers, working out how to hack the system so you could get the full range of weapons without paying for upgrades, then testing it again when they reckoned they'd made it more secure.

I got up each day with a new sense of purpose, and it wasn't just about the paycheck that meant I could buy some decent clothes, get myself a car at last. It wasn't even about being part of a team (I still preferred to work alone). It was just having a purpose, having a deadline.

By the time I stepped onto Flight 79, I was a different person. I knew where I was going. I had a seat in business class, among all those people who never questioned their right to be there. I'm not questioning it either—I finally feel like I belong.

I finally feel important.

TWENTY-TWO

10 P.M. | ADAM

There's a pale moon at the nape of Sophia's neck, where her thick plait has fallen to one side and where the needle now hovers above her skin.

Don't move, Sophia…

I can see the corner of her right eye, the lashes dark on her cheeks. Her thumb has found her mouth, which sucks in time with Becca's gentle rocking.

Don't move a muscle.

"What's in the syringe, Becca?" I'm trying to keep my voice quiet, my tone light so as not to frighten Sophia, as though we're talking about the weather, about Becca's studies, about nothing of any consequence. I'm trying, but the words bleed into one another. I hear an echo of my own voice in my head, and every few seconds, my vision blurs. A second outline of Becca and Sophia stands beside the first, as if I've taken a photograph before they've stood still.

"Insulin."

Insulin? My dad had diabetes. He wasn't good at managing it. Several times a week, he'd get hypoglycemic, sweat breaking out across his brow as he fumbled for a glucose tablet. Sophia doesn't need any more insulin than her body naturally produces; even a small dose could cause her body to shut down.

"How much?"

"Enough."

I think I detect a tremor in Becca's voice behind the quiet bravado, but her face gives nothing away. My body is locking down; I can feel a numbness creeping over me, as though I'm crawling into bed after a double shift and a nightcap. "Why?" I manage. I inch one foot forward. Grandmother's footsteps. *What's the time, Mr. Wolf?*

"The world needs to wake up and see what's happening."

My veins fill with ice. My eyes flick between Becca's cool, unwavering stare and the tip of the needle, hovering over Sophia's pure-white skin. Is Becca on drugs? By definition, you don't spend a lot of time with babysitters. Five minutes either side of the handover, and the rest of the time, they're on their own with your kid. They could be doing anything. They could be anyone.

"For every battle won, there have to be sacrifices."

There's something robotic about her voice, as though she's repeating a script. I'm reminded of a training session I attended at work, on radicalization of teenagers across the UK. The kids on the video spoke like this: spewing out words force-fed by Islamic extremists. Groomed and cultivated, then used as cannon fodder.

What do we really know about Becca? She's looked after Sophia a couple of dozen times since Katya left. Her mum always picked her up on the corner of the main road—didn't like the potholes on our farm track—so I'd get back from work, and Becca would shove her textbooks in a bag and—

I'm twenty-three actually.

She's played us right from the start. Textbooks, A-level angst, arguments with her mum about which uni course to pick… All a pantomime to make us think she was just a kid. To make us trust her.

Katya told her we might be looking for someone to take care of Sophia after school.

Neither of us checked out Becca's story. How could we? Katya didn't leave any contact details; we couldn't have asked her about Becca even if we'd wanted to.

Sophia's breathing has slowed. Her legs, which were clinging, limpet-like, to Becca's waist, now dangle limply by her side. She's falling asleep, lulled by Becca's swaying and her monotone speech.

"We have to act now to prevent a mass extinction."

Mass extinction? I fight down the fear in my chest. She's insane. She could do anything. I shuffle my feet forward another inch. "Okay…"

Another inch forward, my eyes keeping Becca focused. *Look at my eyes, not my feet. What's the time, Mr. Wolf?* My brain can't make the links I need it to, my thoughts like stepping-stones across a rising river, the space between too far to jump.

"What's that got to do with us, Becca?" Use their name, always use their name. Build up a rapport. I can do this. This is my job. I think of the jumper I talked down off the ledge, the kid crouched in his room with a knife to his wrists. *Talk to me. Tell me what you're thinking.*

I should be three steps ahead, planning our route to the door, searching out my keys, a weapon. Making a plan. But my head is thick with pain and drugs, my limbs dragging me down to the floor. I feel wet on my chin, raise my hand clumsily, and wipe away drool.

"Your wife could be fighting for the cause, but instead she's on a fucking plane!"

I struggle to catch up. Someone's tried to recruit Mina? To radicalize her? This is ridiculous. Insane.

"She's on a plane because it's her job." The words slide into one another.

"Exactly!" Becca is triumphant, as though I've given her the answer she wanted instead of looking for one myself.

"You want her to give up work, is that it?" My head spins. I wonder if Becca is part of some obscure cult, some outdated organization that believes women belong in the home. "Okay. She'll give up." *Never make promises*, that's what they say at work. Fuck that. This isn't work; this is my daughter. I'll promise the world if it keeps her safe. I will dance to Becca's tune.

Sophia stirs, her hair brushing against Becca's hand and the needle so close to her neck. "Mummy!"

"Don't touch her!" My arms reach out without my telling them.

Becca screams at me, "Stay where you are!"

"Mummy! Mummy!" Sophia twists in Becca's arms, startled and scared. She's struggling to get free, crying out in confusion as Becca clutches tighter.

"Sophia!" I shout. "Don't move!"

"Daddy!"

I take a step forward, letting go of the counter and feeling the room spin about me. Becca brandishes the syringe. They're less than six feet away—I think; they keep moving, or I'm moving, or the room's moving. All I have to do is grab the arm holding the syringe. If she drops Sophia, it doesn't matter; it's not far to the ground, and it won't hurt her, not like the insulin. How much is there? What will it do to her?

"Don't come any closer," Becca says. "I'll do it. I will. I'll do it!"

The repetition gives me hope. She's frightened. She's trying to convince herself she's got what it takes. I make myself speak slowly and calmly.

"This isn't the right way to convince people to share your beliefs, Becca."

"We're forcing people to have the conversation. That's the first step."

We.

Becca's still young—if not as young as she made out. There's someone else pulling the strings.

"Who's making you do this?"

"No one's making me. I can see it for myself. It's everyone's duty to act."

"Who's in charge?"

Becca laughs. "Typical copper! It's all about hierarchy for you lot, isn't it? The establishment. The powers that be. When will you see that it's the *establishment* that's fucking everything up?"

Sophia is crying. She's trying to get free, but Becca's grip is too strong. They're both panicking, both fighting against each other, and any minute now, that needle's going straight into Sophia...

"If you inject her with that, she'll die, and you'll go to prison for murder."

Sophia screams, and it kills me to be the cause, but I have to get through to Becca before it's too late. Fog swirls around my head, suddenly too heavy for my body. If I pass out, what will happen to Sophia? Where will Becca take her?

"If Mina does the right thing, I'll let her go."

Everything is fuzzy. Nothing makes sense. Mina won't be home for days; is Becca planning to keep Sophia like this till then? "Mina's on a plane. She can't—"

"If she does what she's told, the tracking app will show her plane changing course, and you'll be free to go."

"What...? Do you think—?" I can't formulate a sentence, can't even work out what this means. Mina can't make the plane change course—unless... Realization dawns on me.

Unless she's being threatened too.

"And if the plane doesn't change course?"

Becca makes the smallest of movements with the hand holding the syringe. At the end of the needle, a bead of clear liquid hesitates for a second before dropping onto Sophia's neck. My vision blurs, a dark tunnel between me and my daughter, nothing else around us. Nothing else matters. I have to get to Sophia, have to just snatch her, and if Becca presses the needle in, I'll need sugar I'll call an ambulance I'll call 999 I won't let Sophia down won't let her down... I tell my legs to run forward and they move but not fast enough and I see the ground coming up to meet me and a thick black fog wraps itself around me as everything goes quiet.

TWENTY-THREE

8 HOURS FROM SYDNEY | MINA

There's a collective stirring as Cesca follows me into the cabin, the way the atmosphere in the office changes when the boss walks in. I hear her saying *hello*, and *I hope you're enjoying the flight*, and *conditions are looking good—we might even get in early*, and my head is heavy with guilt. I stop to let a passenger pass, and Cesca does the same, and for a second, we stand side by side, and I see her face on the edge of my vision. Older than me but still young, with high cheekbones and cropped, dark hair with a heavy fringe that sweeps across her eyes.

As the passenger passes, I catch a whiff of sweat and anxiety and too long in one place. It's the Middle Eastern man from 6J, his hands gripping the back of each seat he passes, as though he's climbing stairs. He doesn't respond to Cesca's greeting, continuing through the curtain. My pulse quickens. Is it him? He disappears into the galley, and I want to follow him, but we're already at 4H, where Finley's watching a Pixar movie. He takes off his headset.

"Did you fix them?"

I'm momentarily confused, then I remember the tangle of wires in my pocket. They seem to belong to another time entirely: a time when I was doing my job, and we were heading for Sydney, and no one was threatening my daughter.

"I'll do it, I promise. I just—" I break off, think of all the times Sophia wants me to do something and I preface my answer the same way. *I just need to phone work… I just need to finish this. Okay, I'll play with you; I just need to do something else first.* Why didn't I just say yes?

"I hear you want to be a pilot?" Cesca crouches by his seat. Finley stares at her, confused, and beside him—finally conscious—his mother takes off her headphones. I leave before my lie is exposed, and because if I'm going to follow through with this—and I am, I am, because *Sophia*—I have to do it now. Blood roars in my ears, fusing with the noise of the plane into something unbearable, something that pushes at the insides of my skull hard enough to break through. I pull back the curtain between the cabin and the galley and almost cry out as I collide with the Middle Eastern man on his way back to his seat. He looks as scared as I am, mumbling an apology, then clawing his way back, one seat at a time.

Jamie Crawford and his wife are back in their seats; the Talbots and baby Lachlan are all asleep. I don't see the journalist Derek Trespass or Jason Poke, and although I crane my neck to see the seats at the back, I can't tell if they're empty or if their occupants are lying down. Who is missing? Who is the hijacker?

Cesca is standing up. She's still talking to the boy and his mother, and I wonder what they're saying to her, if she knows that I lied and is wondering why. In the next few minutes—the next few seconds, perhaps—she'll say she'd *better get back* and tell them to *enjoy the rest of the flight*. Maybe she'll invite the boy to visit the flight deck when we land, to sit in the captain's seat and try on her hat. He'll look forward to it, think of the people he'll show the photo to. Maybe he really will think about being a pilot, start dreaming of soaring above the clouds, of being in uniform, striding through the airport on his way to California, Mexico, Hong Kong, the way I once dreamed.

Guilt brings tears to my eyes. They spill onto my cheeks, hot and out of control, and I look for the lock on the door of the bathroom by the flight deck, wanting it to be vacant, wanting it all to be a terrible mistake. Let it be a training exercise, let it be a YouTube stunt. Let me be fired, pilloried, vilified forevermore as the woman who was ready to sacrifice hundreds of people to save her own child. Let it be anything, but please don't let it be real.

The sign reads ENGAGED.

I walk toward it. My movements feel stilted, like the graphics of a computer game, every muscle tensed as though waiting for a bullet. I am inches away from whoever is in there, and I try to imagine what they're doing, what they're thinking. Do they have a weapon? Explosives? Sweat trickles down my spine, my shirt clinging to my skin as I turn.

The door is at right angles to the flight deck. I punch in the code, keeping my head low because surely it's written all over my face, and as the *beep* of the door release sounds, I hear a click behind me. The bathroom door is unlocked.

I feel the weight of eyes on my neck, and I fight to keep a neutral expression on my face as I push open the door to the flight deck. Mike doesn't turn around; he's looking at a paper, doing the crossword. Mike, who may be a father, a brother, a husband. Who shook hands with all the crew, smiled for the cameras.

Mike, who is unlikely to survive the next few minutes.

I step to the side. Fix Sophia's face in my mind as I commit the most terrible act I have ever done. Mike turns. His smile dies before it fully forms, features reflecting first confusion and then dismay, as he looks from me to the man with no manners, the man with the face full of angles, the man playing computer games. The door closes, and for that moment, only three people in the world know that Flight 79 has been hijacked.

I have followed my instructions to the letter. My husband and daughter are safe.

Everyone on this plane is in danger.

PART TWO

TWENTY-FOUR

PASSENGER 1G

The first time I broke the law was at the Women's Peace Camp at Greenham Common, where I was sandwiched between my mother and an octogenarian with a pocketful of flapjack. I threw a stone, and it hit a policeman. Good shot, my mother said. I was nine, and my age absolved me of my act. I remember the surge of power I felt as the policeman turned around, rubbing his shoulder and searching for the culprit. He never once looked at me.

Hiding in plain sight. Beyond suspicion. That's been my aim ever since.

Believe it or not, it isn't in my nature to inflict pain or suffering, but there comes a point where you have to weigh up the consequences of action against inaction. In times of conflict, for example, it is accepted that violence will be used against enemy soldiers and that civilian casualties are a tragic but inevitable side effect of warfare. A bomber plane that fails to meet its target will soon become a target itself.

And we are fighting a war—make no mistake about that. It might not feel like a war, just as the Second World War was a different beast from the First, but it is nevertheless a war, and all the more dangerous for those who do not recognize it as one.

The Criminal Law Act entitles all of us—not just police officers—to use "such force as is reasonable in the circumstances in the prevention of crime," which begs the question: What is a crime? The dictionary would have you know it is an act or omission punishable by law, *but the law of one country is not the law of another. Gambling, for example, is not a crime in the United Kingdom, yet Islamic law forbids it. Chewing gum is illegal in*

Singapore; unmarried couples may not cohabit in the United Arab Emirates. So you see, a "crime" can be many things to many people.

Those of us who have freedom of speech, of movement, have the luxury of choosing how to respond to a crime that takes place before our eyes. Either we can walk on by, or we can call upon the powers issued by the law of the land and act. I choose to act, and I know you would make the same choice. We might not have known each other long, but I can already tell that you wouldn't be able to stand idly by—it isn't in your nature.

As for what is "reasonable" force, that surely depends on the crime. Taking a life is unreasonable in many circumstances—most circumstances, we might say—but what if that stolen life was the life of a murderer? A rapist? What if, by taking that life, you could stop further murders, further rapes?

You see—right and wrong aren't so clear-cut, are they?

Let me tell you something about the war we are waging. It is the greatest war of all time, the biggest, the most dangerous. The crimes are many and their effects far reaching, so that every life already born and still to be born will be at risk.

Doesn't that sound like a crime worth stopping?

What is a death compared against offenses of that magnitude?

Nothing. It is nothing.

TWENTY-FIVE

MIDNIGHT | ADAM

My eyelids resist as I peel them open. I go to rub the grit from them, but my arms are numb and won't comply. My head pounds, and my mouth is dry, and there's a revolting taste in my throat, as though last night was ten pints and a kebab instead of… I shake my head, trying to clear it. What *did* happen last night?

Is it morning even? Darkness drapes around me, thick as a blanket, so that I'm not sure if my eyes are open or closed. There's music playing—a top ten hit from some manufactured band. I'm not in bed—it's cold and hard beneath me. Where am I?

Slowly, memories filter through the fog in my brain. The debt collector. Becca. Sophia.

"Sophia!" It comes out in a whisper, scratched and inaudible. Water. I need water. Am I still in the kitchen? I was there when I fell, wasn't I? My body aches all over, as if everything's broken, everything's bruised.

A sudden image assaults me: the syringe full of insulin, caressing my daughter's skin. Did Becca inject her? Twenty-three, she said, not seventeen, so not an A-level student. Not a student at all perhaps. Who the hell is she?

I picture Sophia screaming as the needle bit, her body convulsing in shock as the insulin seeped into her system.

"Sophia!" The sound bounces back at me.

Where am I? I'm lying awkwardly on my side, the floor so cold, it feels damp, and I struggle into a seated position, blinking in the darkness. Something tugs at my wrists, preventing me from standing.

I'm tied up.

No, not tied—handcuffed. My arms are behind me, pinning me to a wall. I move my fingers over the metal of the cuff's rotating arms, feel the sharpness of the ratchet holding them in place, tight enough that my wrists are sore and my hands have gone numb. Rigid plastic separates my hands. These are police cuffs, or something close to them.

There's an object between me and the wall, something cold and hard that digs into my lower back. A metal bar, or a narrow pipe, with enough space behind for the cuffs to pass. My fingers follow the metal to the ground and then back up, ten inches or so to where it disappears into the wall. I pull at it, but it doesn't give. The music stops, and an advert plays. It's the radio—some commercial station with energetic presenters and the same forty tracks on a loop.

There are stone slabs on the floor, pieces of dirt or sand rough on my fingertips. I kick one leg out into the blackness in front of me, twisting my body and sweeping my leg to the side until it hits the wall I'm cuffed to, then do the same with the other leg, trying to get my bearings. The room is narrow, with a low ceiling that drips moisture onto my head.

I know where I am.

I'm in the cellar beneath our house.

"Sophia!" The last syllable disappears into a sob. I yank at my arms, the cuffs banging against the metal, again and again and—

I hear her.

I curse the cheery presenters, who are discussing today's phone-in topic—*what's the worst Christmas gift you've ever received?*—and screw my eyes shut, focusing on the one sense I need. "Sophia?"

Or maybe it's something you've given! It's only a week till Christmas, and—don't judge me on this, Michelle—I still haven't bought the wife's present.

Trust me on this one, Ramesh. Don't get her the saucepan set.

She likes cooking, though!

See what I'm up against, insomniacs? Call in with your stories and suggestions, and stay tuned for festive tunes. See what I did there, Ramesh?

Underneath the vacuous commentary of Michelle and Ramesh, of Rise FM, I can hear breathing.

"Sophia, is that you? Sweetheart, are you there?"

"Daddy?"

Relief rushes through me. "I'm here, baby. Are you hurt?"

She doesn't answer. I hear a scratching noise—shoes on stone—and I blink the remaining grit from my eyes, slowly letting them adjust. Looking *through* the darkness, not *at* it. Since joining CID, I've spent more shifts behind a desk than on the streets, but I did my time in uniform. I've felt my way through empty warehouses in the dead of night and chased intruders across pitch-black playing fields. The beam of a torch gives a false sense of security, creating shadows in corners and making what isn't lit up darker still. *Trust your eyes*, I think.

Our cellar is around ten feet wide and twenty feet long, with steep stone steps at one end that lead down from the kitchen. When we bought the house, we had grand plans to convert it into a room, knocking out the old coal chute and digging down from the front garden to add a high-level window. The quote was exorbitant, and we abandoned the idea. The cellar is too damp to store anything, and as the temperature falls, the mice come in search of warmth and food. Instinctively, my fingers curl inward.

The worst present I ever received, Michelle, was a hand-knitted sock from my mother-in-law.

Just one, Ramesh?

She'd run out of wool.

"Daddy." A whimper in the darkness.

The walls of the cellar are brick, buried within the foundations of the house. My eyes travel along each side, searching out a difference in the gloom, looking for black against the gray.

There!

She's on the stairs: a child-shaped shadow crouched on the top step, where the faintest of light bleeds from the kitchen beneath the door. It flickers, like a bulb close to exhaustion. Slowly, my eyes adjust.

"Are you okay, sweetheart?"

Sophia's legs are drawn up to her chest, her arms wrapped tightly around them and her head buried in her knees. I pull uselessly at the metal bar behind me. Whatever Becca gave me is wearing off, the brain fog slowly clearing. There's a sharp pain around my ribs, and every time I yank my wrists forward, it takes my breath away. The only way Becca could have gotten me into the cellar is by dragging me to the steps and letting me fall, and every inch of my body feels as though that's exactly what she did.

"I don't like it here, Daddy."

"Me neither. Are you hurt?"

"My tummy feels funny."

"Did she give you anything, Sophia? Anything to eat?" I yank hard at the cuffs, angry with Becca, with myself, with the bloody pipe that won't. Give. An. Inch. "Did she? It's important!" Sophia buries her head again, and I bite my tongue, soften my tone. "Sweetheart, did Becca give you any medicine?"

She makes a movement, but I'm not sure if she's nodding her head or shaking it.

"Is that no?"

"Yes."

"No medicine?"

"No medicine."

I breathe out. "But your tummy aches?"

"It feels funny. Like when you spin me around, or when the bath monster comes, or when I play flying with Mummy." Her voice is thin and scared.

"Ah. Mine feels a bit like that, to be honest." The radio phone-in segues into the weather report, which warns of more snow overnight and a drop in temperature to minus three. Damp from the stone floor seeps into my bones. I'm wearing suit trousers and a collared shirt; Sophia's in her pajamas and dressing gown. At least she has slippers on—my socked feet are numb with cold.

I listen for sounds in the house beyond the radio, but there's nothing. Has Becca gone, or is she still in the house?

"Sweetheart, is the door locked?"

"Yes."

"Could you try again? Really rattle it, so I can see?" Slowly, Sophia gets to her feet, and the slice of light from beneath the door widens. She twists the doorknob, then rattles it hard. The door doesn't give.

"It's stuck." She rattles the handle again.

"Bang on it. Make a fist and bang as hard as you can."

She hits the door, over and over, so loud down here in the cellar that by rights, the whole town should hear it. Becca said that if Mina's plane didn't change course, she'd harm Sophia, but Sophia's here safe with me—if you can call being locked in a cellar "safe." Does that mean Mina followed instructions? Has Flight 79 been hijacked? Fear grips me, colder than the stone beneath me.

Has the plane crashed?

"Sophia, I want you to scream, okay? As loud as you can. I'm going to shout too, so cover your ears and scream as loud as you can. Ready? One, two, *three!*"

The noise is deafening. It ricochets around the cellar, Sophia's high-pitched scream and my furious *Becca!* I don't want to shout *help!*—don't want to make Sophia any more scared than she already is.

"Okay, now shhh—listen."

But all we can hear is "Rockin' Around the Christmas Tree." The flickering light is the digital radio, I realize, pushed close to the other side of the door; the faint fluorescent one is from the kitchen ceiling behind it. I'm trying to fathom why Becca chose to give us the questionable comfort of a radio, when I hear the words…*inaugural flight to Sydney.*

Concern was first raised when air traffic control operatives were unable to contact the pilots, despite communication channels appearing to be in place. Pilots are required to inform ground control when entering and leaving foreign airspace…

"I can scream even bigger than that." Sophia opens her mouth.

"Let me just listen to this."

Shortly after eleven p.m. in the UK, a tweet was sent from an account belonging to the Climate Action Group, alleging that members of their group had hijacked Flight 79 in a protest against climate change.

Climate change. *Mass extinction.* That's what Becca was talking about. I struggle to make sense of it. Planes are hijacked by terrorists. Terrorists are religious extremists, not environmentalists.

And yet…

"*The aviation industry presents the single biggest threat to the environment,*" the tweet reads, "*and world leaders must take action now.*"

"Come and sit on my lap, Soph." That's what Becca meant about Mina choosing not to fight the cause. Not radicalization—at least not from religious fanatics—but pressure to ground planes, stop people flying, bankrupt airlines.

"Flight 79 is Mummy's plane." Her voice wobbles.

Should I lie to her? Tell her it isn't Mina's, it's got nothing to do with Becca, with the fact that we're locked in the cellar? But Sophia's not your average five-year-old—she reads and writes far above her age, she takes everything in, and she knows exactly where Mina is. And besides, I've told enough lies.

Climate Action Group has released a statement denying their involvement. They claim their Twitter account was hacked, and they are currently reviewing their security measures. More on this story as we have it.

As a music track fades up, I hear a sound in the kitchen. A chair, scraping across the floor, as though someone has stood up quickly.

"Becca!"

"Mummy's plane is Flight 79."

"I know, sweetheart. *Becca!*" I yell louder, knowing I'm scaring Sophia but not knowing what else to do. Mina's plane's been hijacked. This should be over.

"Mummy's plane is a Boeing 777. It has three hundred and fifty-three passengers."

"That's right. *Becca!*"

Another noise, closer this time, and I know—I just know—that Becca is right there, on the other side of the door, her ear pressed close to the wood. I force myself to speak more calmly.

"Becca, I know you're there. You've got what you wanted. Whatever Mina was supposed to do, she's done it. The plane's been taken over. You can let us go now."

There's a muffled sound, something halfway between a sniff and a cough, then Becca answers. The pitch is high and harsh, faster than the measured, calculating tone she used when she drugged me.

"It hasn't changed course. I'm supposed to let you go when it changes course."

"It's been hijacked! They said on the radio… Becca, you have to let us go."

"Shut up!"

"You've done what they told you to do. Now—"

"I said shut up!"

"Daddy!" Sophia cries from the steps, and I bite back the expletives Becca deserves, dropping my voice, making it as warm and safe as I can.

"Come and sit with me, sweetheart."

"Why is Mummy's plane on the radio?"

"It'll be warmer on my lap."

Sophia shrinks back. "The mouses will eat me."

Once we decided not to convert the basement into a usable room, we forbade Sophia from going into the cellar. The steps were steep, and there was no light—it was a disaster waiting to happen. *Mr. Mouse will nibble your toes if you do*, I would tell her, nipping my fingers at her feet as she squealed with laughter.

"There aren't any mice," I say now, hoping I'm right. Becca's turned up the radio, the music pumping manufactured happiness through the door. There's no sound from Becca. Is she still there, listening?

Sophia steps gingerly down into the cellar. She curls herself into my lap, reassuringly heavy, and I ache to put my arms around her. I think of the hundreds of times I've longed for her to come to me and how often she's gone to Mina instead. She leans her head against my chest, her mouth opening in an involuntary yawn, and I press a kiss to the top of her head.

"This," I say, in a manner far more measured than I feel, "is a tricky situation, but Daddy's going to sort it, okay? Daddy's going to get us out of here."

I just need to work out how.

TWENTY-SIX

PASSENGER 1G

There are people—not you, I'm quite sure—who cross the road when they see a homeless man instead of stopping to make sure he's okay. Who don't drop a coin in his pot or buy him a sandwich. I don't understand those people, but I imagine they're the same ones who switch channels when an unpalatable advert airs—starving children, beaten dogs, hand-dug wells full of dirty water—because they can't bear it.

If we can't bear to see it, imagine what it must be like to live it.

If we can't bear it, we should do something about it, don't you think? Donate money, sign petitions, join marches.

When those people read the newspaper, do they see the news articles about overcrowded prisons, about the devastation caused by a high-speed rail network? Do they flick past them because they don't notice or because they don't care? It's hard to know which is worse: apathy or ignorance.

Matthew 9:36 says, When he saw the crowds, he had compassion for them, because they were harassed and helpless, like sheep without a shepherd.

It is our job to be the shepherds. It is our job to herd these sheep—be they apathetic or ignorant—into making the right choices. Into saving the world. We have to educate people, because without education, we are all lost.

Back in 2009, I had an epiphany. I switched on the news to see a fire, raging through a Californian forest.

"The West Coast has experienced its warmest temperatures on record," *said the newsreader. "We spoke earlier to Professor Rachel Cohen at the*

University of California, whose recent paper examines the link between forest fires and climate change."

I listened to Cohen while the forest fire raged in a small box above her head, before we returned to the newsreader for an update on the Copenhagen Summit. I watched the United Nations' environment minister declaring climate change to be one of the greatest challenges of the present day, and I felt a surge of adrenaline.

I'd marched in numerous demonstrations in support of marginalized people, but it was in animal rights and environmental campaigns that I had invested most of my time and support. An animal has no voice; a forest is silent. They can't fight for themselves, and so we must fight for them. I had fought for years, but my strategy had been flawed. By dividing my time between so many small protests, I was diluting my energy.

What is the point in fighting to save one greenfield site when acres of rain forest are being destroyed every day? What use saving a children's center from closure when those very children won't have a planet to live on? I'd been bailing out water when all the time there'd been a hole in the bottom of the boat.

Climate change has caused deadly heat waves and raging wildfires. Hurricanes, drought, and flooding. Polluted oceans, melting ice caps. The extinction of a third of all known species of animals.

Climate change is the biggest emergency the world faces and the only one that matters.

Once you know that, you can't cross the road, can you?

TWENTY-SEVEN

7 HOURS FROM SYDNEY | MINA

I waited for the plane to dive, for the bottles to rattle in the racks in the galley as we lurched forward. I braced myself for the screams from the passengers as we plummeted toward the ground.

Nothing happened.

And still nothing is happening.

Through the gap in the curtains, I can see a handful of passengers. Reading, sleeping, watching TV. After she left Finley, Cesca took the opportunity to walk through the plane, chatting quietly to those passengers still awake. No one's looking at me. No one saw what I did.

I can't make myself go back into the cabin. I'm rooted to the spot, guilt hammering in my chest, my brain imprinted with the image of Mike's face when he realized what was happening. He's a big guy, fit-looking. He's not going to go down without a fight. A sob erupts from inside me, raw revulsion at what I've done, at what must be happening, right now, in the flight deck.

Why isn't the plane going down? I need it to be over. I cannot take this any longer.

I picture them breaking the news to Sophia, and tears spill across my cheeks. She's five years old. Will she even remember me? I think of the note I left on her pillow, never thinking it would be the last one I'd leave, the final physical piece connecting us both. I always knew the notes were more important to me than to her, but I wonder now if she'll keep that hastily drawn heart. If this note, at least, will be special.

Tears stream faster. I cry for the days she will come home from school needing me, for the advice she will want and the cuddles she's finally begun to let me have. I cry for her first day at secondary school, for her wedding day, for when she has a baby of her own.

But she will be alive, I remind myself fiercely. *And she'll have her daddy.* I choke back a sob as I think of Adam—not the man of the last twelve months, who lied and cheated his way out of our marriage, but the man I fell in love with.

The man I still love.

We could still do it, he said—*spend the week before Christmas together, buy presents, drink mulled wine. Spend some time together.* And I'd said no. I'd arranged it so that I'd be away—so that I'd be on this damned flight—not because I didn't want to be with him but because I did. Because I still love him, and it would have undone me.

Cesca comes into the galley, half turned as she answers a passenger. *Absolutely—on the homestretch now!* I try to find enough moisture in my mouth to speak even as I grapple for the words I will use. How can I ever explain what I've done? Every second that's passed since I opened that letter—since I found Sophia's photo even—I've been thinking about Sophia, about what I was being asked to do. But now that I've done it, what next? What happens to us now?

"Sweet kid. Wants to know if you've untangled his—" She takes one look at me, then pulls the curtain closed. "What's wrong?"

I can't speak. Can't move. I stand with my back to the flight-deck door, hands pressed against the walls either side as though I'm blocking the way, when really, I'm anchoring myself because I don't feel real. Nothing about this feels real.

Cesca must see something in my expression. Her face hardens, and she moves me forcibly to one side, punching in the code to request access to the flight deck. Will the hijacker even bother to look up at the cameras? Will he see the panic on Cesca's face as the door fails to open?

Behind me, I'm aware of someone—Erik, I think—coming into the galley.

"For fuck's sake, Mike." Cesca taps in the code again, waiting for the click that means he's released the door lock.

"What has happened?" I hear Erik's clipped tones, followed by Carmel's softer ones.

"Is something wrong?"

The four of us cluster around the flight-deck door, and I wonder what we'll do if a passenger wants to use the bathroom or comes looking for a drink. It will be obvious to them that something is terribly wrong.

"Mike's not letting me in." Cesca swears under her breath, her fingers slipping on the keys. Her breathing is rapid and noisy, panic breaking through the surface. A slim wedding ring encircles her fourth finger. "Is he ill, or...Mike!" Her voice is urgent but quiet—he wouldn't hear even a shout—and I try to speak but my mouth is so dry, nothing comes out. Cesca is trying the code again and again, and Erik is looking at me, and he knows. He knows...

"He's got kids," Cesca says. "Why would he..."

"Use the emergency code," Erik says.

"No!" It's out before I can stop it. The emergency code works in the opposite way to the standard request code. Instead of the pilot pressing a button to allow access, they have to press one to stop it. But to do that, they have to know it exists. They have to know which button to press.

Everyone stares at me.

"Don't," I say quietly.

They think it's just Mike in there. That he's ill or that he's lost his mind. They don't know we've been hijacked. They don't realize they could all get hurt too.

"It was her." Erik points an accusatory finger at me.

"I—"

"She did something."

Everything spins, as though I might pass out. I have to explain. "My—my daughter. I—"

"She has been hiding something since we took off."

Where do I even begin? I taste salt on my lips and realize I'm crying again. Perhaps I never stopped. I hear everyone's voices as though we're on a long-distance call: the briefest of delays between receiving the sound and understanding it.

"She was in the bathroom for a long time. Too long," Erik says.

Sophia, I tell myself. *I did it for Sophia.*

"She got a note. From a passenger." Carmel flushes slightly, avoiding my eyes as she tells Cesca. All three of them surround me, and I wish it would happen now, I wish the plane would dive and the inevitable would happen and it would all be over.

Will the investigation uncover how they accessed the flight deck? Will people know the impossible position in which I found myself? I think of the headlines, the photos they'll dredge from somewhere to show the face of the woman who betrayed everyone. Will Adam hide them from Sophia? Will he tell her that I did it for her, to keep her alive, keep her safe? Will she understand that I loved her so much, I would have done anything to protect her? That I died to save her?

"Mina!" Cesca shakes me hard by the shoulder. "If you're withholding information, I order you to tell me this instant."

I open my mouth, but as I do so, the intercom crackles. Everyone freezes.

Ladies and gentlemen, this flight is under new management. My name is Amazon, and I am now your pilot. Only full cooperation will ensure your safety.

The stunned silence is broken by a terrified scream ringing out from somewhere near the back of the plane. It triggers a huge swell of noise, like a dam bursting, as passengers scramble across seats and down the aisles.

"Tell them to sit down," Cesca says, and Carmel rushes to comply, but half the passengers are crowding around the galley already, snatching open the curtains and demanding to know what's going on. *Is this some kind of joke? Are we being hijacked? Is this a terrorist attack?* At the end of the seven business-class rows, framed in the doorway to the bar, Hassan stands with a cloth hanging from one hand, the glass he was drying in the other. Behind him, on the opposite side of the bar, the crew in economy is fighting to keep control. All around, there are people crying and clutching one another, hysteria rising like a tidal force.

Erik and Carmel take an aisle each, and I hear the undercurrent of fear in their voices as they tell people to *please take your seats* and *try not to panic*. The passengers already in their seats are gripping their armrests. Some have assumed the brace position. Several are praying.

I find my voice. "The hijacker is a man who was sitting in seat 7G."

Cesca drags me out of view, pushing me against the lockers. Her fingers handcuff my arms either side of me, the metal doors hard against my wrist bones. "How do you know that?"

I take a breath. Release it in a sob. "Because I let him into the flight deck."

"You're working with him?"

"No!"

"I don't believe you."

"He threatened my daughter. He knew things about her. He knew her school. He had a photograph of her—taken this morning. He had something from her bag. He said if I didn't do it, she'd be killed. What else could I do?" My voice rises, ending with a plea that would be heard in the cabin were it not for the noise already being made there.

"You could have called it in!" Specks of wetness hit my face as Cesca screams at me. "You've put everyone's lives in danger!"

"He said if we cooperate—"

"And you believe him?" Cesca gives a harsh laugh. "I can't decide if you're dangerous or just stupid, Mina."

"My daughter's name is Sophia." I drop my voice.

"I don't c—"

"She's five years old. Just started school. She's really bright, and she remembers everything. She's incredible." I'm speaking so fast, there's no space between words, and I'm not seeing Cesca; I'm seeing Sophia's crazy curly hair and her big, brown eyes. I'm feeling her soft hand in mine, the weight of her embrace in my arms. "She was born to a woman who didn't care whether she lived or died, and she was given to us because we *did* care." Tears choke my words, but I carry on regardless, and I feel Cesca's grip on my wrists slacken a little. "And I swore I'd keep her safe, no matter what."

Cesca lets my hands fall, but she doesn't move. My wrists throb.

"Do you have children?"

There's a long pause, then Cesca nods. "Three."

"Wouldn't you have done the same?"

She doesn't answer. She takes a step back, shaking herself into action. "We need to calm everyone down. Panic isn't going to help anyone. We'll go through the cabin, speaking to everyone individually, okay?"

I nod.

"We tell them we'll be doing everything we can to ensure their safety; that yes, the flight deck has been breached, but that we will be attempting to communicate with the hijacker in order to regain control of the plane. Understood?"

"Yes."

"And, Mina?" Cesca lifts her chin, her eyes drilling into me. "Stay where I can see you."

Beds have been changed back into seats, headsets dangling from abandoned films. Blankets and pillows litter the floor as passengers cluster in small groups, panic written on their faces. Finley has crawled onto his mother's lap, his face buried in her neck.

At the front of the cabin, Leah Talbot holds baby Lachlan, silent sobs darkening the comforter she's wrapped around him. I crouch by their seats, scrabbling for words.

"It'll be okay," I hear myself saying, and I despise myself for the lie.

Leah looks at me, her mouth twisting as she tries to talk. "Ten years, I've been trying for a baby." She rocks back and forward, bent over her baby.

Paul reaches for her. "Leah, don't."

"We can't—we weren't able to…" She's crying, her words punctuated by painful gulps. "Paul's sister carried Lachlan for us. We've been staying with them. Since the birth."

"Leah…" Her husband is close to tears too, but she keeps talking.

"When we checked in for this flight, all three of us, I thought I was going to burst with happiness. We were finally a family. I finally got to bring a baby home."

"It'll be okay," I say again, trying to make it sound true. "We're doing everything we can to get the plane back under control."

"We're going to die, aren't we?" Leah says. She collapses against Paul, letting him rub her back and try for soothing words that are no match for the horror of the situation in which they find themselves, and as I walk away, something changes inside me.

We cannot let this happen.

Every single person on this plane has a reason to be here: someone they're going to see, someone who will cry for them if our plane never arrives. Every passenger has a story. A life to live. I did the only thing I could do, to keep my daughter safe, but now we have to fight.

I wipe my face and make myself mentally step away from what I've done. What matters now is how I deal with it. What matters is getting home to Sophia. Getting everyone else home. The man from seat 7G didn't crash the plane the second I let him into the flight deck, which means they must be planning to take us somewhere else before—

I don't let the thought finish. If they're taking us somewhere else, we have time on our side.

Alice Davanti is writing. She looks up as I approach but returns to her notebook before I've finished, her pen moving frantically across the page.

"Are you…working?" It seems extraordinary, but it is an extraordinary situation.

"A letter," she says curtly. "To my mother."

I catch a glimpse of the first line—*I'm so sorry*—before I leave her to speak to the next passenger and the next. They are, variously, frightened, confused, and angry. Some are all three. Derek Trespass, the balding journalist, is in the aisle, speaking with the eloping couple, who have reached a level of insobriety that is cushioning them from reality.

"Jusht open the door and drag 'im out!" Doug is saying. "I'll do it myself!"

"Don't hurt yourself, baby." His fiancée grabs his arm. Mascara streaks her cheeks.

"It's bloody tempting," Trespass says. "At least we'd be doing *something*."

"I understand your concerns, but we really do need everyone to stay calm. Please return to your seats—"

"Stay calm?" Doug says. "We're being hijacked for Godshshake!"

Only a handful of passengers are sitting down, containing their fear, and craning their necks toward the door to the flight deck. What's happening in there? Is Mike dead? I think of what Cesca said—*he's got kids*—and feel sick to the stomach.

An older woman at the front of the plane stands up and claps her hands, the way a primary school teacher does. "Excuse me!" Her voice is shrill, but there's an authority about it, and slowly everyone turns to look at her. "Panicking is unnecessary and unhelpful." It's the woman with the long, salt-and-pepper hair, who decanted her belongings into pockets rather than put her bag in a locker.

There's a murmur of discontent from somewhere, but for the most part, the cabin is quiet. People need a voice of reason in a crisis, and they are often more ready to trust one of their own than the people in charge. This woman could be helpful. I try to retrieve her name from my memory, but there's nothing there.

"No one will get hurt, as long as you cooperate."

I start to make a plan. There will be other passengers like this woman—authoritative, confident. They can help us keep everyone calm, while we—

My brain catches up with what I've just heard.

You. Not *we.*

"The plane is now under our control." The woman is in her sixties. She looks like a teacher, a social worker, a nurse, not a terrorist. She holds up a hand as a man two rows back makes a move toward her. "We have weapons, and we will not hesitate to use them."

Slowly, the man sinks into an empty seat.

"My name is Missouri," she says. "But I am not alone." She looks around the cabin, and one by one, we do the same. My gaze falls on each passenger in turn. Jason Poke, the Talbots, Finley and his mother. Lady Barrow. The nervous flyer. The petite blond who cried as we took off.

"My friends and allies sit among you," Missouri says. A small smile plays across her lips. "Try anything, and we will know."

My pulse thrums. I had thought I was doing the bidding of one hijacker—of the man with the sharp-angled face now in charge of our plane. But there are more. We don't know how many. We don't know where they're sitting.

We can't trust anyone.

TWENTY-EIGHT

PASSENGER 1G

I prefer working alone, as a rule. It presents less risk (careless talk and all that), and it avoids those circular discussions involving lots of talk but little action.

Some jobs, however, are too big for one person.

Over the years, I had found myself leading a splinter organization of the climate action group I had joined following my epiphany. It had the thrust and energy of a political movement but without the hierarchy or restrictive constitution, and although we were small, we were passionate about saving the planet. I was careful about who joined us: I didn't want mavericks, wild cards, lone wolves. I wanted team players. I wanted followers, not leaders.

Slowly, I was building my flock.

Environmentalists are unfairly stereotyped by the media. They depict us with dreadlocks and beards, bare feet and filthy hands. They have us on benefits, living in woods, hugging trees. They make fun of us, and by doing so, they subtly influence society to make fun of the issues too. If environmentalists are a joke, then environmentalism must be one too.

In reality, we come from all walks of life.

One of my early recruits was a housewife. I was administering a Facebook group, then called Household Hacks. The content had long since been skewed toward avoiding single-use plastic, and I was beginning to introduce more animal images, seeing how much they resonated with the group. Soon, I would change the name of the group to Climate Action and merge it with the main group. In this way, I had already built a community of more than a hundred thousand people from all over the world.

On our own, we are a small voice; together, we can roar.

A woman had posted a crying emoji on a picture of a starving polar bear.

Eight days into my plastic-free month, *she typed.* Struggling tbh, but this has reminded me why I'm doing it!

A mini thread sprang up beneath her post.

Well done you—keep at it!

Thank you 😊 My husband hates the wax wraps on his sandwiches. Any tips for alternatives?

Foil?

Of course! Duh, I'm such an idiot!

She mentioned her husband a lot. He liked things a certain way, it seemed. Including her.

Tried the solid shampoo this morning. Apparently I'm scaring the horses LOL!!!

Individually, her posts barely stood out—the group had three thousand engaged members, and topics moved swiftly down the page—but when you read them carefully, as I did, they built up a picture.

Anyone know how to get grease out of a tie? Please????

Is it okay to replace butter with low-cal spray?

Her profile picture showed a pretty blond with a tiny waist. Clicking back through the years, she appeared to have shrunk, dwarfed by the man by her side in almost every photo, his proprietorial hand on her shoulder.

I messaged her.

—Hi! Thanks for being a top contributor on Household Hacks! I just wanted you to know I really appreciate your posts and comments.

Her reply was instant.

—Wow, thanks! It's such a friendly group. I don't know what I'd do without it!

—Did you get the grease out of the tie?

—No. *This was followed by a sad emoji, a single tear running down its cheek.*

—Ah, well, *I messaged.* Plenty more ties in the sea!

—Tell that to my husband...

We chatted most days. I had a sense already of who this woman was and what her marriage was like, but even I was taken aback when, after a few days without hearing from her, she messaged to say she'd been in the hospital after a nasty fracture to her left forearm.

—It wasn't his fault, *she said.* He's been really stressed at work.

My fingers, poised on the keyboard for what I'd expected to be another chatty session that veered only slightly into therapy on her part, curled into fists. That poor woman. That bastard man.

—Has he done it before?

The screen blinked at me. I pictured her hesitating. Typing then deleting, typing then deleting.

—Most days. Never this bad before.

And so, as if I'd turned on a tap, out it all flowed. All his excuses, all his mistakes. I looked between her lines for the truth and was horrified by what I found. He had successfully isolated her from her friends. He controlled their finances, what they did, where they went. She was completely trapped.

—I run a climate action group, *I told her.* There are thousands of us all over the world, but just a handful who organize things behind the scenes. You should join us.

—I wouldn't be any help. I couldn't pour water from a boot even if the instructions were on the heel, my husband always says!

—You're always coming up with solutions in the Hacks group. You'd be a really valuable addition to the team.

—My husband wouldn't like it.

—Don't tell him. It's all online. I'll give you a pseudonym. It's a great group. I know the others are going to love you.

That was the clincher. What she needed, more than anything else in the world, and it was so simple. She just needed someone to love her.

—Okay then! Thank you so much xxx

Later, she told me she thanked her lucky stars *that I* happened to message her *right when she needed someone to talk to, but there was no luck involved. No fate, no fortune. We are conductors of our own orchestras and can choose who plays in them.*

I did feel responsible for Sandra, though. I was the only person she'd told about her husband's abuse—how could I not help her? She was deeply insecure, but beneath the lack of confidence, I saw a thoughtful, compassionate woman who cared about the environment. I saw a woman at rock bottom. A woman whose crippling self-doubt made her grateful for every crumb of praise. Someone so used to having her own thoughts replaced with someone else's that she could be sculpted into exactly what I needed.

I saw an opportunity.

To the shepherd, his sheep.

TWENTY-NINE

6 HOURS FROM SYDNEY | MINA

The woman who calls herself Missouri is wearing a hand-knitted jumper in chunky, green wool.

The fear pulsing through my body begins to abate—this is not the terrorist I expected. This is someone's grandmother. We are a long way from safe, but if the others are like her…

It's clear that I'm not the only one to have this thought, because those passengers who are standing begin to move toward her as if by some prearranged signal. My mind begins to race, thinking ahead to when we have her on the floor. There are plastic restraint cuffs in the crew lockers, and however many of them there are, there are more of us. All we have to do is—

But then Missouri lifts up her green sweater, and everything changes.

The swell of passengers shrinks back. Beneath the jumper are four plastic bags taped to a wide belt strapped around her chest. The bags are black, the contents pliable enough that the corners of each bend slightly, and two thin wires snake from each one and disappear up beneath her jumper.

"Sit down." Missouri moves to stand at the front of the cabin, by the entrance to the galley. Slowly, every passenger returns to their seats. The terrified silence is broken only by Lachlan crying and by the anxious voices of the passengers at the back of the plane, oblivious to this latest development. I make out the voice of a flight attendant from economy, assuring someone that *everything is under control*, and sweat trickles down the small of my back. Everything is far from under control.

There's a bomb on the plane.

Everyone complains about the security queues. You hear them all moaning as they take off their shoes, see them legging it to their gate because they haven't left enough time for checks. *Do I look like a terrorist?* they say, cross when they're pulled to one side for a search. But terrorists come in all shapes and sizes, and this one wears a green hand-knitted jumper.

"She's bluffing," Cesca whispers. We're in the aisle on the same side as Missouri, a few rows back from where she's standing. I want her to pull her jumper back down, as though not seeing the explosives will make any difference to the likelihood of her detonating them.

"Maybe. Do you want to risk it?" It's a rhetorical question. Neither of us is going to risk it. Airport security systems are rigorous, but no system is infallible. A bottle of hair bleach will be confiscated, but a travel-sized shower gel bottle filled with hydrogen peroxide can slip through the net. You can't bring a knife, but you can bring knitting needles, sewing scissors, metal nail files. There are weapons enough if you want to find a way.

Carmel and Erik are on the opposite side of the cabin, Carmel twisting a ring on her finger around and around. The petite woman from seat 5J—the blond I saw flirting in the bar—is still standing, and I gesture to Erik to tell her to sit. As he approaches, the woman walks instead toward the galley, adopting a mirror image of Missouri's position on the opposite side of the cabin. She looks at Missouri and smiles, then gives a curt nod toward the rest of us. "Zambezi," she says. It takes a moment for me to realize she is introducing herself.

She's dainty and doll-like, her hands slotting together in front of her like a bride missing her bouquet, and I scan the outline of her body for signs of explosives. She's wearing a stretchy dress that falls from sharp clavicles to skim a concave stomach. Beneath it, black leggings bag around her knees.

Zambezi. Missouri. They make an unlikely pair. They make unlikely terrorists.

Missouri walks backward into the galley, never taking her eyes off the cabin. The wires from her vest must run into her sleeve, because in her left hand is a small piece of black plastic into which the wires are secured. She picks up the intercom with her right hand and speaks to the entire plane.

"I am wearing enough explosives to end the lives of everyone on this aircraft."

The only sound is a gentle sobbing, so insistent, it seems to be coming from the very bones of the plane.

"You are all frightened of dying, and yet you waste water desperately needed for crops. You warm the oceans, depleting resources of fish. You drive cars when you can walk, you eat meat when you could grow vegetables, you cut down trees to build houses to contain an out-of-control population. You are killing the planet, and the planet is as afraid as you are right now."

This? This is what they have hijacked our plane for? What they've threatened my family for? The *planet is afraid*? Anger explodes inside me, and it's all I can do to keep it there. I had imagined a religious zealot, a fanatic. Not this. This is what insanity looks like. It looks like a gray-haired woman in a green jumper with lines around her eyes and age spots on her hands. I think of the news coverage I've seen of environmental protests and how quickly I changed the channel, dismissing them entirely. A bit batty, perhaps, but not actually mad. Not *dangerous*.

"Want and need are very different," Missouri says. Her eyes are black beads, her face animated. "None of you *needed* to take this flight. There are beautiful places in your own country and in countries you can reach by train or by boat. You can work with companies across the world by email, by phone, by video. You do not *need* to destroy the planet. It is selfish, it is costly, and it has to stop."

I think of Leah and Paul Talbot, taking baby Lachlan home, and the woman hoping to reach Sydney in time to say farewell to a dying friend. I think of Pat Barrow, escaping her grief. I think of the twenty crew members with mortgages to pay and children to feed. Need is relative.

"How come you're on a plane now, then?"

An audible gasp passes through the cabin as everyone turns to find the source of the question.

"Doug, don't!" Ginny grabs at her fiancé, who is gesticulating like a drunk in a Saturday night comedy club.

"The inventor of the light bulb worked by candlelight," Missouri says, seemingly more amused than irritated by the heckling. "The creator of the motor car traveled by horse and cart. Those of us working toward a better future must use the tools at our disposal in order to discover new ones."

"Why haven't we crashed yet? That's what I want to know." A hysterical voice comes from a seat on the other side of the cabin, each word higher pitched than the one before. "If we're going to die, let's get it over with. I can't bear this—I can't bear it!"

"Someone shut her up," Derek Trespass says. "You heard her—if we cooperate, we won't get hurt."

"She's got a bomb!"

The word sends another flurry of fear around the cabin. As I glance at the doll-like Zambezi, I see a smile play at the corners of her lips. She's enjoying this.

Missouri holds up a hand, and we fall silent. "We have prepared a statement that is scheduled to be released on social media in the next few minutes. Among other things, we ask the government to bring forward their target for zero carbon emissions to 2030 and to issue fines to airlines that cannot demonstrate a commitment toward renewable energy."

The passenger in 2D—the man with the long legs, who told me to cheer up—is leaning forward, his forearms resting on his knees. Instead of the terrified expression on the other passengers' faces, 2D is nodding along with Missouri's speech. I nudge Cesca and jerk my head until she follows my gaze.

Amazon, Missouri, Zambezi, and now the man in 2D. That's four of them. How many more? Are there any farther back, in economy? A sudden thought strikes me: *Are there any among the crew?*

"We are taking only a few hundred people hostage," Missouri is saying. "Our politicians have the whole world's future in their hands."

Across the cabin, Erik has moved. When I last looked, he was standing with Carmel, but he's several rows closer to the galley now than he was before. Zambezi is intent on Missouri's speech, and Erik in turn has his eyes on Zambezi. As I watch, he moves again—one foot, then the other, so slowly, you might miss it. I hold my breath. What is he doing?

"We will continue to stay airborne until the government agrees to our demands, or—" Missouri pauses. "Until we run out of fuel."

There is a moment's silence as our collective imagination pictures the full horror of this threat.

Before anyone can speak, Missouri continues, "I am in no doubt that we will achieve our goal. Intentionally sentencing hundreds of their own citizens to death would be rather an own goal, don't you think?" She doesn't seem to expect an answer. "In the meantime, all you have to do is cooperate."

Erik moves again. Slowly, slowly. Is he number five? I think of how he pulled the curtains around his bunk during our rest period, refusing to play along with the gossip and the games. He said he wanted to sleep, but did he have something to hide?

"And if we don't?" Derek Trespass calls.

Missouri raises her arm, letting the sleeve of her jumper fall to her elbow. The wires speak for her. Jamie Crawford's wife starts crying, noisy wails that make everyone look nervously between her and Missouri, in case the burst of emotion might trigger the hijackers to act. There's a sudden movement toward the galley. It's Erik, running forward and grabbing Zambezi, twisting her arm behind her back. Screams echo around the cabin, and Carmel runs forward, her voice rising above the noise.

"Erik, no. You'll get us all killed!"

Everyone's out of their seats, crying and shouting and pulling in different directions. Missouri crosses the galley and reappears behind Zambezi, grappling with Erik. Carmel's tugging at his arm, hysterical now, and above it all, baby Lachlan screams at the top of his lungs. I take the shortest route across the cabin, clambering over seats, not knowing what I'll do when I get there, not knowing who is where and which way they're pulling, knowing only that someone is going to get hurt if they—

I've never seen so much blood.

It spurts in a wide arc above the seats and leaves a crimson slash on the wall. Someone screams and goes on and on, not stopping for breath. The man with the neatly trimmed beard—his glasses spattered with blood—says, "Help me get her on the floor!" His gray sweatshirt is drenched in blood, his hands on a wound that won't be closed, no matter how hard he presses. Screaming. So much screaming.

Carmel. Twenty-two years old. A head full of accent walls and dusky-pink sofas, of far-flung hotels and a boyfriend who works in the City. Thirty-five thousand feet in the air, her blood pulses through a stranger's fingers, a corkscrew plunged deep into her neck.

THIRTY

PASSENGER 1G

What you have to understand is that I never wanted *anyone to get hurt. But as the saying goes: you can't make an omelet without breaking eggs. Sometimes violence is the only language people understand.*

The corkscrew was insurance: a need for a weapon more immediate, more targeted than the threat of a bomb. I slipped it into my pocket on an early visit to admire the bar, *with no real plan for its use, and I was glad of it the moment I saw the crew's attempt to undermine my plan. The metal pierced the girl's throat with a pop I found curiously satisfying. The first life I had ever taken. Blood on my hands.*

Her death was regrettable, as any death is, but out of everyone on that plane, the cabin crew surely carries the most guilt. Imagine how powerful a statement it would make to the world if airline staff refused to fly? If they demanded lower emissions, renewable energy?

Turkeys don't vote for Thanksgiving, though, do they?

The girl was a sacrifice, just like the man in 1J, who died in order for Mina to understand the importance of our demands. He flipped open his wallet in the bar, proud of his family, and I caught a glimpse of his frequent flyer card. Not as guilty as the crew, but not so innocent either. He chose to generate 5.8 tons of carbon dioxide by flying from London to Sydney. He chose to destroy fifteen meters of polar ice cap. You reap what you sow.

I crushed Rohypnol in his drink, then dispatched him with an insulin overdose, which caused a rather violent convulsion and rapid coma, swiftly followed by death. Insulin mustn't be stored in the hold of a plane, you see, due to its need to be kept at a constant temperature. Whether you're traveling for a single night or six months, your entire supply can be carried in your hand luggage, with nothing more than a doctor's note to satisfy security. It seems quite extraordinary to think that I had to remove my heeled shoes for an explosives check, yet with little more than a cursory glance, I could waltz through with two months' worth of insulin and twenty Rohypnol tablets in a packet marked paracetamol.

Humble weapons, perhaps, but far more easily explained away than illicit poisons, and most effective, as you've seen. Granted, the Rohypnol administered to Adam Holbrook could have taken effect sooner, but Volga hadn't considered his size, his strength. No matter—he succumbed eventually.

Ah, Volga… This is all because of her really. Not that she realized that at the time.

We had already begun to target the aviation industry, achieving notable success when we brought Britain's largest airport to a standstill with nothing but a pair of drones. The press coverage was extraordinary—finally, people were listening—and I knew then that we could achieve something even bigger. Something so big that the powers that be would be forced to take action.

The following summer, I was monitoring the message board when Volga presented me with the perfect vehicle. Literally.

Volga had been with us for some time. She attended marches, seemingly having a nose for wherever disorder was and picking up a criminal record along the way. She was one of those young people who view themselves as indestructible, with a penchant for prescription drugs that enabled me to keep her on a lead.

I know someone who adopted a turtle through WWF for her daughter, *she typed,* but get this: she's a fucking flight attendant!

The conversation had centered around the sorts of middle-class armchair activists who demonstrate a noisy fervor for "retro" glass milk bottles yet think nothing of flying halfway around the world to lie by a pool for the weekend.

Hypocrite! *Ganges concluded, quite rightly.*

She's flying nonstop to Sydney in December. Can you imagine the footprint?

I could imagine more than a footprint…

I googled the route. The coverage was extensive, the tabloids already speculating at the celebrity guest list likely to be heading to Sydney, keen to see their names linked to such an historic flight.

Tickets had just gone on sale.

I messaged Volga privately, squeezing every last piece of information from her and promising her enough opiates to keep a smile on her face till Christmas. She did not know this woman personally; she knew their Ukrainian au pair. Could she, I wondered, manufacture an introduction? If she could get into the house, she could learn more about the family. I knew that Volga was in her twenties, and I suggested she might consider whether she could pass for younger. Society does not credit young people with enough intelligence to be suspicious, I've found, and this apparent innocence can be useful.

The rest, you know. Becca Thompson, seventeen. A-level student (art, history, French). Babysitter. Undercover activist. I was confident she'd be able to hold her nerve, despite her age. She had the element of surprise on her side after all.

In fact, my only concern was that she might go a little too far.

THIRTY-ONE

1 A.M. | ADAM

The first time I took a flight with Mina, we'd just moved in together. We drove to the airport and said goodbye at check-in, not knowing if we'd see each other in two hours or three days.

"Fingers crossed." Mina kissed me, then turned to the guy on the desk, clasping her hands together in front of her in mock prayer. "Whatever you can do, yeah? I quite like this one." I caught a cheeky wink before her emerald-green overcoat swished around and she walked toward security, her wheeled case following demurely. Her hair, which only a few hours previously had been spread across my pillow, was tamed into a neat bun at the nape of her neck, half a can of hairspray choking up the bathroom.

At the gate, I fiddled with my passport as everyone lined up, then disappeared through the tunnel. I stared through the window at the World Airlines plane waiting on the tarmac, picturing Mina welcoming passengers and checking boarding passes.

"Final call for passenger Williams."

As the announcement faded, I listened for running feet. I looked around at those still seated, for the shocked face of someone lost in another world. *So sorry, I was miles away... No problem, sir. Let's get you boarded.* I tried to catch the eye of the staff member on the desk, to remind her I was there, but she was deep in conversation. The flight was due to leave in ten minutes.

I'd call up the lads, I decided, if I didn't get on. See who was around for a beer, rather than moping around in the flat. It'd be a laugh. Might even be more fun than a weekend in Rome.

"Final call for passenger Williams. The flight is now boarded and ready to depart. Final call, passenger Williams."

More fun? Who was I kidding? A year ago, a few beers and a kebab with the boys from work would have been my idea of a perfect night out, but now I was head over heels. Never mind Rome—I'd spend a week on standby for one night in Skegness with Mina.

"Adam Holbrook?" Not the PA system this time but a shout from the desk. I stood up so fast, I tripped over my hand luggage, dropping my phone and the magazine I'd bought for the journey. The flight operative laughed. "I was going to say it's your lucky day, but I'm not so sure now."

"I'm going?"

"You're going."

I boarded to two hundred filthy looks from passengers who took me for the tardy Williams, grinning at Mina as she ran through the safety briefing she once did naked for me, standing over me in bed with a glass of champagne in one hand. *The emergency sexits are situated here, here, and here…*

It was the best weekend. The sort of weekend that goes too fast yet seems to last forever, where you never stop laughing, never stop talking. Our whole relationship felt like that.

Where did it go?

You broke it. And now you might never see her again.

I wish I knew what was happening with Mina right now. I curse the radio for the lack of updates. Why isn't this all anyone's talking about? How can Rise FM still be playing Christmas tunes and Marks & Spencer adverts when hundreds of people could be—

No! They're not dead. Mina's not dead.

I try to picture her, try to replace the horror in my mind with something hopeful, but all I've got is scenes from disaster movies. Guns. Bombs. Planes exploding, diving, slicing through buildings…

I screw my eyes tighter, but the scenes keep coming, and with them, the knowledge that this is all my fault. If I hadn't got into debt and lied to Mina, she'd still love me. If she loved me, she wouldn't be on that plane.

I hadn't been snooping. Mina had met us at the park, to take Sophia home, and I'd persuaded her to come with us for an ice cream. She'd perched on the edge of her chair the whole time, checking her watch and asking Sophia if she'd nearly finished. The pattern was always the same: me stalling for more time, Mina itching to get away. If we could just spend the day together... But Mina wouldn't even consider it.

"I need space," she kept saying.

"How about we do something next month?" I'd said last time I'd seen her. "When Sophia's in school all day. The arboretum, maybe, once the leaves are turning. You love it there." I thought I saw regret in her eyes as she said no, but perhaps it was wishful thinking on my part.

I'd kept pushing. "Or Christmas. I know it's months away, but they'll be doing the rosters soon. I'll book time off the week before, and we can do the markets. Get something nice for Sophia." I thought that might swing it, but she had just said, *I'll think about it,* and shut me down.

Then she was snatching up the bill the second Sophia put down her spoon, taking it to the counter to pay. Her phone buzzed against the table, and instinct made me reach for it—the same auto-response that sees my fingers self-swiping to betting sites on my own phone. I glanced at the screen. It was from someone called Ryan.

Swap sorted with Crew Ops. You're on the Sydney run. Still think I ended up with the better end of the deal!

It wasn't so much that I didn't understand it (although I didn't)—more that it didn't register as being significant. Only as we were leaving, Mina said, "Oh, about the Christmas markets. Don't bother booking time off. I've been shafted with the Sydney flight. I'll be away all that week."

Suddenly, Ryan's message made sense.

As they walked away, I felt crushed. To be hated so much, she'd rather be ten thousand miles from me... My fault, I knew. Even so.

I think of Mina now, at the mercy of hijackers, and I trace the blame backward. I shift on the cold stone, trying to get some feeling back in my legs without disturbing Sophia, who has dozed off on my lap. She was leaning into my chest, but as she grew sleepy, her head slipped to one side, and with no hands to stop her, I had to twist my shoulder forward to stop her from falling. It was awkward at first, then uncomfortable, and now it's almost unbearable, but sleep is the best place for Sophia right now, while I figure out what to do and how much of this is my fault. I'm certain that if I hadn't been so distracted—hadn't been in so much pain from the kicking I got—I'd never have lost to someone like Becca.

I should have told Mina the truth from the start, except that it was never meant to be a lie. Buying a scratch card might technically be gambling, but no one calls it that until it's a problem, and it wasn't a problem until it was. By then I was too worried, too ashamed, too desperate to pay off the debt before Mina noticed.

Water drips from the wall down the back of my shirt, and I shiver involuntarily. Sophia stirs, and I freeze, but it's too late.

She's awake.

"Mummy!" And again, louder. "Mummy!"

"Shh, Daddy's here."

"Mummy!"

I rock her gently from side to side, my shoulder screaming with the movement. Sophia starts crying. "I don't like it here. I want Mummy. Mummy!"

"How about a story?"

"No, I want Mummy!" Her body is tense, and her feet kick against my shins.

"In the great green room, there was a telephone."

"Mummy." Quieter now.

"And a red balloon. And a picture of..." I end the line in a question.

"The cow jumping over the moon," Sophia whispers. She stops kicking.

"And there were..."

"Three little bears sitting on chairs."

How I hated *Goodnight Moon*. I'd taken it away once, slipped it under the rug in Sophia's room. I told myself it would be good for Sophia to have a different bedtime story, to break this ridiculous reliance on routine and repetition. I told myself it wasn't that good a story anyway—there were far better out there. I bought a stack of stories from Waterstones, assuaging my guilt with *The Gruffalo* and *Room on the Broom*. I ordered a copy of *Le Petit Prince*, suggested to Mina that Sophia might like to hear stories in French. "Did your mum speak Arabic to you when you were growing up?"

Mina grinned. "Only when she was cross."

"We could find some traditional Algerian stories for Sophia."

"She likes *Goodnight Moon*."

"Every night, though!"

It wasn't only the repetition that needled me. It was the fact that Sophia only ever wanted Mina to read it. When Mina read *Goodnight Moon*, Sophia would join in. She'd point to the pictures and hold her finger to her lips when the old lady whispered *hush*. I was always a poor second, the reserve player on the losing team. "Goodnight stars; goodnight air; goodnight noises everywhere," I'd finish, and Sophia would sit up in bed. "When is Mummy back?"

"She doesn't say it to hurt you," Mina would say, but it never took away the sting.

"Goodnight noises everywhere," I say now.

Sophia nestles her head under my chin. "Thank you, Daddy."

"You're welcome, pumpkin."

"I'm so cold."

Her body feels warm against my chest, but when I drop my lips to her forehead, it's icy. I jiggle my upper body so she wobbles from side to side. "Come on. Up you get. Exercise time."

She stands up, and I almost cry out at the mix of pain and relief that comes from relaxing my shoulders and pulling my feet up toward my body. "Do you remember how to do star jumps?" She nods. "Give me twenty, then. Go, go, go!" As she pumps her limbs in then out, in then out, I move as much of my body as my restraints allow, pins and needles crippling my extremities as the blood starts to flow. Sophia finishes, out of breath and laughing. "Now run on the spot. Go!"

I make her work out, knowing it won't be long before the exertion makes her hungry but balancing that against her getting hypothermia. She protests when I tell her we've done enough, but if she breaks into a sweat, it'll cool on her skin and make her feel worse.

"Can we play I Spy?"

I look around the cellar, my eyes now fully adjusted to the gloom. Stone. Steps. Locked door.

I spy, with my little eye, absolutely no way out...

"I've got a better idea. How about you be *my* eyes and we go exploring?"

"Outside?" Sophia says hopefully.

"In here for now."

She sighs. Draws out a reluctant agreement. "Okaaay."

"Start in the corner. Over there." Dutifully, Sophia skips over to the far corner of the cellar. "Now, run your hands over the walls. Tell me everything you find."

"I'm scared of the mouses."

"Mice. There aren't any mice, sweetheart. That was a silly story Daddy made up. What can you feel?"

"Bricks."

"Feel on the floor as well. Is there anything there?" A loose brick, a forgotten tool, *anything*.

At police training college, we were taught how to search a house for drugs or weapons. Pairs of officers, starting in opposite corners of a room, then crossing over and going over each other's patch. Dividing the area into quarters, making sure each one's clear before moving to the next.

"Pretend you're a police officer," I say now, "searching for clues."

"I'm going to be a pilot."

"Just pretend."

She finds a nail and a can of Diet Coke from before we realized the damp put fur on whatever we'd tried to store down here. "We can drink it." I'm suddenly desperate for it, my throat scratchy and my lips sore. "Do you think you can open it?"

It takes an age, her little fingers struggling to lift the catch. Eventually, she manages, the can pinned between my feet and Coke fizzing over my socks. Sophia drinks first—excited to be allowed a drink normally forbidden—then she tips it to my mouth too fast, so sticky liquid dribbles down my neck. When we've finished, Sophia lets out a huge burp. She tries to say *excuse me*, but another burp comes, and she claps her hand over her mouth. Her eyes are wide, expecting an admonishment, and she's shocked when instead I make myself burp too.

"Daddy!"

I tell her off all the time, I realize. I tell her to *be quiet* or *be good*, to *eat nicely* and *don't talk back*. I tell her off far, far more than I praise her. Is it any wonder it's Mina she wants?

I burp again. "Sophia!"

"That was you!" She jumps on me, heavy on my legs, and clasps her hands around my face, squashing my cheeks and laughing at the face it makes when I smile.

"I wish I could give you a cuddle."

Sophia tugs at my arms.

"They're very stuck, I'm afraid. So unless you can magic up a key…" I rattle the cuffs against the metal bar.

Sophia lets out the *oh!* of an idea. She scrambles off my lap and picks up the nail.

"Nice idea, pumpkin, but that only works in films." Sophia's face falls, so I twist around, showing her the hole in the cuffs where a key should fit. "Go on, then: do your worst." I lean forward, giving Sophia free rein and wondering if my strange and beautiful daughter is going to surprise me with a hidden talent for lock picking.

We must have been down here for hours. How much longer will we be here?

I call out for Becca again, but there's no reply, and not knowing what she has planned for us fills me with terror matched only by my fear for Mina. Flight 79 was due to touch down at Sydney in a few hours, and all we know from the radio is that it hasn't diverted, and it hasn't crashed.

Yet.

THIRTY-TWO

PASSENGER 1G

Flying a plane isn't easy.

We needed a pilot—that was clear—but attempting to bring an existing commercial pilot around to our way of thinking would have been a struggle, risking the end of our plans before they'd even taken shape. I attempted to find a discredited pilot, but they are not as easy to locate as, say, struck-off doctors, whose details are widely available.

In the midst of my research—mostly involving online forums—it became evident that many aviators shared a love of computer-simulated games. It seems extraordinary to me that after a week in a cockpit, anyone would wish to spend their days off manipulating a pixelated plane across a screen, but there you go. Apparently, modern simulators are so lifelike and so responsive, it's almost like flying a real plane.

I'd been going about this the wrong way, I realized. Why search for a pilot to bring into the fold when I could fashion a pilot from an existing disciple?

There were two possibilities. Yangtze was our resident IT specialist. It was he who had set up our forum on the dark web and ensured it would self-destruct as the flight took off, who had created our numerous Facebook pages, which I'd used to harvest followers in such a subtle way, they hardly noticed.

Unlike most of my group, I had not found Yangtze; he had found us. We operated via a rudimentary message board locked down by a series of supposedly complex passwords. I turned my computer on one day to find a grinning skull pasted across the log-in box. As I attempted to find a way in, the screen dissolved before my eyes, colors puddling on the bottom of my monitor. A ping from my inbox informed me of the point of this clever trick:

I could pay a thousand pounds for the safe return of my website, or he would forward the contents to the police.

I laughed at the audacity. Our exploits, back then, merely skirted around the edges of the law; discovery would have been an inconvenience but not a disaster. A thousand pounds seemed a curiously low amount for a would-be blackmailer, and I replied to the email with an alternative offer. If we intended to carry out more significant direct action, it was clear we would need a more secure online home, and I had found the person to create it.

Yangtze was a strange man. He had inherited a large sum of money from a grandparent, and it had made him both listless and entitled. He was, I discovered, not remotely interested in the reason for our group, only the challenge of hiding it. The combination made him an asset but also a risk, and I would no sooner put him in control of a plane than I would give him a gun.

Amazon, too, was rather a wild card, but I had succeeded in taming him in a way I never had Yangtze. As with most of the others, I'd found him online, deciding early on that the group could benefit from his skills. He was a difficult man, with bouts of mania that made him quite unstable.

The key to recruitment is matching desire with fulfillment. On a basic level, this is your salary—you need £28,000 per annum; I'm paying £28,000—but a shrewd employer will go a step further. Skilled headhunters will scour social media accounts to identify their targets' weak points before going in for the kill. We have an excellent childcare scheme, on-site gym, medical package... We have team drinks every Friday. We work from home. We dress down...

Amazon's weak spot was interesting.

I just want to game! read the one-line bio on his profile. I took in the rest of his feed. The lack of interaction from others; the posts he shared and then deleted. No, I thought, you want recognition. You want to be liked. You want to show your parents you haven't wasted your life. I looked at his other posts too—the shares of far-right "patriotic" images and the many, many petitions signed for scattergun causes—and I knew that here was a man whose anger and frustration could be channeled in any direction I chose.

I sent a link to my Grand Theft Auto profile. I figured he wouldn't ask questions, and he didn't, just added me that afternoon. As we played, I scattered thoughts like seeds.

—Fucking lefties stopping people wearing poppies, can you believe it?!

—Did you see that bint in the paper? Accepted drinks all night then cried rape?!

—International Women's Day? When's International Men's Day, then?!

He grabbed each one and ran with it, confirming my suspicion that he had no thoughts left of his own, that years of gaming had dulled his mind to such an extent that he now needed opinions fed to him, like a patient on a drip. Slowly, I filtered the content until my prompts were purely environmental, until it was him, not me, who introduced them.

When I was confident he was one of us, I went in for the kill.

—Friend of mine's looking to employ gamers—some software company needing to test how robust their systems are. Interested?

Of course he was.

For a year, I "employed" him, tasking him with hacking the levels on an FPS game, then sending the exact same game, saying the security had been tightened.

—You're amazing! *I told him when yet again, he beat the system.* I don't know what I'd do without you.

It cost money, of course, but our income was good. The starving polar bear image—such a hit on our Household Hacks pages—resulted in a regular stream of donations. People who give money "for the environment" don't ask how it will be used.

Moving Amazon from shooting games to flight simulations was a struggle (Where's the fun if you can't kill people?) but by then, he was conditioned to accept whatever work I gave him. I sent him up and down the country to try out actual flight simulators until he felt as comfortable in a flight deck as in his gaming chair, then booked a series of lessons in light aircraft—never at the same airfield twice.

—The instructor said I was a natural! *he messaged after his first go.*

I took a moment to reflect on how far he'd come in such a short time. I'd never met Amazon in person, but I imagined he was standing a little straighter, holding his head a little higher. The same had happened for Zambezi, who was a far cry from the battered wife I'd picked up from the floor. Our work—our important, world-altering work—was transforming people's lives closer to home too.

It takes around sixty hours of flying to get your private pilot license, and Amazon must have clocked up thousands of gaming hours that year alone. By the time he stepped onto Flight 79, he had a private license and dozens of hours in Boeing 777 simulators. More than enough for what I had in mind.

After all, how much training do you need to fall from the sky?

THIRTY-THREE

5 HOURS FROM SYDNEY | MINA

The screams have given way to a silence laden with fear and disbelief. Derek Trespass has made all the passengers move away from Carmel, across to the left-hand side of the cabin, roaring, "Show some respect!" when nobody responded. Erik, Cesca, and the man in the gray sweatshirt are on the floor in the aisle with me, Carmel lying between us.

"It is slowing down," Erik says. The spurts of blood that have covered us all are less regular, less forceful. The man with the glasses is still pressing around the wound in Carmel's neck, blood bubbling up around his fingers. The corkscrew is from the bar, a simple metal twist with a wooden handle. It seems barbaric to leave it sticking out of her, but the hole it would leave would make the blood loss even worse.

The decision is academic.

"It isn't slowing," Cesca says grimly. "It's stopping."

We watch Carmel's life ebb out of her, the convulsions slowing as her organs fail and she loses consciousness. Her eyes roll back in their sockets, the skin around them clammy and tinged with blue. Her rescuer takes his hands from her throat and slumps back on his heels. He pulls off his glasses, rubbing sweat and blood across his brow, his face racked with horror.

I touch his arm, and he flinches, still locked in the nightmare we've just lived.

"You did everything you could."

"I could have held the wound firmer maybe, or—"

"You did everything you could." My voice breaks on the last word.

"Stupid girl." Like the rest of us, Missouri is splattered with Carmel's blood, but unlike us, her face is impassive.

I stare at her. "How could you?"

"That's what happens when you ignore instructions."

"She did nothing wrong, and you killed her!"

"It wasn't—"

I scramble to my feet, sickened by the excuses. "You're a monster."

"Shut up, Mina, for God's sake!" Erik snaps.

I round on him. "You're a fine one to talk! Carmel was trying to stop you. This is all—" I break off, my conscience refusing to allow the remaining words. It isn't all Erik's fault. It's all mine. He knows it, and I know it.

The bearded man is still staring at Carmel.

"What's your name?" I say gently.

He looks at me blankly for a second, then shakes himself. "Rowan. We should move her. We can't leave her on the floor like this. It's not right." He blinks rapidly, then wipes his glasses ineffectually on his sweatshirt before putting them back on.

Cesca looks toward the door that leads to the pilots' rest area. "Could we—"

"We'll put her in a seat," I say quickly. Ben and Louis are safer where they are—half the cabin crew too. Why risk them getting hurt when there might still be a chance we can land safely? The pilots still have another hour to go before they're due downstairs, but I suddenly realize that the relief cabin crew were due on shift an hour ago. Where are they? No sound travels between the cabin and the bunks, but could one of them have come down for a drink? Opened the door, just a crack, and seen what's going on? I imagine them retreating, closing the door, making a plan.

Cesca's quick to follow my train of thought. "Yes, let's do that."

"She can go in my seat," Rowan says. He points to where a film plays silently on the screen. "Somehow, I don't think I'm going to be watching the end."

Cesca presses the button to slide it into a bed, and between us all, we move Carmel from the floor. I tuck a blanket around her, choking back my tears.

I'm so sorry, Carmel, so sorry.

If I could turn back time, what would I do? Knowing how much blood would be spilled, would I have opened that door? I stand with my hand resting on Carmel's still warm body, and for one horrific moment, I force myself to see Sophia lying here instead, and I know without a shadow of a doubt that I would do the same again.

Any parent would.

The atmosphere in the cabin has changed. Passengers huddle in terrified groups, no longer in their own seats but crammed on the opposite side, where Derek has herded them. I catch a glimpse through the bar. A figure stands on the far side, guarding the rear cabin, just as Missouri and Zambezi have resumed their aisle positions at the front of business class. The coordination makes me shiver. These people must have spent months planning this—how can we hope to overcome them? The noise from economy has subsided, and I hope the crew is cooperating. I hope they realize what might happen if they don't. I wipe my hands on my skirt, leaving dark streaks of blood across the fabric.

I make my way across the cabin. I have to know Sophia's safe, that all this hasn't been for nothing. Missouri raises her hand as I approach, the plastic trigger visible in her fist. Panic flutters in my throat, but I keep walking. I have to know.

When I'm close enough to speak without being overheard, I stop, open palms raised to show I'm not a threat.

"Where is my daughter?"

Nothing.

"You promised she'd be safe if I did what you wanted. Please—" It sticks in my craw, but I say it again. "Please, is she okay? Has anyone hurt her?" I fight to stop myself from crying, not wanting to show any more weakness than I have to. Missouri still isn't answering, her face barely registering she's heard, and anger swells inside me. "You promised. I did exactly what you asked!"

"How rude of me." A cruel smile spreads across Missouri's face, and she raises her voice, her words ringing out into the cabin. "I never thanked you for making our hijack possible."

"What?" The sharp voice comes from Jason Poke.

"Mina here was most helpful. We couldn't have taken control of the plane without her assistance."

"You're *one of them*?"

"No, I—"

"I knew it!" Jamie Crawford says. "Didn't I say, Caz, there was something off about her? You fucking bitch. Where are you from anyway? You're not English."

"What's that got to do with it?" Derek Trespass says.

"She looks like a Muslim, that's what, and since we're in the middle of a fucking terrorist attack, I'd say that's pretty fucking relevant, wouldn't you?"

"They're environmental activists, not jihadis, you idiot."

"Semtex is Semtex, mate, wherever you're from, and I'm telling you: she's a fucking terrorist." He jabs a finger toward me, and I jerk back despite the rows of seats between us.

It isn't the first time I've been viewed with suspicion. I was flying back from Dubai, tensions high after a bomb scare in Qatar the previous week. We'd been delayed taking off, and a group of lads were already borderline pissed. Two hours later, they were well oiled. I heard them egging each other on, each taunt more outrageous each time I passed.

"*Allahu akbar!*"

"What's the difference between a terrorist and a woman with PMS? You can negotiate with a terrorist."

"Come over here, sweetheart. I've got something in my pants that'll go off if you touch it."

They arrested them at Heathrow for offenses under the Terrorism Act. I made myself look them in the eye as they were walked off the plane, even though my knees were trembling so much, I had to lean against the wall.

"It was a fucking *joke*!" one of them hissed as he passed.

There were enough indignant passengers, with enough mobile phone footage, for their solicitors to persuade them to enter a guilty plea, and I was spared the anxiety of giving evidence at court. I told the boss I was fine, but the incident rattled me for months afterward, and the hatred in the footballer's eyes now sends me straight back to it.

"What about you?" Crawford turns on the Middle Eastern passenger from 6J, whose eyes instantly widen in fear. "Are you one of them too?"

"Jamie!" Caroline's horrified tone is echoed in the gasps from several of the passengers around me. "Don't be so racist."

The man from 6J drops his head in his hands. I feel a stab of shame at having distrusted his claim to be a nervous flyer. Whatever disasters he anticipated can't possibly have been as bad as the reality.

"You can hardly blame us." Crawford is on a roll. He's looking around for support, and I'm grateful to see that he finds little. Most people are avoiding his eyes, looking at the floor. "It's always you lot, isn't it?"

"'You lot'?" says Derek Trespass. "You need to watch what you're saying."

"I don't care whether you're Muslim or Hindu or Jehovah's bloody Witnesses," says the woman on her way to spend Christmas with her dying friend. "But if *she*"—she points at me—"helped them, then she's one of them, pure and simple."

"They threatened my daughter," I explain, trying to hold it together. "They said she'd be hurt if I didn't do what they said."

"And what about *my* child?" Leah Talbot screams across the cabin. Everyone turns to look at her. Tears course down her face as she carries on, the words broken by choking sobs. "Do you know how long I waited to be a mother? Eleven years. Eleven years of miscarriages, of fertility treatment, of being told we weren't right for adoption." She snatches Lachlan from Paul and brandishes him in front of her. "Doesn't his life matter? What makes him less important than your daughter?"

Paul reaches for her, wrapping his son and his wife in his arms as Leah collapses into cries that rack her whole body. I'm trembling, remembering how desperately I wanted a child, how the pain in my womb each month was echoed in my heart.

"They are all important!" Lady Barrow is on her feet, and despite her diminutive stature, she is a commanding presence. "All our children. Whatever this young girl did, any number of you would have done too, if it had been your child at stake." In any other situation, I might have laughed at being called a young girl, but I'm silent as Pat shouts down the self-righteous roar her statement has provoked. "Stop it! All of you, stop it! I for one don't want to spend the remaining hours of"—she falters for a second, at the last moment changing *my life* to—"this journey fighting."

The cabin falls silent. Throughout all this, Missouri has watched with a small smile on her face. She's enjoying this, I realize with a wave of revulsion. Maybe she even planned it, wanted to see us turning on one another instead of on them.

"The man in there." Alice Davanti points toward the flight deck as she addresses Missouri. "Is he a trained pilot?"

"Do you think we would jeopardize our own mission? He knows how to fly the plane."

"That's not the same thing."

Fear crosses the cabin like fire, a murmuring that grows in volume, hysteria building into worst-case scenarios.

"Amazon is a skillful pilot; he will take us to our destination without mishap, as long as you comply with our instructions. If you don't..." Missouri looks pointedly toward Carmel's body, and everyone swallows their fear.

Several TV screens are still playing, headsets trailing uselessly across empty seats. I watch Zac Efron mouth angry words at an equally angry and silent woman. Slowly, small groups of passengers form again, comforting one another or exchanging fevered whispers. As the focus of attention shifts away from Missouri, away from me, I ask her once more, hating the begging tone I hear in my voice.

"Please just tell me she's okay."

Missouri sighs, as though I'm an irritant. "It's not my department."

"But you promised!" *You promised.* As though it were an ice cream, a new bike. I should never have believed them; they're criminals, terrorists. My hands curl into fists, and Cesca touches my arm, as though she can sense what I might do.

"May we hand 'round some water?" she asks Missouri. "It might help to calm down the passengers."

Missouri considers this for a moment. "Fine. But quickly. And don't try anything." Raising her voice, she sends Erik and Rowan across to the other side of the cabin, leaving the aisle clear as she walks toward the middle of the plane.

Cesca releases my arm. "She'll be okay," she says softly, and even though she can't possibly know that, it steadies me enough to take a step back. My breathing stabilizes, and I blink away the lingering tears.

I have to stay calm. I have to focus.

I've done all I can to save my daughter; now we have to save ourselves.

I promised Sophia I'd always come back to her.

Somehow, I have to find a way to keep that promise.

THIRTY-FOUR

2 A.M. | ADAM

Sophia's "worst" turns out to be a sharp jab with the nail in the fleshy part of my hand, prompting a yell of pain and the metallic tang of fresh blood. I tell her it's no big deal, pressing the wound hard to the back of my shirt and wondering when I last had a tetanus shot. But she's already screaming, as if she's been holding it all in and now it's flooding out in tears and homesickness and misplaced rage.

I'm the first to admit I've never handled Sophia's meltdowns well. Even after I knew the psychology behind them—knew that she wasn't being deliberately badly behaved—I still struggled to cope.

"It's like shaking up a fizzy drink bottle," the counselor said. "Every new encounter, every challenge shakes it up a little more. The lid can only stay on for so long; sooner or later, it's going to blow."

The solution, she said, was to open the lid very slowly—to give Sophia a chance to let off steam in a controlled way. *Take her to the park after nursery, or stick her on the trampoline for ten minutes*, was the advice, which was sound in principle but useless in the face of a child who would sometimes throw herself to the floor the second we left the school grounds, screaming till she was physically sick.

"Sophia, that's enough!" I'd tell her, knowing even as I did it that I was making it worse but somehow unable to stop it.

"Come on, baby. Let me carry you," Mina would wheedle, as though Sophia were ill instead of angry, and out of my frustration and helplessness would grow an argument.

"Mummy!" Sophia cries now. "I want Mummy!"

"I want her too!" The ferocity of my response shocks her into silence, and for a second, we stare at each other, until I realize I'm crying. I drop my head, wiping my cheeks with my shoulders. *Mina, Mina, Mina...*

Soon after Mina started flying, there was a hijack attempt on another airline. Everyone was scared. Every time she flew, I'd feel as though I was holding my breath till she landed, and I begged her to look at roles in other parts of the industry.

"I love my job, though."

"But I love *you*. And I'd quite like to know you'll come home in one piece."

Still in one piece, she'd text after that, the second they landed. Slowly, we relaxed, the years bringing false confidence, until by the time Sophia arrived, I hardly thought about the risks at all. There hadn't been another significant attempt since, and so the whole world believed there wouldn't be. Couldn't be.

Now there has been.

Sophia pulls her dressing gown sleeves over her hands and wipes away my tears. She whispers as if she's afraid to hear her own words. "Has Mummy's plane crashed?"

I take a sharp intake of breath. "No, sweetheart, it hasn't crashed." The news has run every twenty minutes, and every time, I've braced myself, only to hear the same script. *No communications... No deviation from the scheduled route... No new information.* A spokesperson from Climate Action Group has denied all knowledge of the hijack. *Our ethos is passive resistance and civil disobedience*, he said. *We do not condone or encourage acts of criminal violence.* There's been no sound from Becca, and I picture her hunched over the tracking app, waiting for the plane to divert. The fear I heard in her voice hasn't reassured me; it's done the opposite. A frightened felon is a dangerous one. An unpredictable one.

"Is Mummy okay?" Sophia crouches by my side, her face so close to mine, I can feel her breath on my skin. A lump forms in my throat, and I feel my nose prickle with tears again. I don't know what to do, whether to tell her.

Mina would know.

A fierce wave of love surges through me, erupting in a howl that hurts my heart and bends me double, as I remember the arguments, the harsh words, the bitterness of a relationship I ruined with my lies.

"Daddy?" Sophia touches my head, and I can hear how frightened she is, but I can't speak because I'm fighting to find my breath, to find *myself* beneath this mess of a man who cries like a baby. How could I have let this happen? If I hadn't gotten into debt, I'd never have gone to loan sharks. Katya would never have been threatened; there would have been no secrets to tear Mina and me apart, no thug at my door with fists that didn't care what they broke. Becca wouldn't have been able to drug me; she'd have failed before she'd even started, and Sophia and I wouldn't be here in this cellar, with no way out. This is all my fault. Becca may have turned the key, but for months, I've been locking myself away.

"Daddy, I'm scared."

I need to pull myself together.

Slowly, I get my breathing under control. I flex every muscle, stiff with cold and lack of movement. I can hardly feel my fingers now.

"And I'm hungry."

"Me too." There's a break in my voice, and I cough and say it again, trying to convince myself—as much as Sophia—that I'm holding it together. I look around the cellar, as though food might miraculously appear in the dim light my eyes have now grown used to. "We're going to try shouting for Becca again, okay?"

Sophia's bottom lip wobbles.

"She's the only one who can bring us something to eat. I won't let her hurt you, okay?"

I take her silence as acceptance and shout as loudly as I can. "Becca! Becca! Becca!" I pause—I think I can hear movement, but I can't be certain. "Becca? We need food! Water!"

We listen. There are footsteps above, and a shadow falls across the narrow strip of light at the base of the door. The radio stops abruptly.

"Sophia needs food and water."

Nothing. But at least the shadow is still there.

I try again. "Just some water. Please, Becca."

"I'm not opening this door. You'll try and escape." There's a tightness to her voice that sounds like stress. Because she doesn't know what to do?

Or because she knows she's already gone too far? I need her to be calm. If she's calm, maybe I can talk her around.

"I can't move. How can I escape?" I pull at the pipe behind me, the metal making a dull clank against the handcuffs.

"You'll try something."

"Please, Becca. Just something for Sophia." I look at my daughter. "Go on," I whisper, "you try."

"Please, Becca, I'm so hungry."

The shadow moves away from the door. I think for a moment that she's gone, but then I hear movement from the kitchen—the sound of cupboard doors, the cutlery tray, the fridge. The radio goes back on: a truncated chorus of "Last Christmas" before a segue into what it's like to be lonely at *this special time of year*.

Time to think fast. This could be our only chance.

"Sophia, we're going to get out of here." She searches my face for the promise, and I wonder how much I can ask her to do. "How fast can you run?"

"Really really fast. I'm the fastest in the school."

"And can you be super still?"

In response, Sophia sits cross-legged, her arms folded and her lips pressed tightly together, the way they do when the register is called.

I smile. "Very impressive. We're going to play a sort of game, okay? First, you're going to be super still, then you're going to run as fast as you can."

The cellar door opens inward into the stairwell. If Sophia flattens herself to the wall behind it, Becca won't see her.

"Take off your dressing gown and put it over there." I nod toward the darkest corner of the cellar. "We're going to pretend you're lying on the ground."

Sophia obliges, her teeth already chattering as she arranges the dressing gown. It's not perfect, but Becca's eyes will be adjusting to the darkness, and all I need from her is a few steps into the cellar...

"I'll tell her you're sick," I tell Sophia. "That she needs to help you. As soon as she comes down the stairs, you run into the kitchen and straight out of the house, okay? Don't stop for anything, you understand?"

"And you too?"

"You're going to have to do this one on your own, sweetheart." I lock my eyes on hers. "You can do it, I know you can."

The light beneath the door flickers, Becca moving about the kitchen. We haven't got much time.

"Behind the door, now, sweetheart. Quiet and still as a mouse."

Sophia scurries to take up position at the top of the stairs, pressing herself into the wall. The light is too poor for me to see her face, but I know she's looking at me, and I wish I could give her a thumbs-up instead of the encouraging smile she won't be able to make out. A door bangs upstairs. "Ready?" I whisper.

"I'm ready."

Too late, I realize I only told Sophia to run, not *where* to run. Mo won't open her door at this time of night, and the third cottage in our terrace is a holiday house, rarely visited. The next nearest house, as the crow flies, is across the park to the housing estate. Even if Sophia makes it across the park, whose bell will she ring? Her friend Holly lives somewhere in the estate, but even I struggle to find it amid the maze of streets. What if she gets lost?

What if Becca catches up with her?

I'm about to risk another urgent whisper across to Sophia when there's a scraping noise and a loud *thud*. I look to the top of the cellar steps, but there's no shadow, no movement across the strip of light beneath the door, and suddenly I feel a gust of cold air from above my head. Becca's outside the front door, by the old coal chute. The entrance—an opening around two feet square—is hidden in the grass by the front wall of the house. It emerges around halfway up the cellar wall, the sloping angle of the chute itself making it impossible to see the outside world. The cold air is close enough to feel, yet I can't see it, and I think how the opposite will be true for Mina.

Something drops from the ceiling, hitting my shoulder, then bouncing onto the floor. I hear the concrete slab being dragged back across the opening, and the air changes, as though a window's been closed.

I stay still for a moment, listening to Becca's footsteps running back toward the house. The front door bangs, and despair floods through me. Our only chance to escape, and Becca made damn sure we couldn't take it. I call Sophia back.

"But when she opens the door, I have to be ready."

"She's not going to open the door, sweetheart."

The package that hit my shoulder is a supermarket carrier bag, its handles tied tight in a knot Sophia can't unpick. She rips at the plastic instead, taking out a bottle of water and two foil-wrapped sandwiches, one of which she hands to me.

"You're going to have to feed it to me."

"Like a baby?"

"'Fraid so."

Sophia takes a sandwich in each hand, already eating hers as she holds out the other to my open mouth. It's cheese, roughly cut and with no spread to moisten the bread, and my first bite sticks in my throat. I have a fleeting panic that I'm choking before the lump moves down my gullet and I can breathe again. Sophia copies me, an exaggerated gulp that uses her whole body, before she tears off another mouthful of sandwich.

"Better?"

She nods, her mouth too full to answer. The soothing tones of the graveyard shift radio presenter tell us they have *more on tonight's breaking news story*, and I shush Sophia, jerking my head toward the radio.

The prime minister tonight called an emergency meeting following the confirmed hijacking of a Boeing 777 by climate change activists. More than three hundred and fifty people are believed to be held hostage on board Flight 79, the first-ever scheduled direct flight from London to Sydney. The hijackers have stated that they intend to remain airborne until the fuel runs out unless the government concedes to their demands to bring forward their target for zero carbon emissions to 2030 and to issue fines to airlines that cannot demonstrate a commitment toward renewable energy. A few moments ago, the prime minister gave this statement…

"Daddy, that's Mummy's plane."

As the feed switches to an on-the-ground reporter, we hear the muted sounds of a crowd—cameras clicking, journalists talking—and the indefinable crispness of night air. I picture the prime minister standing in a floodlit Downing Street, the severity of the situation bringing the country's media out of bed.

Just say yes, I urge him silently. *Whatever they want, just agree to it.* He doesn't have to keep his word, does he? These people are criminals. Terrorists.

Just say yes. I tug at the metal around my wrists, frustrated to be made a bystander in my own crisis. Each radio update makes me feel more helpless.

"I would like to extend my sympathies to the families of all the passengers and staff on board Flight 79. World Airlines are making personal contact with all next of kin, to ensure that updates are passed as swiftly as possible."

My mobile is upstairs, and the charge was already low when I picked up Sophia. Have they tried to call me? Then again, maybe I'm not listed as Mina's next of kin any more. I imagine her emailing Human Resources, giving the number of a friend, her father... *Following my recent separation, please update my personnel file.* I feel a flash of anger, not toward Mina but toward myself. My marriage crashed around me, and I could have saved it. I wasn't thousands of miles away, I wasn't listening to radio reports, I wasn't shackled to a pipe six feet underground. I was right next to Mina—a copilot, not a passenger—and I did nothing.

The prime minister continues.

"Indonesian air traffic control operators have identified the hijacked aircraft and obtained authorization for a military intercept, and we are in the process of establishing what action has been taken since Flight 79 failed to maintain radio contact."

Having neatly passed culpability, he leaves the sort of silence that introduces a soundbite.

"Make no mistake." Another pause. *"This is an act of terrorism."*

Yes. I didn't vote for the PM, I didn't vote for his party, but at least he's calling it what it is. Not activists or environmentalists or laughable hippies stopping the traffic with rain dances. Terrorists.

"And we will not be held to ransom by terrorists."

What? No! No, no, no, no...

"Environmental issues are a key part of my party strategy, and we are working across the aviation sector to achieve lower carbon..."

I don't listen to the rest. There's a roaring in my head. All I can see is Mina; all I can hear is the words of a man who doesn't have anything at stake, doesn't have someone he loves on a hijacked plane. Someone who is thinking about political spin, about point scoring and vote winning and the upcoming election.

We will not give in.

Where does that leave Mina?

THIRTY-FIVE

PASSENGER 1G

I found it interesting to see the passengers turn on one another. How quickly the layers of human decency strip away, how swiftly raw instinct and prejudice take over...

Their leap in thought to Islamic terrorism was a natural one, and in fact, I have studied such acts in depth, learning much about their devotion, their patience, their methodology. The 2008 Mumbai bombings were the result of almost a year of training and planning. There are, however, distinct differences between a jihadist's actions and ours. They are motivated by belief; we are motivated by science. The facts are unarguable, whether or not you choose to listen to them.

The business-class passengers quieted down once they saw the lengths to which they had forced me to go. I had not planned to kill Carmel, but her death reinforced our position of power, and I felt that things would be easier from then on. As the remaining crew was occupied fetching water, I took advantage of the opportunity to pay a visit to the economy cabin. Just as I was entering the lounge, I witnessed a movement behind the bar. I pulled up short.

"Who's there?"

Slowly, a man stood up, his raised hands shaking so violently, he looked like he was dancing.

"What's your name?"

"H-Hassan."

"Move!"

The man responded instantly, ducking under the hatch, and half running, half falling the few feet toward the economy cabin, where Niger was holding the left-hand aisle.

"Get him back with the rest of the crew."

Niger acknowledged this with a curt nod, stepping aside as Hassan lunged past, then giving him a shove in the small of his back, which sent him running down the aisle. At the back, by the entrance to the galley, a cluster of uniforms pulled the hapless barman to the floor. Niger had made the crew sit in the aisle, where he could more easily see any movement, and I was impressed by his initiative. Living on the streets had given him an edge over the others, a hardness that meant he wasn't easily intimidated. When I met him, at a global warming demonstration, he was smearing Vaseline over the windscreen of the police riot van, parked down a side street while its occupants tried to prevent a perfectly lawful protest. Our eyes had met just as he was sliding off the bonnet. He wore a balaclava; I had a beanie hat and a scarf across my mouth, making it hard for him to read my mood.

"Fucking pigs," I said, for quite possibly the only time in my life.

He nodded approvingly. "There's another one in Bridge Street."

"Lead the way."

He'd grinned then and chucked me the Vaseline. Fearless and clever. I had yet to find a weakness. I caught the tub neatly, and we ran together, united against a common enemy. By the end of the day, I had a new recruit (not that he knew it at that point), and he had somewhere to live, after I'd called in a few favors. He never associated his part in our organization with that chance meeting—never knew when we chatted online that we'd already met in person—and that was just how I liked it. I knew everyone; nobody knew me.

In stark contrast to Niger, I was already nervous about Ganges. He was young—still in his twenties—and although he was a psychology graduate, working at the time as an NHS clinician, I frequently found his judgment to be skewed. I watched him finally take up his own position—guarding the entrance between economy and the bar—and saw he was shaking with nerves. It was clear he had contemplated abandoning us altogether, and I knew I would have to watch him.

I looked around the plane, counting off team members, cross-checking positions with names, names with faces. There appeared to be more compliance in the economy cabin than in business class, and I wondered if passengers in the latter carried a sense of entitlement that resulted in more *challenges. Perhaps I was overthinking it; maybe the tightly packed seats simply lent themselves more easily to a hostage situation.*

A number of the passengers were fiddling in vain with mobile phones, presumably still imagining that the Wi-Fi was indeed "temporarily down," as they had been informed early in our flight. I could see them stabbing buttons in desperation, even holding their handsets high above their seats, as though the additional height might provide them with a signal.

Communications were a key part of the operation, of course. I decided we would not attempt to hack the flight-deck radio. Yangtze was quite sure it was possible and indeed was champing at the bit to try, but it seemed an unnecessary gamble. Once the hijack was in progress, air traffic control would be largely powerless, and there was always the risk that Yangtze's interception could be noticed too early and the authorities alerted.

It was far more important to bring down the Wi-Fi in the cabin. Mina's role was crucial to the success of our mission, and it relied entirely on her being unable to communicate with Adam. It left her frantic, of course, but that was precisely the point.

And as it turned out, she was better off not knowing.

THIRTY-SIX

4 HOURS FROM SYDNEY | MINA

As Cesca and I move around the galley, filling jugs with water, I glance at the door to the flight deck. What's happening in there? There's been no indication that we're not still in the hands of an experienced pilot, and I wonder whether that's because the man they called Amazon knows what he's doing or because we're still on autopilot.

Could Mike still be alive?

I'm clutching at straws, I know, but if he is alive—knocked out, tied up, but *alive*—then I owe it to him to put this right. I have to find a way of turning this around. I can't see Missouri, but the blond woman—Zambezi—is watching me, dividing her gaze between Cesca and me and the passengers in the cabin. She can't be more than five foot five and slim with it, but she stands like a boxer, and there's not a flicker of nervousness about her face. Rather, she sports a small smile, as though she's saying, *Come on, then. Show me what you're made of.*

The long-legged man from 2D gets up and stretches, as though he's just going for a stroll instead of hijacking a plane. He walks into the galley and leans against the flight-deck door, taking in the scene. He nods at the blond woman.

"Yangtze." The corners of his mouth twitch as he looks her up and down. "A woman, huh?"

"No shit."

The reply is terse, and I glance at Cesca, trying to make sense of their conversation, but she's as confused as I am. I try to see whether the tall man has explosives. He's wearing a T-shirt, and there are no wires, no bulges around his chest. He sees me looking and raises a suggestive eyebrow. I turn away before he can see the revulsion on my face.

"No glass." Zambezi gestures to where Cesca is filling a tray with the goblets we use for business-class passengers. Wordlessly, Cesca replaces them in the locker and finds a stack of paper cups. I open cupboards with deliberate slowness, my hands pulling out water bottles and bags of pretzels while I mentally go through every area of the galley to find something we could use as a weapon. Food and drink, an oven, a coffee maker, the chiller cupboards…nothing I can easily take and use.

If I could break a glass, I might secrete a shard somewhere, but how can I do that with the pair of them watching us? There are port glasses in the cupboard—narrow stems that would snap easily and quietly. Would it be obvious if I dropped one in the pocket of my jacket? I slip a hand in to remove the pair of cotton gloves Dindar likes us to wear when we're serving food.

"Get a move on."

My fingers are still sticky with Carmel's blood. They close around the note I found with Sophia's flapjack. I want to take it out, but I can't bear the thought of the hijackers snatching it from me, this fragile link between me and my daughter.

For my mummy.

In my pocket, I press the note between my hand and my hip, remembering the weight of her as a toddler as I carried her from the car, half asleep. Legs dangling either side, her head flopping on my chest. I let out a slow breath.

I'm coming back for you, Sophia.

I repeat it to myself as I walk with Cesca through the cabin, pouring water under the watchful eyes of the hijackers. *I'm coming back for you.* Every iteration makes me feel more like it's possible, more like I'm strong enough to survive this.

"Are you okay?" It's Rowan, the passenger who helped with Carmel. He's taken off his blood-soaked sweatshirt and put on a near-identical one in a slightly darker shade of gray. "They let me get it out of my hand luggage." He looks at my spattered uniform. "Would you like something? I always have a few spare bits in case my luggage goes AWOL."

"Thanks. I'm okay." Having Carmel's blood on my clothes feels like a penance I deserve and a reminder of what's already been lost.

"I don't think the others have explosives." Cesca speaks in a low voice, her eyes fixed on the cabin. "I can't see anything in their hands."

The hijackers are roaming up and down the aisles, shouting at passengers to keep their hands where they can be seen. I scan each of them in turn, watching the way they throw their arms about. Impossible to say if they're wearing anything under their clothes, but she's right: they're not holding detonators.

Could we overpower Missouri and get it out of her hand before she has the chance to set it off? My pulse quickens, sweat breaking out across my forehead. The chances of success are tiny, and if we fail... I think about all the times Adam has tackled violent criminals, telling me about it afterward as though it were nothing. Just fists, just needles, just knives. Quietly courageous.

I'm coming back for you. I repeat my silent mantra, and this time, it's not only Sophia I'm thinking of.

When Missouri reappears in the aisle, we snap to attention, the sight of the plastic and wires in her hand enough to make us comply.

"I want you in economy. Get rid of that water." She turns toward the cabin, claps her hands again in that disconcertingly prim way before shouting the order again. "Everyone at the back of the plane. Move!" She shouts the last word, provoking a panicked scramble to get from business class across the bar to economy.

"Change of plan," I hear Missouri say to Zambezi as we pass. "I want them farther from the action."

In the bar area, they divide us roughly into two groups, herding us into either side of economy. I'm pushed toward the right-hand aisle, along with Cesca and Rowan and the two journalists. The Middle Eastern man from seat 6J is in front of us, but he isn't moving. Every muscle is tense, and as we file past, I catch the acrid scent of stale sweat. At the back of the plane, I can see the remaining on-duty crew, huddled together on the floor. The door leading to the relief bunks is still closed. Have they realized what's happening and stayed hidden?

"Sit down. Now!"

We drop down between the rows of economy passengers, and the sudden lack of space makes me feel as if I can't breathe. I'm at the front of the aisle, Cesca behind me, then Rowan, Derek Trespass, and finally Alice Davanti.

"Hands on your heads."

Hundreds of pairs of elbows snap to attention. Lachlan is screaming again, the loud wails of a hungry baby. Elsewhere in the cabin, muted sobbing spreads like fire.

The long-legged Yangtze is still in the bar area. He gives a mock bow as Missouri approaches, his heels clicking together. "Yangtze, reporting for duty."

She doesn't miss a beat. "You took your time."

"I figured you had it all under control."

Missouri's face twitches, as though she's trying to decide whether to be flattered or annoyed, and the odd exchange between the two hijackers in the front galley suddenly makes sense.

A woman, huh?

No shit.

"They don't know each other," I say to Cesca. "They're meeting for the first time."

The Middle Eastern man is still standing, his eyes darting around the cabin. I'm trying to make eye contact with him, trying to convey that he's putting us all in danger, when Missouri hisses at him.

"For fuck's sake, Ganges, pull yourself together."

Ganges?

The man nods, planting himself firmly in the center of the space, his eyes fixed on the far end of the cabin. A chill runs through me as I think of how I ignored my suspicions, how I felt guilty for them.

Missouri repeats her instruction to a man standing on the opposite side of the cabin. "Niger, hold the aisle."

Ganges. Niger.

Rivers, I realize, finally making the connection. Missouri is the ringleader, standing in the bar with the blond Zambezi and the long-legged Yangtze. Ganges is the young man whose feet are inches from my knees. Average height and slightly built, Ganges has the soft, unhealthy skin of someone unaccustomed to exercise. He wears gray, wire-framed glasses, and his black hair stands on end, as though he has just run his fingers through it. He shifts from one position to another, his hands fiddling with his pockets, his buttons, his collar. He scratches his neck, chews his lip, glances across the aisle and back toward the two hijackers at the rear of the cabin. Perhaps feeling my eyes on him, he looks down. I try a smile, and he flushes, snapping his eyes away and resuming his nervous fidgeting. Across the aisle is the man Missouri referred to as Niger. I only caught a glimpse of him before we were made to sit on the floor.

I turn and whisper to the others, "I've counted six of them, including the one flying the plane."

"Do you think there are more?" Derek says. He's younger than I thought, I realize, his hair prematurely thin and worry lines scoring his brow.

"Everyone else has their hands on their heads." Rowan kneels up, looking back along the aisle. All the passengers are sitting down, either in their seats or on the floor, and there's an eerie quiet. He looks back toward the hijackers and shudders. "To think that they were sitting among us for all that time, and we never knew."

"*Some* of us knew..." Alice Davanti glances in my direction, but no one takes up the baton. We have to come up with a plan.

Soon after I started work, World Airlines rolled out a training package designed to equip us with the skills required to handle a hijacking situation. Run by a former pilot and martial arts expert, the setup took place in a hangar on a private airfield in Gloucestershire, using the front half of a decommissioned B747. We shivered away the morning in our coats, sitting on plastic chairs next to the plane, while the instructor took us through pop psychology and negotiation skills. After lunch, we were split into two groups—cabin crew and passengers—and introduced to a troupe of actors who would be playing the other passengers and the terrorists. I recognized a man from *Hollyoaks* and the woman from the previous year's John Lewis advert.

"The scenario you're about to experience is as close to a real-life situation as we can get," said the instructor. "You won't be physically hurt, but you may find the experience psychologically distressing. If you need to leave, blow your whistle, and we will stop the scenario." We exchanged nervous smiles, all privately hoping we wouldn't be the ones to put a stop to the fun.

I thought we'd feel silly. Self-conscious. I thought the acting would be hammy, the responses scripted, and perhaps it was a little, at first. Those of us playing cabin crew boarded first, greeting our passengers and checking their boarding passes, which had been faithfully reproduced for maximum authenticity. We carried out the safety briefing, moved to the jump seats, and then we "took off." Sound effects and a low vibration hummed throughout the plane.

The seat belt sign went off with a *ping*, and suddenly we were starting a mock drinks service, and the buzz of conversation across the aisles made it feel so real and all the more shocking when there was a loud bang and a scream, and I looked up to see a man in a balaclava holding a gun. A second man had a knife to the throat of a woman, dragging her to the flight-deck door, and a third threw something into the aisle in front of me. I screamed and ducked down behind the trolley I was pushing as a cloud of smoke mushroomed out across the seats. There was more shouting, more screaming, and at no point did I have space to think, *It's just pretend.*

I wish I could blow a whistle now.

Lachlan's cries increase in intensity, and a man at the back, crouched like us in the aisle, shouts for someone to *shut that fucking baby up!*

"Shut up yourself," Paul Talbot shouts back.

"It's been screaming for hours. It's so fucking inconsiderate." It's Doug, more sober now but just as vociferous, his fiancée leaning toward him, pleading with him to be quiet, not to draw attention to himself.

"Inconsiderate? We're about to die, and you're talking about etiquette?" Paul gives a hollow laugh.

"I can't do this." Doug stands, looking wildly around, as if he'd throw himself out if only he could get to a door.

"Hands on your head!" the hijacker at the back of the aisle yells at him, but he takes no heed.

Ginny pulls at her fiancé. "Baby, sit down! It's the only way we're going to get through this."

"Get through this? We're not getting *through* anything. We're going to die, Ginny."

Sobs echo around us as hysteria spreads through the cabin. Those who aren't crying are watching Doug and Ginny, and I wonder if this might be our chance to get past Missouri and into the flight deck. But when I look for her, she's still holding her position, not remotely distracted by the sideshow.

"No." Ginny lifts her chin, determined to stay positive. "We're not going to die. We're going to get to Sydney, and we're going to get married and—"

"I can't marry you."

There's a horrible silence, and even with everything that's happening, my heart breaks to see Ginny's face crumple.

"What do you mean?"

Doug hangs his head. "I got carried away. It all happened so fast, and you were so excited. I didn't want to hurt you, but…"

He stops, and Ginny's voice hardens. "But what?"

"I'm already married." He sounds as though he might cry, but there's no sympathy on any of the faces around him.

"You bastard," someone says from a few rows behind.

"Talk about timing," Derek mutters.

Ginny bursts into tears, and a woman next to her puts her arms around her. I wait for one of the hijackers to shout at her to put her hands back on her head, but they either don't care or haven't noticed.

I look up at the hijacker guarding the front of our aisle. He looks almost as shaken by Doug's revelation as poor Ginny, and I wonder if it's served to show him that we're people, not just hostages. I manage a smile. "What's your name?"

"Ganges."

"Your real name."

"You don't need to know that."

"I'm Mina. Short for Amina, but everyone's always called me Mina." I remember that much from the scenario debrief: *Use your name as much as possible. Tell them details about your life; make them think of you as a real person.* I try to hold Ganges's gaze, but his eyes slide away. "Can you tell us what's happening?"

He glances at the opposite aisle. I'm too low to the ground to see who he's looking at, but it's clear Ganges feels out of his depth. "Cooperate, and you won't be hurt." He has the faintest of accents—the barely there intonation of someone who's lived in their second country far longer than their first.

"Where are you from?"

"You don't need to know that either."

"How come you've never met one another before?" I'm met with stony silence, but I persevere. "She knows you, though, right? Missouri? That doesn't seem fair. She knows you, but you're not allowed to know—"

"She knows our positions, that's all." His response is muttered, a dart of his eyes checking to make sure Missouri isn't listening. "She knows our names from where we're standing."

"I see. So you guys have only chatted online, right?"

Cesca shuffles forward, into the gap to my right. "It isn't too late to back out, you know," she says quickly. *Too soon*, I think, turning to her, trying to convey through my eyes alone that she needs to be quiet, that I was sure I could get somewhere. "If you're having second thoughts, you could help us instead, and I'm sure the police would—"

"Quiet!" He raises a clenched fist, bringing it down swiftly, then stopping a hair's breadth from Cesca's face.

Too soon.

"Consider that a warning."

Cesca retreats, the others clustering around her. But I'm watching Ganges's face and the flicker of alarm that crossed it, not when Cesca spoke but when he raised his fist. He didn't stop because he only wanted to warn her; he stopped because he couldn't bring himself to carry on. *He doesn't want to hurt us.*

We're too close to Ganges to talk about him. I indicate as much to Cesca and the others, and we begin to make some space. Derek kneels up and stretches, his hands still dutifully on his head. When he returns to a seated position, he is a full row behind his original spot. Alice waits until Ganges is looking away—something he does every few seconds, as though he's searching for answers elsewhere in the cabin—then slides swiftly back into the space Derek has left. Slowly, we all move backward, and Ganges either doesn't notice or is relieved not to be at such close quarters.

Next to me, in the central aisle seat of the third row, a pregnant woman is sobbing quietly to herself.

"Are you okay?" I ask, even though she clearly isn't. None of us are okay.

"My husband didn't want me to fly. But he's working over Christmas, and the baby's not due for six weeks, and I figured it would be nice to be home and let Mum take care of me for a bit, you know? And now—"

She doesn't finish. She doesn't need to. I wonder if her husband knows—if any of our families know. Unless Missouri's pilot is proficient enough to maintain comms with air traffic control, it would only have taken around half an hour for someone to notice that we were out of contact. Maybe it's on the news already. I picture Adam in the sitting room, glued to the television; I imagine the journalists standing at the airport, the sea of holidaymakers incongruous with the solemnity of the report.

"I'm so sorry."

"It's not your fault. It's theirs." She directs this last to the bar, where Missouri can be seen talking to the other hijackers. "They're insane. And climate change, for God's sake! Of all the stupid, stupid reasons…"

"There is no climate change, you know." The man in the next seat leans forward. "They've disproved it. It's just a natural cycle. Give it another hundred years, and they'll be moaning that we're heading for another ice age."

"What is this—debating society? *This* is real!"

"Try to stay calm," the man says. "Increased blood pressure isn't good for the baby."

The pregnant woman stares at him. "How many times have you been pregnant?"

"Well, none personally, obviously, but—"

"Then fuck off." She stands up and shuffles into the aisle. I half stand, too, as she approaches Ganges, unsure if she's likely to help or hinder.

"I need to pee."

"You'll have to hold it. Sit down."

"There's six pounds of baby pressing on my bladder. My pelvic floor isn't holding anything."

Ganges turns a deep shade of red. He backs into the bar, keeping his eyes on the pregnant woman as he mutters something to Missouri. She rolls her eyes and comes forward, grabbing the woman's sleeve and propelling her into the loo. She stands in the doorway, and I see a man in the front row turn away to give the poor woman some privacy.

I turn around, the distraction giving us a brief chance to talk. "We have to do something."

"Like what?" Rowan says.

"Force our way through."

"What?" Derek laughs. "The five of us against six terrorists, at least one of whom is wearing explosives? And God knows how many more of them there are on board!"

"Derek's right." Alice looks at me despairingly. "Even if we got past Missouri and the others, what would that achieve? The door to the cockpit's locked, isn't it?"

"There's an emergency access code," Cesca says. "It overrides everything."

We all look toward the flight deck, and I push up onto my knees to get a better view. There's ten feet between us and Ganges, and behind him the bar in which Missouri stands, surveying her team. Behind them, the length of a tennis court stretches out before the flight-deck door. How far would we get before Missouri pushed the button?

Ganges glances again at his conspirator on the other side of the cabin. I follow his gaze. Slowly, I rise up, so I can see over the central seats, careful to stay lower than the passengers next to me. My arms are aching, and I lock my fingers together on top of my head to relieve the strain.

"And you know the code?" Rowan asks Cesca.

"Of course. I just don't see how we'd get close enough without her detonating that bomb."

"Sit down!" Ganges snaps. I sink dutifully to the floor. But I've already seen the man Missouri called Niger. And I recognize him. I recognize the baggy combat trousers with the heavy boots and the tight T-shirt that strains across his biceps, and I'm almost completely certain I know something about him Missouri doesn't.

Now I just have to figure out how it could help us.

THIRTY-SEVEN

3 A.M. | ADAM

"Shall we do some baking together when all this is over?" I'm talking with my mouth full, but I figure normal rules don't apply when you're trying to distract your five-year-old daughter from the fact that you're locked in a cellar, at the mercy of an increasingly unstable maniac.

After Becca closed the coal chute, I heard her running back into the house, slamming the door like the teenager she'd pretended to be. She is moving about the house now, pacing this way and that, and I feel a charge in the air that makes me fearful of what she might do next.

"Daddies don't do baking." The words are indistinct, as though she's about to cry, and I wonder if I've said the wrong thing—reminded her of Mina perhaps.

"Lots of daddies do baking. And I'm sure I could give it a go. Not dandelions, though—yuck. Silly Becca. Who wants to eat weeds?" The more I try to make Sophia smile, the quieter she becomes. She puts her hands to her face.

"Daddy!" It's barely a whisper, choked with emotion.

"We'll see Mummy soon, pumpkin. I promise." My own voice breaks at what feels too much like a lie. It must be possible, surely; there must be a chance that she'll get out of this alive. I can't bear the thought of losing her.

"Da—" Sophia's fingers flutter around the front of her throat, and I suddenly realize it's not emotion in her voice, it's panic. Her eyes widen, she shakes her head, and I can see her lips swelling, as though she's been stung by a bee. Elephant falls to the floor beside her.

"What was in your sandwich?"

Again, louder, because she's frozen, terrified eyes locked on mine. "Sophia, what was in your sandwich? Let me taste it—now!" I pull at my handcuffs as though they might have magically unlocked.

Sophia scrambles for the crusts she's stacked neatly on the floor, and they've barely touched my lips before I can smell it, taste it.

Peanut butter.

"We shouldn't even have it in the house," Mina had said when we got back from the doctor's, three-year-old Sophia blissfully unaware of the potentially fatal diagnosis she'd just been given.

"Her allergy isn't *that* bad." There were some people, the doctor told us, who couldn't be within ten feet of a nut, who could feel their lips swelling the second a packet was ripped open in the pub.

"But what if she opens it? She's too young to understand the difference between a spread she can have and a spread she can't."

"I'll keep it on top of the fridge. She won't even see it." Peanut butter was my guilty pleasure, spooned from the jar before a long run or smeared on toast on a Sunday morning.

Since her diagnosis, Sophia's only had one allergic reaction, when a thoughtless parent at a coffee morning gave her a biscuit without checking with Mina.

"It was terrifying," Mina said afterward. She shook her head as if there were a fly trapped inside. "I used the pen, and I suddenly thought, *What if it doesn't work?* You know—we have these pens, and you just assume they work, but what if we've got a rogue one? An off day at the factory. The one duff pen."

"But it did work," I reminded her, because her words were racing as though she'd forgotten that Sophia was banging pans around her toy kitchen, the excitement of the day already forgotten.

"Yes, but—"

I moved to hold her, physically stemming her panic. "It worked."

As Sophia got older, she knew not to take food from anyone but us. She got used to taking a packed lunch on days out, learned to ask at parties if the cake contained nuts. We relaxed. Became complacent. But the peanut butter jar stayed on top of the fridge, safely out of Sophia's reach.

"Stay calm. Try and breathe slowly."

She's hardly breathing at all. I know that her chest will be tight, as though someone's sitting on it, her throat swelling so that every intake of air is forced. She moves her lips, but no sound comes out. Her eyelids have already puffed up, closing her eyes to narrow slits.

"Becca!" If I shouted loudly for our food, it's nothing compared to how I shout now. I get on my knees, as though the tiny increase in height will carry the sound farther, and bang my handcuffs against the metal pipe again and again and again. "Help!"

It can take anything from a few minutes to a few hours to die from an anaphylactic attack. The first time it happened, we drove her straight to the GP, where we were rushed past the queue to an efficient doctor who whipped out an EpiPen and dialed 999 at the same time. We were given our own pen at the hospital.

"What happens if she doesn't have the epinephrine? How bad would the reaction be?"

"Impossible to say. Let's not find out the hard way." The doctor was young and thoughtful, empathy in her eyes. "Best to get a spare pen."

We have five in total. One at school, one in Sophia's school bag, one in Mina's handbag, one in my car, and one in the kitchen drawer along with spare keys and loose batteries and three-year-old toys from McDonald's Happy Meals.

"Help!"

In the kitchen, the radio snaps off midway through "Fairy Tale of New York."

I don't wait for Becca to call out.

"I need Sophia's EpiPen. You gave her nuts, you stupid, stupid—"

"I gave *you* nuts! There wasn't enough cheese, so I—"

"Quickly! There's no time. She could die, Becca!" I regret my words the second I see Sophia's face, swollen and panicked and now fighting for what little breath she's managing to find. "It's not true, sweetheart," I add in a low voice. "I just said it because we really need your pen."

There's noise upstairs. I hear a clatter of keys, and I picture the contents of the kitchen drawer spilled on the floor. I yank at my handcuffs, fear and frustration lending strength to my stiff arms. What will I do if Sophia stops breathing? If her heart stops?

"Hurry!"

"I can't find it!"

Mina must have moved it. I feel an unjust spike of anger that she didn't tell me, that we didn't talk about it, say, *I was thinking it might be better to keep it in the hall, in the bathroom, in the cupboard.*

"In Sophia's school bag!" I yell.

Becca makes a sound that's midway between a sob and a scream. "It isn't there! It's on the plane. I took it last night when I babysat. I was just told to leave it by a bench in the park and someone would pick it up."

"It's wh—" This is no time for questions. "My car!" Sophia makes a strangled sound that might be *Daddy*, and my arms yank instinctively against my restraints as they try to reach for her. "In the glove box!" I'm hoarse from shouting, but I can hear Becca's footsteps running outside, I hear the *beep* of my central locking and a car door opening.

"It's okay. It'll be okay, sweetheart."

More feet, then the scraping sound as the paving slab is shifted from the entrance to the coal chute, and a clatter as the pen slides down into the cellar.

"Pick it up, pumpkin. Take off the cap. That's it, just drop that. Now straight into your thigh."

Sophia looks at me, not moving, tears falling down her swollen face.

"Come on, sweetheart. I can't do it for you. See that Action Man on your pajamas? There. The one above your knee—higher, higher, *there.* Stab it, then keep the pen there till I tell you to move."

I know my daughter is brave. She doesn't cry when she scrapes a knee or wakes in the night with a fever. She's fearless at the playground, hanging upside down and running across to try the "big slide." But I didn't know quite how brave until I see her lift her hand, fist wrapped around the EpiPen, and plunge it into her own thigh. I choke back a sob, scan her face for signs that she's going to be okay, but her face is still swelling, and she's gasping for breath. Her fist's clamped tightly around the EpiPen, and I can't see if she's done it properly. I don't know if the pen's worked, if the needle's in the right place.

I don't know if it's enough to save her.

THIRTY-EIGHT

3 HOURS FROM SYDNEY | MINA

I press my fingers against the note in my pocket. I picture Sophia lying on her stomach in her bedroom, the tip of her tongue poking out as she forms each letter, carefully looping the tail of each *y* beneath the line, the way I taught her.

For my mummy.

It isn't the first time Sophia has hidden some of her baking for me—I unpacked in New York last month to find a piece of banana cake wrapped in a napkin and slotted into one of my shoes—but it's the first time she's included a note. The letters I leave on her pillow when I go away barely seem to register, and I've often wondered if she even looks at them, but maybe she's learning something from my leaving them. Maybe we're finally making progress.

I close my eyes for a second, drawing strength from the thought and from the note in my pocket. I murmur silent affirmations, pouring all the energy I have into them, as though commitment alone will make them true. *She's safe. You kept your side of the bargain to keep her safe. Adam won't let anything happen to her.*

Adam's name brings into sharp relief all the things I love about my husband, all the things I've missed since we separated. Before Katya, everything was good. He'd have done anything for me; I'd have done anything for him. That's how it works when you love someone.

That's how it works…

I look past Ganges, along the stretch of empty aisle to where Yangtze now stands by the flight-deck door, and the beginnings of a plan flicker around the edges of my mind. I'm fairly certain I know something about the hijackers that even Missouri doesn't know, and it might just get us into the flight deck. I picture Cesca sliding into the captain's seat, her now-familiar voice over the PA, telling cabin crew to prepare for landing, and my heart surges with the promise of home.

"I've got Wi-Fi!" A cry goes up from somewhere on the other side of the cabin. I stand, clumsy in my haste and heedless of the hijackers, my urge to speak to Adam far stronger than that of self-preservation. I see an arm in the air, a mobile phone triumphantly aloft. "I've been trying ever since we took off, and I finally got a connection!"

There's a surge of activity: passengers scrambling under seats for their bags, unclipping their seat belts to open overhead lockers. Incongruously cheerful tones sound as devices are turned on, their screens lighting up faces. I look at the hijackers to see how they're taking this news, but Missouri is staring at her own phone screen, her brows knitted together as she taps furiously with two thumbs.

"They switched it back on," Rowan says.

"Why?"

He shrugs. "To communicate their demands perhaps?" We both look toward the bar. To one side of us, the pregnant woman is FaceTiming her husband. Tears stream down his face as he reaches out and touches the screen.

"I love you so much," he says.

"I love you too."

I choke back a sob and turn away, unable to bear the torture of watching someone else's goodbye. The noise level in the cabin is rising as more people get through to their loved ones. There are messages left on voicemail, declarations of love, requests for forgiveness. *If I don't make it, tell the kids I love them...*

Cesca's sending a text, biting back the tears I can see threatening to break through her controlled facade. My hand itches for my phone, zipped in my bag at the front of the plane, and I wonder how long the network will cope with so many people trying to call home.

My mother phoned me the day before she died. It was less than a year after I'd dropped out of pilot training, and I couldn't handle another interrogation about trying again, couldn't deal with her gentle but insistent questions about what had happened that day in the air. I watched her name flash up on my screen, and I let it go to voicemail. I'd call her later or in the morning.

Only I didn't, and I've never forgiven myself for it.

Images flash through my mind. Adam, standing at the altar, turning to see me walk down the aisle. Meeting Sophia. Bringing her home. Playing bath monsters, walking to school, Adam and I each with a hand, swinging her high in the air. My mother wasn't there to see me marry Adam, never met Sophia, never knew me as a mother myself. I don't want that for Sophia. I want to be there for her—it's what I promised her the day we brought her home.

I'll never leave you. You'll never be on your own again.

"Here."

I look 'round. Rowan is holding out his phone. I reach for it, even as politeness makes me say, "I couldn't—you must want to—"

"You first. Call your husband. Your daughter."

"Thank you." I swallow hard.

Adam's mobile is switched off, and I hang up and call the landline. I imagine Adam stirring, wondering who on earth is calling at this time of the night. I picture him stumbling downstairs, glancing through the open door of Sophia's bedroom to make sure it hasn't woken her.

*You've reached the Holbrook family. Sorry we're not here to—*I hang up. Press redial. Where are they? I did everything the hijackers wanted me to do. I did it for Sophia, to keep her safe. Where is she?

You've reached the Holbrook family. Sorry we're not here to take your call. Leave a message, and we'll get back to you as soon as we can.

"Adam? If you're there, pick up. Adam!" I told myself I wouldn't cry, but I'm powerless against the sob that rushes up and drowns my words. "The plane's been hijacked. They said they'd hurt Sophia if I didn't—oh God, Adam, if you're there, if nothing's happened, go somewhere safe, please. They say they're going to let the plane run out of fuel, and—" I'm speaking so fast, the words are tumbling over one another, and I jab at the phone to end the call, angry with myself for losing it.

Rowan puts a hand on my shoulder. "Breathe."

Behind Rowan, Alice is typing feverishly on her phone's keypad. I breathe. "Can I call back?"

"Of course."

...Leave a message, and we'll get back to you as soon as we can.

"Adam? If I don't make it, tell Sophia I love her. Tell her she's brave and beautiful and clever and that I'm in awe of her every single day. Tell her I did everything I could to keep her safe. I promised I'd never leave her, and I need her to know that I'm sorry. I'm sorry I broke my promise. She's going to do so much in her life, and although she won't be able to see me, I'll still be there, watching out for her. I love her so much. And—I love you too." I swallow, then speak louder, each word fiercer than the last. "But you won't need to tell her that. Because I'm coming home, Adam. I'm coming home."

I wait for a moment, imagining the answerphone playing in the empty kitchen. And then I hang up, and I take a deep breath. *I'm coming home.*

"Are you okay?"

I nod mutely at Rowan. How can I be okay? How can any of us be okay?

"What happens when the fuel runs out?" Derek says quietly. We're sitting in a tight circle—me, Cesca, Rowan, Derek, and Alice—squashed into the aisle between the seated passengers. Alice is still typing on her phone. Around us, snatches of farewell calls fill the air with fear and grief. I think of the six hijackers I've counted and wonder how many have yet to make themselves known. Derek is, if it's possible, even more disheveled than earlier, his shirt rumpled and his glasses at a slight angle, as though they've been knocked.

Cesca hesitates. "We'll crash," she says eventually.

"But what happens?" Derek persists. "How will it feel?"

I shiver.

"Don't." Alice screws her eyes shut.

"The engines will stop. One, then the other, within minutes—maybe seconds—of each other. The plane will become a glider."

"We won't just drop out of the sky, then?" Derek says.

Alice winces again. Her eyes are still fixed on her screen, fingers moving faster than I can follow. A memory surfaces, and my pulse quickens, the buzzing in my ears taking me back to training school, back in the hot, cramped cockpit of a Cessna 150. I let out a breath, counting to ten and digging my nails into the flesh of my palms until I'm back in control. Cesca's still talking.

"A Boeing 777 has a glide ratio of, I don't know…maybe seventeen to one? So for every seventeen thousand feet we travel, we'll lose around a thousand in altitude."

"How high are we?"

"Around thirty-five thousand," I say quietly. There's silence as we all try to do the math.

"It's not an exact science. The glide ratio's dependent on weather conditions, altitude, weight…" Cesca trails off.

"But eventually," Derek says. "Eventually, we'll crash."

He speaks matter-of-factly. As if he doesn't care. As if, I realize, he *wants it to happen*.

"At the moment," Cesca says, "the plane's still on autopilot. Anyone could be in that flight deck, and you wouldn't know the difference. But landings are different. The plane needs to be configured for landing or ditching—"

"Ditching?"

"Landing in the water," I say.

"—and the nose needs to be kept up for as long as possible. If we go into a death dive—" Cesca stops abruptly, her bottom lip caught between her teeth. "Well, that's going to be hard to come back from."

There's a long silence.

"People do survive plane crashes, though, don't they?" Alice looks at me, her fingers still poised above her keypad. "Those safety briefings you do, that we all ignore—that's what we'll have to do, right?" Her head nods furiously as though she's answering her own question.

"The ones in seats maybe," Derek says. Alice looks around the cabin, where the economy passengers all have their seat belts on. Several of them are leaning into one another, twisting as far as their restraints will allow, hands clasped above their heads. "The rest of us will be thrown around like rag dolls. We'll be dead before we hit the ground."

I glance up at the pregnant woman. Silent tears spill over her lower lashes.

Cesca glares at Derek. "Do you want to start a mass panic?"

"Alice has a point," I say. "Depending on how and where we land, we stand a chance of surviving this, but if we're not in seats, the injury potential is significantly higher."

"So we need seats." Alice's voice has gone up a notch. She kneels up, head swiveling like a meerkat on lookout. "I read somewhere the back of the plane is the safest place to be, so that's something."

"The plane's full," I say.

"But we paid more!" She looks at us all in turn, seemingly oblivious to our incredulous faces. "We paid more for our seats. So if they won't let us back into business class, it stands to reason that—"

"No." Rowan holds up a hand, palm raised toward Alice as though he can physically stop her from saying anything else. "Just stop." She glares at him, then resumes typing. I'm just wondering who she's saying goodbye to when she stops, stares at her screen for a moment, then presses a final key.

"There," she says with a long exhalation. "Filed."

Derek stares at her. "You have got to be kidding me." He looks at the rest of us, who aren't following. "She's written it up for the paper."

"Let's face it," Alice says. "You'd have done the same if you'd thought of it. I bet it's never been done before. A hostage's account of a hijacking while it's actually happening."

There's a stunned silence. I wonder how long it will be before Alice's article goes online. Might Adam read it?

"We could ask for the life jackets from business class," Derek says. "That would be something at least."

Cesca and I exchange glances but say nothing. We're a little over two hours from Sydney—well over northern Australia now. If we crash now, life jackets are going to be about as much use as a spoon in a knife fight.

"Sure," I say. There are already flashes of yellow in the seats around us. I see Alice eye up the life jacket nearest to her, worn by an ashen-faced teenager, and I picture the journalist ripping it off him, the cost of her ticket justification for increasing her own chances of survival.

"I'll go," Rowan says.

"No." Cesca and I speak at once, fueled by the same feelings of duty, responsibility.

"This is my job," I say simply, getting unsteadily to my feet, my hands raised in surrender. *And my fault.*

Slowly, I walk the few feet from the third row to where Ganges is standing. He's sweating profusely now, shifting his weight from one foot to the other.

"I'd like to get the life jackets from business class," I say.

"No one leaves this section of the plane."

"It will help keep the passengers calm." He wavers but shakes his head, clear in the instruction Missouri has given him. I change tack. "Who's at home, waiting for you? Are you married?"

"I live with my parents." He stops abruptly, as if he spoke by mistake. A muscle spasms by his left eye.

"They must be proud."

Angry red spots appear, high on Ganges's cheekbones. "They will be. They'll be proud that I'm standing up for what I believe in."

"By sentencing hundreds of people to death?"

"No one's going to die!"

"They already have." I think of Carmel, the life draining out of her in seconds. No one else, I think. No one else can die.

"That was—" Ganges flounders. "That was an accident. If you cooperate, no one will get hurt. The government will agree to our requests, and Amazon will land the plane safely."

"You'll go to prison."

"We'll have saved the planet."

I shake my head. "How old are you? Twenty-five? Twenty-eight? Your whole life ahead of you, and you've been brainwashed into throwing it all away."

"Climate change is the biggest—"

"—threat to the planet. I get it. But this isn't the answer."

"Then what is? Talking? Meetings? Words don't bring about change; action does. You can be part of the problem if you want, but I'm proud to be part of the solution."

"Sit down!"

It doesn't come from Ganges—breathing hard now, as if he's on the final furlong of a marathon—but from Missouri. She glares at me as I drop to the floor, then barks at Zambezi, "Stay with him."

Zambezi rolls her eyes but complies. Behind her, Missouri is striding toward the front of the plane. I peer between Ganges's and Zambezi's legs and see her knock on the flight-deck door.

It opens, and Missouri disappears.

What's happening in there?

The man flying the plane—the one calling himself Amazon—knows enough to be able to let Missouri in, but do either of them know how to override the emergency access?

"I hear you used to fly." Cesca has moved to sit next to me, mirroring my position.

I look at her sharply. "Who told you that?"

"One of the cabin crew, sometime in the autumn. I mentioned I was doing the London–Sydney, and he said he was rostered to do it too but had swapped. Said you were *mad for it*." She imitates Ryan's accent, a small smile on her face.

"Right." I relax a little. Ryan doesn't know the whole story, only that I started my training, then dropped out. Trust him to pass on even that tiny bit of gossip. "I had my first lesson in a Piper Warrior. A present from my parents. I cadged a few more in my late teens, mostly in Cessna 150s."

"He said you started commercial pilot training." Her expression is curious but not unkind, and I think about telling her everything. I wonder how I'd feel to admit everything after all these years. Confession given to a priest, as death waits in the shadows.

The choice is taken from me by the crackle that precedes an announcement from the flight deck.

"This is your pilot speaking."

It's a woman's voice. Missouri.

"Why is she flying the plane?" Cesca says.

I look up at Ganges, but the confusion on his face tells me he doesn't know. "Does she know how?"

"I don't know," he whispers. I picture him in his parents' house: his bedroom bearing the memories of school, teenage friendships, music played too loud. Next to him, Zambezi is looking across the plane to the opposite aisle, and I think, *Yes, I'm right. I had it right.* A plan is slowly taking shape.

Missouri's voice continues.

"I regret to inform you that the British government will not comply with our demands to impose fines on airlines unable to demonstrate their commitment toward renewable energy."

I spin around, exchange horrified looks with Cesca and the others. What does this mean?

We don't have to wait long to find out.

"We remain on course for Sydney," Missouri says. "There, we will show the government the true impact of their failure to act by flying into the iconic Sydney Opera House."

Ganges spins around to look at Zambezi, whose horrified face matches those of the other hijackers.

They didn't know. This wasn't part of the plan.

My stomach lurches.

A man in a window seat stands up, his phone in his hand. "They've scrambled fighter jets! It's all over Twitter."

"It's the Air Force!" someone shouts from across the cabin. "They've come to rescue us!" A cheer goes up—defiant, emboldened—and I exchange glances with Cesca, whose face is taut and pale. My stomach twists. With Missouri gone, people are dropping their arms, rubbing stiff muscles.

"What will the jets do?" Derek asks, his sharp eyes catching our concern.

"They could force us to divert to Brisbane," Cesca says. "Or they might escort us to Sydney airport and stay close till we land."

Rowan leans in, making a tight quadrant that leaves no room for Alice. "And if Missouri tries to make for the Opera House, like she says?"

"They won't let us get there." Cesca pauses. She drops her voice so only the four of us can hear, knowing that we need to keep the cabin calm, that what she's about to say isn't something the other passengers should hear.

"They'll shoot us down."

THIRTY-NINE

4 A.M. | ADAM

Mina's voice is beautiful. She speaks in the luxurious way that linguists often do, their words velvety with the knowledge of the path each phrase has taken. She considers English her first language, having lived here her whole life, but it is interchangeable with French—the language her parents spoke at home. She claims not to speak Arabic, although she can understand it, but every now and then, she'll slip in a word or two that *just doesn't translate* into English.

"Everything translates," I said. It was pre-Sophia. Pre-marriage.

"*Ishq*," she countered without a beat.

"What does that mean?"

"Love, only—"

"See—it does translate!"

"—it's so much more than that. *Ishq* is your greatest passion, your other half. The word for ivy comes from the same root. *Ishq* is a love so great, you cling to each other." She smiled at me. "*Ishq* is what we have."

Ishq, I think when I hear Mina's voice through the answerphone. Not confident now—not rich and velvety—but thin and scared, tears thickening her words and blurring them into one rapid, terrified note.

"Tell her she's brave and beautiful and clever and that I'm in awe of her every single day."

Her words play over a jarring bed of Mariah Carey. *All I want for Christmas is . . .*

"And—I love you too."

The knot in my chest twists tighter. There's never been anyone but

Mina. Girlfriends, yes, before I met her, but the moment I did, the memory of them melted so far away, I struggled to name them. I'd been waiting, that's all. Waiting for Mina.

Sophia lies on the floor, her head on my lap and my eyes fixed on the barely there flutter of a pulse in her neck. A gentle rasp accompanies each shallow breath, her face so swollen as to be unrecognizable. I want so badly to hold her, to trace her features, to cup her cheeks in my hands.

"Is she okay?"

Even through the coal chute, I can hear the panic in Becca's voice. I want to tell her, *No, she's not okay.* I want to let her think that she killed her, want her to go through just one-hundredth of the pain I went through, watching my daughter have an anaphylactic attack. Instead, I let the silence speak for me, my focus fixed on Sophia's closed eyes, on the weight of her body on my lap. The skin on my wrists is rubbed raw from my efforts to pull myself free, sweat and blood sticking dirt to my fingers.

"I thought you'd check." Becca's voice bounces off the metal-lined walls of the chute. "You normally check!"

Six feet below, I watch the drug take hold, and I send up a silent prayer as Sophia's body rejects the poison almost as swiftly as she ingested it. Light from the front of the house spills down the chute to puddle on the floor by my outstretched feet.

"It was practically pitch-black!" I yelled back. "We were starving. These are not normal circumstances!" My own voice bounces back at me. Sophia takes a sudden, huge breath, letting it out in a sob that tears my heart in two. I could have lost her. I might still lose her.

"I'm going to make sure you know what it's like to be locked up." My face is upturned toward the beam of light, and it's as though I'm shouting to the gods; gods who strike indiscriminately, who punish a child who's done nothing to deserve their wrath. "I'll pull every string I can to get you the maximum possible sentence."

"The planet is dying because of people like Mina."

"You're insane. Mina has nothing to do with climate—"

"She has everything to do with it! If all the pilots and cabin crew stopped work—"

"There would be others to take their place!"

"—the planes couldn't fly, and if the planes couldn't fly, the ice caps wouldn't melt. Don't you see? It isn't too late to redress the balance. That's what's so awful: we know the damage aviation is doing, yet we keep doing it. It's like being diagnosed with lung cancer but continuing to smoke!"

There's a quality to Becca's voice that scares me. It's the sort of tremor I've heard in street preachers or door-to-door fanatics. It's a fervor that tells me she really believes what she's saying. And if she really believes it, what else is she capable of?

"Don't *you* see that you're being manipulated? Whoever's pulling the strings isn't the one facing prison. They don't care about you; they've set you up to take the rap. You're cannon fodder, Becca, nothing more—a pawn in someone else's game. You've been brainwashed."

"You're wrong. You don't know what they're like."

"What who is like?"

For a second, I think she's going to give me a name, but she swallows the word. "Our leader."

Our leader, as if it's some kind of cult.

"Do you know what they do to people like you in prison? People who hurt children?"

I wait, long enough for the thought to take root. I think of the times I've sat across an interview table from muggers, murderers, rapists, and how—no matter how awful their crimes, how much I've been sickened by their actions—I have never before felt the way I feel now. Never before felt my muscles tense with the urge to fight, never before wanted to pin someone down and make them pay. Never before wanted to kill someone.

But then, never before has anyone threatened my daughter's life. My wife's. I try to imagine what's happening on board Flight 79, but all that fills my head is the image of a plane crashing into a building. It plays on a loop: fire and screaming and twisted metal.

"How can I go to prison," Becca says, "when no one even knows I exist?" There's a mocking tone to her voice that serves only to enrage me more, and I feel fresh blood trickle to my fingers as I wrench my wrists against metal.

"We'll find you. *I'll* find you."

"You don't even know my real name."

Sophia's breathing is more even now, and as she slips into sleep—exhausted by the anaphylaxis—I find a clarity previously clouded by fear that she might die. I switch off the hijack disaster movie playing in my head, and I remember who I am, what I'm good at.

"Your mother drives a red Mini Cooper with a pom-pom hanging from the rearview mirror."

The silence that follows turns my speculation into fact, the win giving me courage. I'd just clocked off when I saw Becca at Tesco. I'd promised Mina—promised myself—I'd go straight home, but the urge to gamble was too strong, and I found myself driving in the opposite direction, toward the hypermarket on the outskirts of the next town, where I was less likely to bump into someone I knew. I had a pocketful of loose change, and somehow that made it okay. What was a scratch card, really? Thousands of people bought scratch cards. I wouldn't log on to my online account, I wouldn't spend more than a tenner, wouldn't buy again if I lost the first time…

So many promises, so many deals with myself.

Was this how an alcoholic felt? I wondered. *It's okay if I have a beer—a beer's not vodka. It's okay if it's a half—a half's not a pint. It's okay if I'm with friends, if it's after five, if the day has a Y in it…*

I emptied my pocket on the counter, not meeting the cashier's eye in case he saw right through me, and I sat in my car, thirty miles from home, scratching the silver foil from seven worthless cards. *The first step is acknowledging you have a problem*, everyone says. Only no one tells you what the second step is.

If I'd gone straight home, I'd have missed her. But I sat in the car for a minute or two, fighting the sweat that prickled my skin, the guilt, the shame, the desire for more. I found a quid in the glove box, a bunch of twenty-pence pieces in the defunct ashtray, waiting for a parking meter. Cobbling together enough for two more cards, I got out of the car, hating myself but doing it anyway. I'd get different ones this time. The Match 3 Tripler ones. I'd judge the queues, try and get a different cashier. If I got the same one, I'd give a rueful smile. *The missus said I got the wrong ones*, I'd say. Let him think I was henpecked. Better that than the truth. I passed Becca on my way in. She was looking at her phone, walking toward a car parked in the disabled bay. The woman in the driver's seat had the same neat nose, the same curve in her top lip. Sister, I thought at first, then I clocked the gray roots above the blond, the lines around the mouth. I looked away, not wanting to get into conversation, not wanting to do anything but win something, anything, to justify my actions.

"What are you talking about?" Becca says now, but it's too late. Her pause told me everything. I close my eyes, put myself back in that covered walkway that runs from the store into the car park. Becca didn't see me—wasn't looking—and she walked right past me and into her mum's car. I wasn't concentrating—didn't care, only cared about the scratch cards, about how if I won a fiver on Match 3 Tripler, I'd only be four quid down—but a bit of me was still in work mode. A bit of me is always in work mode. I remember her hair was tied back—she'd worn it loose the couple of times she'd sat for us—and she had a zip-up hoodie with some kind of logo on the breast. Dark jeans.

No—not jeans. Trousers. Navy-blue trousers. What kind of teenager wears navy-blue trousers? Something slots into place. Becca calling Mina out of the blue; Mina being so grateful, she didn't question it.

She's a friend of Katya's—they used to work together. Apparently Katya told her we might be looking for someone to take care of Sophia after school.

"You work at Tesco," I say.

If I'm wrong, I've lost. No more upper hand, no more bargaining power.

She says nothing.

I'm right.

"So even if you've given them a false name and address, it'll be a simple matter for me to request the CCTV from the supermarket and get your mum's registration number. I expect you'll be on the electoral roll there, won't you?" I keep talking, faster and faster, gaining in confidence, falling back into the job I do day in, day out. "That'll give us your full name and date of birth. Oh, and of course, we'll have a record of when you've been in our property, so I'll get our broadband supplier to provide me with the details of all devices logged in at the relevant times."

It fits me like a second skin. Investigator. Father. The two halves of my self merging in the most awful way but in the most perfect way too. And in that second, I know that we'll get out of here, and I'll track down

Becca—whoever she really is—and I'll make her pay. Not with the fists that itch to be used but with the bread and butter of my working life.

The sound of running feet interrupts my thoughts.

"Becca?"

There's a sound from inside the house now. I see a flicker of shadow across the strip of light beneath the cellar door as she passes it—one way, then back again. I call her name, over and over, knowing I've pushed her too far but hoping it's not too late. The front door slams, feet running down the path. I hear the swing of the gate and the metallic clatter as it swings back into place, then the sound of trainers on tarmac growing fainter and fainter until they disappear altogether.

I listen for sounds within the house and hear only the house itself. The water pipes creaking; the gutters dripping as the snow melts; the low hum of the fridge.

Sophia stirs. She opens her eyes, still narrow from the swelling, and runs a tongue over her chapped lips. "Where's Becca?"

"She's gone."

I pull at my handcuffs. Becca's gone.

And nobody knows we're here.

FORTY

PASSENGER 1G

I would be lying if I said I wanted to die. It would be more accurate to say that I was prepared to. I hoped the politicians would see that they had no alternative but to agree to our demands, the ticking clock of the fuel gauge sufficient to concentrate their minds. But it seems that for our government, a few hundred lives are disposable. An embarrassment, perhaps, but soon surpassed by more pressing matters. Bad news buried.

As for the others, you must see that I couldn't have told them? They might have backed out or buckled midway through our preparations; they might have raised the alarm—unwittingly or otherwise—with tearful goodbyes to their loved ones. They might even have let something slip to a passenger, prompting the sort of knee-jerk reaction that might have caused us to crash-land in the ocean. Better for the passengers to believe there was a chance they could be saved.

—No one is going to die, *I told the others when I outlined our plans.* The government has to believe we'll allow the plane to run out of fuel so they take our demands seriously. The passengers have to believe they will die in order for us to maintain control. But of course, that isn't the plan!

It wasn't a lie, technically speaking. That wasn't the plan.

But nor was the one I gave them.

—Amazon will divert to a location deep in the Gibson Desert in Western Australia, *I told them,* where climate action comrades will be waiting with jeeps. We will evacuate the plane and disappear, leaving the passengers to be rescued. We will shed our assumed identities and escape undetected.

Had it been the real plan, it would have been torn to shreds. Escape detection? With half the Australian army deployed to surround us? But it wasn't the real plan. It was pure fantasy, mine to embellish with whatever I needed to allay the concerns of my ever-faithful followers. Every problem they threw my way, I caught deftly, knocking back an answer that shut down their line of questioning.

—We'll be climate heroes! Ganges posted. *Much virtual cheering followed.*

I doubt many of my disciples would have accompanied me in this mission had they known my true intentions. One or two, perhaps—the less mentally stable, the more fanatical environmentalists, but not the others. The others— Zambezi, certainly; Congo, for sure—were here for the new life they'd been promised.

I was fond of Congo. I found him during an open mic night at a comedy club organized in support of Greenpeace. The bar was busy and heckling was fierce, and by the time Congo had hauled his bulk onto the stage and got his breath back, he had already used two of his allotted five minutes. Laughter began to build. There was the inevitable chorus of, Who ate all the pies? *as our comedian of the moment finally took the mic from the stand.*

"Get a move on!" someone shouted.

His material was weak and his timing off, every joke punctuated by a wheezing cough. But he didn't give up. And when the slow clapping started, he didn't flush or stutter. Instead, he took a long, sweeping look around the room, dismissing them all with a loud, "Fuck you, you cunts. I could eat the lot of you and still have room for a kebab." It got the loudest laugh of the evening.

I followed him to the taxi rank, marveling at his ability to put one foot in front of the other—albeit painfully slowly—when each thigh wrestled for space and his ankles bulged above his trainers. He bought a burger from a kiosk and took it into an alleyway, where he demolished it in three bites, all the time wiping away the tears that glistened in the streetlamp's glow. I had never seen a man so miserable yet so brave.

His website showed nothing on the "upcoming events" page, but his blog was rich with material. He had become more guarded in recent years—perhaps when he began touting himself about as a stand-up—but his early posts were honest and raw, recounting a sorry tale of bullying and victimization. He was a staunch environmentalist—hence his appearance at the charity open mic night—and he wrote passionately about climate change.

—I saw your gig tonight, *I wrote.* You're funny.

I styled myself as a twenty-five-year-old blond from a town far enough away to be safe. Single. Interested. I modeled my interests around everything I'd found in his blog and expressed my delight when he found us to have so much in common. I introduced him to the group and encouraged him to play an active part in our plans.

—You're amazing. You're so brave. So clever. You're making such a difference.

He wanted to meet. Of course he did.

—Afterward, *I told him.* In Australia.

I had never used my real name online, borrowing for my activism work the identity of a student who committed suicide, many years ago, midway through the Michaelmas term. Sasha's family lived abroad, and as I boxed up belongings, it occurred to me that a spare birth certificate and passport might be useful. I had so far managed to avoid surrendering my fingerprints and DNA to the police, but as my political activism grew, so did the risk. Far better, I decided, for poor Sasha to retain any criminal record I might inadvertently pick up.

I adopted several online pseudonyms, providing each recruit with an appropriate mentor. In one guise, I, too, had lost a brother at the hands of the police. I shared a love of computer games in another. For Zambezi, I was the supportive friend; for Congo, the would-be lover. I slipped in and out of each persona, giving each what they needed, playing one off against the other.

I had my sock puppets argue with one another, had the majority round on an outlier, defending my own plans. Once, I staged an eviction, intimating to the others that loose lips had resulted in an unfortunate end for one individual. The compliance was instantaneous.

My recruits were no longer individuals but one homogenous mass, to be moved in whatever direction I pleased. But I knew their obedience could only be tested so far. A dog can drive his sheep for miles without losing a single one, but a fox will still scatter them in an instant. I couldn't tell them the truth, even though truth would make the headlines we all wanted.

Two thousand people were making their way to the Concert Hall at Sydney Opera House for a community choir service. For three months, more than fifty separate choirs had met in churches, offices, pubs, and houses to practice the same ten songs. I imagined the performers, coming together for the first time backstage, all dressed in black, the only identifiable difference the colored rosettes denoting their respective towns. I imagined the guests—the celebrities, the journalists, the "friends of the Opera House"—forgoing their cocktails in favor of this special treat.

Why the Opera House?

People.

A terrorist doesn't bomb an empty building, a shuttered shop, a closed-down factory. A gunman doesn't blaze through a school on the weekend, a shopping mall in the small hours of the morning. Hearts are won by people, not the buildings that house them, and those people must be the right people.

Do you think the burgled single mother on the sink estate gets the same response times as the toffs in the town house? Look at the coverage given to a missing child when she's pretty and white, then look at the ugly ones, the disabled ones, the brown ones, and tell me people care as much.

I needed to make them care. I needed politicians around the world to sit up and think, We have to do something about climate change. *I needed them to say:* More people will die if we don't radically change our approach. *It should have been enough that the* planet *was dying, but I had long understood that it wasn't.*

As the cockpit door closed, I said a prayer. Not to a god but to Mother Earth. I thanked her for her blessings, for continuing to provide for us, even as we abused the privilege and took more than we needed. I felt the plane quiver beneath me, as though it, too, was on my team.

Of course I was afraid. Wouldn't you have been? Haven't you been scared on a fairground ride, even though you stepped onto that ride of your own free will? I breathed through the fear; I embraced it. Instead of pain and panic and fear, I visualized the headlines and the summit meetings. I imagined the conversations that would be held around the world—conversations that would begin even as people lay in the rubble, their rosettes torn and tattered. Those people would change the world for future generations. They would be heroes.

The thought was inspiring. I allowed myself to focus more clearly on what needed to happen for my goal to be achieved. I thought of the "death dive" that would send us toward our target. I thought of the twisted metal, the shattered glass, the iconic sails of the Opera House turned to dust. The broken limbs, the staring eyes, the stillness. They took life from Earth, and Earth would take life back.

The symmetry was rather beautiful, don't you think?

FORTY-ONE

When Missouri finishes speaking and the PA goes silent, there's a beat like an indrawn breath. Then somebody screams.

The first scream triggers a second and a third, and now the plane shakes with the panic of 353 passengers faced with the certainty of death. Next to me, a man draws himself into a ball in his seat, his voice a high-pitched wail of fear. I turn around, see Cesca's horrified face. Rowan slumps against the seats, one hand gripping Derek's arm as the older man tries to shake him off.

Alice is tugging at the seat belt of a woman in an aisle seat, wild with desperation. "Get out! Get out!"

The woman grips her seat belt clasp, fending off Alice with wild swipes of her hand.

"My newspaper paid six thousand pounds for a seat!"

The woman's elbow finds its target, and Alice reels back, blood pouring from her nose. Cesca pulls Alice away, and I move to help, but she collapses against Cesca.

"I paid for a seat," she sobs.

"Everyone did." Cesca lets go of Alice, who falls onto the floor of the aisle, clutching the base of the seat as though her fingertips alone will stop her from being flung from the plane.

There is nothing we can do.

Had we been faced with a controlled landing in water or on unsuitable ground, I could have handled it. This is our bread and butter after all, even if we hope never to face it. Life jackets, emergency exits, slides... I could do it with my eyes shut.

But when Missouri flies us into the Sydney Opera House, there will be nothing I can do to protect the passengers on this flight from the impact of a 350-ton Boeing 777 hitting Australia's most celebrated building.

The pregnant woman has her hands over her bump, tears flowing from her closed eyes. Beyond her, in the other aisle, I see the Talbots in a tight embrace around their baby boy. I'm suddenly aware of how many children are on this flight, from barely walking toddlers to terrified teens. Missouri is ending lives that have barely begun.

"I was going to kill myself in Australia," Derek says suddenly.

The rest of us exchange glances. He carries on talking, fast, as if he's worried he won't have time, as if he just *has* to spill whatever's been eating away at him. "I don't have a commission for this gig, you know. I paid for my own ticket. My brother lives in Sydney, and I thought I'd book on the flight, then try to place a feature in one of the travel supplements. But they all said no, one after the other." His voice cracks, and Cesca squeezes his shoulder.

I know I should be offering similar comfort, but I can't work him out—can't reconcile this broken facade with the man I thought I caught a glimpse of. I take Finley's headphones from my pocket and start unpicking the knots, my fingers working out the tension in my head. Alice has stopped texting and is staring at Derek in horror, as though whatever he's got might be catching.

"I lost my job, last year. The editor said I'd lost my *edge*. Said my reporter's instinct wasn't sharp enough to keep up with the younger crowd. I tried to go freelance, but when I sent in ideas, everyone was already doing them in-house, or they didn't have a budget but did I want to write it up for the website? Someone suggested I start a blog." His laugh is hollow.

Rowan lands a fist bump of camaraderie on Derek's upper arm, but Derek ignores the gesture, pointedly turning away. Experience has made him bitter and untrusting, I realize, and I feel a sharp tug of solidarity toward him. Our reactions are shaped by the people around us, by the way they behave toward us. I think of Adam and of all the bitterness I've felt, and I feel it begin to peel away. I don't know if I can forgive, but I think I can forget.

If I'm given the chance.

"Tough times," Rowan says, a little uncertainly. He glances at me, and I give a tiny nod, trying to convey that I understand—that he's simply trying to help. I don't think anyone can help Derek now: he's determined to get out his story, to catalogue his descent to a place where life was no longer worth living.

Derek looks at Cesca. "I just felt…useless—you know? No, not just useless. *Pointless*."

Alice has gone back to her phone, bored by the story.

"I decided I'd take the flight anyway and visit my brother in Sydney, and then I'd lock myself in a hotel room with as much booze and pills as I could take, and that would be that. I was looking forward to it, in a funny sort of way."

"And now…" I don't finish, but he nods, a bitter smile at the corners of his mouth.

"Ironic, isn't it? I suppose it focuses the mind rather, being faced with death. Turns out I'm not so keen on the idea after all."

"None of us is," I say grimly. I stand, looking toward Ganges and Zambezi, raising my voice to make sure they hear. "You didn't know, did you? You didn't know she was planning this."

Ganges looks over his shoulder toward the flight deck, then across to Niger, who puts up his hands to fend off a passenger who has clambered out of his seat and down the aisle, still doing his job, despite this turn of events. They've been radicalized, I realize—so effectively that even now, they're reluctant to stop doing Missouri's bidding.

I see Paul Talbot put baby Lachlan in his wife's arms and urge her toward the vacant seat, but before she can move, Jason Poke leaps into it, belting himself in and assuming the brace position.

"We have to do something," I say, as much to myself as anyone else.

"Do what?" A passenger in the front row screams the question at me, his mouth twisted in fear. "There's nothing we can do!"

Ganges takes a step back, then forward again. He's not sure what to do, where to go now that his leader has gone. This is our chance, surely? I turn to Cesca and the others. "We need to get into the flight deck."

"But the explosives…" Rowan starts. "The second we get close, she'll…"
He clenches his fingers into a ball, then opens his fist in a sudden starburst.

"And if we don't," Derek says, "she'll crash into the Opera House."

The pregnant woman is listening. "Either way, we're fucked."

"If she triggers the bomb now…" I swallow, hardly able to put words to what I'm thinking "…it's just us. The plane will break up, and okay, there might be casualties on the ground, but there might not. Whereas if we let this happen, we *know* people are going to die."

"She's right." Cesca stands up. "There are thousands of innocent people heading for the Opera House right now. We can't let—"

"What about the innocent people on this plane?" comes the voice from across the cabin. There's a clamor of agreement, angry voices shouting across one another. Rowan looks at me, two lines deepening at the bridge of his nose.

"You think we should give up," I say.

He closes his eyes for a second, as though seeking strength from within. When he opens them, they're dark with despair. "No. I think we've already lost."

Farther back in the cabin, a woman in a pink top stands up, as though she's about to offer her seat to someone. I steel myself for more shouting, more arguing, but when I look more closely, I feel calmer: it's the doctor who responded to our call for assistance. She puts her hands on the back of the seat in front of her, like a preacher in the pulpit. I wonder how it feels to be unable to save someone's life. If it haunts her, or if she's seen enough death to be numb to it.

"All the talking!" Her face is creased in irritation, and the cabin falls silent. I remember how reluctant she was to speak to me, the flush on my face as I apologized for disturbing her. "Should we storm the flight deck; should we stay here…" The doctor's voice is whiny, a cruel mimic of our machinations. Unease darts through me. "Just do it. She's going to take us down anyway."

"Easy for you to say," Jamie Crawford shouts across the seats. "You didn't see the suicide vest she's wearing. It's rammed with explosives."

The doctor throws back her head and laughs. The sound is manic, and slowly the truth dawns on me. I've been reassured by the presence of a doctor on the plane. I thought how she'll help us save people, how she'll protect the injured and do her best with the dying.

"Have you any idea how hard it is to get explosives on to an aircraft?" she continues.

I look at my watch. Two hours until our scheduled arrival in Sydney. In the cabin, everyone's looking at the doctor, hoping for a plan, for something that will save us.

"It's fake, you idiots," she says. "We don't have explosives—it's just wire and plastic bags. There is no bomb."

We don't have explosives.

She's one of them.

There's no time to think about what that means—about who else might still be sitting among us, hiding the truth.

Missouri's bomb is a fake.

If we can get into the flight deck, we can overpower her, and Cesca can take us safely down.

We still have a chance.

I can still keep my promise to Sophia.

FORTY-TWO

5 A.M. | ADAM

I've fucked up. Again. Just when it didn't seem possible that things could get any worse, that I could do any more damage to my family—to myself—than I've already done, I fuck up even worse.

"Is Becca coming back?" Sophia's sitting up, her voice steadier now. She's far from her usual self, but who could be themselves, down here?

"No, pumpkin, I don't think she'll be back." *Shit, shit, shit.* I'm cursing myself for shooting my mouth off. I wanted to frighten Becca, sure. I wanted to show her she'd be easy to find so she'd come to her senses and let us out. And it felt good, that I was back on top of my game, doing my job, the way it felt before my head was full of debt and my failing marriage. I caught a glimpse of the old me, and I let my mouth run off, and now I've made it worse…far, far worse.

I wonder where she's run to. She might have a car, parked out of sight. She told us she didn't drive, but she told us a lot of things. I picture her getting home, letting herself into her parents' house, and creeping up the stairs. Lying on top of the covers, fully clothed, waiting for her pulse to subside.

Maybe she's not such a kid as I think. Maybe she doesn't live at home. Tesco could have been a holiday job, a temporary fix—a cover story even. I imagine her in her own place—some squalid room in a shared house—throwing meager possessions into a rucksack. Where will she go next? Where *do* these people go, these professional protestors? I remember reading about some corporate bigwig so incensed by the European referendum that he jacked it all in and moved down to London. Sold all his possessions, sofa-surfed with friends, and spent the next three years shouting into a megaphone outside the Houses of Parliament.

I don't understand it. I get that people feel passionate about certain causes, that they want to see justice done—I wouldn't be a police officer if I didn't care about putting things right. But these people dedicate their lives to their beliefs; they go to prison for them.

The hijackers on Mina's plane must know they're going to die. They're taking hundreds of people with them, and presumably they're okay with that—a small battle lost in the midst of a war. I can't imagine what I could ever feel so passionately about.

Yes, I can.

Sophia.

I would fight for Sophia. I *will* fight for her.

But how? I've pulled at my cuffs so hard, there's no skin left around my wrists, and the pipe on the wall isn't budging. If I could get myself free, I could break down the door at the top of the steps, it would be easy...

A news bulletin breaks into the playlist, and I feel Sophia tense, as I do the same. *Please*, I beg silently. *Don't let it be this way that she hears she's lost her mother.*

We've just this moment had an update on Flight 79. The Telegraph's *travel editor, Alice Davanti, has released a first-person exclusive of scenes inside the hijacked aircraft.*

I'm so flooded with relief that the plane hasn't crashed that I miss the first few words of Davanti's statement, my focus snapping back when I hear Mina's name.

"Mummy!"

...many people will condemn her for putting her own family's safety above the lives of the hundreds of passengers on Flight 79. As I write this, I am surrounded by parents, grandparents, children. The families of these passengers will no doubt struggle to understand why their loved ones' lives should be worth less than that of one woman's child.

The radio cuts back to the presenter, who promises *more on this very soon*, and Sophia struggles to sit up.

"Daddy, what's that woman saying about Mummy?"

Rage surges through my veins. I am not putting this on Sophia. I won't let her feel guilty; I won't let her think badly of her mother, when Mina did what any parent I know would have done.

"She's saying—" I stop, just long enough that what follows isn't swallowed by a sob. "She's saying Mummy loves you more than anything else in the whole world."

The sound of a car engine cuts through the night air. The farm track doesn't lead anywhere: no one comes down here unless they live here, and no one lives here except us, Mo, and the woman who comes a few weekends a year. Is the car hers? Why would she arrive at this hour? I've lost track of time, but it can't be far off dawn now.

For a second, I feel a rush of hope. Perhaps Becca had a change of heart. Maybe my words struck home and she realized the police would catch up with her sooner or later, so she—

Except that the engine I can hear isn't diesel, which means it's unlikely to be a police car.

Becca's parents? Or one of the other activists perhaps. If they've come to move us somewhere they think will be safer, we'll have a chance to escape. They'll have to release one of my hands to free the cuffs from the pipes. I need to be ready. I picture myself swinging at whoever comes—right hook, left hook, whichever is freed first—knocking them out cold and pulling Sophia up the steps, into the kitchen, through the hall, and out.

There are footsteps outside. Quiet ones. Careful, thoughtful. Pacing the width of the house. Peering into windows maybe, to make sure no one's in, that it's just us, locked in the cellar. No one to hear us scream.

Where will we go when we escape?

Becca used my car keys to get the EpiPen. If she dropped them back where they were, I can snatch them up as we run through the house, drive to the central police station—where I work—where teams operate around the clock.

But she could have put them anywhere. She might even still have them, stuffed in a pocket. Hunting for them could cost valuable time. Better to run. The back door, perhaps, where they won't be expecting. Over the fence and across the park, where we can't be followed in a car. Maybe that's the best way to go anyway: not waste time looking for keys. Just get out.

I start flexing the fingers on each hand. They've been held in this position for hours now, and I can hardly feel the tips of each one. I straighten, then curl each in turn, and slowly the numbness becomes the tingle of pins and needles. I roll my shoulders—backward, then forward—flex, then point my toes, pull my knees up to my chest.

"What are you doing, Daddy?"

"Exercising. Want to join me?"

Sophia shuffles her bottom so her back is against the wall. She puts her hands behind her back, into invisible cuffs, and together we lift our legs and tilt our heads from side to side. In her haste, Becca didn't replace the paving stone over the entrance to the coal chute, and I'm grateful for the light from the porch and for the breeze, despite the cold. The air down here feels stale and overused, and even though I know it couldn't have been airtight before, it still felt as though we could run out.

"Now we're going to make a sort of triangle, okay? Move your bottom forward, that's it, then straighten your legs and lift them up, and see if you can touch your toes. Keep your back straight—that's it." I form two sides of my triangle, while Sophia forms three, and my heart bursts with love for her. "That's brilliant. How long can you hold—"

We look at each other, startled, as the strains of the doorbell die away.

"Someone's at the door."

"I know, sweetheart."

"We need to answer it."

Why are they ringing the doorbell? Something doesn't feel right. If Becca's gone to the others for help—or even if she'd had a crisis of conscience—they'd know where we were. We're hardly likely to answer the door, are we?

Who is it?

The question is answered in the very next beat, with a thump on the door that reverberates through the house.

"Open up, Holbrook!"

Sophia looks at me, recognition of her surname lighting up her face. I shake my head in warning, whisper a *shhh*, while I figure out what's happening, although the lurch of my stomach has already told me.

The loan shark.

He hammers on the door. "I know you're in there. I can hear the radio."

"Daddy!" Sophia scrambles to her knees and shakes my shoulder. "Shout! Someone's here. They can rescue us!"

"Sweetheart, that man won't rescue us. He'll—" What? Leave us? Beat me up? Hurt Sophia? It's too horrific to imagine.

It started with text messages—*your payment is overdue*—then evolved to WhatsApp photos of my car, the house, Sophia's nursery. I tried my best to make the payments, but it was so hard when Mina didn't know—couldn't know—what I needed the money for.

"There's hardly anything in the joint account," she'd say. "Can you stick in a couple of hundred?" She'd do the same, and I'd sweat for a couple of days, pretending I'd forgotten whenever she asked, then taking out yet another credit card. I earned more than her. We'd worked out a system, in the beginning, when we took out our first mortgage, that meant each of us contributed the same proportion of our salary toward joint bills. *Aren't we grown-up?* we joked.

The first visit came six months after the WhatsApp photos started. I walked out of work, and as I turned toward the bus stop for the park and ride, I became aware of someone watching me. A man in a black bomber jacket, like a nightclub bouncer, raised a hand in something far from a wave. A warning. *I know where you work. I know you're a copper.*

You'd think sorting out trouble would be easy when you're a police officer. I know all the right people, all the right laws, right?

Wrong.

Debt—particularly the sort of debt I have, without contracts and credit checks—puts coppers at risk. It makes us ripe for corruption, vulnerable to approaches from the underworld. It makes us beholden to the very people we should be arresting. Getting myself in the shit isn't a disciplinary offense, but not telling the bosses about it is.

After that, they didn't hold back. I'd look in the rearview mirror and see one of them following me; I'd hear their footsteps as I walked through the alley to the bus stop. There were three of them—three that I saw anyway—and they never did anything, just raised a hand, then turned off. It was a message, that was all. *We know who you are, who your family is, where you live, where you work.*

It's not in a loan shark's interest for you to pay off your debt too fast. Far better for you to rack up the loan, every day another hundred quid, until there's no way you can pay it. And all the time, their scare tactics are paying off. Six months down the line, I would have done anything. Almost anything.

"I need you to do a little job for me," the voice down the phone had said.

"What sort of job?"

"One of my boys is up for something he never did. I need you to disappear the evidence." The voice was low and gruff. Was it the same man who gave me the money? Standing in a stairwell in the roughest part of the roughest estate? Could have been.

"I can't do that." Sweat trickled down my forehead.

That was the day they threatened Katya. They could have beaten me up, but instead they followed Katya and Sophia. They knew it would have more of an effect than a black eye or a broken nose.

"He said you owe him money," Katya said afterward, when she'd stopped crying and I'd finally convinced Sophia that the *bad men* had gone and wouldn't be back. "Lots of money."

"I do."

"Then how you know he not come back?"

"I don't."

She was too frightened to stay. I told Sophia it was nothing, told her not to tell Mummy because *she might be worried, and we don't want to worry her, do we?* and hated myself for doing it.

Three days later, the same man rang.

"I'm outside your house, Holbrook. You got my money?"

"I'm getting it. I told you." I was at work, in the CID office, waiting for someone's brief to tell them to go no comment.

"Getting it ain't got it."

He didn't answer. Instead, I heard the unmistakable sound of a lighter. The hiss of gas, the click of the flint. I snatched the keys to a pool car and ran, calling Mina again and again as I drove to the house. She didn't pick up.

When I got there, my heart pounding, the house was in darkness. I couldn't smell smoke, couldn't see the flicker of fire—had it been an empty threat?

The light went on in the bedroom window, and I called Mina's mobile again. I had to know she and Sophia were okay. She canceled the call, and I stood on the farm track, wondering if I should go back to work.

But what if the threat hadn't been empty?

She opened the door as I was walking up the path. No fire. Only Mina—suspicious, angry, unharmed—and a doormat soaked in petrol.

"Holbrook! If you're in there, open the fucking door." More hammering.

"Daddy," Sophia whispers now. "Is it the bad man again?"

"I think so."

"You were told midnight! Have you got it or not?"

Her face crumples, a tremor seizing her upper body. As long as I live, I will never forgive myself for putting her through this.

"I'll take that as a no, then," the man yells.

"We need to be quiet, sweetheart. He mustn't know we're in here."

She nods, and I ache to put my arms around her. These bloody handcuffs. Again and again, I pull against the pipes, glad of the blood, of the pain, because it's no less than I deserve.

The sound of an engine makes me stop. I look at Sophia. Was that it? Has he really given up so easily?

"I think he's leav—" I start, but something catches in my nostrils, an acrid smell that fills me with fear and makes me pull at my handcuffs again.

Smoke. I can smell smoke.

The house is on fire.

FORTY-THREE

2 HOURS FROM SYDNEY | MINA

The vest isn't real. It's not a bomb. The words in my head are echoed by the voices around me, as though the more it's repeated, the more we'll all believe it. *It's not a bomb. She's not wearing a bomb. The vest isn't real.*

Or is it?

How can we trust this woman, this pseudo doctor more likely to take a life than save it? How do we know this isn't part of the plan, designed to push us toward our own demise?

Sweat's running down the side of Ganges's face, soaking into his collar. He's breathing fast, rocking on the balls of his feet, but I'm not worried about him—he'll fall the second he's pushed. Behind him, in the entrance to the business-class cabin, Zambezi stands firm, and across the cabin, Niger waits, every muscle poised. He watches me, and I know he'll move the second we do, but I can stop that. I've planned for that. These people stand between me and my daughter as surely as if I could see her behind them, and nothing is going to stop me reaching her. Eleven years ago, I made a terrible mistake, and I've lived with it ever since. I shouldn't be here, but I am, and I have to make it count.

"What did she tell you?" I address my question to Ganges, the most likely to answer me.

"Just what we needed to know." His answer is slippery, like Adam's when he'd come home hours after his shift finished, telling me he went to see a mate, ran into traffic, had a problem with the car. I know what a lie looks like.

"Missouri told us the plane would be flown until the UK government gave into your demands or until we ran out of fuel. If that was the case, all of you would have known there was a chance you'd die, but that's not what your faces said just now. You never thought you'd die, did you?"

Ganges doesn't answer. His eyes dart from side to side, mouth working as though he's chewing gum. I wonder how many fighter jets there are, whether they all fire at once—the way firing squads do—or whether one person has to live with the knowledge that they've brought down a plane. I wonder what it'll feel like, whether it will be fast, whether it's better or worse than crashing into a building. I imagine the sky, spinning around me, the panic rising as the altitude drops down, only that isn't my imagination, it's a memory and—

I ground myself. *Stop this. Focus on now. On here.*

There are hundreds of passengers. Half a dozen hijackers. We can do this.

And yet.

Most of the passengers are still hunched in their seats, clinging to loved ones, frantically messaging everyone back home. Can I rely on them to rally when we need them? I think of Carmel, her life cut short in the cruelest way. Explosives aren't the only way to kill.

"She lied to us!" The shout comes from halfway down the cabin, where a vastly overweight man is getting to his feet. He fills the aisle, damp circles around his armpits and in dark crescents beneath the bulge of his chest. "She said the plan was a bluff. No one would get hurt."

"You stupid fucking gorilla!" Niger says. "No one's supposed to—"

"—tell them the plan?" The big man's tone is sarcastic. "Well, guess what, dick-brain? There is no fucking plan!"

"We have to trust Missouri." Niger looks around the cabin at his comrades. "We have to follow her. This is everything we've worked toward. Remember what we're fighting for!"

Zambezi is nodding feverishly, her gaze falling between the cabin, Niger, and the locked flight-deck door. The other hijackers are looking to Niger now, too, in the absence of Missouri, and I can feel us losing them. If they see Niger as a replacement leader, we'll lose any chance of getting back control of the plane.

We have to move. As soon as the authorities know what Missouri has planned, the fighter planes will be given the order to fire.

"Stay calm," Niger says. "Hold your positions."

"You're going to listen to him?" I say, turning to take in as many hijackers as I can see. "He's been lying to you."

"What the fuck are you—"

"He's been seeing her, behind all your backs." I point to Zambezi, who looks at Niger for help, her mouth working wordlessly. As soon as I saw him properly, I'd immediately remembered the two of them in the bar, the familiarity of the way she looped her thumb into his pocket. It had struck me as odd that two people who had clearly met before were traveling in separate cabins, and I'd wondered if perhaps my instincts were off the beam—if memories of early dates with Adam were coloring what I was seeing.

"None of us has met before," the big man says. He's shaking his head, insistent but confused. "I'm Congo. Did any of you know that?"

Ganges backs him up. "We're not allowed. Missouri doesn't—"

"Fuck Missouri!" The shout comes from the doctor, who's out of her seat and pushing past to get to the front of the cabin. "You piece of shit, Niger. You finished with me because you said it was jeopardizing the operation, and all the time, you were shagging *that*!"

"Lena—" begins Niger, but there's an outraged gasp from Zambezi, who leaves her post to stand next to him, and I turn and look at the others, because if there's ever going to be the right time, it's surely...

"Now!" I say, and I run, the sudden movement beside me telling me that Cesca, at least, is coming with me. Yangtze's blocking the flight-deck door, but Rowan and Derek are coming too, and they grip the younger man's shoulders and drag him out of the way. He's tall, but there's no substance to him, and he crashes to the floor even as he's throwing a punch, limbs splayed like a discarded mannequin. We have nothing to lose now, and the knowledge gives us all strength.

Cesca taps in the emergency code to the keypad on the flight-deck door.

I hold my breath. Under normal circumstances, the pilot would be looking at the cameras right now. At the first sign of anything amiss, they can override the access, but there's every chance Missouri won't know how to—

Click.

We're in.

The sun's coming up, a hint of gold tinting the clouds that swirl around us, endless and dizzying.

Here, let me show you...

If Lena was lying, this is where it ends. In the release of a trigger, in a sharp explosion. In fire and shrapnel and too many shards of bone and metal to ever be pieced back together. My chest feels tight, blood roaring in my ears so loudly, it drowns out the sound of the plane.

Here, let me show you...

I shake away the memory, but I still can't move. I'm transfixed by Mike's body on the floor and by the slumped body of the sharp-faced hijacker—Amazon—in the left-hand seat. Both men are dead. There's an angry ligature mark around Amazon's neck, and the same around Mike's, and I think how easy it is to bring a weapon on board a plane—an innocent piece of cord inside a drawstring bag or hooded top.

Missouri's in the right-hand seat, her hand on the yoke and a piece of black plastic hanging uselessly from her sleeve. Cesca and I move as one, but the flight deck is cramped, and Cesca steps on Mike's arm, flung out across the floor. She stumbles, crying out with the horror of it all, and I reach to pull her back—

Too late.

There's a terrible noise—a guttural, primeval scream. Cesca stands upright for a split second, blood pouring from a gash in the side of her head. Then she falls.

Missouri has the fire ax, taken from its clip beside her seat. Sharp enough to cut its way out of a wreckage, sharp enough to break a skull, to pierce a brain. She places the ax across her lap.

No.

I say it out loud, roaring it, shouting it for this time and the last time and for every time I should have said it.

Sun pierces through the glass, a rainbow carving the flight deck in two, separating the dead from the living. Everything slows until I'm aware of every breath, every movement, and as Missouri's hands touch the steering yoke, I reach into my pocket.

Here, let me show you...

No, I think. Let *me* show *you.*

Finley's headphones pull against Missouri's neck, the ends wrapped around my fists. Her hands claw at her neck, fighting for the wire, but I pull harder, dropping to the floor and bracing my legs against the back of the seat. I can smell the metallic tang of Cesca's blood, feel the tangle of limbs against mine, but still I keep pulling. I try to imagine Missouri's bulging eyes—her lolling tongue—only it isn't her I'm seeing, it's a man. Another pilot.

There's a sudden feeling of weightlessness as the wire snaps, and I fall back. I scramble to get up, pain in my arms from the force I've been using, but Missouri isn't moving. Have I killed her? Is it over? The space around me feels at once too small and too big, the clouds moving so much, it feels as though I'm the one who can't be still. I'm aware of Rowan and Derek moving around me, dragging Mike and Amazon outside. Sound comes back to me as if my ears have been blocked, everything taking on a clarity it's never had before, and I crouch by Cesca, who isn't moving. Derek hands me a cloth, and I press it to the wound on her head.

"Stay with us, Cesca," I whisper, hot tears stinging my eyes. We're so close now. So close. I look up to find Rowan standing there. "Upstairs," I tell him. "There are two more pilots." I give Rowan the code for the relief bunks.

Cesca's eyeballs flutter beneath closed lids, a network of tiny veins visible beneath the taut skin.

"Help me get her into the galley. There's a first aid kit in the big locker by the fridge."

We're half carrying, half dragging her out of the flight deck when there's a sudden bang, and the door to the bunks flies open. I choke back a sob of relief. We're going to be okay. I can get a message to Adam, to Sophia, and they'll know that I kept my promise. That I'm coming home.

Only it isn't Ben or Louis in the doorway.

Rowan looks between me and Derek, his mouth fighting to find the words.

"The two pilots," he says eventually, shaking his head as though he could deny his own truth. "They're dead."

Blood roars in my ears.

Ben and Louis are dead.

Cesca's unconscious.

We have control of the plane, but no one on board knows how to fly it.

FORTY-FOUR

6 A.M. | ADAM

The fire crackles above our heads, like footsteps on a carpet of dry leaves. Sweat slicks my palms, my back, my brow.

"Daddy?" Sophia looks at me with that mix of curiosity and wariness, and I shape my lips into something meant to reassure. There's a crash from somewhere inside the house. The hall stand? A picture? The hall is carpeted, thick drapes at the door to keep out the draft. Too many coats, heaped on too few hooks. Plenty to catch alight.

"Daddy, what's wrong?"

I've seen fires like this before. Fires fed by lighter fuel, with petrol cans, by grease-soaked rags. I've watched cars burn out till only the carcass is left, stark against the ground like the bones of a vast animal, the meat picked off by carrion. I've watched tower blocks burn stubbornly despite the hoses turned on them, and I've stood in the mortuary after an arson attack, my eyes fixed on the body of a child trapped on the top floor a minute too long. I don't need to see it to know what's happening.

I choose my words carefully. "I think there's a fire upstairs." *I think.* As though there's some doubt. *A fire.* Like the one in the sitting room, with its glowing metal coals, or our campfire pit, built for marshmallows. A little fire, that's all. Nothing to worry about. *Upstairs.* A whole staircase away.

I hear the insistent *beep beep beep* of the smoke alarm and think of Mina standing on a chair, wooden spoon in hand to reset the switch. *Burned the bloody toast again. At least we know they work.*

"We have to go!" Sophia tugs at my sleeve.

"Yes." The disconnect between my words and my thoughts is so great, it could be someone else speaking. I have to stay calm. I have to. For Sophia's sake, and because if I don't stay calm, how will we ever get out?

The fire will travel upstairs. Flames licking at the carpet, first one step, then the next, and the next. Chasing along the banister and around the doorframes. Splicing itself into pieces, each snaking into an empty room, only to swell and fill the space with searing heat that blackens the paintwork and sets the curtains ablaze. Dividing and conquering.

"Daddy!"

The crackle is a roar. The secondhand sofa, the cushions Mina piles on the floor to lean against when she's watching TV. Boxes of Lego, melting into one brightly colored mass. The kitchen table, the chairs, the family calendar with a column for each of us.

"Daddy!" Sophia grabs my face with both hands, and I jerk as though I've been slapped. We have to get out of here.

It won't be the fire that kills us but the smoke. Already I can see a wisp of it drifting beneath the door. Right now, it'll be rising to the ceiling; for a time, it will still be possible to crawl through the kitchen with your face low to the ground, but soon there will be more smoke than air, and that's when it will find its way into the cellar.

"I'm going to get you out," I tell her.

"What about you?"

"Then you'll get help, and they can come and get me out," I say it with more confidence than I feel.

Sophia takes a deep breath. "I'll knock on Aunty Mo's door. She'll call nine nine nine, and the fire engines will come and—"

"No," I cut in, trying to think of another option. I picture Sophia, banging on the door while Mo sleeps and our houses burn.

"Do you think it's too isolated?" Mina had said when the estate agent sent us the details of this place.

"It's peaceful," I'd replied. "No neighbors, but we can still walk to the pub."

Now, I look at my terrified daughter. "You know where the police station is, right?"

"No, I don't—"

There's a crash from upstairs. "You do!" Sophia flinches, and I say it again, softer this time. "You do, sweetheart. You know where it is. The bookshop, then the empty shop, then the estate agent where they sell the houses. The butcher's, then Sainsbury's…" I let the last syllable rise, passing the chorus to Sophia.

"Then the shoe shop, then the fruit and veg shop." She sounds uncertain, and I rush to reassure her.

"Good girl! And after that, the police station. There won't be anyone working there at this time of night, but outside the door is a yellow phone. All you need to do is pick it up—you don't even need to dial a number. Tell them there's a fire in your house. What's our address?"

"I—I don't know."

"You do." I make myself stay calm. I can taste the smoke now, bitter on my tongue. "Number two…"

"Farm Cottages."

"Good girl. What's the town?"

"Hardlington."

"Say the whole thing."

"Number two, Farm Cottages, Hardlington."

"And again."

She repeats it, more confidently now. If she panics, if she forgets, they'll send a police car to the station to make sure she's okay. And maybe they'll help her remember where she lives, and if they can't… My chest tightens. Well, at least one of us will be safe.

I want to go over the route with her again, but there's no time. I have to trust her. "Tell them your dad's trapped inside so they know to send someone quickly."

"I'll say you're a policeman," she says earnestly, and I smile, despite everything. "I'll say you're a real policeman and you have a number but it isn't on your uniform and it's eight three nine."

I look at my daughter, and I think of all the times I've listened to her reciting plane numbers, all the times she's talked me through Mina's routes and routines. I think of the petty jealousy I've felt each time. "You know my shoulder number."

"You're Detective Sergeant 839 and you work on CID and you used to drive a Vauxhall Astra with flashing lights but now you've got a blue car with no flashing lights, and it corners like a bloody tank."

"Sophia Holbrook, you never cease to amaze me." I take a deep breath. "Time to go, pumpkin. You know how you and Mummy play airplanes?"

She nods.

"And you can balance so brilliantly on Mummy's feet—like you're flying?"

Another nod.

"We're going to do some balancing now, and you're going to be really brave, okay?"

Her eyes are pools in the darkness, the light from the coal chute serving only to shadow her further. "I'm scared." She breathes in, bottom lip wobbling.

"Me too."

The coal chute is high—too high for Sophia to reach by standing on my shoulders while I'm seated, and with my hands fixed to the metal pipe, I can't stand up. I twist around instead, my back on the floor and my legs against the wall. I have a sudden, painful memory of Mina doing the same one evening after work. *My back's killing me.*

I shuffle back toward the wall till my shoulders are as close to the brick as I can get them, my feet as high as they can possibly reach while I'm still cuffed to the ground. "Ready to play airplanes?"

"Y-yes."

I bend my legs close to my chest, keeping the soles of my feet horizontal. "Can you kneel on my feet? That's it. Don't worry about hurting me."

She scrambles over me, squashing my face as she clambers onto my feet, Elephant clutched in one hand. Smoke catches at the back of my throat, and it's all I can do to stop myself from catapulting Sophia upward. "Ready? We're going to fly!"

Slowly, so she doesn't fall, I push my legs straight, my thigh muscles straining with the unaccustomed action. Sophia clutches at my feet, and as she leans to the side, I fight to keep her balanced. I lock my knees into place. "Can you stand up?" I can't see the entrance to the coal chute, but I know we're not high enough.

Not yet.

"It's all wobbly!"

"I need you to stand up, sweetheart. Please try."

For a second, I think she won't do it. Can't do it. I think it's all over, and I'll have to lower her down and we'll stay here—we'll die here—in this concrete tomb.

But I feel her move. Slowly. Carefully. One tiny foot pressed against mine. She gets her balance, then I feel the other foot on mine. My toes curl around her slippers as though that alone will stop her from falling.

"Can you see the tunnel?"

"It's right by my head."

Another big breath. "This is it, then, sweetheart. Time to crawl out and get help." It isn't a long chute. With her feet in the entrance, she can stretch up through the shaft and—

She's *five years old*.

What am I doing?

I have no choice. If she stays here, she'll die. Outside, it's freezing, snow on the ground, and Sophia is in pajamas and slippers. She's walked to school every day for a whole term, she knows every turn, every shop off by heart, but can she do it on her own? In the dark?

Even if she doesn't, she'll be away from the fire. Away from the smoke. She'll be safe.

I feel the sudden lightness on my feet as Sophia lifts first one, then the other leg into the chute, blocking off the light as she crawls out onto the grass. "Don't run!" I call after her. "You'll fall!"

Maybe she'll get help to me in time. Maybe she won't.

It's the biggest gamble of my life.

FORTY-FIVE

PASSENGER 1G

I cannot be confined. Arrested, interrogated, thrown in a police cell. I couldn't sit in the dock of a criminal court and hear my life's work torn apart. I couldn't let it end that way.

There would be no trial, no lawyers, no photograph in the paper for me. There would be no handcuffs, no arrest.

I had never believed in the existence of fate, but it seemed I was at the mercy of fortune. A different ending awaited me, and I embraced it.

I was ready.

FORTY-SIX

90 MINUTES FROM SYDNEY | MINA

"She's dead." Derek takes his fingers from Missouri's neck.

"Are you sure?"

He nods.

I killed her.

I feel a crushing sense of despair at the bloodshed, at the lengths to which we've been driven. Beneath it, keeping its distance, as though it knows it shouldn't be there, is an eerie calmness. For eleven years, I have carried my guilt rather than shouldered it, and now culpability slips over my shoulders like a second skin. *I killed her.* There is no disputing it.

This time.

Rowan and Derek drag Missouri from the first officer's seat with a thud and out of the flight deck. For a moment, I'm alone, the space simultaneously cavernous and claustrophobic. Sunlight paints the sky a thousand shades of gold, and it should be beautiful, it should be incredible.

Here, let me show you...

My body begins to shake, tremors juddering my joints and rattling my teeth. The vast array of instrument panels shrinks before my eyes, until all I can see is the artificial horizon and I'm remembering how I kept my eyes on that line till I couldn't bear it anymore, till I had to close them—

"Mina!"

I spin around, my mouth open in a cry that dies away when I realize it's Derek and Rowan. On the floor in the galley, I see Missouri's body, and I feel a wave of resentment that she won't face trial, won't spend the rest of her life in jail. Anger concentrates my mind. Panic is still rising, threatening to engulf me, but I can't let it win. I have to focus on what matters: on getting home.

"Someone needs to check on the relief crew." I think of the pilots' bunks above us—Ben's and Louis's lifeless bodies—and fear grips me as I imagine what lies in the crew's bunks at the other end of the plane.

"What are we going to do?" Derek's looking at me as though I have all the answers, when I don't have a single one.

"What's happening back there?"

"The economy crew is keeping the hijackers the other side of the bar, but I don't know how long they can hold them. Without Missouri, the rest don't know what to do. They're turning on one another."

"And Cesca?"

"Hanging on. Your colleague's with her. Erik, is it?" Rowan looks at the instruments in front of the pilots' seats. "Have you told anyone what's happened?"

I shake my head numbly. I haven't moved from this spot, my feet rooted to the floor.

"Erik's spoken to the rest of the crew," Derek says. "There's no one with any flying experience."

"They'll attempt a talk-down," I say. My voice is cracked, as though it hasn't been used. "Ground control will try to take us through each step, with the aim of getting us safely down."

"The *aim*?" Derek looks at me. I don't say anything. I don't know how many talk-downs have been attempted and how many have succeeded. I do know that staying in the air is the easy part; landing requires a skilled pilot.

Rowan squeezes past me, sliding into the right-hand seat. "Is this the radio?"

"You're not seriously going to try and fly this plane?" Derek says.

"Someone has to."

"Someone who knows what they're doing! Mina, you must know—"

Rowan turns to look at him. "Don't you think she's been through enough? It's not fair to put this on her as well."

"You can fly a plane, though, can't you?" He doesn't wait for an answer. "I heard you talking to Cesca. You trained to be a pilot."

"I *started* training! I was in the classroom for weeks and then... I've flown light aircraft, that's all, Cessnas, Pipers..."

"It can't be that different—"

"It's completely different!" I gesture at the switches that cover every surface of the flight deck, light-years away from the two dozen controls that sit on the small instrument panel in the cockpit of a light aircraft. Derek's frowning, his anxiety heaping pressure on me, because I know he's right. I know I need to get in that seat but...

Here, let me show you.

"She's having some kind of panic attack." I hear Rowan's voice, calm and reassuring. "Get her back into the cabin and sitting down. Make her eat something—she might have low blood sugar. I'll try and make sense of the radio."

She had a panic attack...

I remember walking away from the Cessna, my legs unsteady and my head numb, Vic Myerbridge's arm around me, strong and confident. *Don't beat yourself up, Mina. The trick is to get back on the horse as soon as possible. Don't let it get the better of you.*

I shake off Derek's arm. "I'll do it."

Rowan starts to speak. "I really don't think—"

"Let her. Out of all of us, she's the best placed to do it."

There's a loaded silence as the two men glare at each other before Rowan holds up his hands and gives in. He sends a warm smile my way, and as I clamber into the captain's seat, I hold on to the tiny ray of confidence it gives me, pushing my memories aside. Behind me, I can feel Derek's presence. He's not a big man, but the flight deck is small, and a band tightens across my chest.

"Can you stay in the galley?" I turn to him. "And close the door?"

He shoots a stony look toward Rowan but does as I ask, and immediately, I feel better without a presence over my shoulder. I think about Derek's suicidal confession, and I'm uneasy about his insistence that I take the helm. Does he want me to do it because he thinks I'm bound to fail? Because he *wants* me to fail?

My hands trembling, I put on a headset, grateful for the times I've brought coffee into the flight deck, catching the pilots' movements as they speak to control. This, at least, I can do.

"Mayday, mayday, mayday. This is World Airlines 79."

There's a brief pause after I'm connected, as though the operator is too stunned to speak. And then: "World Airlines 79, what's your situation?"

I let out a breath. The last time I piloted a plane, it set in motion a chain of events I'd do anything to have changed.

"The aircraft was hijacked. We have control of the flight deck again, but three of our pilots are dead, and the fourth is critically injured. We have no other technical staff on board. Repeat: we have no technical staff on board." My voice rises as I finish transmitting, and I swallow hard.

"You're doing great," Rowan whispers, but I'm breathless with fear, the band around my chest squeezing all rational thought from me.

"What's your name, World Airlines 79?"

"Mina. I'm cabin crew."

"Understood," she says. "Wait one, World Airlines 79."

The wait is an eternity. In the distance, I can just make out where land and sea meet, although the line is blurred with a golden haze. I can't see beneath or behind us. I think of the Air Force jets, scrambled to intercept, and sweat prickles the back of my neck. They don't know that I'm not one of the hijackers or sitting here under duress. For all they know, there's a hijacker right next to me, telling me what to say. One wrong move, and they'll take us down…

"World Airlines 79, this is Brisbane Center." The new voice is male, the headset pouring it into my ears as though he were right next to me. I start to tremble, and I slide my hands under my thighs to keep them still. "Mina, my name's Charlie. I'm a triple seven pilot, and I'm going to help you get safely down."

I blink back the tears. "Okay."

"First things first. I want you to tell me how much fuel we have. See the two glass screens in front of you—right in the middle?"

I scan the vast instrument panel, a sea of levers and knobs and screens. *Here, let me show you…*

"Mina?"

"Y-yes."

"On the top to the right, you'll see a bunch of around eight buttons. Right in the middle, you'll see one marked FUEL."

Rowan reaches toward the button just as I see it and looks at me inquiringly.

"Push it," Charlie says. I nod to Rowan. "Now read out the figure on the bottom of the two screens." I do what he says, the figures meaningless to me, and there's a silence long enough for me to think I've lost him.

"Okay," he says at last. "We're good for a couple of hours."

"Is that enough?" I exchange panicked glances with Rowan, who's looking at his watch.

"Next up is really important, Mina. Around your right knee, you'll find a dial marked *autobrake*. Once we're on the ground, that's going to stop the plane. Can you see it?"

I remember calling Adam at work once, when I needed to cut the grass and couldn't for the life of me work out how the new mower worked. *I can't see it*, I kept saying, and he'd patiently go back to the beginning and talk me through it again. Charlie's using the same voice: slow and clear, patient but not patronizing.

"I see it." I realize that Charlie didn't answer my question about the fuel level.

"Push it in, then turn it to three. Tell me when it's done."

"Done."

"Great job. Now, we've got some time before we start our descent, so I'll give you a tour of the instruments you're going to be needing. Things are going to get a little busy later." He tells me how to extend the flaps and change the speed and where the lever is for the landing gear. Each time, I reach out and touch the relevant control, trying to commit it to memory. It's so different from a light aircraft, like learning to ride a motorbike, then getting in a car. I look at Rowan, who nods, silently noting the location of the switches.

I look through the window, but my head starts to spin, and I shut my eyes to quell the feelings of nausea it prompts.

"Are you okay?" Rowan asks.

I nod, although it couldn't be further from the truth.

"Shall I take over?"

"It's okay."

He touches my arm. "Your daughter will be okay. I'm sure of it."

"You don't know that!" A painful sob erupts through the words, everything I've been trying to keep at bay forcing its way to the surface. I've been trying hard to keep Sophia and Adam out of my head, to concentrate on getting us down safely. I can't think about how much I love them—how much I need them—until I know for certain we're coming out of this alive.

"I'm sorry, I—"

"Please! Just—" I squeeze my eyes shut, pressing my fingertips to my head as though they have the power to change what's inside. Rowan falls silent. I let out a slow, juddering breath, then press the button to speak to air traffic control. "World 79."

"Go ahead, Mina."

"We're going to need an ambulance the second we land. One of our pilots is in a bad way."

"Ambulance, fire, police, military—you're getting the full cavalry, Mina."

"We have a number of fatalities on board as well. Two hijackers, one passenger, and four staff."

Only the briefest of pauses indicates the implications of my transmission have hit home. "Copy that."

"Charlie?"

"Go ahead, Mina."

I swallow. "The hijackers made threats against my family."

I leave the sentence hanging, waiting for Charlie to jump in, to tell me that he knows all about it, that Adam and Sophia are safe, have been safe since the moment I did as I was told. Waiting to hear I did the right thing.

"If I didn't comply with their demands," I say, when it's clear Charlie needs me to finish, "they said my daughter would be hurt. I need—I need—"

I let go of the radio button, pressing my head into the back of my seat and squeezing shut my eyes, my chest burning with the tears I'm holding back.

"You need to know she's okay." He can't see my nod, and a second later, he speaks again. "We'll get on it." I let out a breath. "Right now, I need you to change frequencies. I'm going to send you over to Approach—"

"Please don't leave!"

Hysteria laces my words, but Charlie doesn't waver. "You don't get rid of me that easily. I'm walking from one desk to another, that's all, and when you hear my voice again, I'll be able to see you on close radar."

The promise is reassuring, and I follow his instructions to change the channel, but nevertheless, it's the longest thirty seconds of my life—as though I've been cut loose from my moorings and am drifting out to sea.

"Ready to start our descent?"

Relief makes me smile. "Ready."

He talks me through each step, and we drop first to twenty-five thousand feet, then to fifteen thousand. Charlie guides me to a button marked IAS MACH, and I drop our speed to two hundred and fifty knots. I manage to keep my breathing steady, but I can't look outside, and each time Rowan moves or Charlie breaks the silence, my pulse gallops.

The flight deck smells of coffee and cleaning products, of sweat and plastic-coated seats. My vision blurs, black spots around the edges, and my head spins.

Eleven years since it happened.

"What do you mean, you're dropping out?" My father was angry, my mother confused. "You've got top marks in all your ground training. You scored top of the class in your last set of tests."

"I just don't want to do it anymore."

I said I'd pay them back, but even if I were to manage it, the house they sold to pay for my training was long gone.

I hated myself for giving up. Giving in. I tell myself being cabin crew is the next best thing, but it's more penance than consolation prize. A constant reminder of the choice I made.

"Mina?" Charlie's voice in my ear, Rowan tugging at my sleeve. They're talking at me, these two men, but I can't hear the words. The instruments blur into a mass of brown and gray, and the voices belong to another time, another man.

Vic Myerbridge.

I met him in the White Hart. Nice enough, but not my type. Old enough to be my father, for a start, and possessed of a confidence that tipped too often into arrogance. But we talked about flying, and he made me laugh, and it was a pleasant way to spend the evening after a friend had bailed on me.

"I'll walk you back to your block," he said. The bar was close to the training school—technically public, but pretty much entirely populated by student pilots or qualified ones who paid to keep their own aircraft on site, and I guessed he fitted into the latter category, although he hadn't said.

"Not going to invite me in?" he said when we got to my room.

I laughed. Why did I laugh? I felt awkward, I suppose. "It's a bit late. Thanks for a nice evening."

He tried to kiss me, and I stopped laughing. Brought my knee up, hard, and then he wasn't laughing either. I shut my door and locked it, poured myself a stiff drink, and vowed to avoid the pub for a few days until he'd moved on.

Two weeks later, we were assigned the instructors for our first dual flights.

He didn't say anything. Not when we were introduced, not when we shook hands. Not when we walked out to where the Cessnas were lined up waiting. Not during the checks or when we were taxiing out. He had forgotten, perhaps, or not recognized me—or perhaps he was mortified by his behavior and thought it best to move on.

At nine thousand feet, he told me to concentrate more on how the plane reacted to my controls, to *feel* its response.

"Every action has a reaction. Here, let me show you." He reached across and put his hand on my breast.

I froze.

He circled my nipple, then pinched it hard between thumb and finger. "Feel the response?" His voice came through my headset, so close to my ear, I thought I could feel the dampness of his breath.

"No."

"I think you can." He tweaked my nipple again, as if its hardened state were evidence of my lie. My hands shook on the yoke and, at that moment, crashing seemed the better of my options. When he moved his hand to between my legs, I told myself it was happening to someone else. The cockpit of a Cessna 150 is a little under three feet wide, the two seats pressed close against each other. From your seat, you can reach out and touch both sides of the cabin, the front, the back, the ceiling. There is nowhere to go. I kept my eyes fixed on the artificial horizon until I couldn't see through my tears, then I closed my eyes and let him take control.

"Mina?" Rowan shakes my shoulder.

I find my voice, eleven years too late. "Get off!"

He jerks back, confused, and even though I know it's not him, I know, too, that I can't be in the flight deck with Rowan—with anyone—if I'm going to bring this plane down safely.

"You have to get out," I tell him.

"Mina, calm down."

"Don't tell me to calm down!" I rip off my headset. Rowan reaches for me, but I throw off his hands because it isn't helping. Blood roars in my ears, and the flight deck isn't the triple seven anymore but the tight confines of a Cessna, and Rowan isn't Rowan, but—"Get out! Get out! Get out!" I swipe at him wildly, not stopping until he pushes his seat back, his arms raised against my fists, all the time telling me to *stay calm, it's okay, everything's okay.*

It is not okay.

Everything is not okay.

It isn't okay until Rowan is gone, and the flight-deck door closes, and I'm finally alone. But no sooner does the roaring in my head subside than something else takes its place. An alarm—the *whomp whomp whomp* of a warning siren and lights flashing from the instrument panel.

Panic grips me once again as I read the message on the screen.

We're no longer on autopilot.

FORTY-SEVEN

Don't run, you'll fall.

Past the park, up the hill. Wait for the green man, not yet, not yet...

Now!

Cat in the window. Like a statue. Just the tiniest tip of his tail moving. Twitch, twitch, twitch.

Another road to cross. No green man, and no lollipop lady—she should be here...

Look both ways. Not yet, not yet....

Now!

Don't run, you'll fall.

Postbox, then lamppost, then bus stop, then bench.

Big school—not my school, not yet.

Bookshop, then empty shop, then the 'state agent where they sell houses.

Now the butcher's shop, birds hanging from their necks in the window. My eyes squeezed shut so I don't have to see theirs staring back.

Dead. All dead.

There's dead on the plane—the man on the radio said. Daddy talked so I wouldn't hear, but I did hear. I did. And now the birds are looking—I sneaked a look, and they're staring at me, staring as I get near, and I don't care what Mummy says I have to shut my eyes and I have to run as fast as I can because of the birds and the bad people and Daddy in the ground and—

Smack!

Hit.

Hard and hot and stinging. Tears on my face. Blood in the snow.

The 'state agent, then the butcher, then...then... Then where?

It's all different. Dark and covered in snow and shadows in shop doors I don't want to pass. They're still staring at me, the birds with their black bead eyes like ink poured in their heads. There are dead rabbits in there too—I've seen them. And the three little pigs' feet. All of them watching from the shop. Waiting for me.

Snow on my slippers. Snow on me, on my dressing gown, on my pajamas. So cold, so so cold.

Where now?

FORTY-EIGHT

30 MINUTES FROM SYDNEY | MINA

The plane starts to bank, the siren as loud and insistent as the panic in my head that tells me this is it—this is the end. I can't breathe, a sudden, overwhelming claustrophobia made worse by the endless sky taunting me through the windows.

Whomp whomp whomp. It goes on and on, drilling into a head already full. Eleven years of bitterness, of anger, of the raw sense of failure that followed me home from training school and never left. If only I hadn't swapped flights with Ryan, if only I hadn't gone back to work after Sophia arrived, if only I hadn't frozen that day eleven years ago. If I'd trusted myself, trusted my instincts. If I'd made a complaint, stood my ground. If only. This wouldn't be happening.

Whomp whomp whomp. There must be a hundred switches in front of me, their unfathomable names etched in tiny white letters. FLIGHT DETENT. STAB TRIM. VERT SPD. F/D ON. One of them is the autopilot— but which one? I try to make myself look systematically, one row at a time, but my eyes dart around, losing my place. I can't see it. It's not there.

I pull on the headset. "Charlie!" There's no time to waste on call signs and radio etiquette, and the siren's loud enough to speak for me.

"I hear you, Mina—that's the autopilot." He could be telling me the kettle's boiled, his voice is so calm. "Look at the top strip of instruments, right below the glare shield."

"Charlie, we're dropping." In front of me is a large screen that shows an artificial horizon. Slowly, the plane is dipping to the left; the altitude readout on the right-hand side is dropping steadily. *Nine thousand eight hundred, nine thousand seven hundred...* Sydney stretches out beneath the sunrise.

"To the right of the top panel—"

Nine thousand six hundred.

"VERT SPD, V/S, HOLD." I read the litany of white letters, all the time waiting for the plane to tip headlong into a dive we'll never come out of. "A/P ENGAGE?"

Nine thousand five hundred.

"A/P ENGAGE. There are three buttons—you want the left one. L CMD. Press it."

I press it. Instantly, the siren stops, the warning lights extinguished. I still don't trust myself to breathe.

"Are you okay, Mina?"

"I—I think so." My hands are shaking. "I don't know what I did, Charlie."

"It's okay."

"I had a panic attack. I didn't mean to turn it off. I didn't think—" I let go of the transmitter, my words as confused as my thoughts. I don't remember what I touched, only that I had to be on my own, had to get Rowan out of the flight deck.

"Hey, it's over. It's all okay now."

After I left training school, I'd continued to look at their website, continued to google for snippets of news from the small private airport from which they operated. It was how I learned that a pilot had lost control of their light aircraft. A member of the public saw the plane come down, but by the time the emergency services were on scene, the fire had taken hold. There were no survivors.

The instructor was Vic Myerbridge. His student was a new female pilot. Cass Williams.

When recordings of the plane's transmissions were played at the inquest, it became evident that there had been some kind of a struggle, and although the coroner recorded death by misadventure, it was enough for the school to quietly remove the glowing obituary they had posted on their website.

In the months that followed, I was haunted by the knowledge that by doing nothing, I had at once saved my own life and caused Cass to lose hers. I had been spared, but I had none of the euphoria that should accompany a near miss: instead, I was held hostage by the weight of my guilt. Even without fighting back—without putting my own life on the line—I could have told someone. There would have been an investigation, Myerbridge would have been suspended; Cass would never even have been in that plane with him.

Instead, I allowed him to put his arm around me, to walk me off the airfield as if I were an invalid. I allowed him to talk over my head, to tell people I'd *had some kind of panic attack*. I allowed him to make me doubt my own memory.

I never told Adam. I couldn't bear to see the judgment in his eyes. My own was more than enough to bear.

"Mina," Charlie calls up. "We're ready to start our approach."

I think of the passengers back there in the cabin—the pregnant woman FaceTiming her husband; Lachlan and his parents; Lady Barrow; poor Ginny and her reluctant fiancé. My finger hovers above the controls for the PA, knowing I need to tell the passengers something but not trusting myself to give them the reassurance they need.

I press the button and fight to keep my voice steady. "This is your pilot speaking." Let the passengers think I have everything under control; let them at least *believe* we'll get down safely. "We will shortly be starting our final descent to Sydney, so please return your seats to the upright position and fasten your seat belts." The familiarity of the patter calms me, and when I replace the handset, I look out at the vast sky ahead of me. I can do this. I think of the desperate phone calls I heard in the cabin—of the promises, the confessions, the declarations—and I know that I owe it to them to get us safely down. I owe it to Sophia, who I promised would never again be without a mother. I owe it to Cass Williams, who wouldn't have died if I'd only had the strength to fight back.

I owe it to myself. I have to prove to myself that I can fly.

Charlie's upward inflection fills my headset. "Mina, can you take us down to five thousand feet?"

My mind is momentarily blank, then I remember the ALT button, and I drop our altitude and then our speed. "Okay—done."

"Look for a knob marked HDG. We're going to use that to turn."

I see it before he's finished speaking—below the glare shield, left of the autopilot button—and I turn it a hundred and eighty degrees before pressing the button, as instructed. Almost immediately, the plane begins to turn.

"Good job, Mina. Remember I told you where the flap lever was?" I reach across for it. "Lift it up, then move it down one slot." There's a grinding noise and a thud as the flaps find their place, noises I would normally find reassuring. I picture where I'd be, had this flight gone to plan: walking through the cabin, checking seat positions, tray tables. Looking forward to my hotel room, to a walk around Sydney. Now all I want is to be safely on the ground.

"Four thousand feet."

I do as Charlie says, repeating the instructions in confirmation. *Heading zero-seven-zero. Three thousand feet. Flaps. Heading zero-three-zero.* With each new heading, the plane makes a farther turn, until I can see the airport ahead of us.

"Look for a button marked APP," Charlie says. "That's our approach button. It'll capture the localizer and the glide slope, which will take us safely down on an autoland."

It takes me a while to find it—just below the autopilot button—and as I'm pressing it, Charlie's already on the next instruction: to lower the landing gear. The handle's in the middle position, and I pull it out and then down, the rush of air making a long rumbling sound.

"Mina, did you press the APP button? Is the bar beneath it lit up?"

I look at the panel. Nothing's lit up.

"I pressed it, but…"

"You've missed the intercept. We'll need to go around again. How much fuel do we have left?" I find the right button and read out the figure from the bottom screen. I picture Charlie, sitting at a computer in Brisbane, watching an LED light move slowly across the screen. There's a long pause, and when he speaks again, the calm in his voice sounds forced. "Okay, Mina. Let's try that again."

"Do we have enough fuel?"

A beat. I close my eyes. Think of Sophia and Adam. Charlie hasn't told me if they're okay, and I don't know if it's because he doesn't know or because he knows they're not.

"It's tight, Mina. I'm not going to lie."

I take a deep breath. It has to be enough. We can't get this close only to fail.

"Heading zero-nine-zero."

"Zero-nine-zero," I repeat once I've made the turn. We're flying at three thousand feet, the air clear below us. The ocean is navy blue, tiny, white horses galloping across the waves. It seems impossible that we only set off from London yesterday; so much has happened in twenty hours. My tiredness feels as solid as me, a greatcoat draped around my shoulders, weighing me down, my alertness a sham fueled by fear, like the temporary burst of energy after coffee.

"One-eight-zero."

"One-eight-zero."

"Three-one-zero."

I make the final heading, and the plane's nose moves slowly toward the airport. I am not flying this plane but guiding it, and I wonder at the feat of engineering that allows us to maneuver several hundred tons of metal through the air, from one country to another.

"Now press the APP button."

I press it firmly, releasing it only when I see the horizontal bar light up beneath my finger. In a few moments, I feel the plane turn and line up with the runway as we finally capture the localizer. I breathe.

"Flaps all the way out now, Mina."

As Charlie gives me our final speed, the plane goes nose-down, the top of a glide slope that will take us to the runway. I sit on my hands, knowing that the slightest jolt of an instrument will switch off the ILS.

Parallel runways protrude into Botany Bay like a two-tined fork, and as we descend, I see that the left has been cleared of aircraft, the planes grounded on the adjacent runway. A bank of emergency vehicles waits to one side.

The automated countdown begins. *Fifty, forty, thirty…*

I've never been a religious person, despite my mother's entreaties to join her for Mass every Sunday. But as the runway rushes up to meet us, bright-blue ocean either side, I keep my eyes on the center line, and I pray.

FORTY-NINE

7 A.M. | ADAM

How long has it been?

I tried to keep track of the minutes by counting the seconds, but every crash from above made me lose track, and it feels as though Sophia has been gone for hours. The electrics have tripped, the strip of fluorescent light beneath the door flickering twice and then disappearing, the radio cutting out, midway through more breaking news.

As Flight 79 approaches Sydney, air traffic control operators have made contact with members of the crew. It has not been confirmed whether the aircraft remains under the control of the hijackers. Emergency services are on standby at Sydney airport.

The cellar is pitch-black, the darkness dense and oppressive. I can't see the smoke, but I can feel it. I can taste it. It catches at the back of my throat, making me cough until I retch, the convulsions jerking my wrists against their metal cuffs. I can no longer feel my hands or feet—a combination of pins and needles and the cold—and my head feels heavy, the way it did after Becca drugged me, although I don't know if that's the smoke or just exhaustion.

Sophia must be in town by now. I recite her journey, second-guessing where she's gotten to. *Bookshop, then empty shop, then the 'state agent where they sell houses.* I picture her outside the police station, breathless from running, above her, the blue glass lamp that's been there since Victorian times. The old cells are filled with lockers now, and the station's only staffed three days a week, but the yellow phone outside goes straight to the control room, and all she has to do is lift the receiver…

Come on, come on!

There's another crash from upstairs. The staircase? The first floor? I think of Mo next door, still fast asleep, unable to hear anything until it's too late. The postman comes around eight, but there's no light coming through the coal chute now the porch light has gone, so it must still be early.

It's all on Sophia, and there's so much that could go wrong. Even if she remembers the way, there are roads to cross and well-meaning strangers—let alone predators. What if she can't reach the phone or it's out of order? I picture my brave, beautiful daughter, in her Action Man pajamas and her unicorn dressing gown, her slippers wet with snow, and I let my tears fall.

At first, I think I'm imagining the sound of sirens.

They fade in and then out again just as quickly, and I close my eyes and listen so hard, I think I'm hearing it only because I want it so badly. But there it is again: the shrill pitch of a fire engine, and alongside it, the rhythmic peal of a police car. There's another crash from above me, but the sirens are building and building, and now I can't hear the roar of the fire anymore, only the sound of help.

Sophia must have told them exactly where I am, because there's a burst of torchlight through the coal chute, falling like a spotlight just beyond my feet.

"In here!" I try to shout, but my throat won't comply, acrid smoke making me choke. The coal chute's too small for an adult to use, and I feel panic rising inside me. What if they can't get me out? The creaking and cracking I've heard, the crashes from above…is the house collapsing? I imagine being buried beneath piles of rubble, no way out as long as I'm chained to the wall.

"Adam? Hang on in there, mate. We're coming."

There's a flicker of light near the top of the cellar steps. I pull my knees up and bury my head as an almighty crash echoes through the house, sending dust and debris across the cellar. I feel a hand on my shoulder, another lifting my head up and slipping something over it. Suddenly the air is cleaner—the breath doesn't catch in my throat—and my eyes stop stinging. There are two firefighters in the cellar. One of them gives me a thumbs-up, and I nod a response, then she gestures for me to bend forward. The other is already looking at the cuffs, and I bend as low as I can, shuffling away from the wall to give them some space. There's a spray of sparks and a sudden grinding noise, and I brace myself for a slip, but instead there's a jolt, and I fall suddenly forward, finally free.

They've cut the pipe, not the cuffs, and I stumble as I try to get up, unbalanced with my arms behind my back. My ankles buckle beneath me, stiff from inactivity. Just as I'm wondering how I'm going to walk, let alone run, I'm pulled unceremoniously from both ends and lifted onto a stretcher, straps pulled tight across my chest and legs.

They pull me up the stairs—the wheels at the base of the stretcher bumping up each step—and through the wreckage of the cellar door. I catch a glimpse of the kitchen before we're into the hall, flames licking at the wallpaper that runs up the stairs, and water—water everywhere—then we're out. Blue lights flash from every direction as I'm dragged through the snow, a paramedic running by my side. Even as he's pulling off my smoke hood, I'm shouting, "Sophia—where's Sophia?" but no one's listening.

"One, two, *three*." There's a jolt and a sliding sensation as they put me in an ambulance.

"I need to see my daughter."

"He's got handcuffs on—look like police ones. Can you get someone over here with a key?"

They talk over me, and a wave of exhaustion engulfs me as I shut my eyes and let them do their job. I feel my head being lifted and an oxygen mask placed over my face, then I'm turned to the side as the paramedic examines my bleeding wrists.

"You wanted a handcuff key?" A woman's voice filters into my subconscious. There's a tug at my wrists before the blissful sensation of release, swiftly followed by the intense pain as I try to move them. The woman's still talking, and I recognize the voice but I can't place it.

"...absolutely distraught, poor thing. Okay to bring her in?"

"Sophia!" I scramble to sit up just as a mass of dark curls peeps around the open door, accompanied by DI Naomi Butler.

Sophia stares at me, eyes wide and scared, and I lift up the oxygen mask so she can see my face. She's wearing Butler's leather biker jacket, the sleeves hanging down to the ground. It's zipped up, Elephant poking out beneath Sophia's chin.

"I fell over," she says. Her bottom lip wobbles.

"You did so well, pumpkin."

"A teenager picked her up." Butler lifts Sophia into the ambulance, and she runs to hug me. "Lives next door to the butcher's—apparently she met Sophia in the park last night? Good kid. She called it in right away."

"I tore my pajamas."

"I'll take you shopping. Buy you some new ones."

"Mummy too?"

My heart pitches. I open my mouth and flounder, looking at DI Butler, who smiles and hands her phone to Sophia.

"Do you want to show your dad?"

Sophia beams. "Mummy flew the plane." She taps play on the little screen and presses her head against mine, and together we watch Mina bring Flight 79 safely to land at Sydney.

FIFTY

CHRISTMAS EVE | MINA

"I'm nervous." I look up at Rowan. "Isn't that silly?" We're standing in baggage collection at Gatwick, a place I've stood a hundred times before—watching the same cases go around and around. In the center of the carousel is a Christmas tree decorated with cardboard cutout suitcases.

"Because of the press?"

"Yes," I say, although I hadn't thought about the press. It's the prospect of seeing Adam that's filling me with anxiety. We've spoken every day for the last six days, the poor connection doing nothing to help the awkwardness between us. I look at his face on my screen and it's the same old Adam, yet so much has happened since I last saw him.

He's told me everything. The gambling, the loan sharks, the dizzying interest rates. The lies he told at work; the fact that he might lose his job. When he told me how the man had threatened Katya, and I remembered how Sophia's night terrors had started that very week, I couldn't take anymore. I ended the call and turned off my phone and sat in the bar of my hotel, emotions heightened by one coffee after another.

They put the crew in the same hotel as the passengers, an entire ground-floor corridor cordoned off for interview rooms. We moved like invalids through the restaurants and lounges, shepherded between doctors, police, and journalists, and—whenever we needed it—counselors.

"The relationships between you and the other crew and passengers will be complex," said the first psychologist. She was talking to us all in a conference room at Sydney airport, arming us with tools to *survive the next few days*—just in case we had thought our ordeal over. "You might hate one another, because the very sight reminds you of what's happened," she said. "Or you might feel closer to one another than you do to your own family. You've been through hell over the last twenty hours. Whatever you're feeling right now is normal, I promise."

I feel anything but normal. Guilt consumes me, from the second I wake to when my eyes finally close, exhausted from the interviews, the anxiety, the compulsion to go over and over what happened. The hotel was full of traumatized passengers, meeting in corners of the lounge to say, *I keep remembering when…* Every day, a cluster of tourists would arrive to check in and we'd stare at them, wondering what it felt like to be arriving in Sydney for a holiday, to emerge from a flight with nothing more than jet lag.

Adam gave me space. I ate dinner with Rowan and Derek, wishing Cesca were there. The blade of the ax missed her brain by millimeters. Her condition was still critical, the doctors said, and it remained to be seen what long-term damage had been caused, but she was going to live. They'd keep her in ICU in St. Vincent's until it was safe to bring her back to the UK. I wanted to visit, wanted to get out of my head the image of the last time I'd seen her, blood matting her hair, but they wouldn't allow visitors until she was more stable.

We fell into a routine, like holidaymakers on a cruise, meeting for meals then disappearing to our rooms, never leaving the confines of the hotel. I detected—rightly or wrongly—an animosity toward me from the rest of the crew, and it felt no less than I deserved, so I was glad of those passengers who offered gentle support. As long as I live, I will never come to terms with what I did.

"Anyone would have done the same," Rowan said. We were having a drink after dinner, Derek having retired for the night. I needed to sleep, but I was frightened to be alone, frightened of what I'd see in my dreams.

"But they didn't. I did." I was haunted by the look in Carmel's eyes, by the senseless deaths of Mike, Ben, and Louis. So many lost lives.

"So many *saved* lives." Rowan was a teacher—*math, for my sins!*—and I could see he was a good one. He had the sort of eyes that crinkle with a smile and a way of explaining things that made them suddenly clear. Single. Not that it mattered to me, of course. "Never met the right woman," he said and grinned, then his face grew serious, and my breath caught in my chest. We both looked away at the same time, both wondered aloud if we shouldn't call it a night. Headed off down separate corridors to our separate rooms, and I lay awake, too tired to sleep, wondering if things would ever feel the same again.

I called Adam the next day, the urge to see him greater than the anger I felt at the danger he'd put our daughter in. I thought about the years I'd lied to him—to everyone—about why I'd abandoned my dreams to be a pilot. What made one lie worse than another?

"I miss you," I said.

"We miss you too."

I was desperate to get home. Adam promised me Sophia was fine, and I believed him, but the thread that tied me to my daughter was tugging at my heart. *One more day of interviews*, they kept saying. *Just one more day, then you can go home.*

World Airlines suspended the direct route *as a mark of respect*, and we changed planes at Shanghai. Their stock fell by 42 percent, and I wondered how long it would take to repair the damage Missouri and her team had done. I guess that means they won, in some sense.

Dindar booked out the whole of business class for our flights home, leaving empty those seats surplus to requirements, the way they do for security when the Queen flies. The full crew and those passengers whose travel plans changed after our hijack ordeal. The pregnant woman opted to fly home to her husband, who—given the extenuating circumstances—was granted leave for Christmas. Doug came home, leaving Ginny to lick her wounds at the five-star resort he'd booked for their "honeymoon."

Rowan had been on his way to Sydney for a conference he never got to attend. "Not much point staying now," he said when the return tickets were offered. None of us could imagine hanging around to sightsee.

Jason Poke came back to the UK too, along with a handful of other passengers, including a family with economy tickets who thought it might be their only opportunity to fly business class. I wasn't the only one to feel a sudden, desperate need to be home for Christmas.

Finley and his mum had adjacent seats. I handed him a small gift just before takeoff, and as he tore off the paper, his eyes lit up.

"Airpods! Awesome!"

"I thought you'd like them," I said, grinning, watching him slip the wireless buds into his ears.

"Thank you. You're very kind," his mother said. She didn't take her eyes off him the whole flight. When he grew too tired to stay awake, she lay on her side, the partition lowered between their seats, and watched him sleep.

I was worried about Derek. I sat in the lounge at Sydney airport, remembering the despair in his voice when we were huddled on the floor in economy. He'd changed his mind, sure, but was that simply the pressure of the situation? The lack of control? The day of the press conference, he had shared a link on Twitter to a blog post. It was a series of goodbyes from the airplane, poignant and blackly humorous, and it moved me to tears. Had he changed his mind again? Was this his suicide note?

Then, minutes before the gate was due to be announced, he barreled into the lounge with a carry-on suitcase and a newspaper. He'd been offered a column in the *Times*. He made light of it, but his shoulders were straighter, his expression lighter. I was glad that something good had come of it, for him.

They gave us five-star treatment on our flights home, complete with a counselor and a doctor who gave me a sleeping pill when I was too frightened to shut my eyes. When I woke, sweating and crying, Rowan talked me down off the ledge I'd climbed onto.

I wasn't the only one to scream in my sleep or to shake uncontrollably when the pilot announced we were *facing a little turbulence—please fasten your seat belts*. I wasn't the only one to look at my fellow passengers, making sure I recognized each one, that none of Missouri's team had somehow slipped through the net.

My suitcase rounds the corner, and I step forward, but Rowan gets there first. "Let me."

As we turn the corner into Arrivals, the noise is deafening. Camera flashes light up the hall with a dizzying intensity, and I'm glad of the sunglasses Rowan had suggested we both wear. It had felt foolish—like wannabe celebrities—but the onslaught is terrifying, and my instinct is to hide. Rowan steers me toward the exit, his hand firm and safe on the small of my back. There are shouts of *over here!*

I see Alice Davanti talking on her mobile. She skirts around the mass of reporters and heads directly for the exit. She'll be going straight to the office, I expect, getting the scoop on the hijack of the decade. *As the first hijacked passengers arrive back in Britain…*

"Mina, will you be facing criminal charges?"

The room swims, a sea of faces moving in and out of focus. I feel myself fall. I'm back on the plane, I'm opening the flight-deck door, I'm seeing Mike's face…

"Medic!"

A convenient collapse, one of the more unpleasant newspapers will call it. *Overwhelmed by her heroic landing*, another will say. I could have given them different headlines. Terrified. Haunted. Guilty.

Rowan helps me to my feet, and I brush off the enthusiastic first aider who has rushed to my side. Because I've seen something, among the chauffeurs' boards and the journalists' tape recorders, and it's the only medicine I need.

The sign is painted on cardboard, Sophia's careful letters filled in with red paint and glitter.

welcome home mummy.

Taped around the edges of the sign, overlapping like petals, are dozens of smaller pieces of paper. The notes I've put on Sophia's pillow every time I've left her. She's kept every single one.

I let go of my case, and I run. I run as fast as I can toward the sign, toward my daughter, toward home.

"Mummy!"

I pick her up and squeeze her so tight, crying into her hair, smelling her shampoo, her skin, the very essence of her. She's crying, and I'm crying, and then I feel an arm around me and I know the weight so well; I know the *feel* of it so well.

"What took you so long?" Adam says softly.

I squeeze my eyes shut and force out the horrors of Flight 79 and instead focus on the familiar arms of my husband and on the soft body squashed between us. This is my family. This is my life.

"Sorry I'm late."

FIFTY-ONE

THREE YEARS LATER | ADAM

"Let's have a look at you." Mina brings her face level with Sophia's, and with a jolt, I realize she no longer has to crouch. Sophia's gotten so tall. "You look perfect."

"Daddy did my hair."

"Clever Daddy."

At Sophia's insistence, I've been teaching myself via a series of YouTube tutorials. Today I've attempted French plaits, the parting beginning in the center and meandering first left and then right. The frizzy ends stick out below her ears, one big and one small.

"It looks great." Mina grins at me, then drains her coffee and dumps the mug in the sink. It was six months before we could move back after the fire. The insurance covered everything, thank God, and when we finally stepped through the door, there was no trace of what had happened. The new kitchen was different, and we pushed a dresser up against the wall so you'd never even know there was a cellar. I thought I'd see Becca everywhere I went, but the three of us had spent so much time deliberating over the choices that now made up the ground floor of our house that all I saw was home.

Butler gave me that Christmas off—*given the circumstances*—and the three of us drove from the airport to Mina's dad's house, where he'd left folded towels at the end of the spare bed, the way her mum used to do. On the floor was a single blow-up bed for Sophia.

"I'll make some coffee," Leo said, leaving Mina and me standing in the room, our bags on the floor between us.

"I never told him we'd separated," she said.

"Sophia can go in with you. I'll take the mattress."

"No, it's okay." She hesitated. "If it's okay with you, that is."

I felt my heart skitter. "You mean..."

She nodded.

We slept fitfully, Sophia abandoning her blow-up bed to curl up like a comma between Mina and me, giving us another excuse not to talk. For two individuals whose jobs revolved entirely around talking to people, I thought, we were spectacularly bad at communicating.

We did speak, though, in fits and starts over the following few days. And when Leo took Sophia for races along the windswept beach, throwing anxious glances back at us as she whirled in the wind, I thought that perhaps he had known after all.

I wasn't suspended. I was sent back to uniform, with a fierce command from DI Butler to *sort yourself out, then come and get your job back.* There was a referral to welfare and for counseling, an introduction to a debt management advisor. The intelligence I provided in relation to the loan sharks I'd used led to several arrests for associated criminal activity and a laconic *nice work* email from Butler.

Mina wasn't charged with any offenses relating to the hijack, despite the witch hunt led by Alice Davanti's paper. It was a year before we knew—a year of sleepless nights and *what if I go to prison?*—but eventually, two quietly dressed men came over and said the CPS felt it *wasn't in the public interest* to prosecute her for opening the flight-deck door. The decision didn't lessen her guilt. Rowan put her in touch with a friend of his who specialized in PTSD cases, and slowly she came to terms with what she'd been forced to do.

Even slower was the unravelling of what had happened during her pilot training. I'd wanted to punch something—or someone—when she told me about Myerbridge.

"We should complain to the school. Or to the aviation authorities."

"What would that achieve?" Mina was more sanguine than I was. "It was a different world back then. They have policies in place now—I've checked." She was letting it go, and so I did too.

"No more secrets, though," I said. "From either of us."

"No more secrets," she agreed.

Surprisingly, Sophia seemed to be the only one of us who escaped relatively unscathed. We took her to counseling, but she was pragmatic about Becca and the fire and proud of the special commendation she'd received from the police. Her experiences as a baby had given her a resilience that made me at once proud and sad, and I hoped that one day, she would lose these memories altogether.

"Ready?" Mina says now.

I look at Sophia, who nods. "Ready," I say. I pick up the car keys.

"My name is Sandra Daniels, and when I stepped on Flight 79, I left my whole life behind."

The woman in the dock is tiny—under five foot five—and almost unrecognizable from the photograph in the paper of the hijacker known to the world as Zambezi. The months on remand have faded her tan to nothing, and her hair has grown dark brown, the blond ends dry and brittle. Beside me, I feel Mina tense. Daniels is the first of the defendants to give evidence, a part of the trial expected to last at least another two weeks. This morning, the final witnesses were called, including Sophia.

She was allowed to give evidence via video link, her unblinking eyes seeming vast. She stared directly into the camera, the only sign of nerves a twitch as she nibbled at the inside of her bottom lip.

"How long did you spend in the cellar, Sophia?"

She frowned. "I don't know."

"A long time?"

"Yes."

"An hour? Longer?"

Sophia's eyes flicked to the side, looking for help she couldn't have, from Judith the court chaperone, who had gray, bobbed hair and sweets for afterward. Mina had held Sophia's hand as they walked with Judith through a maze of corridors to the vulnerable witness room. As Sophia gave her evidence, Mina sat on a plastic chair in the corridor, while across the Old Bailey, I watched my almost nine-year-old daughter being cross-examined.

"A lot longer than an hour."

We didn't want Sophia in court. Her evidence had never been

contested, and although the six surviving hijackers had entered *not guilty* pleas, Becca had held up her hands without a fight. They'd found her at her mum's, frantically trying to wipe the search history from a laptop that tied her neatly to the purchase of the restraints she'd used to keep me in the cellar.

"I'm sorry," she'd told the arresting officers. I wish I'd been the one to tighten her cuffs.

It was the CPS barrister who called Sophia as a witness. "She's very articulate," he'd said, as though this might be news to us. "I think she'll make a good impression on the jury."

Sophia wasn't called to give evidence. She was called to make the jurors' hearts melt, to win them over with her earnest responses and innocent understanding. She was called to help them see the human cost of the hijackers' actions, even though their plan ultimately failed.

"No further questions."

Sophia's face remained blank, but the twitch of her bottom lip ceased, and I could finally breathe. She's missed a lot of school, called to court only to wait around all day, her slot pushed back again and again. Now that the defendants have been called, we are taking turns to hear their evidence, Sophia spending her days in the parks and cafés close to the court, looked after by Mina and me in turn, or, when we both had to be in court, by Rowan, Derek, and Cesca, whom Sophia adores.

It was touch and go for Cesca, but she made a full recovery. They'd taken her off the plane first, strapped to a stretcher. As the waiting air ambulance took off, the armed police moved in, removing each hijacker to a separate armored vehicle.

Weeks after Mina came home, I found her watching the news footage, the tiny figures marching across the screen of her phone. "It doesn't seem real," she said. Quietly, she named each handcuffed figure. *Ganges, Niger, Yangtze, Zambezi, Congo, Lena.* The passengers followed, ashen-faced and trembling, and then the crew, blinking as they appeared in the bright Sydney sunshine. Not quite the arrival photograph Dindar had planned for them.

"Enough," I said to Mina, but she shook her head.

"I need to see it."

She cried when the body bags were brought out. Roger Kirkwood,

Mike Carrivick, Carmel Mahon, Ben Knox, Louis Joubert. Names everyone in the world now knew as well as they knew the names of their attackers. The postmortem confirmed that the two relief pilots had been given the same drug as Roger Kirkwood, the first man to die. It was likely one of the hijackers had slipped the crushed-up pills into the drinks Carmel had made for the pilots to take upstairs, although we'd never know for sure. With Missouri dead and her plan shared with her conspirators on a "need to know" basis only, there were a lot of questions with no answers. The relief cabin crew had been found, stiff, dehydrated, and terrified but thankfully safe, up in the cramped sleeping area—the door to the cabin jammed shut by one of the hijackers.

Photographs of the nine conspirators—the eight from the plane plus Becca—fit neatly onto a full page of the *Daily Mail*, above their real names and, opposite, a world map with helpful arrows denoting the etymology of each hijacker's alias. The *Guardian* devoted several days of internet content to the critical status of said rivers, accompanied by pleas for donations so they could continue to educate people about the climate emergency.

It took almost three years to reach trial and two hours to read all the charges leveled against the defendants sitting in the two rows of seats within the glass box at the side of the court. *Preparation for acts of terrorism, fundraising offenses, possession of articles for terrorist purposes, murder, conspiracy, kidnapping...* The list went on and on, right down to offenses of using false instruments—the passports Missouri obtained for each of her team.

The trial itself has taken five months. We've lived with the aftermath of what happened for so long that sometimes I'm not sure we can be any other way, that we're capable of talking about anything other than that week's evidence.

Sandra Daniels's defense—that she didn't know the extent of the group's plans—falls apart during cross-examination, leaving her to claim mitigation due to years of trauma caused by an abusive marriage. Over the next two weeks, we hear other similar excuses from the remaining defendants— promises made, escape routes planned—and a picture emerges of manipulation, grooming, and radicalization at the hands of one woman.

Missouri.

Every tributary leads back to her, and although she had covered her tracks well—the hijackers' dark web message board was never recovered—police found paperwork in her house that tied her to each of her accomplices.

On the final day of the trial, when we're called in to hear the judge's verdict, I look around the courtroom at the people who have become as familiar to me as my own family after six months in court. Derek has a suit on today—he must be doing an interview later. He's moved seamlessly from print to television, in stark contrast to Alice Davanti, whose career crashed into oblivion after one of the passengers leaked video footage of her trying to claw her way into an already-occupied seat.

Jason Poke has done better. He gave a heartfelt and impassioned public apology for all the *insensitive jokes* of his past and pledged to atone for his seat grabbing on Flight 79. "When you think you're about to die," he said on *Good Morning Britain*, "your whole life flashes before your eyes—and what I saw didn't make me proud." He's become the go-to presenter for disaster documentaries, traveling the world to find the *human stories* behind tsunamis, earthquakes, forest fires... *Woke Poke*, the tabloids have dubbed him. A born-again empath.

Caroline and Jamie Crawford haven't returned to hear the verdict. Jamie left straight after giving evidence; Caroline hung around long enough to announce the launch of the Crawford Youth Sports Foundation. Their divorce sounds messy. SCREWED OVER FOR SCREWING AROUND, one tabloid said, listing the millions Jamie had signed over to his wife's charity, only for her to give him his marching orders.

I thought the media would grow tired of the case, but the coverage has been relentless. With the hijackers on remand, it was the passengers who provided fresh copy, from AUSTRALIAN HIJACK HELL SURROGATE COUPLE GIVE BIRTH TO MIRACLE TWINS, to the haunted face of Carmel's parents: WE'LL AVENGE OUR DAUGHTER'S DEATH.

The judge gives them life. Although really, he is taking it away, bestowing each with a minimum sentence of forty years. I squeeze Mina's hand.

Even Becca (I still think of her as that, despite her real name being plastered across the papers), the youngest defendant, will be in her sixties when she gets out. She'll have no children, no career, no life.

We don't cheer. There's no feeling of euphoria as we leave the court; the length of the trial has sapped us of adrenaline. There's just the overwhelming feeling of relief that it's finally over.

"That's that, then." Derek looks almost disappointed. He claps me on the back, turning it into an awkward man hug, before kissing Mina on the cheek. "Brave girl."

There are few people Mina would allow to call her a girl, but Derek is one of them. He has slotted into our lives like an additional uncle, and I like to think he sees us as family too.

"Cesca's turn for dinner, I think?" he adds.

"It certainly is," she says. "I'll ping an email around."

The monthly dinners had begun as a one-off, a few weeks after Cesca left the hospital. They were Mina's idea, to introduce Sophia and me to Cesca, Rowan, and Derek. Conversation was stilted to begin with. We scratched about for small talk that kept us away from the very thing that had brought us together.

It was Sophia who broke the ice. "What will happen to the 'jackers?"

"They'll go to prison," I said firmly.

"They should send them on an airplane and tell them it was going to crash so they would be as scared as you were. And then put them in a horrible freezing cellar and set fire to their house and see how they like it."

There was silence after this little speech. I wasn't sure whether to applaud my daughter's sense of justice or worry I was bringing up a psychopath, but when I looked at Mina, she was laughing. "I couldn't agree more." She raised her glass. "To Sophia."

"Sophia!" we echoed.

"Maybe you should be a judge when you grow up," Rowan said, but Sophia shook her head.

"I'm going to be a police officer." She'd smiled at me, then looked at Mina. "And a pilot."

"Busy woman," Derek said.

"And an environ…" Sophia stumbled over the word "…mentlist."

She might as well have said *Macbeth* in a roomful of actors. Derek flinched, Cesca closed her eyes, and Rowan—usually so unflappable—lost his eyebrows somewhere beneath his hair.

"They've been doing it at school," Mina said. "Ice caps, single-use plastic, that sort of thing." There was an apology in her voice we all understood.

"I'm in charge of recycling for the whole school."

"And she's persuaded the milkshake shop to switch to biodegradable straws."

Three pairs of eyes stared at Sophia. We were used to this. Proud of it, I suppose, as though we were entirely responsible for the genes that gave our daughter the intellectual capacity of someone twice her age. And if sometimes the looks were more wary than awestruck? We could handle that too. We loved Sophia because of her quirkiness, not in spite of it.

"Well," Rowan said suddenly, a fist on the table adding an exclamation mark to the word, "I, for one, think it's remarkable." He looked at Cesca and Derek, gathering their enthusiasm. "Five years old—"

"Nearly six," Sophia said.

"Nearly six years old and already bringing about change."

"*Brava*, Sophia!" Derek added. "Future pilot, police officer, and environmentalist!" We raised our glasses for the second time that evening, before Sophia was dispatched to brush her teeth.

"Will you read me a story—"

Mina had put down her glass in readiness.

"—Daddy?"

I'd been unable to hide the joy I felt, and I scrutinized Mina's face for signs of jealousy as Sophia was saying good night to our guests. I knew what it felt like, after all, to play second fiddle. But there was nothing. As the weeks passed, I realized I'd had it all wrong. I'd been looking for fairness—for equal love, equal attention, equal *status* from my daughter. I'd been thinking about what I needed from her instead of what she needed from me. From both of us. Sometimes Sophia wants me to read to her; sometimes she wants Mina. Sometimes she reaches for my hand; other times, she pulls away, not wanting me near. Attachment disorder isn't cured overnight, but slowly we're making progress.

That first dinner turned into monthly get-togethers, and by the following summer, the occasional spontaneous game of rounders or sunny pub lunch. It was hard for outsiders to understand a tenth of what we'd been through, so much easier to not have to say it. It was good, too, for Sophia to see how we'd all come through it, and that adults, too, had the occasional setback. I liked to see her deep in conversation with Cesca or Rowan and watch her burst into laughter as the serious turned into the absurd. It was good for us all, I realized.

We walk away from the Old Bailey now, an awkward group on a too-narrow pavement, and retrieve our phones from the travel agent that acts as a left-luggage center for the court. Sophia is talking to Cesca, pointing to each of the signs in the window in turn.

"Athens. That's in Greece. Rome is in Italy. Barbados is...Africa?"

"The Caribbean."

Sophia frowns, although whether at Cesca or her own mistake, it isn't clear.

"Bright kid, that one," Rowan says.

"Runs rings around me." I grin. "Did Mina tell you she wrote to our MP last month? All on her own. Got a letter back and everything."

"Incredible. I'd put money on her going into politics, wouldn't you?"

Rowan's expression is guileless, but nevertheless I tense. "Ah, I'm not a betting man," I say lightly. I don't know if Mina told the others about my gambling problem. I don't want to know. I still go to meetings, and apart from a tiny slip when we learned the extent of the fire damage, I haven't placed a bet in almost three years. The odds of the three of us escaping with our lives had been as low as they could go—I won't be throwing down any more chips.

We part ways on the corner, Cesca running for a train, Derek off to meet his editor in town. Sophia ends the earnest conversation she's been having with Rowan, pulling a paper bag out of her rucksack.

"These are for you."

Rowan looks inside. "Biscuits? Thank you."

"She spent all weekend baking," Mina says. "Honestly, I'm going to end up the size of a house."

I'm about to tell Mina she looks pretty fabulous when Rowan tuts at her joke. "You're beautiful," he says, and I force a smile. Saying anything now would sound like an afterthought.

"Bye, then," I say to Rowan. Mina raises an eyebrow at me, but Rowan shakes my hand and takes no apparent offense at my abrupt farewell. I wonder where he'll go now—who he'll share the verdict with. Despite his close friendship with Mina—and, by proxy, Sophia—I don't think I know him any better now than I did three years ago. I'm not sure if it's Rowan who's kept his distance, or me: either way, we're guarded with each other, as though we're adversaries, not friends.

There are more handshakes and claps on the back, and Rowan gives Mina a hug. His hand rests lightly on the small of her back after he releases her, and I have to fight the urge to put a proprietorial arm around her. It would be easier if Rowan were unlikeable. If he were arrogant or bigoted or annoyingly smarmy. But he's none of those things, and I don't need a therapist to tell me that my watchfulness is borne not from Rowan's actions but from my own inadequacies. Rowan was there when I wasn't. While I was cuffed to a pipe in the cellar, relying on my five-year-old daughter to save me, he was storming the flight deck with my wife. In the immediate aftermath, I supported Mina through a video screen; he took her for dinner in their Sydney hotel, held her hand when she cried on the flight home.

Mina was upfront about the time they'd spent together. "I don't know what I would have done without him. And Derek and Cesca," she said, but the addition was for my benefit, and we both knew it.

"I'm glad they were there for you," I said. And I meant it.

"Good luck back at work," Cesca says to Mina now, kissing her on the cheek. Dindar was good to Mina after the hijack. She was off work on full pay for six months, spending time with Sophia, before taking an admin role, away from the airport. It fit well with school pick-ups—neither of us was ready to use a babysitter again—but I knew she missed flying.

"I think I want to go back," she'd said. "After the trial."

"Then go back."

She smiled. Said I reminded her of her dad. "I'm a bit scared, of course." She still had nightmares about Missouri and the others. "But you can't let them win, can you?"

"How about fish and chips when we get home?" I say now once Rowan has turned the corner and it's just the three of us again.

Sophia's eyes light up. "Yay! As long as it's—"

"—sustainably caught, I know." She is wise far beyond her years, my daughter, and the last three years have made her wiser. We fight it to a certain extent—we encourage her to play, to be silly, to be a child—but I'm proud of our clever, passionate, perceptive girl.

I hail a cab, thinking of that day walking home from school, when she wouldn't hold my hand, when she wanted Becca, not me. I think of how much it hurt and how far we've come since then. How much closer I am now to Sophia. I wouldn't wish what happened on my oldest enemy, but as silver linings go, it's a good one.

"Love you," I say, more fiercely than I'd planned. The taxi pulls up, and I open the door, letting the girls in before I follow.

"Love you too." Mina squeezes my hand.

Between us, Sophia sighs happily. "Love you three."

FIFTY-TWO

PASSENGER 1G

A life sentence. I confess I hadn't expected that. Standard for terrorism, yes, but is it terrorism to protect the Earth? Is it terrorism to open people's eyes to the devastation their actions are wreaking upon the world?

The courts say it is.

They see no difference between our cause and religious mania, between saving the planet and destroying it. They are blind to the truth that is so clear to those of us who care about the future we're leaving for our children.

It will be forty years before parole is even a possibility. Who knows if I'll even be here to see it? Forty years behind bars, no contact with the outside world. It's barbaric. Inhumane. Surely death would be preferable?

In that respect, Missouri won. She escaped. Beat the system by dying.

You didn't think it was Missouri's plan, did you? That it was Missouri in charge of the complexities required to pull off a project of such magnitude, such significance?

I wouldn't blame you if you thought that. After all, she did. She saw herself far more as a leader than as a follower, and it was easy to plant the seeds and let her nurture them. Missouri saw herself as the shepherd, when all the time, she was simply another of my sheep. Should anything go wrong, it ensured that all roads would lead back to her, my own hands kept clean. Our online discussions were secure, but I kept meticulous paper records of every contact, every decision, making the judicious decision to visit Missouri's house after she left for the airport in order to leave the file in her study.

I'm not the first to have a fall guy, and I certainly won't be the last. We see them everywhere, from the corporate world to the political sphere, and we watch them crash and burn when their time is up. Around them, CEOs walk away unscathed to invest in new ventures; political führers pledge allegiance to a new puppet. The true leaders aren't on the stage; they're pulling the strings.

The others respected Missouri—or rather, they respected what they thought she was. They listened to the words I put in her mouth and the plan I allowed her to present as her own. I'm not good with words, *I told her.* It'll sound better from you. People listen to you. You're a natural leader.

People see what they want to see. Believe what they want to believe. Missouri was used to traveling the world, commanding high fees to speak about injustice. She was used to people hanging on her every word. Her ego hung her and kept me hidden.

Forty years, though.

Would I have done the same again, had I known we would fail? That the prison doors would slam, trapping so many futures inside?

The number of major natural disasters has increased threefold in my own lifetime. Island nations are disappearing under rising sea levels. Bees—those humble pollinators to which we owe so much—are vanishing. A terrifying two thousand species are under threat of extinction because of climate change. The world is dying.

So would I do the same again?

In a heartbeat.

And I will.

Because I wasn't stupid enough to let myself get caught.

There were times when I was worried, of course. Times when I—momentarily—lost control and risked exposing myself as the real master-mind behind the plan. As I knelt by the body of the young flight attendant, my hands pressed around the wound in her neck, my pulse soared. I waited for the hand on my shoulder, the accusation, the truth. Killing her had been reckless—any one of those passengers could have seen my hand around the corkscrew—but their eyes were focused on Missouri. By the time they settled on me, I was trying to save the girl's life. A hero, not a threat.

The investigation was extensive—the backgrounds of all passengers were looked into—and I felt the hot breath of counterterrorism on my neck. But it came to nothing; I had covered my tracks with an expertise I have honed over the years. Rowan Fraser has been a model citizen.

It wasn't the ending I wanted, of course. I wanted us to plunge dramatically into the Opera House. I wanted footage of our actions—the most important political statement ever made—to be replayed for decades, across every continent, in every house, every school, every institution. I wanted "breaking news" headlines, a spotlight on climate change so bright, no one could avoid it. Missouri wanted it too. She was tired of fighting for justice for her brother—also an environmental activist. She was tired of trying to make people listen to the same message that had gotten him killed more than two decades ago. One final act, she said. For him.

It amused me to see the passengers shrink back from Missouri's rudimentary piece of fancy dress. We have the jihadists to thank, I suppose, for creating such hysteria around a glimpse of wire and plastic. Her "bomb" was nothing but socks in dog-waste bags, strapped to an elastic luggage strap, the colored wires ripped from earphones. Each item innocently passed through the X-ray machine at security and assembled in the bathroom of the plane.

Perhaps if Lena had never known the explosives were fake, it might have been enough to keep the crew at bay… Hindsight is a wonderful thing, is it not?

I did my best to keep Mina from storming the flight deck. I hadn't counted on her ridiculous desire to "make good" the events of the preceding hours. I could have neutralized her. Even, perhaps, Mina and Cesca. But Mina, Cesca, and Derek? When it became apparent that they were committed to their entirely unplanned rescue mission, I realized that joining in with them, getting into the flight deck with them, was my last chance to make the headlines we needed.

I confess, I had rather expected Mina to fall apart emotionally. I could see it happening, tried to push it still further. I reminded her of her family, exploiting what I knew to be her weak point, just when she needed to hold it together. The controls were almost mine, the mission so nearly complete.

Did I push her too far? Her reaction to my needling was extreme, a screaming tantrum so wildly disproportionate to my own behavior that I can only assume she was in the grip of hysteria. I gave up, then. Even the toughest troops know when to withdraw. Regroup. Better to live to fight again. To fight better.

We won small battles amid the lost war. After the hijack, the UK government banned air miles, a small but significant step toward deterring people from flying. They introduced tax breaks for businesses shipping their products by sea instead of air and added VAT on the purchase of new aircraft.

We made that happen, I tell myself in my darker moments.

I'm telling you now. We made that happen. *That's the power of protest. Don't ever think that you can't effect change, can't truly make a difference in the world. To the world. Your children's children are counting on you.*

Nevertheless, it is time for a new approach. Protests have changed since my mother took me to Greenham Common; legislation has changed, technology has changed. We can be cleverer. Quieter. More powerful.

Over the last few years, since our hijacking mission, I've noticed a sea change in attitudes toward climate change. You must have seen it too. More coverage in newspapers, more documentaries, more celebrities standing up to be counted. The tide is turning, and the time to ride the wave is now.

But I'm not the one to ride it.

Branding is everything in this world of consumerism and social media, and it has never been my style to take center stage. What's needed is someone young, someone passionate, someone whose purity shines through for the world to see.

Someone like you.

I know you're ready for this. You've listened to my side of the story, and you understand the issues. You see that it's the cause that matters, not the people.

It's daunting, I know. But I'll be there, in the wings. I'll help you write your speeches and prepare for meetings. I'll teach you how to carry people along with your energy and your innocence, until they believe every word you say. I'll be behind you, but you'll take the credit. You'll be known the world over, making nations sit up and listen because you are the voice of reason. The voice of the future.

Consider this an apprenticeship for now. I'll talk, and you'll learn, and meanwhile you'll be winning hearts, so that when the time is right, people will follow you wherever we wish to lead them. I'll show you how.

Your parents?

Oh, Sophia, they're not your parents. They're carers, that's all. No more a part of your family than your teachers are. It is their job to look after you. Nothing more. Adam and Mina wanted a child, they wanted any child—they didn't choose you. Not like me.

Yes. That's right. I chose you.

I chose to tell you all this while the others watched the trial.

Why?

Because I can see your potential. Because together we're going to change the world, and I know you're strong enough not just to lead those changes but to cope with the bloodshed along the way. I chose you to be my second-in-command, to be the future of my campaign.

I chose you. So what do you say?

Good girl. You're making the right decision.

They're looking at us. I have to go. Don't tell them what I've said, will you? It's our little secret. Just sit tight, and don't breathe a word. Be who they want you to be. For now.

I'll let you know when it's time.

EPILOGUE

SOPHIA

I'm squashed between Mum and Dad in the taxi. It's like I'm the net in the middle of a tennis court, words bouncing from Mum to Dad to Mum to Dad. Over and over.

Over my head.

That's what people say if they don't understand something. *It goes over my head.* Like water when you're drowning.

Grown-ups think what they say goes over my head. They think that because I'm little, I don't hear what they say. They think I don't understand. I listened to Dad talking to Derek one day. I heard Derek say, *There's just something about him* and Dad say, *Mina won't hear a bad word against him.* When they saw me, they stopped really suddenly, and Derek said, *Do you think—* and Dad said, *Don't worry. It'll go over her head.*

It didn't.

They were talking about Rowan.

I'm not stupid. I listen really hard. I listen all the time, and when I don't understand something, I find out what it means. Mostly, I ask Mum and Dad, but sometimes...sometimes I ask Rowan.

Rowan doesn't think I'm too little to understand. He tells me about climate change and why the prime minister isn't any good and why bad things happen, like fighting and wars. Lots of grown-ups use a different voice when they talk to children, but Rowan doesn't. *You're a clever girl,* he says, *I don't want to patronize you.*

I don't know if I'm clever. I'm interested in stuff. I find things out, and then my brain remembers it. Like before Becca locked us in the cellar, when we were having tea and Dad was talking about making cakes with me, and Becca said you could make biscuits from dandelions. *There are loads of websites*, she said.

Mum lets me use the internet to look up recipes, so I looked. Becca was right. It's called *foraging*, and it means eating weeds. You can eat loads of weeds. Nuts, berries, nettles...loads. I made acorn muffins. Mum and Dad said they liked them, but then I heard Dad say they tasted like someone cleaned out a hamster cage, and I was so angry, I almost burst.

There are nettles in the park, just behind our house, and blackberries and flowers you can eat, like violets and sweet rocket and mallow.

Not foxgloves, though. Foxgloves are poisonous.

But how can I know that? I'm only nine years old...

Rowan's taught me loads. Like how to find things on the internet without anyone seeing you were looking. Like how to stop Mum and Dad from thinking I'm up to something.

He's good at acting. Mum really likes him, but Dad doesn't, even though they shake hands like they're friends. Rowan says soon Dad will start playing the lottery again, and *look what happened last time*.

When Mum first said she was going to start flying again, I thought Rowan would say something—he was so angry—but he kissed her and said, *Well done. I know what a big decision that was.* After, we went to the park, and he said how Mum could have protested against climate change, and instead, all the papers were writing about the *brave flight attendant* going back to work.

"You should tell her," I said, but he shook his head.

"I'm working on a better plan."

He wouldn't tell me what it was, not for ages and ages. Instead, he said he had a big secret—a huge secret I couldn't tell anyone. Not Derek or Cesca and especially not Mum or Dad.

It was all him. The hijack, Becca, everything. He was sorry about us being in the cellar—said I had to understand it was all *for the greater good*. When the trial started, Mum and Dad often spent all day in court, and Rowan and I waited in the café and drank hot chocolate. *There's more to the story*, he said. *I think I can trust you to do the right thing.* He gave me a chapter each day, like bedtime stories.

I'll let you know when it's time, he said.

He's forgotten what he said about when *he* broke the law. When he threw a rock at a policeman. *My age absolved me of my act*, he said. I had to ask what that meant. It meant he was nine. Too young to be arrested.

My age.

So I can't wait, can I?

I baked the biscuits at the weekend. Mum was *glad of the distraction*, she said and pleased I wasn't *finding the court case too much*. Dad came into the kitchen when I was putting in the flowers. "What's cooking?" I had four mixing bowls, with a different flavor in each one.

"Shortbread," I said. "With edible flowers." I suddenly felt all hot, sure they could read my mind. Did Rowan feel like this when he threw the stone at the policeman?

"Looks awesome," Dad said.

I decorated my biscuits with bits of petal, pushed into the top of the shortbread. Yellow pansies on some, blue borage on another one, pink roses on the last one.

And on the final batch, a tiny piece of purple foxglove petal.

That's something else Rowan taught me: hide your secrets where people are looking.

The police will find out, you see, afterward. I'm not stupid. There'll be an investigation, and they'll do blood tests and find foxglove, and they'll know I put it in my biscuits, quite a lot of it in fact, so it would look suspicious if three of my batches had the right flower on them, and the foxgloves ones were plain.

They'll know it was me. But they can't arrest me.

I'm only nine years old.

Our taxi moves forward, then stops again. Dad sighs. "It would be quicker to walk."

"Sophia's exhausted," Mum says. The window is open, and I can smell the dirty fumes from the cars around us choking the streets. "If we miss the train, we're definitely eating. I'm ravenous."

"I've got my biscuits," I say, as though I've just remembered. I open my rucksack and take out the paper bags. One for each of us.

"What would we do without you?" Dad grins. I smile too, but my heart is going *pitter patter pitter patter*. I wonder how long it takes to die from foxglove poisoning. I wonder how much it hurts.

We munch the biscuits, and our taxi moves another tiny bit.

It's done.

I feel better now. Sometimes you have to do something bad, to stop more bad things happening. Just like Rowan did.

"These petals are just lovely," Mum says. She leans across to see Dad's and then mine. "Oh—you gave Rowan your favorite ones." She looks at Dad and laughs. "She wouldn't let me pinch one!"

"Well, it was nice of him to look after me during the trial," I say. "And he told me loads of interesting stories. He lives on his own, and I don't think he has anyone to make him biscuits. And I really, really wanted him to have the purple ones."

My parents exchange a glance that says *bless!* and I know they're thinking how much they love me. What a good girl I am. "You're very kind." Dad puts an arm around me and squeezes me against him. I look at them both, and I give them my sweetest smile.

"That's okay. I think he deserves them."

AUTHOR'S NOTE

Sometimes an idea for a book floats around for a long time before it's ready, like a seed germinating in the ground, waiting for just the right combination of sun and water. Like lots of writers, I keep a notebook of ideas, many of which never take root. Within the first few pages of that notebook are a handful of phrases. *Flight attendant. Hijack threat. Save the child, or save the plane?*

Some time after I wrote those words, I saw an article about the preparations for the first direct flight from London to Sydney. At that point, the longest flight I'd ever been on was thirteen hours, and the thought of adding another seven filled me with horror. I couldn't help but think of Agatha Christie's *Murder on the Orient Express*, where passengers are trapped on a snowbound train with a murderer in their midst. The idea of being thirty-five thousand feet in the air with nowhere to hide terrifies me, so naturally I decided to spend a year writing about it.

I love travel, and I'm very lucky that my job requires me to do a great deal of it. Lately, though, I've become increasingly concerned about the environmental impact of the flights I take, prompting me to evaluate whether each trip is truly necessary from a business point of view. I take trains where I can, and I try to offset my travel by making numerous small changes at home. Every little bit helps. I often sit in airport lounges, watching my fellow passengers and second-guessing their reasons for travel. Whether or not a flight is "necessary" is a subjective question, and in writing this book, I wanted to take a look at some of the perceptions and judgments that surround air travel and environmentalism. As I wrote, COVID-19 hit, and slowly countries shut down. Planes were grounded, airline staff furloughed or laid off completely.

The skies cleared. Last year, I visited thirteen countries; this year, my diary is empty. It has been both unsettling and inspiring to write about an anti-aviation movement at the very moment the industry ground to a near halt, and I have been struck by the positive environmental impact evidenced in such a short space of time. It is impossible to know how the world will look in the future, but I'm quite certain it will change the way we travel forever.

I'm aware that—to put it mildly—the environmental activists in my novel are not heroes. They are fundamentalists, and fundamentalists are rarely sympathetic. So why write about extremists rather than the legion of scientists and ecologists doing valuable work in a measured, perfectly legal way? The short answer is: that would make for a very dull crime thriller. The longer answer has its genesis in Oxford, when I was a newly minted police officer. I had joined the force at a time when protests against animal testing were an almost daily occurrence, thanks to the numerous laboratories housed within university buildings. As a law enforcer, one is required to separate personal beliefs from professional exigencies, and regardless of my own views on animal testing, I was duty-bound to protect those scientists in the firing line. The vast majority of demonstrators were law-abiding, exercising their legitimate right to protest. A vocal few, however, were not. I found it fascinating that a person who cared so deeply about animals that they would devote their life to protecting them could at the same time care so little about a human that they would set fire to a family home. Is it okay to kill a person if you save an animal? How about if you save a forest? A river?

Later, I worked as a protest liaison officer: the point of contact between police and campaigners. I would sit in a room with a representative from the English Defense League, Unite Against Fascism, or Fathers for Justice and try to find common ground amid our—very different—objectives. It was fascinating work that taught me a great deal about the psychology of protest.

As I was writing the first draft of this book, a protestor grounded a London City plane bound for Dublin, delivering a lecture on climate change as cabin crew attempted to remove him. I think we'll see more demonstrations at airports and on planes as the effects of global warming worsen: environmentalists taking more extreme action in an attempt to make their voices heard. Whatever your views on protests, it is hard to argue with the science (although a surprising number manage it). We must take action now to save the planet for future generations. Take trains, ban single-use plastic, eat less meat...there are a hundred small changes you could make today to make a big difference tomorrow.

Finally, a note of reassurance to anyone of a nervous disposition who is reluctant to get on a plane after reading this book. *It is all make-believe.* You are ten times less likely to be in a hijacked plane than you are to be struck by lightning, and unless you make a habit of weather watching from the middle of an open field, that isn't very likely at all.

Thank you for reading. Safe travels.

Clare Mackintosh

READING GROUP GUIDE

1. Sophia's care before her adoption creates added challenges for Mina and Adam. Do you think adoptive parents and biological parents have different approaches to supporting their kids?

2. What was your first impression of Adam? Why do you think he was first introduced through Mina's perspective? How did your opinion change throughout the book?

3. Mina calls the protests just outside the airport pointless because they only reach people who are already committed to flying. Who are the protestors trying to reach? Is there anywhere else that would be more effective?

4. The disagreement in the bar highlights disparities between business and economy class passengers, and Mina insists the economy passengers return to their seats. Why do these divisions exist? Do you think there was another way to de-escalate the situation?

5. When Mina receives the note, she thinks through some of the training she received to deal with hijackers. Why didn't she follow that training? What would you have done in her place?

6. Passenger 1G discusses the way they groomed the other members of the group and coaxed them into participating in the plan. What did all the members have in common before they boarded the plane? How does the internet enable radicalization?

7. The terrorists hold the airline employees, the passengers, and the airline itself all equally responsible for the London–Sydney flight. Can personal choices, like eating less meat or flying less often, make a significant difference to ecological health? Why do we focus on individual choice more often than corporate responsibility?

8. How do you feel about the dictate "Never negotiate with terrorists"? What are the short-term and long-term impacts of that stance?

9. How is business travel changing after the COVID-19 pandemic? Would you argue for or against the continuation of regular business travel?

10. Do you think the characters all got justice? Did you want a different outcome for anyone?

A CONVERSATION
WITH THE AUTHOR

Sophia's attachment struggles are a poignant thread throughout the book. How did you learn about the adoption process? How did that compare to your research process for airlines and flights?

I have a number of friends who have adopted children and who were generous enough to speak openly to me about their lives. Some families encounter no significant issues as their adoptive children settle in and grow up, but several of my friends have found it a challenging—although no less rewarding—experience. My time in the police had exposed me to the long-lasting impact of childhood trauma, and I wanted to explore this area. I was particularly struck by one friend's account of how her daughter, adopted at birth, had asked for a hug for the very first time at the age of ten. Attachment disorder is deep-rooted and long-lasting, and I wanted to write about the impact of this on a relationship.

Researching the aviation side of the book was equally interesting. I based the layout of my fictional aircraft on a combination of real-life planes and quickly fell down a rabbit warren of online resources. Flight attendants are extraordinarily indiscreet on message boards, and there is a surprising amount of information about how to deal with a hostage situation. I spent hours on the brilliant NATS.aero website, where their "Plane Talking" page enables you to listen to air traffic controllers guide a real flight into London Heathrow.

Adam and Mina anchor the majority of the narrative, but there are plenty of other points of view. Did you have a favorite character to write? Did anyone capture your attention more than you expected?

I usually have the most fun writing the "baddies" in my books, and

I very much enjoyed those sections in *Hostage*, but it was Sophia who really came alive for me. I have a particular soft spot for children with big vocabularies and questioning minds, and I loved giving her a voice and agency in the story.

The terrorists in this book come from a wide variety of backgrounds. Do you think that everyone is susceptible to radicalization on some level? What do we miss when we define terrorism narrowly?

Radicalization is manipulation, and all manipulation is based on identifying the target's weak spots and offering a solution to them. It could be financial security or a roof over someone's head; it could be a father figure or a friend with a listening ear. Everybody needs something, which means everyone has the potential to be manipulated...

The word "terrorist" immediately makes us think of religious extremists, but a terrorist is someone who uses violence or intimidation in the pursuit of political aims. Such a broad definition encompasses so much more than religion, and although I've chosen to highlight environmental extremism in this novel, the cause could have been any one of a number. Throughout 2020, as the COVID-19 pandemic devastated the world, I was horrified by the number of "COVID deniers" I came across on social media. I watched as they blocked people who held opposite views to their own, creating an echo chamber that would strengthen their beliefs. The internet has made it very easy to find one's tribe.

You point out that fundamentalist activists are rarely sympathetic. When you worked as a protest liaison officer, what strategies were most effective in gaining public sympathy and support for a cause?

No one is without flaws, and few of us have no redeeming features. I was fascinated by the workings of extremists and had a reluctant respect for their passion and single-mindedness. The most successful causes play on the emotions of their targets. Think about the times you've given money to a good cause: nine times out of ten, it's because a photograph, story, or statistic has made its way to your heart. For the organization hoping to secure sympathy, research is the key. They have to know their audience and understand how to push their buttons. A demonstration held by a right-wing organization gathered huge support in an area with high unemployment by sowing the seed that unwanted immigration was responsible. We all have a responsibility, I think, to do our own research and to ensure we are not being swayed by someone else's agenda.

In general, does your background in police work change the way you write?

Absolutely. I am fascinated by the gray area between good and bad and firmly believe we are all capable of committing terrible crimes if the circumstances were right. I explore this in much of what I write, which means you can never really trust any of my characters...

How often do you come up with new ideas for a book? How many of those ideas would you estimate make it to a full manuscript?

I'm constantly thinking of "what if?" questions or extraordinary situations in which I might drop ordinary people to see how they cope. A fraction of those are right for a novel, and I have several half-finished books behind me, where the idea simply wasn't enough to continue. *Hostage* is one of the rare times when I had the idea and knew almost immediately what would happen and how it would end. It made it a hugely enjoyable book to write and, I hope, to read.

As a writer, at times you've challenged yourself to step outside crime fiction and suspense. How does genre affect the way your stories develop? Do you think your suspense generally and *Hostage* specifically have benefitted from writing other types of books?

I am a firm believer that story is what matters, not genre, and I always think it is a shame when a reader staunchly refuses to read a particular type of book. Some of my favorite writers segue between, say, crime and literary fiction, and some of my favorite novels are a hybrid of two genres. My fourth novel, *After the End*, is a family drama, not a thriller, but it is every bit as suspenseful as a crime novel. The only difference I found in writing it was that the story was led more by the characters than by the plot. This pushed me to spend more time considering who the protagonists were and why they made the choices they did. As I came to write *Hostage*, I found myself naturally spending more time on the backstory for Adam and Mina, and I think the novel is richer for it.

How has your writing process changed since your first novel? Do you have any advice for new writers?

Sometimes, at a literary event or writing workshop, I read a section from my debut psychological thriller, *I Let You Go*. I remain exceptionally proud of that novel, which is published now in more than forty countries, but that doesn't stop me wincing at some of the prose... Ten years of writing full-time has taught me a great deal, and I hope the next ten will teach me even more. Just as my prose—and plotting—has developed, so my process has changed. I am more analytical, more commercially aware, and quicker to abandon something I can see isn't working.

I have two bits of advice for new writers: the first general and the second very specific and practical. First, read everything. Read the bestsellers, read books your friends rave about or your librarian recommends. Read nonfiction, crime novels, sci-fi, and historical romance, regardless of the shelf on which you see your own work sitting. Understand why these books make you want to turn the page—or why you can't wait to put them down. Read, analyze, re-read. A good writer is a good reader.

When I started writing, I was still working full-time, and most new writers will know how difficult it can be to find time. Many authors are insistent that writing every day—no matter how few words—is the only way to be productive, but if that doesn't work for you (it didn't for me—I was too exhausted at the end of a police shift to string a sentence together), my second tip might be helpful. When you finish a writing session, don't finish at the end of a chapter. Stop in the midst of a scene—halfway through a piece of dialogue even—and jot down a few bullet points for what follows. When you next sit at your keyboard or pick up your notebook, whether that's the next day or a week later, you can plunge straight into your manuscript and make the most of your precious writing time with no fear of the blank page.

ACKNOWLEDGMENTS

As always, I owe an enormous debt to a great number of people, without whom this book would not have been possible. Two readers donated to charity for the privilege of seeing a name of their choice appearing between these pages. My thanks to Tanya Barrow, whose mother-in-law, Patricia, truly is a Scottish Lady, and to Mike Carrivick, a former Qantas employee who worked on the very first London to Sydney flight in 1989. Your fictional demise was a noble one, Mike. Their generous donations were in support of Aerobility, a superb charity enabling people with disabilities to take to the skies. The work they do is truly groundbreaking, and it was a privilege to help with their fundraising efforts.

I'm grateful to Rhonda Hierons, for sharing her experiences of attachment disorder, and to friends who have spoken to me about adopting children. The impact of a chaotic, neglectful, or abusive start in life is profound and long-lasting, and I am in awe of parents who give such children a safe and happy home.

There will be many pilots, aviation engineers, and crew keen to tell me what I got wrong about cabin configuration, shift patterns, landing procedure, and much more. I respectfully refer you to the (fictional) customer services department at World Airlines, who will be delighted to handle your complaints. For my part, I am tremendously grateful to air traffic controller Charlotte Anderson and air crew training specialist (Emirates) Gillian Fulke for their advice and expertise, and to Tony and Athena for welcoming me to the Emirates Aviation Experience, where my son Josh and I got to land a B777 at Sydney airport in the precise conditions faced by Mina in this book. Several pilots from around the world helped with my research, and one in particular—who has asked not to be named—was incredibly generous with his time. He sent annotated photographs with Mina's precise descent path, talked me through the landing, and answered numerous questions about everything from fighter jets to cloud cover. I hope he knows how grateful I am. All mistakes are mine, made mostly for the benefit of the story.

My thanks, too, to my eagle-eyed agent Sheila Crowley, for pointing out that footballer Jamie Crawford couldn't possibly be jetting off to Australia at such a critical time in the season, and to Graham Brown for confirming that even if Jamie were injured, he would be required to stay and support the training. Thus Jamie retired gracefully somewhere between drafts two and three.

Sheila Crowley, of Curtis Brown Talent and Literary Agency, isn't just a football (and rugby) fan. She's an incredible agent, mentor and strategist, and a dear friend. There is no one I would rather have in my corner than Sheila, and my thanks go to Sabhbh Curran and Emily Harris for their hard work as part of the CB team.

I have been fortunate enough to have the same editor—Lucy Malagoni—since my debut novel was acquired in 2013. She is astute and ambitious and pushes me a little harder with each book, which is exactly the way I like it. She is just one in an outstanding team of passionate and hardworking people at Little, Brown Book Group, by which I am very proud to be published. There isn't space to acknowledge every person in the art department, sales, marketing, accounts, publicity, audio…but I value every single one of you. Particular thanks must go to Gemma Shelley, Brionee Fenlon, Kirsteen Astor, Millie Seaward, Rosanna Forte, and Abby Parsons, and to Linda McQueen, copy editor extraordinaire.

Thank you to Andy Hine, Kate Hibbert, and Helena Doree in the rights team, who have collectively brought my books to readers in forty countries and counting. I have some truly brilliant editors across the world and love seeing how you shape my books for your market.

I don't have room to thank each of my publishers individually, but I want to make a special case for my U.S. team. The moment I started talking books with Shana Drehs and Molly Waxman, I knew I'd found the right home for *Hostage* in Sourcebooks Landmark. Their passion and responsiveness has been amazing, and I'm so grateful for their faith in me. Production editor Jessica Thelander and proofreader Sabrina Baskey spotted an embarrassing number of errors, thereby saving me from abject humiliation. Thank you, Jessica and Sabrina! Working closely with the Sourcebooks team has been publicist extraordinaire Meagan Harris, who is a joy to work with and who has helped me reach more readers than I could ever have hoped for

That brings me neatly to the most important people of all: readers. Whether you've been with me from the start or whether this is the first of my books you've read, whether you read ebooks, borrowed books, audiobooks, hardbacks, paperbacks, whether you read one book a year or a hundred—thank you. You are the reason I am able to make a living doing something I love. Please keep leaving reviews, keep supporting independent bookshops where you can, keep using libraries. Keep reading. If you're not already a member of my book club, I'd love to see you there: claremackintosh.com/jointheclub.

Last but by no means least, thank you to Rob, Josh, Evie, and George, for putting up with me.

ABOUT THE AUTHOR

Photo © Astrid di Crollalanza

Clare Mackintosh is the multi-award-winning author of four *Sunday Times* bestselling novels. Her first three novels were all Richard and Judy Book Club picks. Translated into forty languages, her books have sold more than two million copies worldwide, have been *New York Times* and international bestsellers, and have spent a combined total of fifty weeks on the *Sunday Times* bestseller chart. Clare lives in North Wales with her husband and their three children.

For more information, visit Clare's website claremackintosh. com or find her at facebook.com/ClareMackWrites or on Twitter @ClareMackint0sh.